Dear Reader,

This month we're delighted to welcome best selling author Patricia Wilson to the ***Scarlet*** list. With over 40 romance novels to her credit, we are sure that Patricia's new book will delight her existing fans and win her many new readers. You can also read *Resolutions*, the conclusion of Maxine Barry's enthralling 'All His Prey' duet. And we are proud to bring you books by two talented new authors: Judy Jackson who hails from Canada and Tiffany Bond who is based in England.

You will possibly have noticed that some of the ***Scarlet*** novels we publish are quite sexy, while others are warmer and more family oriented. Do you like this mix of styles and the different levels of sensuality? And how about locations: is it important to you *where* an author sets her ***Scarlet*** book?

If you have written to me about ***Scarlet***, please accept my thanks. I read each and every one of your letters and I certainly refer to your comments and suggestions when I am thinking about our schedules.

Till next month,

Sally Cooper

SALLY COOPER,
Editor-in-Chief – ***Scarlet***

About the author

Tiffany Bond lives in the heart of Yorkshire with her fiance, five Newfoundland dogs, two cats and a horse. When she isn't writing, she is walking or training her dogs for shows, and, if the mood takes her, riding her mare, Roxy. Although Tiffany has no children herself, her fiance has a son and a daughter whom she loves very much.

Tiffany's first romance novel was written at the tender age of eleven, and featured a hero called 'Crazy Horse' and his true love 'Snowstorm'. When she left school, the author was involved in accounts work, all the time continuing to write romances for pleasure. Then 'the call' became so great, Tiffany finally gave up work to write full time.

She has travelled to Greece, the setting of *An Improper Proposal*, many times and finds the place has a charm all of its own. She's also visited Australia, the Philippines and Bangkok. Closer to home, she loves to travel the length and breadth of the British Isles. As Tiffany says: 'Life itself is one exciting journey of experiences.'

TIFFANY BOND

AN IMPROPER PROPOSAL

Enquiries to:
Robinson Publishing Ltd
7 Kensington Church Court
London W8 4SP

First published in the UK by Scarlet, 1997

A copy of the British Library Cataloguing in Publication data is available from the British Library

ISBN 1-85487-906-5

Printed and bound in the EC

10 9 8 7 6 5 4 3 2 1

CHAPTER 1

A grey shadow of doubt settled unceremoniously onto Carrie's slim shoulders. Was she doing the right thing? There *was* no other alternative. She'd gone over this with a fine-tooth comb since her return to Greece, and each time she'd come up with the same answer. Alexis Stephanides held the key; he was the only man rich enough!

'Miss O'Riordan, Mr Stephanides will see you now,' said the pleasant dark-haired girl, in heavily accented English, as she emerged from the office with CHAIRMAN engraved on the gold plaque of the heavy mahogany door.

Taking a deep, steadying breath Carrie thanked her, automatically threw the latest edition of *Hello* magazine back onto the coffee table and stood up. Pushing her streams of white blonde hair away from her face, she afforded herself a grin. Glancing up into the full plate-glass window above her she drew her shoulders back in an effort to look cool, if not sophisticated.

Maybe she should have tied her hair back? But no, a little voice reminded her, Alexis loves your hair, adores your blue eyes. Remember, he told you so the last time he was in London. Running her shaky hands down her stark white sundress, Carrie swallowed deeply. The heat outside had been oppressive, but, even in this air-conditioned office the thought of facing Alexis had her running a temperature.

If only it were that easy, she thought. Alexis may love her hair and her eyes, but after her cruel rejection of him and all her outrageous insults she was surprised he had even agreed to see her.

'Do I have to wait an eternity for you to grace me with your presence? I only have so much time for you to grovel at my knees, *Thespinnes*,' grated the dark, earthy tones of the man lounging in the doorway.

So he knew! thought Carrie. The Greek shipping grapevine had done its job well, it seemed, and that at least made Carrie's task a little easier.

Raising her clear, icy blue eyes to his, she straightened her back and moved past him without uttering a single derogatory word in response. He was baiting her and she knew it!

His cologne tickled her nostrils as she floated past him with the grace of a young gazelle. She was trying with all her might not to look up into his face. Instead she concentrated on the subtle scent of his cologne, which was fresh and clean and had the strangest effect on her knees, making them wobble uncontrollably.

He threw an appraising look at her. His dark brooding eyes stung her, sending conflicting messages to her brain as they rested fleetingly on her covered breasts and then travelled down the full length of her sundress to her shapely legs. Carrie refrained from meeting his gaze.

'Would you like to sit, or would you prefer to get straight to your knees and begin to grovel? From what I can gather your godfather is in need of a miracle.' His gaze finally settled on her lips.

Carrie's mouth pouted in consternation; it would seem he wasn't going to listen to what she had come to say and only wanted to get his revenge after the episode in London.

Squaring her shoulders, she said softly, 'I didn't come to grovel, as you put it, Alexis. I came to ask you to help an old friend. Is that too much of a problem for you?'

Sea-blue eyes met and held Alexis's burning gaze. He waved his hand at her, indicating she should sit, as he moved to occupy his grey leather chair.

Once seated he rocked back, shrugging large athletic shoulders as his eyes connected with hers once more, singeing her with a contempt still harboured from their last meeting. Carrie knew he would never forget that.

'I will give you the opportunity of explaining your case to me,' he assured her, with just a touch a sarcasm in his deep sombre voice. He was going to make it hard for her, that much was clear.

Carrie closed her eyes for a moment. Alexis was not an ordinary man by any means. Taller than most, more powerful both in build and personality, he resembled a wild animal of the jungle, sleek and dangerous, so alive and vital that at times he scared the living daylights out of her. He was also very proud of his Greek heritage, and he didn't like being insulted – no Greek did. But Carrie, being Carrie, always seemed to be insulting him. Whatever she said, it always came out wrong.

She squirmed under his dark look, knowing this wasn't going to be easy. Spreading her hands in a helpless and futile gesture, she sighed. But her voice, when it came, was clear. If she were to be successful in persuading him to do the right thing she would have to act as if she were confident.

'As you are aware, Petros is in need of financial help. He's run into a few problems over the last year, and the business has suffered.' She shrugged her slim shoulders, almost bare but for the shoelace straps of her dress.

'Go on,' he said, sounding maddeningly at ease.

'He needs to sell off some of his shares, needs to raise some capital,' she explained softly, her voice catching in her throat at his intense scrutiny.

'How much capital would your godfather need – ' he paused momentarily – 'and what percentage of his shares would he be willing to sell?'

Carrie stuttered, her mouth parched. 'I d-don't know. We haven't discussed that.'

Alexis nodded his head but his eyes hooded over until they were icy slits of revenge. 'Then I suggest, *Thespinnes*, you go home and ask him to contact me. I will not bargain with you, he is foolish to even think of sending you.'

Her look implored him as her attempts at staying unemotional became impossible. 'He doesn't know I'm here.'

'I see.'

'Oh no, you don't see at all! If you did, you would have helped him before now.' She lashed out at him bitterly, no longer managing to hold onto her calm façade.

She was standing now, slamming both hands down on his desk as she violently spat out, 'You don't understand at all. You've never understood!'

His diary went flying to the floor, as her hands swept everything out of her way in angry waves of emotion.

'Miss O'Riordan, I warn you . . .' he began menacingly. But the papers continued to fly off his desk as her Irish voice rose in temper. At last he stood, clamping his hands firmly around her flailing wrists.

'Carrie, for God's sake, calm down! It surely can't be that bad?' Several seconds passed in which Carrie tried to get a hold of herself. He motioned her to sit.

'I can't, I have to go,' she cried, biting her lip as she saw the aftermath of her outburst – paper was strewn all over the floor. Suddenly her shoulders sank in defeat and shame as she reached for her bag.

'Sit!'

When she ignored his order, he repeated it so softly, so dangerously, that Carrie paused in fear.

'Sit down and explain yourself.' His voice sliced through her like a red-hot knife and she found herself obeying him. Dropping her bag to her side she perched on the edge of the chair, ready to run, to make her escape should he become angry again. She'd only seen him really angry twice before and that was enough for any lifetime.

Her words were a shaky declaration of hope. 'I heard you were looking for a fleet to invest in. I beg you, Alexis, help him. Make him an offer. He's an old man now, and I know the shame of all this will kill him, I just know it. He needs your help.'

His black eyes gave nothing away. He punched at his intercom, quickly reminding his secretary that he had ordered two Greek coffees to be sent in. His voice was soft, yet full of command.

Then he stretched back languidly, arranging himself more comfortably into his chair, reminding Carrie of a lean black panther, his muscles taut against the fine white silk of his shirt.

'And tell me, what do I get for investing a very hefty sum into a – a *what*? A failing old shipping fleet? Petros has done nothing for five years but take from it. Where are my rewards for rebuilding such a thing?' He was shaking his head. 'No, Carrie, it's too high a price, even for friendship.'

The knock on the door stopped Carrie from replying. Sinking her teeth into her bottom lip quite viciously, she held back her temper. Only after the Greek girl had politely stepped over the scattered papers, placed the coffee on the desk, and then departed without so much as a raised eyebrow, did Carrie spit out, eyes blazing angrily, 'But there is no one else. Alexis, Petros needs you.'

Alexis simply pushed the small cup of coffee and the tall glass of iced water towards her, his denial emphatically projected across the desk, forcing a gasp from her lips as he uttered, 'I said no!'

'Do I have to beg? I will, you know.' She made a move, as if she were about to drop to her knees.

Moving around the desk faster than Carrie had seen anyone move before, Alexis pulled her roughly to her feet, his grip on her upper arms painful as he spoke harshly.

'You little fool, you think something so trivial as falling to your knees would make me reconsider? There is only one thing that would make me change my mind. One thing, Carrie.' His head descended swiftly and his cruel lips met hers.

Carrie steeled herself not to respond, but the kiss was not demanding a response, it was dealing out punishment, a demonstration of power that was quick, hard and devastating to the soul.

Pushing her shocked, pliant body back into the chair, he once again took his seat. Dark eyes searched her face, his scowl the living proof that he was annoyed. Swiping a strong, tanned hand irritably through his black hair, he caught and held her gaze, but said nothing.

'This one thing, what is it? Can I help? Would I be able to change your mind, Alexis?' Carrie persisted with a glimmer of new hope.

Alexis studied her in a deathly silence, taking in her classical feminine features. She had high cheekbones, a gently turned-up nose, soft full pink lips that quivered under his scrutiny, and those amazing blue eyes, with thick, luscious, dark blonde lashes. He inclined his head.

'Yes, it is only you who can change my mind,' he returned softly, his eyes lingering on the low-cut neck of her sundress, on her pronounced and yet fine-boned shoulder, and the pulse that was beating furiously in the hollow of her throat.

He had her full attention. She'd do anything for Petros, anything at all. 'How?'

Alexis pondered slightly, then a frown wavered around his brow and a smirk touched the side of his lips. 'I want you to have my baby. Give me an heir to my empire, and I'll give Petros a deal that will save his skin,' he murmured softly, his keen eyes watching as her lips formed the word.

'*Baby*?'

'Yes, a *baby*, Carrie, *our* baby.'

Carrie screwed her eyes up as if she had suddenly realized what he had said. Her hand flew to her mouth in open astonishment.

'You must be stark raving mad!' She floundered for words, utterly shocked by his proposition. 'I couldn't marry you!'

Raising a sardonic eyebrow, his low voice drifted across to her like a slow slap to the face. 'I want a child, not a wife!'

This was ridiculous! The man was clearly crazy! Petros and he were such good friends, why couldn't he help him? Why couldn't he invest in the company? He had enough money. Why on earth did he want a baby?

'A baby,' she echoed softly. Licking her bottom lip, Carrie looked across at him. He was deadly serious, she saw. He meant every word, it was obvious in his eyes. She coughed softly, suddenly reaching for the thick dark coffee and then the iced water, anything to wet her parched and angry throat.

Placing the glass back on the tray with shaking fingers she questioned faintly, breathlessly, 'Let me get this straight; I, I mean *we*, conceive a baby, and when that baby is born you take him away from me. Is that it?'

A slight smile touched softly at his lips when he confirmed, 'Something like that.' He drank his own coffee and then caught her eyes. He was silently laughing at her. 'How do you know you will have a boy?'

'A what? Oh, a boy! I don't know,' she said absently, staring through him almost as though he weren't there. Her thoughts drifted. Then, as if recognition dawned, she attacked him. 'But I do know why you're doing this. This is some kind of petty revenge, isn't it? Some kind of sadistic act, all because I rejected you in London. But men like you leave me cold. Do you hear me?'

He did hear, his indifferent shrug mortified her almost to the stage that she would have liked to slap the arrogant, smirking face.

'So you say, but from what I could see, you were certainly putting it about in London. But they were all only boys, my dear Carrie, only boys. One more sexual encounter wouldn't hurt you. Unless of course you don't like older men. Men with experience know exactly what a woman needs,' he taunted, his voice like dark chocolate. He shrugged those large, strong shoulders, his words insolently suggestive. He added, 'Of course, you don't have to enjoy it.'

'Oh,' she gasped in outrage, 'as you so crudely describe it, I *put it about* with who the hell I like, and I don't like *you*, Alexis Stephanides, nor would I like sex with you!' She threw her silky blonde hair away from her eyes and looked at him challengingly.

Alexis stood up, hardly seeming to notice her cruel words. Steadily he moved across to the window to stare down at the hustle and bustle on the streets of Athens. When he turned back to her he looked thoroughly bored with the conversation. 'Your reason for rejecting my offer of making love is because you're scared of your own reactions to me, and not because I leave you cold.'

Carrie jumped up from her seat, outraged by the truth in his words, knowing she would never admit it.

'Believe what you want. I told you that night in London that I would never go to bed with you. You think you've got me over a barrel with your threats, don't you?' she sneered, her small hands balling into fists at her side, the nails digging hard into her palms.

He raised a dark eyebrow, and his voice became silk-soft, sending shivers of apprehension up and down Carrie's spine. 'Now there's an interesting thought.' He laughed wickedly and turned back to the window. 'You have until Friday to make your decision. After that, you really could beg and I wouldn't entertain you.'

'You're disgusting!' she shouted in temper at him.

Alexis spun around, his frown warning her, his voice threatening her to be silent. 'Shut up! Stop your screaming: you know what I do to screaming children.' He moved towards her like the sleek hunter he was and she backed away as if his touch would burn her.

'You touch me if you dare, I'm not a child any more,' She spat the words out like an alley cat, wild and hurt.

Alexis gave her a look full of contempt as he walked swiftly past her to the door. There, he turned slightly, throwing over his shoulder, 'Then stop behaving like a child.' He glanced down at the gold watch on his wrist. 'I have a meeting. Friday is the deadline, Carrie. At noon!'

Carrie stared open-mouthed. Eventually she found her voice. 'That's too soon.'

His gaze travelled her full length. 'If you truly love Petros, having my baby will be a worthy sacrifice!' With that he left, leaving her shocked and devastated.

CHAPTER 2

Petros was sitting by the pool when she reached the island. His tired face was gaunt with worry and again it was obvious that he'd turned to the brandy bottle for solace.

'Oh Petros, what have I told you about the brandy? It won't help you,' Carrie admonished softly, lifting the bottle from his hands.

He smiled, but there was no humour, no hidden sparkle in his eyes. 'My child, I have failed you. I made a promise to your father on his deathbed that I would care for you, and now I find you caring for me.'

'How can you say that, Petros? You've been the most wonderful person in the world to me. You've stuck by me through thick and thin. Don't worry, something will turn up, just you wait and see.' She bent and tenderly kissed his tired face. 'Come with me, my dearest, sweetest Petros. It's time to eat.'

Later at the dinner table the *kleftiko* fell apart as she picked the meat delicately from the bone. Neither Carrie nor Petros had done justice to the spiced lamb that Christina had cooked for them. Instead Carrie had concentrated on her Greek salad, rich with crumbly feta cheese and the olives which once she hated but now loved. She ate with great attention, hoping to chase Alexis's ultimatum out of her mind.

It had been at this table that she first met Alexis. She had been fifteen. She was wild, totally spoilt and out of control. Poor Petros had not known how to handle her after her parents' death. She had been a wicked minx!

Carrie fingered the polished surface that still held traces of the scars that she had inflicted upon the otherwise perfect wood. In the mirrored images of the table her mind slid back to that fateful day.

'But I don't want to go to my room!' she had pouted, pushing her bottom lip out sulkily and folding her hands behind her back. 'I want to stay here, Petros!'

'No, Carrie. We've already discussed this. This is a business meeting, not a party for children. Now be a good girl and go to your room,' said Petros gently, while he apologized to his six guests.

Carrie stamped her foot to the floor, a snigger crossing her lips as she heard the men gasp in horror. Greek girls nearly always did as they were told, or so it seemed.

'I want to stay at the party!' she chanted like the spoilt girl she was.

All but one man, sitting to her left, seemed perturbed. He was younger than the others, yet seemed infinitely more dangerous.

'Carrie, I will not repeat myself to you again!' Petros threw his hands in the air when she ignored his words. 'Alexis, what would you do with such a disobedient child?'

Alexis turned in his seat, his eyes floating over the youthful teenager with obvious distaste, taking in the thin boyish figure dressed in pink silk pyjamas.

His words were sharp and to the point. 'Slap her, my friend, the child has no manners. I would not tolerate such insubordination in my home.'

'We are not in *your* home!' piped Carrie insolently, throwing her shoulders back, and swishing her long hair dangerously close to his face.

'A great pity, young lady, for you would be over my knee at this very moment.' Brittle, dark eyes encompassed her childlike face. 'And you would be very, very sore when I finished with you.'

'Your puny threats don't frighten me. I'm not a Greek girl, I won't obey any orders,' she said scathingly as her Irish temper rose.

Petros gasped, swearing in his own language. 'Enough of this. Do you hear?'

But Carrie didn't know when it was time to retreat. Out of sheer temper she picked up the knife which lay near the breadboard and scraped it along the polished table, amidst the stares of the shocked men.

Her voice carried, a nasty, childish message, 'I don't care about your so-called *party*. You can stuff it as far as I'm concerned!'

Just as she would have run from the table in a fit of tears, a firm tanned hand clasped around her wrist like a band of inescapable steel. Her wild eyes connected with Alexis's. His were cold and evil.

'Petros, may I?' The sheer strength in his voice terrified Carrie.

Petros looked from Alexis to Carrie, and to the polished table with the large gouge scored out of it. Absently he nodded.

'No! Petros, I'm sorry,' Carrie's pleas came too late. Within seconds she was hauled to her room, her screams ignored, her kicks ineffectual against the big man. He threatened to turn her over his knee, but she didn't receive the spanking she feared. He simply dumped her unceremoniously on her bed, and told her in no uncertain terms to stay in her room or he would be back. And if he had to return, he warned menacingly, she would receive that spanking.

Touching the table, she trailed her finger along the jagged line of the otherwise perfect wood.

'I wonder what you are thinking?' said Petros softly, his eyes tinged with the first sign of humour since she'd arrived three weeks ago.

Carrie smiled, the warmth oozing out of her beautiful blue eyes, her voice reminiscing when she said, 'I was very naughty nine years ago. Wasn't I?'

Petros nodded and emphasized, 'You were very naughty indeed.' He shook his head. 'I wonder if you will ever forgive Alexis. He humiliated you. You screamed at him when he hauled you out of the room, and when you screamed a second time at him, he merely tucked you under his arm. He put you to bed, which is what you deserved.' Petros smiled. 'But do you know Carrie, I think he made you a better person after that. You were far too spoilt in those days.'

Blushing to the roots of her hair Carrie chose her words carefully. It was obvious that Alexis had furnished him with a different version of what had really happened. If she *did* consider Alexis's outrageous offer she wouldn't want Petros to think she was holding a grudge.

'That was a long time ago. Alexis and I have made our peace over that. I saw him in London a few months ago and he took me out to dinner,' she declared, and then wished she'd never said a word.

Instantly hope gleamed in Petros's eyes and Carrie knew what he was thinking, knew immediately what he was planning. Under normal circumstances she would have stopped her godfather there and then, but at this very moment she didn't have the heart. He needed something to hold on to.

'Excuse me, Mr Simari, the telephone for you. It is Mr Stephanides calling from the mainland,' said Christina as she interrupted their chatter. She was a small robust woman with dark shining eyes, eyes that searched Carrie's face. Christina practically read Carrie like a book, and knew of her visit to the mainland today. Carrie knew she didn't believe that she had been shopping.

Petros looked at Carrie with a grave smile.

'Go on, Petros, go and talk to Alexis, I'll take a walk on the beach,' she insisted gently, a quiet sigh escaping her lips. Speak of the devil and he will appear, she thought derisively as she watched Petros's small figure stride out into the hallway.

So now he was planning his attack. The phone call had to be something to do with today's conversation. Alexis Stephanides never did anything without having a battle strategy.

Carrie needed to walk, her mind was full of conflicting messages. His proposition was outrageous. She knew it, and yet it kept pushing to the forefront of her thoughts. Like a drifting boat she was caught up in the fantasy of having his baby; she loved children.

From the moment she'd set foot on Greek soil three weeks ago she'd felt like she had come home, but she wasn't sure of the reason. Perhaps it was simply the welcome she'd received, or perhaps it was something far more complex. Perhaps it was her destiny.

'Carrie, my darling, it's so wonderful to see you.' Even with his obvious joy at seeing her again, Petros's words had not hidden his pain and worry when he met her at the harbour, and Carrie knew now how deep that worry was.

Slipping off her shoes she let the fine golden sand encompass her toes. London had been fine for a few years, and she had been quickly caught up in the hustle and bustle of everyday life. The fast living, catching the tube from one place to another, making new friends. Reading *Vogue* magazine.

She had thought she was really settling down in the city, until the night when Alexis had turned up at her favourite London night club. Of all the people to bump into when she had been feeling so vulnerable, it had had to be Alexis Stephanides!

She'd been dancing the night away with several of her colleagues. They were all laughing and giggling, having fun and wasn't that what birthday celebrations were all about?

'Come on, Carrie, let's go wild' cried Timothy as he cavorted across the dance floor.

It was then, while she was dancing, that she saw him, dressed in the expensively-cut dinner suit, dark and dangerous. He was standing by the bar, blatantly watching her move, his gaze sweeping over her appraisingly.

At first glance she thought he was an apparition and she continued dancing in the hope that if she ignored him he'd disappear into thin air. When she realized he wasn't about to do a Houdini act, she began to dance for him, suggestively spinning and hugging herself in the tight black dress. She danced provocatively, flirting with her glances, teasing with her body.

He'd looked bored at the first instance, calmly raising the glass of amber liquid to his lips in a mocking salute, but she continued her swaying until she could see a new, hungry light his eyes.

It had been then, at that moment, that he had placed the empty glass on the bar and walked purposefully towards her, his long cool strides hypnotizing her as she watched him draw nearer.

'Come here, witch,' he'd whispered, as if his voice came direct from his soul.

As he pulled her into his arms seconds later, she gasped for breath against the solid wall of silk-covered muscle. Alexis had never done this to her before; he'd always had a reserved manner in her presence.

'So you flirt and cavort about the dance floor with these men. This is such a perilous game, isn't it, little one? Didn't anyone ever tell you that this is a very dangerous pastime?' He breathed the words softly in her ear, the sensation sending a hundred different messages searing around her brain.

Carrie pulled back in his arms, laughing up into his face, her eyes sparkling, as she purred, 'Alexis, I don't know what you mean?'

He tilted his head slightly to one side, surveying her with a hot, dark look. 'No? Come now, don't pretend to be naïve, Carrie. I've seen you! You have openly flirted with all these boys – ' he swept his hand around and then brought it back to prod his own chest – 'and now with me.'

Carrie laughed again, until he squeezed her close and her breath was suddenly lodged in her throat. 'These *boys*, these boys are men!' She pointed to Paul. 'Paul over there, why he is married!' She muttered the words indignantly, all the time hoping he would release her soon. She didn't like the breathless effect he was having on her.

'So, you play the field? This is the correct term, is it not?'

The mischievous giggle echoed in Carrie's throat. He thought she was dating these men, and not just one, but all of them. The urge to elaborate and tell just a few white lies became paramount.

'Not *all* at once, you understand!' She laughed up into his face, trying to wriggle away from him.

Alexis snorted angrily, his accent getting stronger with every word, 'Petros should never have let you leave the island! Poros is your home!'

'Petros couldn't stop me and nor could you,' she responded. Anyone would think she was dancing with her father, not a man a mere seven years her senior!

Alexis looked down at her along his strong arrogant nose and his dark brows came together in a disapproving frown. He shook his head, admonishing her for her words. 'I could have stopped you, I merely wanted you to stretch your wings. Remember the mistake you made when you were fifteen. I was the only one who stopped you then.'

Carrie's faced flushed with colour as her voice became waspish with the memory, 'Oh, and what was that?'

He caught her chin in his cruel fingers, his body stilled as the music stopped. She was forced to look into those frightening eyes as he retaliated softly, 'You underestimated my powers.'

'That wasn't power,' spat Carrie, trying to pull away from him although his grip just tightened. 'That was brute force. You were a bully, Alexis Stephanides! I was just a child. I was distraught; my father, my mother and my baby brother had all died within months of each other and I needed company. I needed loving, not thrashing!' To Carrie's utter chagrin tears formed in her eyes.

Alexis saw them, swearing in his native tongue before dragging her back into the circle of his arms. 'You were naughty, just as you are being tonight,' he mocked softly in her ear. 'And I did not *thrash* you, little one. I could have, but I didn't.' It was a softness Carrie had never heard before. A softness she could have liked.

He straightened, pulling her with him. 'Quickly, come with me. I fear you've had too much wine and would be easy pickings for the men around here.'

This time Carrie did pull out of his arms, right out of his grip, almost stumbling on the darkened dance floor. 'No!'

'Carrie,' his voice warned silkily.

But Carrie stood her ground, staring mutinously at him. 'I'm staying here. Leave me be, Alexis. I will not be ordered about!'

She watched, fascinated, as a muscle moved dangerously in his cheek. His eyes glittered a warning at her, but she ignored it.

Eventually he nodded his head, his low voice an angry affirmative, 'So be it.'

Turning, he walked swiftly away from the dance floor. His retreating figure was gaining welcoming gasps from some of the female clientele as he disappeared from view, and although Carrie instantly dismissed what they were appreciating, it seemed that from there on the evening went downhill. Her friends soon split up and went their separate ways and it seemed there was only Carrie who had travelled some distance to get here, and she would have to get a taxi back home.

Since Alexis had walked away, all she had done was dance until she was fit to drop. She had been so angry with him that she had danced wildly, disobeying all the doctor's advice, and now she was paying for that abandon.

Collecting her jacket minutes later she managed to safely manoeuvre her way down the steps of the club. She felt extremely dizzy, maybe even a little tipsy, although she had only drunk two glasses of wine. Now she felt deflated and rather sad, but she had no idea why.

The blast of cold air from the open foyer doors made her gasp and look up. Even before she drew close to the commanding figure standing tall in the doorway, she knew it was Alexis. The hairs that stood up on the back of her neck had told her so!

'Oh go away!' she muttered indignantly.

Sighing, she made to move past him, but she was caught by a band of steel around her upper arm. Firm, strong fingers held her still through the soft silk of her jacket.

'Alexis, I don't need a nursemaid,' she threw at him furiously. 'I will see you home,' he insisted, his voice low. He pulled her back into his arms to allow others to pass and she fell against his rock-hard muscles. Inhaling, she suddenly felt the dizzying effects of the virus she was suffering from. Sinking against him, her fingers curled inside his jacket, his laughter tickling her ears.

'What's so funny?'

'You are, Carrie. Why, I think it's the first time I've ever seen you drunk,' he admonished softly, amusement lifting his voice slightly.

'I am not drunk! I'm ill!'

Urging her to move, he ignored her remark, keeping a tight hold around her waist as he hailed his limousine.

The cold night air almost knocked Carrie off her feet. She shivered and looking around the illuminated street in a hazy stupor, she suddenly felt much worse.

Alexis opened the car door, ordering her to get in. Feeling faint, she caught the heel of her shoe on the curb and would have fallen had he not come to her rescue again. Once inside the comfort of the expensive car he rapped out orders to the driver. 'My hotel!'

Carrie couldn't understand why she felt so light headed. Her legs looked perfectly capable of moving, and yet they felt numb. She prodded one in sheer horror and fascination.

'Like I said, it's called being drunk, my sweet, little Carrie,' he admonished teasingly; he wasn't annoyed, there was amusement in those hidden depths.

'I'm not drunk! It's a virus, I tell you,' she protested weakly.

'If you say so, Carrie,' he agreed softly.

She turned on the soft leather of the seat to study him. He'd always been so aloof with her, so unreachable, as though he regarded her as an infant. She knew now that they'd come to a crossroads in their relationship, his look confirmed it.

Laughter lightened his mysterious expression. He'd always been dangerous; she'd known that from the very first day she'd met him, but for now Carrie chose to ignore that danger. Weak but intrigued, she ran her fingers up the soft fabric of his shirt, to his bow-tie.

Her unsteady fingers pulled the bow-tie from its knot. It hung loose against his shoulder as she undid the top two buttons of his shirt. It was then he stopped her, his tanned fingers covering hers, squeezing gently.

'No, Carrie, think about where we are. You must wait, be patient, my sweet one. I know we have waited too long for this to happen. Just be patient a little longer,' he whispered quietly, drawing her safely to his side.

Carrie didn't object. She simply submerged herself in the deep masculine aroma of his body. She stared at his muscular chest. She knew it was warm and inviting, and, strangely, a safe haven. Closing her eyes she fell against him, surrending to unconsciousness.

Carrie splashed her toes in the gentle ripple of the Aegean under the moonlit sky. She'd always thought London was her home, having been raised there since she was four years old when her parents had brought her across from Ireland. But when she did eventually return to the big city after her years in Greece, she found it was no longer the home she envisaged. For years she went about like a lost and very unhappy soul. That was until she'd met Peter. She missed Peter, but at least she knew he was safe. Audrey was looking after him.

The call from Petros had been a distress signal, a two-way street, thought Carrie, as she'd been in distress since well before seeing Alexis, and the first excuse she had, had taken her back to the island. Alexis had somehow brought back the joy and passion for life that living in Greece made her feel. The simple pleasures. She felt her destiny was in the hands of this beautiful place she knew she could call home.

'Carrie, *ela, ela,*' called Petros. 'Quickly come here, I have good news for you.'

Carrie walked barefoot through soft golden sand towards her godfather. He'd aged even over the past few weeks. He was worried, not only because his livelihood was being pulled from under him, but also because the livelihood of many crew members and office staff were also at stake.

'Yes, Petros, what is it?'

'Alexis, he's coming to see us. He wants to discuss business. He says it's only a preliminary enquiry, but he could be interested in investing in the *Aphrodite* fleet.' Petros took her outstretched hand and pulled her up the few steps from the beach, a smile transforming his worried features.

'That would be wonderful!' She smiled at the man who had been a father to her in so many ways. 'When are we to expect him?'

They walked back up the terraced gardens towards the illuminated swimming pool.

'Tomorrow afternoon Alexis will arrive by hydrofoil, and he's accepted my invitation to stay for the night. He asked after you, my dear.' Petros turned and looked across at Carrie. 'I'm beginning to think our Alexis is fast losing his heart to you.'

Carrie snorted. 'That will be the day. That man can't even love his own mother.'

'Carrie, that is a terrible thing to say, and you know it's not true,' he chastened. 'I know Helena myself, she is a beautiful, if rather arrogant woman,' he confided.

'She's just like her son, arrogant *and* overbearing. I met her, remember, when we joined them for a day on his yacht? She was stuffy with me at first but I wouldn't listen and I just sat down and read to her.' She smiled at the thought of Helena. She'd been so pleased to hear the operation to restore her sight had been successful.

'I remember vividly how Alexis stared at you. No one had spoken to his mother like that, ever, not even him. He was amazed at the way you just carried on, ignoring what she said and by doing so, making her very happy,' said Petros thoughtfully. 'You impressed him that day.'

'Did I? I do remember you all sat and listened to my stories.' She smiled, an impish amusement in her eyes. 'You all clapped. Do you remember, Petros? But then he went and spoilt it all with that horrible game of Cluedo.'

'Yes, I remember only too well. You screamed at him for cheating, and he embarrassed you.'

Carrie ignored his comment about the game and Alexis. One day she would get revenge for that. He'd made her blush terribly. Perhaps it had been her lewd teenage thoughts about the man sitting opposite which had caused her to blush. The thoughts she had been having about Alexis had been interesting, to say the least. Then Alexis had spoilt it all and said in that midnight voice, 'Colonel Mustard did it in the library with his dagger,' then added softly with a wicked laugh to Carrie, 'He did it to Miss Scarlet, with his dagger.' Carrie blushed at the thought. She'd been Miss Scarlet that afternoon, the one murdered in that game.

'He did not embarrass me, Petros. Now do you remember the story or not?'

Petros nodded and laughed. 'Of course I do, but remind me.'

Sighing, Carrie began, 'The story I told her wasn't in the book, it was one my father had often told me. It was called the Child of the Sea. He loved the sea, didn't he?' she mused thoughtfully. 'Ironic, that the sea caused his death, in a round-about way.'

'The sea didn't *cause* his death. He died of a heart attack whilst at sea. Or more likely a broken heart. He missed your mother so much. We all did, Carrie. She was a wonderful woman,' said Petros softly.

Her mother had been a true Irish colleen, blue eyes and a tongue that could strike the bravest knave to his knees. She died in childbirth with her second child, leaving Carrie and her father devastated.

Her father was a descendant from an eighteenth century Scandinavian family. His great, great, grandparents having moved and settled in southern Ireland, hence Carrie's white-gold hair. The same hair that Alexis had run his fingers through that morning in London.

Carrie smiled to herself. If she were honest with herself, she was still reeling with the shock of Alexis's proposition. It was true she'd gone to his office to persuade him to help Petros, and she would have used her womanly charms to do it, but to have his baby was something else!

Her womanly charms indeed! She couldn't suppress the giggle; she wouldn't have had the first idea how to charm him. Despite what Alexis thought of her, Carrie's experience was limited. He was the second man she had ever kissed, let alone made love to, and the nearest she'd got to that was the night Alexis took her back to his hotel in a state of exhaustion. He'd been too much of a gentleman to take advantage of the situation.

'Sleep, Carrie,' he had whispered in her ear as he carried her up to his room.

She'd woken up in a strange room, the heavy cotton curtains holding the daylight at bay. There had been a mild throbbing around her temples as she peered from under the cotton sheet to look around. She need only look to the right side of her.

'Alexis! His name had dropped from her lips in total, breath-stopping shock.

He was asleep on top of the bed, dressed in only knee length, figure-hugging cotton shorts. She stared at him; he looked every bit as good as the men who modelled them in advertisements.

Carrie's colour deepened at where her eyes had strayed. She tentatively put a hand to her throbbing head and dropped her lashes, and as she did her memory began to flash back moments of the previous evening's fiasco.

'Too much to drink, sweet one,' whispered Alexis's earthy tones in Carrie's ear.

She jumped, instinctively pulling the cover closer and shaking her head. Alexis was too close for comfort.

'Tut, tut, you were hardly bothered with modesty just a few hours ago. In fact you were only too willing to remove your clothes,' chided Alexis as he moved to rest on his elbow and look down at her with those dark, sombre eyes.

'I was *not* willing!'

Tucking a stray tendril of platinum hair behind her ear, Alexis murmured, 'Oh yes you were. Do you know how much I love your hair? And those beautiful Irish eyes, especially when they're flashing angry fire at me.'

She felt a sudden flush of embarrassment as his gaze rested on her lips. She flicked her bottom lip nervously with her tongue, and realized too late that Alexis had taken that as an invitation.

'Don't,' cried Carrie as she saw his intention, but her plea lacked conviction.

Very slowly he dropped his head and sought her lips, drowning swiftly any further denials with masterful kisses. He always liked to be in charge and this was no different. He pinned her to the mattress.

'You were very willing last night, Carrie,' he said between kisses that had a drugging effect on her. Carrie tried hard to fight that effect but the mere potency of his lips denied her the will to win that fight. It was only as she felt the hardness of his potent arousal through the thin cotton of the sheet that she shunned any more advances.

She tore her mouth away, pushing frantically at the wide breadth of his bare shoulders.

'Alexis, no, I don't want this!'

Pushing himself up on his elbows, Alexis looked down into her face, his voice whispering above her, 'Of course you do, I could have had you only a few hours ago, but I wanted you to witness the act of lovemaking and, of course, participate.'

Carrie pushed herself away, dragging the sheet up to her chin to save her embarrassment. 'I was dizzy and sick then. No gentleman would have, have made love, as you call it, to a woman who is ill!'

Alexis laughed harshly. 'You have a lot to learn about men if you think that. Some men can satisfy their needs by using a woman as they see fit.'

Carrie's face distorted with revulsion. 'That's disgusting! And what's more it's repulsive. It's just like you; you're a repulsive man for even bringing me here.' Carrie had put her hands up at him. The ultimate insult to a Greek!

Alexis snorted angrily. He jumped up from the bed with a Greek oath, and delivered a message that chilled her soul. 'I will make you eat those words one day my wicked Irish fireball. No one insults a Stephanides!'

'I just have.' She always pushed him to the limit.

He stood there, all muscle and tanned bare flesh but for the briefs. He was magnificent in his anger, and he was very, very angry with her, she had no doubt. For the second time in her life Carrie thought she had pushed him too far.

His expression frightened her as his fingers clasped into fists at his side. Instead of reaching for his prey, he had thankfully reached for the telephone, crisply ordering a car to take Carrie home.

Alexis turned on her, whispering dangerously soft words. 'I want you out of my room by the time I finish my shower, or by heaven, girl, I'll teach you a lesson you'll never forget!' He strode into the bathroom, closing the door behind him with a definite click.

Within minutes a shaking, confused Carrie was down in the lobby of the hotel amidst the chattering gossip of the early morning staff. Her hair was ruffled, her wide eyes anguished for fear he might follow her, and her clothes were terribly crumpled. She knew what the hotel staff thought. She could read their minds from their stares and whispers. For the first time in her life Carrie felt cheap. Raising her head high, she marched out of the door.

CHAPTER 3

'Alexis, how nice to see you again.' The words were choked out from behind a very flimsy smile and Carrie hoped fervently that Petros could not see beyond that smile, for he would be shocked at the animosity lingering beneath the jewelled depths of her warm blue eyes.

Alexis, however, was left untouched. His eyes sliced through her smile, down into her upturned face, and somehow he delved into her soul. Even before he dipped his head and brushed his cool lips against her cheek, he had her shaking violently inside.

'Carrie, my darling, you become more beautiful by the day,' he said, his voice carrying the distance from the harbour side to where Petros was waiting near the car.

'You think you're very clever,' hissed Carrie softly, her eyes blazing up at him as he held her. Her hair was gently blowing in the sea breeze and she pushed it impatiently behind her ears as he let her go.

'I don't *think* it, little one. I know it!' He said softly before turning and reaching for his leather holdall. 'Come, let us join Petros and see what an excellent actress you can be.'

Carrie wished with all her heart that she could hit him. As always, her anger never penetrated beyond the first layer of his arrogant features. He could handle her in a way no other man ever could.

'Petros, my friend, I do believe your god-daughter is even cheekier than she used to be,' declared Alexis as he greeted her godfather and then slid his arm around Carrie's waist. He smiled at her astounded stare. 'Cheekier and more beautiful, which is why she is getting away without reprimand.'

Carrie blushed, fighting hard to hold her waspish tongue. Why did he have to remind her of that fateful day?

Petros was looking at them both, a new hope lingering in his expression, and because of that she smiled at Alexis. But she was unprepared of her own response when he returned her smile. It touched her deeply, her gaze lingering on the perfect white teeth and the sensuousness of his full lower lip. Her pulse skidded out of control at the mere sight of his smile, and suddenly she was wondering how it would feel to be loved properly by those lips.

Petros laughed. 'Yes, my friend, but Carrie tells me you have made your peace over her little misdemeanour.'

Alexis gave a shout of laughter and hugged her into him. 'It was forgotten soon after I'd administered the punishment. Although you paid dearly for your rudeness, didn't you, little one?' He pinched Carrie's nose affectionately. 'I fear it took you a little longer. You were still weeping when I looked in on you before I left that night, though I suspect some of those tears could have been your wicked Irish temper. I've heard the Irish are renowned for their tempers.'

Carrie instantly paled; she'd always thought it was Petros who had hushed her cries as she was near to sleep, and Petros who had gently kissed her forehead. And, damn the man, Alexis was correct in his assumption that most of her tears were tears of rage.

Petros interrupted with a soft cough, alleviating the atmosphere by cleverly changing the subject. 'And may I ask why you are using the hydrofoil? Are you coming down in the world?'

Alexis frowned. 'No, my business is booming, as you well know. However, my mode of transport today is caused by having an unruly sister who has brought a dozen or more university friends onto my motor yacht.'

'Ah, I see! So the strong, hard-hearted Greek does have some vulnerable places within his soul,' Petros said with mischief.

Alexis laughed and his hand tightened around Carrie's slim waist. 'I guess I'm a little more tolerant than I used to be.'

Carrie looked from one man to the other. Alexis was no more tolerant now than he had been years ago! He was a cruel heartless beast!

'Tolerant, my foot,' she mumbled, and was thankful only Alexis heard her retort.

At last Carrie escaped the confines of his arm and watched in furious dislike as his lips lifted in a slight, but maddening smile. Petros couldn't see Alexis's expression of mocking glory, his eyes sparkling with a hidden danger.

'Come, we will go up to the villa. Christina has some refreshments ready, Alexis. Your favourite pastry if I'm not mistaken,' said Petros happily.

Alexis nodded his head while discarding the grey linen jacket of his suit. 'First, Petros, I need to speak to you in private, and then I must have a swim. I have been in meetings all morning and need some refreshment.'

Petros nodded and preceded him around the car.

To Carrie's consternation Alexis occupied the seat next to her in the back of the shining red Mercedes. Her godfather had taken the seat next to their driver George, Christina's husband.

She thought the inside of the Mercedes was large enough to escape him, but she soon became aware of the heat of his hard muscular thigh, even through his grey linen trousers as it brushed against her leg, bare beneath her short cotton skirt, and the unwanted effect it was having on her. He'd removed his tie and was now unbuttoning the classic-cut shirt, and turning back the sleeves to reveal the strong dark hairs on his tanned forearms.

Carrie swallowed as she witnessed the action, her breath catching in her suddenly parched throat, her body revelling in the intimate closeness of her sworn enemy. His closeness affected her so much, and she hated herself for her own weakness against him.

Alexis turned to her in the seat, his question sending butterflies' wings fluttering down her spine. 'Will you swim with me, Carrie?'

Carrie's eyes opened wide. Before she had time to react Petros turned back in his seat and stated, 'Of course she will. Carrie never misses a chance to swim with our guests, do you, my dear?'

She was speechless. Her eyes flew to Alexis. She could see his dark, wicked amusement and wished she could say no.

'Good, I'll look forward to it,' murmured Alexis as he threw her a charming smile. He lifted her hand to his lips, and it was all she could do not to snatch her hand away.

She looked across at her godfather; there was hope in his eyes, a life and sparkle she had thought had been lost forever. But he still wasn't the same old Petros she had come to cherish, and because of that she didn't have the heart to refuse him. How could she?

It didn't matter which bathing suit she wore; they were all ridiculously high cut. What in the world had come over her to buy these things in the Harrods sale? But she had, and only now was she regretting her impulse buy. Her old costumes were too tight as she'd filled out nicely since her teens, when she'd been rather waif-like.

Reluctantly she donned her lemon one piece, and impatiently threw a large baggy T-shirt over it. She slipped into her comfortable thongs and made her way out onto the terrace.

Alexis stood at the edge of the steps looking out to sea. Carrie feasted her eyes upon the masculine shoulders which were well tanned from plenty of exposure to the Grecian sun. The expanse of his chest, his muscular arms and tapering waist were all too familiar; she remembered every detail from London. She suspected he was aware of her scrutiny as he stood, quite at ease in front of her, his brief black shorts stretched across the tightened muscles of his thighs.

He turned, a smile lighting his eyes in such a wicked way, as he versed, 'Just think, my dearest Carrie, what pleasures this body might give you, if only for a short time.'

Carrie scowled, saying bitterly as she passed him to walk to the beach, 'I don't know what you're talking about. You know how I feel about you and this ridiculous idea. It's a pathetic solution. Why can't you just help him, he's an old friend?'

The light in his eyes disappeared and taut lines crossed his brow. His mouth tightened visibly. 'You know the deal, my lovely. Isn't it about time you helped Petros considering he's spent the past nine years paying for your expensive education and life-style, keeping a promise to your father that he could not afford, and bailing you out when you ended up in trouble.'

Carrie gasped. He made it sound as if it was all Carrie's fault! How could he know about her foolish investment in the production of that play that flopped? And what was all this about Petros not being able to afford the university fees, and the allowance he insisted on giving her?

'That's a lie! Petros always assured me that my education was worthwhile, and my, my – '

'Your what, Carrie? You were suckered into some foolish scam by a con-man. I wonder if you're still as naïve, but then, I saw you cannot be, in London. You were nothing more than a tempting, little . . .' Alexis didn't finish, because Carrie suddenly turned and reached up, bringing her palm angrily forwards to slap his arrogant face.

She was breathing heavily, anger drenching every pore in her petite body as she attacked him. 'You know nothing! Nothing about me!' With that she fled down the beach, dragging her T-shirt off and running out of her thongs into the sea. She struck out as if the devil himself was after her, and little did she know, he was!

With each stroke her arms cut through the crystal water as she neared the moored raft which bobbed about in the blue-green bay. Instinct told her that Alexis was hot on her heels. She felt the fear that attacked her when a predator was patrolling the deep and sometimes dangerous waters that surrounded her. This predator wouldn't kill her, but he would certainly damage her, if not maim her for life.

Breathless, she was within yards of her haven when he was upon her. Strong arms encircled her waist, causing her to submerge and swallow some of the salty sea.

Panting and coughing as she surfaced, she screamed, 'Get off me! Leave me alone.'

They both submerged again and came splashing to the surface, their eyes caught and held as the water streamed down their faces, when Alexis gasped, 'Swim to the raft, you little witch, and then you can sit and listen to a few home-truths.'

In a frantic effort, she grabbed for the side of the raft. Her chest was heaving with exertion and she didn't have the strength to lift herself from the water.

Alexis hauled himself onto the raft. With one swift movement her arm was caught in a painful grip and she too was pulled up out of the water.

Carrie wanted to cry out, but she wouldn't give him the satisfaction. Her muscles were beginning to complain at such a long, fast swim. She hadn't done this in years, and she knew how foolish she'd been.

It was Alexis who eventually broke the damning silence. His voice was rough with emotion. '*Now* you're going to listen to me, and this time you'll not get away from the awful truth about Petros and his debts. It's far, far worse than you think.'

Carrie bit her lip. She dared not meet his eyes; if it were true about her school fees and monthly allowance, she would never be able to face Petros again.

'Look at me, Carrie,' Alexis said softly.

She did, reluctantly, her tongue gliding across the salty skin of her lips. Swallowing deeply she shrugged and said rudely, 'So talk, I won't know if you don't tell me.'

He frowned heavily and his voice became a silky warning that he was losing his patience. 'Don't take that tone with me, Carrie.'

Carrie sighed heavily and surrendered in a temporary truce. 'I'm sorry, Alexis, and although I don't want to hear this, I guess I have no choice.'

Alexis was shaking his head. 'I talked with Petros only a few minutes ago. He's a broken man, Carrie. He's sold almost all of his assets, the villa is the only thing left, barring the *Aphrodite* fleet which as it stands is almost worthless.'

Carrie closed her eyes and the tears filled behind them. 'Go on; you said he couldn't afford to keep me. But my allowance – I thought that was from my father's money?'

But Alexis was shaking his head. 'Your father left you very little money.' He looked down at his hands, as if he was finding it hard to explain. 'Petros didn't want you to think he was being charitable. You were so stubborn about things like that, and so he let you believe that the allowance was part of your father's estate. It wasn't.'

'I see.' Her voice was edged with raw emotion. Had Petros lied to her all these years just to make her happy?

Alexis reached across to push the wet tendrils of hair from her face. She shivered and raised her huge eyes to his, a pained expression within their depths.

'It wasn't your fault,' he offered gently as his thumb massaged her cheek, 'and it certainly didn't bankrupt him. It was everything else on top of that. The catastrophes that have happened over the years. But you must understand he has never owned a big shipping fleet, or ever diversified into any other fruitful business. Your father was the driving force behind his business and when he died, Petros's shipping fleet withered.'

She swallowed and could still taste the saltiness of the sea. Her voice was steady but her heart was crying when she asked, 'Is he bankrupt now?'

Alexis turned away from her to look back towards the villa. Carrie followed his eyes. Silently they both watched Petros watching them.

'Alexis, please tell me if he is bankrupt?' she repeated more insistently.

'He will be if someone doesn't bail him out soon.' He studied her reaction to his words and added quietly, 'But you could stop all this, Carrie. You have the power.'

Carrie closed her eyes. She was trying hard to forget about his proposal, it seemed so unreasonable.

'You don't understand, Alexis. My having a child and giving it up is totally out of the question,' she said breathlessly. It seemed the whole subject made her breathless just thinking about it. How would it happen? When and where, and who would their baby take after? More importantly, would she figure in his or her future?

Alexis surveyed her through hooded eyes and drawled silkily, 'Then there is nothing more to be said on the matter. However, the deadline remains Friday at noon.'

The dark glint of disapproval showed in his expression but he said nothing more.

So, he was still insisting that she think about it, but how could she? Having a baby with him was such a foolish idea. Or was it?

Alexis suddenly caught the back of her neck and began pulling her towards him on the small confines of the raft as it swayed to and fro. He growled roughly. 'The least we can do is give the man some hope. He's still watching.'

It had been so sudden. One second she had been dangling her legs over the side of the raft. The next she was being dragged towards Alexis and laid across his knee while he lowered his head.

'No, Alexis, this is false hope, he doesn't need this,' she returned frantically, but no amount of reasoning was enough. He would not listen to her objections, nor would he be deterred from his mission.

Gently he rubbed his thumb over her bottom lip, puckering it to reveal her shiny white teeth. As she let out a reluctant sigh he covered her lips with his.

He was so gentle, so careful, biting and nibbling her bottom lip, running his tongue lightly over her teeth until she moaned out loud and allowed him full entry.

Carrie was not only shocked to the very core, she was reacting in a way she thought was impossible.

The tingling wouldn't stop, it just wouldn't stop! It spread down into her breasts, her thighs, her legs and deep inside her soul.

She looked up as he lifted his lips a mere whisper away from hers. 'You have the power to help Petros, you and only you.' Abruptly he lifted his head. 'Come, we must swim back to shore, and you must cool off – such wanton responses!'

With his last remark he tipped her into the blue Aegean sea, his laughter following her under the deep water.

Holding her breath Carrie dived. She'd teach him a lesson or two! It was about time the tables were turned! She held her breath under the raft and knew that soon he would begin to get worried. She'd played this trick many a time on her father and Petros and it had never failed her.

She saw Alexis's shadow leaning over the side of the bobbing raft. Then, suddenly, his fantastic body was cutting expertly through the water. He searched frantically, and then he turned in the water. Carrie wasn't sure what she saw in his eyes during that timeless moment. Whatever it was, it unnerved her to the extent that she surfaced quickly, gasping for air and clinging to the raft for support.

He was beside her in a moment, but now there was a hint of laughter in his warm look that made her stomach lurch, and she shook her head as she saw his eyes on her lips.

Alexis laughed softly. 'When will you learn? The

more you run, the better I like it. Now swim back to shore, sweet Carrie, for if you don't I won't be responsible for my actions.'

Carrie swam back, aware that Alexis was just a stroke behind her all the way. Instead of feeling chased, she found his presence was reassuring in the long haul back to the beach.

They walked breathlessly back to the villa in a comfortable silence. It was only as they climbed the steps to the terrace that Alexis took her hand and linked his strong, firm fingers in hers, denying her attempts to free herself and warning her to be still with a sharp frown.

Looking up, Carrie saw the reason in front of her. Petros was sitting in the shade, watching them and smiling.

'Enjoy your swim?' the older man asked Alexis.

'Of course, the water refreshes both mind and body,' he replied, releasing Carrie's fingers as he helped himself to a fresh orange juice from the tray. 'Carrie, may I pour you one?' His dark eyes assessed her, and a cynical smile hovered around his lips.

Carrie waved her hand in denial. It seemed stupid, but now she was suddenly aware of the scanty lemon costume she was wearing. Quickly she said, 'No I'm sorry, I must shower and change and make myself beautiful. Maybe then I'll come back and join you.'

Alexis smiled, his eyes straying idly over her slim, and yet shapely body, 'You look beautiful without ever having to make yourself so. Doesn't she, Petros?'

'Without a doubt. Why do you think I called my

fleet after her? She is the Aphrodite of Poros,' he laughed. 'Her father often called her the child of the sea,' he reflected, 'and soon after she arrived here I bought my shipping fleet. The same fleet you may be interested in, Alexis.'

Carrie's heart twisted painfully when she saw the eagerness in Petros's eyes, heard the wanting in his voice. Alexis, who had lain back on a lounger, shrugged slightly at her. His look said: The ball is your court now. *Your* court!

CHAPTER 4

The sleeveless, lilac taffeta dress brought out the lavender hue in her eyes and Carrie knew without a doubt that she looked stunning. Her hair was pinned up in a loose chignon, her make-up minimal. She wore the simple diamond stud earrings that had belonged to her mother, and the more extravagant necklace that Petros had bought her for her twenty-first birthday. This might be the last time she could wear it.

'You look so beautiful. I am so proud of you, my child,' said Petros as he entered the *sala*.

His voice was tired and immediately Carrie noticed he was not dressed for dinner.

He was shaking his head, 'Forgive me, I do not feel too good. Can you entertain our guest for me, Carrie?'

Tears pricked the back of her eyes; he looked so pale under his tan, his greying hair seemed more pronounced and his eyes were tired. At that moment she would have done anything in the world for him.

'Petros, are you not feeling well?' Alexis asked as he joined them. The concern in Alexis's voice sounded real, and yet how could it be?

Petros waved his hand away as Alexis went to his side. 'I'm fine, Alexis, too much sun maybe. Or maybe I'm getting too old for all this. Parties are not my strong point these days!' He weakly shrugged his shoulders. 'When Christos realized you were visiting the island he insisted we go to the taverna.'

'Sit down, we can call this dinner off. I am sure Christos will understand.' Alexis's eyes caught Carrie's, burning her with a cold derision. She could almost hear him chanting, 'You can stop all this.' But of course he would never say anything in front of Petros.

'No! You and Carrie must go, just please make my apologies,' insisted Petros adamantly as he rested his weary bones in the white cushioned armchair.

'As you wish, Petros, but first we must make you comfortable. Do you ache anywhere? Can we get you a doctor?' Alexis persisted with his gentle but assertive interrogation.

'No! No doctor. I visited the doctor a while ago. It's just my age, Alexis. I need to slow down,' Petros protested.

Carrie watched them both. Alexis was in charge of the situation, in fact had taken charge since walking into the room. He easily slipped into his role as a leader. His authoritative manner and sheer stance would have had most men obeying his every wish, but not stubborn Petros.

Tears suddenly bubbled up in her eyes and it was only Alexis's cutting whisper of, 'Pull yourself together. Don't let him see you like this,' that stopped her from breaking down.

Christina and George came through and promised they would watch Petros. Only because Christina gave her word to care for him, was Carrie soon sitting in the taxi with Alexis, making their way to the Acropolis Taverna. Turning to one side, he swept a lazy look over his escort. Carrie was so aware of him looking at her she felt uneasy, nervy. Her senses were again reeling from the shock of feeling his thigh so close to hers.

'I didn't have time to tell you how beautiful you look, Carrie,' said Alexis, his tone more gentle as he attempted to caress her with his words.

'You can save the cheap compliments. I'm here because Petros asked me to be here, and for no other reason!' she hissed at him in the subdued light of the taxi.

Alexis laughed, dropping a casual arm around Carrie's shoulders as he confirmed, 'So you're still fighting me, my sweet little kitten, even with your godfather ill with worry.' He caught her chin, forcing her to look up at him, 'Could he be matchmaking? Maybe he's feigning his illness, had you thought of that, my sweet?'

His fingers held her chin firmly and she couldn't hide the quick triggered alarm of her pulse hammering in her neck. With each breath she could taste, feel and inhale the very essence of the man at her side.

There was a subtle scent of his aftershave and the fresh coconut of shampoo. He was gloriously relaxed in a black silk shirt and designer jeans. He was gloriously sexy too, something she couldn't fail to notice.

She met his eyes, allowing him to search her soul before she retaliated breathlessly, 'Don't be stupid. Petros knows my taste in men; he's seen enough of them.'

'Ah I see,' he pondered quietly. 'He knows what kind of man pleases you. Is this so?' asked Alexis. His calm inquisitiveness was infuriating.

Why did she feel she was going to come out of this looking foolish? *Had* Petros been ill? Had he encouraged Alexis at all? Could he truly be feigning his illness?

'Of course Petros knows the kind of man I like,' she assured him crossly.

Alexis released her suddenly. Carrie wished she could rub away the effect he had, and was still having, on her pulse.

'In that case refresh my memory of the men that turn you on. I seem to remember that they were weak, thin, stick-like boys, youngsters, as a matter of fact, a few arty-farty types with long straggly hair.' Carrie wanted to wipe the amused arrogance from his face.

Her hackles rose. 'At least the men I like have not had a charisma-bypass operation! They're real men who can have fun and laugh, and they have a challenge in their life.' She forced herself to meet his look and shuddered when she saw his eyes were darker still. 'And what's more they treat me like a lady, not like a prize brood mare!'

Alexis laughed out loud, so that the taxi driver suddenly glanced round briefly, to stare at them with amused interest.

Alexis threw Carrie a look which she couldn't read and chuckled softly, as his eyes slid insolently over the bodice of her dress, 'Let me assure you, I could have lots of fun with you. You are an exciting challenge in my life, and in spite of your tantrums and your beautiful flashing Irish eyes I do believe I could bring myself to treat you as a lady.'

'But I'd be nothing more than your prize . . .' She was stopped as he put a finger over her lips. She was tempted to bite him, but she didn't because somehow the episode had made her breathless and flushed. His touch was intimate, exciting, even exhilarating. It was infuriating, perplexing. She so desperately wanted to dislike him!

'You would be the mother of our child,' he said minutes later, while his eyes trailed idly across her lips.

Carrie turned away quickly, looking at the lights of the town in the distance. Tears threatened and she was momentarily speechless. Why had he sounded as if he genuinely cared for her, when he wanted her to bear their child and then leave them, having nothing more to do with either him or their baby? Carrie couldn't do that, never in her life could she do that. She would raise any child of her own herself.

The taverna, in all its splendour stood at the edge of the beach. The pale grey marbled steps and columns situated at the front entrance were almost unreal, draped as they were with a mixture of shadow and moonbeam. Traditional Greek music drifted towards them, shrouding them in an atmosphere of romantic charm.

Around the back in the eating area the diners faced a moonlit sea, glittering and gently lapping against the golden sand of Love Bay.

Alexis ushered Carrie from the taxi, an arm on her elbow guiding her up the stairs.

Carrie pulled her arm away, sniping bitterly, 'I can manage; I'm hardly old or infirm.'

Alexis smiled down at her, but there was a bitterness around his mouth. 'Keep this behaviour up and you won't live to see your next birthday.'

'Promises, promises, ouch! You, why you . . .' Carrie was speechless that her sarcastic little comment could cause such retribution. He'd slapped her bottom upon entry to the taverna and now there was no way she could retaliate because Christos was waving them into the kitchen.

Alexis dropped his head a little, whispering in Carrie's ear as he slipped a stray tendril of hair back in place. 'I have a thing about your bottom in that dress, I would much prefer to peel the dress down and kiss you right there!'

Colour dashed into her cheeks at the thought of him doing just that. It flustered her, made her drop her lashes to hide the shock that would have illuminated her eyes. She didn't want him to know what effect he had upon her. The truth was, her reaction shocked her to the core. The emotional earthquake that had just swept through her frightened her. She didn't want to be attracted to him, and yet she was.

Alexis laughed triumphantly. 'So, at last, I have you at a loss for words!' He pondered thoughtfully as he walked towards the kitchen over the marbled floor of the restaurant and threw her another interested look, 'Such an experienced woman and one that blushes still; that's a rare combination. There is something that I haven't fathomed about you yet. But I will, have no fear.'

Carrie was spared the need to reply when Christos came out to greet them. 'Carrie, my lovely, lovely girl.' He kissed her soundly on both cheeks and then turned to Alexis. 'My friend, I'm so pleased you could grace my taverna.'

Alexis bowed his head slightly and smiled. 'The pleasure is all mine. However I must apologize that Petros cannot be with us this evening. He is feeling a little under the weather.'

Pleasantries were exchanged and eventually they were seated near the balcony overlooking the beach. Carrie could hear the splashing of the tide, feel the evening breeze around her shoulders and shuddered involuntarily as she looked up at the full yellow moon.

'A penny for your thoughts,' Alexis asked inquisitively as he poured her a glass of wine.

'Oh, I was just wondering when you're going to turn into a vampire. You're the ideal candidate.' She raised the glass to her lips.

'I am?'

'Yes, of course!'

'And pray tell me why?' he taunted silkily.

Carrie went on, surveying him openly. 'You're arrogant, conceited, dark, and very attractive, to some women, you understand. Vampires are always attractive.'

He laughed softly. 'Is that all?' He raised his midnight-black brows in question.

'No! I think you're cruel and heartless. Like I said you're an ideal candidate,' she returned fearlessly.

Alexis turned the wine glass around in his fingers, making the red liquid swirl 'Isn't it true that once a vampire gives you the kiss of death you belong to him and only him? Once he drinks his victim's blood.' He downed the glass of wine as if to prove his point and his eyes latched onto Carrie's.

They didn't talk for several taunting minutes; they just watched each other. All the other guests might have been a million miles away. The music was drowned out by their electrified silence. Passion surged through every cell of Carrie's body as she eyed the man she truly wanted to hate.

'Do you know that bats are a protected species in many countries, Carrie?' Alexis said as he finally broke the deliberate silence that stretched between them. It was a silence that was charged with a dangerously high voltage.

'Doesn't surprise me; the devil himself would protect you. In fact you could be him!' she told him fiercely.

Alexis rumbled a laugh, his amusement annoying her intensely. 'You have a very low opinion of me. I wonder if this came about when you were fifteen? Because I called your bluff and turned you across my knee and I know for a fact you've resented me ever since, so don't deny it.'

'You did not call my bluff and I certainly don't resent you. I deserved more. I was a horrible spoilt child, and I know it!' She raged at him because he was right. Then she looked up, paused and said in a soft childlike voice, 'I thought you were an honourable man. I thought you stood by your friends. I guess I'm upset because I was wrong about you.'

Fresh bread and several dips were placed in front of them on the gingham-covered table. Alexis viciously broke a chunk of the bread and sampled the *tzatziki* before he gave his reply.

'There is always a price to pay. I have helped people before but you must understand this is a heavy investment, and one I need returns on. You know my price, sweet one. The ball is in your court,' he confirmed with a finality in his voice that warned Carrie the conversation was well and truly over.

They were soon joined by a party of old friends. The women swooned over Alexis as always, especially Anna, who pushed her chair rudely between

Carrie and Alexis, not that Carrie minded much. The German girl was welcome to him!

Minutes later, to Carrie's profound indignation, she realized she was actually feeling a twinge of jealousy. She hated the sight of the woman with her arms around his neck, leaning against him intimately and whispering sweet nothings in his ear while he laughed. The voluptuous redhead was practically maul him in front of a table full of friends, and he was *laughing*!

It was Alexis who eventually put a stop to it by suggesting that Christos show Anna how to dance to the Greek folk music played by the live *bouzouki* band. Almost all the guests at their table got up and danced, and they were left alone.

'Carrie, would you like to dance?' he asked softly.

'No thanks, I'm not in the mood. I'm sure your German friend over there would dance with you!' she retorted angrily.

His eyebrows shot up, the smile on his face only fuelling her anger. 'Do I detect a note of jealousy in that voice?' he smirked.

'Don't be absurd!'

'No?'

'Why would I be jealous? You have to care for someone before you can be jealous,' she confirmed wickedly, her eyes shooting sparks at him. 'And I don't care for you, Alexis Stephanides, not one bit. You're a cad, do you hear me!'

His mouth tightened visibly as if he was holding tight to his temper, 'One day, one day, my girl I'll make you eat those words.'

With that he scraped the chair back on the mosaic tiles and marched across to the dance floor with anger permeating from every taut, lithe muscle.

Carrie watched him retreat, a breath rushing from her lungs. She watched in fascination as he interrupted one of the waiters and took Danielle, Christos's wife, into his arms. He never once looked back.

Blatantly she looked on, unable to keep her eyes off him. He was laughing and chatting with Danielle, looking down into the dark girl's face with interest. As they danced she watched how he moved. Even though he was a large, strong man, he wasn't clumsy. In fact he was in perfect control, had perfect co-ordination.

'Why don't you go and dance with him? I know you want to,' said Christos as he joined her at the table and took a seat.

Carrie looked at Christos scornfully. 'Don't be stupid. Why would I want to dance with him?'

Christos sighed heavily. 'Let me see. How about that you are attracted to him?'

Carrie's eyes opened wide. 'I am not!' she denied too quickly.

'Come now. You're talking to *me*, Carrie. Christos who helped you through a rough adolescence, listening to your woes, advising you when you needed help. Go and dance with him, or are you afraid?' he taunted, his green eyes smiling with a devilish fun.

Carrie lifted her chin and scowled at her friend. 'I dare do anything, you know I dare.'

'Then do it, and tell my wife while you're at it that I would like to spend some time with her, while she's still slim,' he laughed.

Carrie already knew that Danielle was pregnant. She looked across at Alexis and stood up, brushing her taffeta dress into place.

Why was it so hard to interrupt them? Why was her heart missing beats at the prospect? She stepped forward just as the music stilled. 'Danielle, I have a request from your husband. He'd like the next dance.'

Danielle smiled and thanked Alexis. He stood there looking down at Carrie as Danielle left. He was still angry. 'Excuse me,' he said gruffly and made to go, but he stopped as Carrie caught his arm. 'Alexis, I. . . I guess I owe you an apology. Please may we dance?' she stammered, suddenly nervous and shy.

He bowed slightly, his words an affirmation, his eyes sparkling with wicked humour. 'Apology accepted.'

Taking her into his arms they danced for what seemed like ages to Carrie. She had never danced as close as this with him, and certainly never enjoyed it as much.

With unbidden courage she looked up and found him looking down at her. There was the hint of a smile hovering dangerously close to his lips when he said tauntingly, 'If this is another way of trying to persuade me to help Pexros the answer is no. We play my game or no game at all! And you've no need to deny it, this is a trap, but I won't be taking the bait.'

Carrie looked astounded. 'I wasn't trying to . . . to bait you.'

His growl made her jump in his arms. 'That hurt tone in your voice will not alter my course either. My game, Carrie! My rules!'

That did it! Carrie pulled away from him and turning swiftly she ran down the back steps of the taverna to the beach. She didn't wait for his response, nor did she hear his call.

Minutes later she walked along the tree-lined beach listening to the whispering breeze and the quiet lapping of the water.

It was as she stood listening to the silence that she heard the noise behind her. Something rushed past her at speed, whimpering and crying, and on its tail three hard-headed youths.

'Quick, get it!'

'Where did it go?'

Carrie was quicker than the pup's assailants. She knew exactly where it had gone and went running silently after it.

'Oh baby, what have they done to you?' whispered Carrie, her voice gentle and caressing as she crouched down and touched the dog's face with open palms.

The puppy cried and cowered, rolling its eyes in pain and still she crooned, 'Hush, baby; I won't hurt you.'

'I will!'

The voice behind her curdled the blood in Carrie's veins. 'I don't know who you are, but you will not touch this puppy. It could be dying and you have caused this!'

The drunken voice of the second youth jeered, 'Who's going to stop us, lady?' He looked around, The moonlit beach was well and truly deserted but for the three youths and Carrie.

Carrie stood up. She was neither very tall nor very broad and hardly dressed for a fight, but fight she would! 'I suggest you go back to your hotel, and thank your lucky stars that I don't report you,' she said calmly, hoping that she could defuse the situation.

'No! The damn dog bit me. It bit me! Let's get it!' called the third.

'No, you'll have to get past me first.' Carrie shouted into the air, with false bravado.

There was a silence, suddenly broken by a hard-edged voice; 'Go back to the hotel. Do as the lady says, boys, the police will already be on their way. And besides if you touch one hair on my lady's head or on the pup for that matter, I'll skin you all alive! Is that clear!'

He'd arrived out of thin air, tall and threatening and to Carrie a welcome sight. Her small shoulders relaxed a touch.

The leader of the gang eyed Alexis for a while before backing down and calling, 'Let's split!'

Carrie stared mutinously up at Alexis disregarding the silvery glint in his eyes. 'I was managing quite well without your interference!'

'So I see,' came the terse reply.

She immediately bent down to the puppy. It had gone all limp. 'Alexis. Oh dear God, I think it's dead. Oh no please don't be dead.'

'Carrie, let me see,' he muttered roughly as he knelt down by her side and gently probed the blood-soaked dog. 'There is still a pulse. Let's get it back into the light.'

He strode off up the beach back towards the taverna where he lay the pup on the steps with gentle hands. Christos and Danielle were soon with them inspecting the injured dog.

'I have called Jonathan, he will take it back to the clinic and maybe put it out of its misery,' confirmed Christos dispassionately.

'No!' cried Carrie as she knelt by the puppy.

Alexis watched her stroke its blood-stained head, 'Carrie, be sensible. It will hardly last the night out. I don't even know how it managed to run to the beach. We saw them chasing it, which was why I followed. I knew you would intervene if you saw it.'

How could anyone be so cruel? That was the question running through Carrie's mind. Tears trickled down her cheeks, and she shook her head. 'We have to give her a chance, please; Alexis, please give her a chance.'

'Who will want her? Isn't it because she's homeless that she was scrounging? People are cruel, Carrie, that is a fact of life. Now if you want to be useful get me some towels from the kitchen.' He turned to Christos as he watched Carrie reluctantly leave the dog's side. 'Do you know those boys?'

Christos nodded. 'They are from the campsite down the road.'

Alexis nodded and said nothing further. Carrie brought him the towels and fifteen minutes later Jonathan, the local vet, took the pup away to his clinic.

'Come, it's time to leave, Let's say goodnight to our friends,' urged Alexis as he returned from seeing the young vet off.

Carrie ignored him; she had wanted to accompany the puppy, but Alexis had refused and unless she was prepared to cause a scene she had to let the situation pass.

'Carrie,' he warned softly as he bent his head and whispered near to her ear, 'I thought we'd established that when I say go, I mean get off that pretty backside and move. We have a taxi waiting for us. Now thank our hosts.'

It was good manners that made her respond to his wishes, not the warning note in his voice, nor the arrogant glint in his eyes.

The taxi driver played traditional Greek music for them. It was a good thing he did for the silence that surrounded them was awful. Carrie was brooding about the cruel way the pup had been treated and Alexis was none too happy with her for disobeying him.

She shot him a look from under her long lashes. The stubborn planes of his face were illuminated as the street lights flashed by at intervals.

'You could have at least let me talk to the vet,' she accused softly, her blue icy stare meeting with his head on.

'You seem to be under the wrong impression. Time was an important factor for the puppy, any more lost time could result in its death,' he frowned.

'But you said . . .' She was interrupted by his soft, gentle comment.

'No, Carrie, I said you should be sensible. If the puppy could not be saved then would it not be much kinder to save her more suffering?' he said caringly.

Tears sprung into Carrie's eyes. 'But I don't want it to die. It's not fair, it was a baby.'

Carrie dashed the back of her hand impatiently against her eyes and sniffed, but her tears wouldn't stop. The word baby suddenly meant more to her than she'd thought, but she didn't want Alexis to know that.

Words seemed unimportant when he pulled her into his arms for comfort. The clean white hanky was pressed gently against her cheeks and she was reassured that he thought her tears were just for the pup.

'Dry your eyes. I'll phone Jonathan tomorrow and check on its progress. Will that suit you?' When she nodded, he smiled and allowed her to pull back from the comfort of his arms.

'Yes, I'd like that.' He had more compassion for the dog than he did for Petros, and that was something Carrie found very strange indeed.

True to his word the next morning Alexis telephoned the clinic. His face was serious and rather grave as he spoke.

'Yes, I think that would seem the only option you have, Jonathan, and of course I will take care of it as before,' he assured the young vet.

Carrie had just walked into the room, her eyes sweeping over Alexis's tall frame, as he stood with the telephone to his ear. She tried hard not to appreciate the taut muscles she could see through the thin khaki linen slacks and the white short-sleeved shirt that clung to him.

'If that's Jonathan I'd like to speak to him,' she said hastily, but already Alexis was replacing the receiver.

He shook his head. His voice had a warmth about it as if he was speaking to a child, and yet as he swept his glance over her shorts and T-shirt he wasn't looking at or appreciating a child: 'I'm sorry, Carrie, Jonathan is too busy, he's transporting the puppy to the mainland. She's still in considerable pain.'

Carrie opened her eyes wide, her voice husky when she asked, 'Why? What can be done on the mainland? I don't understand.'

Walking across to the old carved sideboard he poured orange juice into two crystal glasses and handed Carrie one as he sat at the table.

'She needs a plate in her back leg. They have far better facilities on the mainland, and at least that will give her a fighting chance. You realize they're not sure if the operation will be a success? If it's not – ' He shrugged his large shoulders and left the words unsaid.

Carrie sat down at the table opposite him. She was concentrating on her orange juice until she composed herself and fought back the tears that would betray her feelings.

Minutes later Christina walked into the dining room with fresh, homemade bread and fruit. There was a selection of delicious sliced cooked ham and cheese on the board just waiting to be eaten, home-made preserves and fresh ground coffee to delight their tastebuds.

Alexis smiled at the portly woman, his words courteous and as always pleasant: 'Christina my dear, you do me proud. Always there is something special, and your bread is already making my mouth water.'

Christina laughed. 'Go away with you! You'd eat my bread if it were old and stale, you've always had impeccable manners. Pity you can't teach Carrie a few.'

'What do you mean?' asked Carrie, eyes blazing. 'I never refuse the food you make me!'

'Oh I know you never refuse it, but you only pick at it; you haven't got a healthy appetite like Alexis,' Christina qualified with utter calm.

'Nor do I have the build to fill, unlike Alexis here – ' she spread her hands in a futile gesture – 'I eat what I can, when I can.'

'Which is not very much these days. Humph, not only will Petros be ill, you will be ill too if you're not careful,' complained the cook as she stomped out of the room.

Alexis was watching Carrie with a maddening smile on his face. 'You can hardly be upset because the woman cares for you. I noticed myself you hardly ate yesterday evening. However, I had hoped it was the effect of having me close to you.'

'Don't flatter yourself, Stephanides. It's the lingering effect of the virus I had. I did tell you in London that I wasn't drunk, but, as always, you disregarded my words as lies,' she said, once again back on the defensive.

Stern lines appeared on his forehead. 'You mean you're still unwell four months on?' He studied her as she sipped at her orange juice. 'I think you should see a doctor, Carrie.'

Carrie opened her delightful blue eyes wide. 'It's nothing, really, Alexis. I sometimes feel a little tired, that's all. Nothing to get all bossy about.'

He examined her face, noting the paleness of her usually rosy cheeks. 'I could insist,' he continued softly, dangerously. 'However, I shall ask Christina to keep me posted, and I absolutely forbid you to go swimming out to the raft when you're feeling this way.'

Carrie was about to reassert herself when Petros entered the dining room. Her retort would have to wait.

His face was drawn, but still, he looked better than he had yesterday, and his presence at the table was a welcome distraction.

'Petros, my friend. Come, sit here and have breakfast with Carrie and me,' urged Alexis as he ushered him to a chair.

'What's all this about a dog, Carrie? Christina tells me you want to fetch it home. You know we can't keep a dog here. As much as I would like to oblige you, child.' He gave a slight shrug.

Carrie grimaced. 'Christina talks too much, Petros. I was just concerned for an injured puppy. I thought we could, well, maybe keep her a little while until I find a good home for her.' Carrie stumbled over her words but Petros was shaking his head again.

Carrie let the matter drop. The only irritating thing about her godfather was his attitude to animals in his home.

Alexis had watched her reaction with some tolerance. He would have intervened had she caused a scene, and Carrie knew that. Instead she bit into a piece of buttered bread and poured out the coffee that was tantalizing her with its rich aroma.

Thoughtfully she poured three coffees. Petros's finances had been uppermost in her mind, and had kept her from sleeping until well into the early hours of the morning. There was only one way out of this mess, and he was sitting opposite her. Strong and reliable, but for how long? Until she'd had his child, or until the child was grown up?

Pushing back her chair she moved out towards the pool, leaving both men to talk.

'More coffee?' The deep timbre of his voice had her shaking even before her eyes caught his in combat. He laughed. 'From the look of those flashing eyes I should be shaking in my shoes.'

Now was her chance to put him in his place. 'I just want to make it perfectly clear to you that I will not be ordered about. If I want to swim to the raft, I will. You are not my keeper,' cried Carrie, venting her anger upon Alexis for the unfairness of his proposition, and for the guilt she'd feel over Petros if she refused.

Alexis mused thoughtfully to himself, holding his chin. 'Let me see. Are you really angry with me for ordering you about? I think not!'

Colour flared into Carrie's cheeks as she looked up into those relentless brown eyes of his. 'Of course that's the reason!'

He was standing over her, close enough to brush the back of his hand down her neck, to rest it on the wild beating of her pulse. He smiled, content with her reaction as he whispered, 'Oh no, little one, you're angry with me for pushing you into a corner. A corner that's very difficult to get out of. I can read your mind, Carrie O'Riordan.'

Carrie pushed his hand away and turned to march off into the garden, hoping to rid herself of his touch once and for all. She needed to breathe the fresh scent of flowers, to see the bright colours and revel in them. To forget Alexis Stephanides, if only for the moment!

Again he grabbed her wrist in his iron grip, but this time he wasn't about to take her to her room for being naughty. Reluctantly she looked up at him. His look scorched her with passion. 'Tomorrow I expect an answer. Twelve noon, no later. Time is fast running out for you, Carrie, and you'd better believe it!'

CHAPTER 5

Alexis rested his arms against the harbour wall. The stiff breeze was welcome, even though it was warm. There was still time for the night air to cool, still time for the blood to settle within his veins. He'd been so angry earlier with Carrie he'd almost done something he was sure he would have regretted. Tipping her into the pool fully clothed had been such a temptation. If only she would come down from that high horse and see he was not asking for the world.

Damn Petros! Damn the whole situation. If she'd been more cordial when they'd met in London there would be no reason to go to these lengths.

He smiled; he'd told her there was no way he would want a wife, he only wanted an heir to his fortune. And yet when she laughed with him as she had this afternoon when they were playing water volley, she'd teased him with the ball and he'd lunged at her, and both had become submerged only to surface mere inches from each other, their eyes catching, holding for several beautiful seconds

. . . It was times like that made him reconsider his own statement of intent.

He watched in silence as he saw Jonathan skirt the edge of the harbour. He waved a salute to the younger man. Tonight he needed the company of his friends. He just needed to drive all thought of Carrie out of his head.

'How is she?'

Jonathan smiled. 'She's doing extremely well considering the extent of her damaged bones. I'm afraid it will take a while to heal fully, but she's on the best antibiotics a vet can prescribe. I'm pleased Carrie found her when she did.'

'And the donkey?' asked Alexis soberly, already reading Jonathan's face, who shook his head sadly.

'I had to destroy the donkey.'

Alexis sighed. 'Yes. I thought as much.'

Jonathan leant on the wall with him, throwing a glance at the man who'd been his salvation. 'Alexis, you can't save all of them, as much as you'd like to. You do enough paying for all the hospital treatment. And the sanctuary you've built hasn't exactly been cheap.'

'Money is something I can donate, and if some of my countrymen need to learn better techniques, then we must provide better education in animal husbandry. At least I can do that for the animals of Greece,' he said thoughtfully. 'My project team are working on the education side. They may need your input soon.'

Jonathan nodded. 'Why don't you tell Carrie? She would love to be involved. Why keep her in the dark?

The first donkey we ever rescued was one she'd seen on Cos. Thin as a coat-hanger. Do you remember? We transported it on the *Challenger*? Damn thing nearly had both of us overboard, and you'd said it was nearly dead. Dead my foot!'

Alexis grinned. 'Yes. I remember. I remember having rope burns, and having to sit with a bucket of apples for the damn thing to eat.' He pondered, frowning as Carrie's face came clearly to his mind's eye. 'I remember Carrie wailing over the donkey when we'd seen it on the cruise. She stamped her feet at me when I'd told her nothing could be done.' He frowned again. 'But always remember, Jonathan, Carrie sees me as an out and out bastard. I couldn't destroy her perfect image of me as the devil. Now could I?'

Jonathan laughed and shook his head. 'I can't see the need for you to hide the real you, Alexis. Carrie should know you as the good man you are!'

'I don't think so. Maybe if things were different, maybe then.'

His subdued look worried Jonathan. 'I'm forever grateful to Carrie, at least for bringing the plight of the animals to your attention. She's saved me a lot of fund-raising work. Sad thing is she's never seen the sanctuary. Nor Dooly. She deserves to see the first donkey her wailing rescued.'

They both laughed.

'She will. One day, she will,' promised Alexis. 'Now how about some supper? Georgio is waiting for us at the Taverna Leki. He feels like smashing plates too.'

Both men grinned. Maybe the Greek dancing would lift their spirits.

Pushing his hands through his dampened hair, Alexis put the power tool down. He'd been working on this particular wall for five hours and still his thoughts were with a blonde-haired Irish girl with a foul temper. The evening with Georgio and Jonathan had ended at three in the morning. He'd thought he was exhausted then, but trying to sleep had taken its toll and he'd decided to work off his energy by attacking the wall with a vengeance.

It was now 7 a.m. Would a cold shower dampen the fire in his loins? Up to now nothing had dampened his imagination. Yes, it was definitely time for a shower, then straight to the office. Relaxing wasn't on the menu today; not when Carrie had his deadline looming over her. Petros was convinced she would say yes to his ludicrous suggestion but Alexis had his doubts. What they were doing between them was tantamount to blackmail, and Alexis had agreed to it!

Petros had pooh-poohed Alexis's idea about him courting her. Time was of the essence, he'd said. Time was something he didn't have, which was why Alexis had agreed. He'd been emotionally blackmailed too by the man who'd to all intents and purposes been more of a father to him than his own. His own father had often left his family to their own devices, and when Spiros had been killed Petros had been a rock to all the family.

He went upstairs to his 'en suite' bedroom. No one really knew about this building, it was his secret, his hideaway. A place where he could be himself. Even rich men needed their own private space from time to time.

He stripped off, letting out a husky sigh. Yesterday afternoon he'd seen Carrie appreciating his body, as she had done, in fact, several times lately. He'd seen it and he'd revelled in it. After London he'd had doubts about Petros's suspicions, but if he dug deep enough, he knew they'd always shared a certain something, a basic sense, or instinct.

Switching on the shower, he washed away the dust and began preparing himself for a day full of appointments, or was it disappointments? He wasn't so sure Carrie would come up trumps, even for Petros.

'Nina, give me an outside line,' demanded Alexis, waiting for the burring of the line before impatiently punching out the international code and number.

'James,' Alexis said brusquely.

'Alexis?'

'Yes. Good to speak to you. How is it going?'

'Fine.'

'No more suspects, I take it? Then maybe we'll have to revert to plan B. So, you'll come here and travel with the ship on her next journey, just as we said,' suggested Alexis, a frown creasing his handsome brow.

'Sounds good to me.'

With the pen in his hand he began doodling. First the word *baby* appeared, then *Carrie*. He circled them both, linking them with a downward sweep.

'They seem pretty consistent, don't they? What we don't need is for them to smell a rat. I think plan B could go well. See what you think. I'll await your report.'

'Okay buddy. I'll call later.'

The call ended.

Absently Alexis looked down at the two words he'd scribbled and linked. He looked at his watch: 9.30 a.m. No wonder James had sounded groggy; it was the middle of the night in the US. Scrubbing out Carrie's name he sighed; he didn't have Petros's faith. Carrie wouldn't fall for a trap like that, not the Carrie he knew.

Waiting like this was hell. Why hadn't he said the deadline was 9 a.m.? He felt like he was waiting for a judge to pass a life sentence. Maybe he was.

'Nina,' said Alexis through the intercom, 'bring me some coffee, and bring your shorthand book.'

'Yes, Mr Stephanides, of course.'

'Bring yourself some coffee in too,' he added softly. He could feel the smile in her voice. 'At least someone seems happy with my endeavours,' he voiced softly to himself.

Nina brought the coffee in, quietly placing it down in front of him on the huge desk. The delicate bone-china cups were crested with tiny shamrocks in the shape of a heart. A gift from Alexis to Alexis when he'd visited Ireland earlier this year.

'Shall I pour, sir?' asked Nina. This was only the second time she had shared coffee with the big boss! Her hands were still shaky from that first time too, even though he'd been very amenable that day.

'Yes, please. You can play mum if you like,' he teased softly then sat back and regarded her at some length before adding, 'So tell me. Have you and Stephan sorted out your problems yet?' He had seen the anxiety bubbling up in his young secretary; several times lately she had looked close to tears, and something always hit him in the gut when he saw a woman cry, especially those he was fond of.

Nina looked up – she wasn't surprised he knew. Stephan had tried hard to keep their secret affair just that: secret, but it hadn't lasted the course, neither the secrecy, nor their affair. Nina had known her boss would find out somehow, they were, after all, the talk of the office.

'No. Stephan is acting like a schoolboy,' she said stiffly. 'And no doubt you'll side with him, sir!'

Alexis laughed, shaking his dark head. 'You're too young, Nina, much too young to know which way I'll jump. But I shall enlighten you!'

He stood up and paced the room. 'Stephan is a fool. I told him Caroline was not the girl for him years ago when he was besotted as a student. I was proved right, but he had to make his own mistakes. We all do, life can often be a cruel *merry-go-round*. When you want to get off, it goes faster. When you need the speed, it stops.' He smiled. 'Let us hope he doesn't make the biggest mistake of his life by losing you.'

Nina looked aghast. 'But I thought . . .'

Alexis smile. 'Yes I know. I'm the devil incarnate in business. In other people's lives I'm a sentimental fool. I like things neatly tied up, for others. Take my advice, wait. Don't rush him, just wait. If he loves you, he'll come running eventually. My cousin is very proud, let's hope his pride is not a brick wall.'

'He wanted me to be his mistress. I refused. My parents would be so upset if I did that,' she said honestly, confiding for the very first time in someone who'd always seemed unreachable.

'His mistress?' Alexis raised his brow. 'And did this include children?'

Nina shook her head. 'No! He wanted me to be there at the click of his fingers.' She sipped her coffee, raised hurt eyes to Alexis. 'He said I would never get another job, if I refused.'

Alexis gasped. 'He said *what*?'

'Exactly that. I've been really scared, sometimes too scared to look at you.' She dropped her eyes.

'How dare he?' Alexis took his seat opposite Nina once more. 'My cousin is getting ideas above his station. That decision is mine to make. You stay, you hear me?'

'I'm sorry I judged you so harshly. Only a shallow man would act on the whim of Stephan. I should have known my job was safe.'

Alexis drank deeply from his cup, then indicated that she should refill it 'Maybe he's having second thoughts. He's not mentioned anything to me and you argued well over a week ago.'

'Well, I'm not so sure he won't. He only phoned me yesterday to tell me my job was on the line,' she said softly, then she looked at Alexis, the tears that had been held back for so long now brimming over in her deep brown eyes. 'I fell in love with your cousin. That has no connection to my work, does it?'

'No, Nina. I will be the one who terminates your contract, should the time ever come, but I can see you drawing a pension here! Don't worry.' Alexis laid a hand over hers.

His frown was darker than ever before. Stephan had taken his role as PA too damn far this time!

Alexis smiled, gently handing his handkerchief to Nina. 'Do you feel like working?'

Nina sniffed back her tears and wiping her eyes she nodded frantically. 'I must keep my mind off him. It's the only way. I'll just go and wash my face, if I may?'

He nodded, watching her go out of his office. Shaking his head, he looked down at the blotter. Quickly he turned it over to a fresh clean sheet. By tea-time he knew it would be scribbled on too. Doodling was one of his many habits.

As the telephone rang, he pressed the connector, 'Alexis here.'

'Alexis. It's Christina.'

'Christina. Is everything all right?'

'*Ne*, *Ne*. *Oxhi*. Oh I don't know, Alexis,' she cried softly.

'Christina, calm down. What does yes, yes, no, mean? *Is* everything all right?'

'Petros has had a turn, and Carrie has run off. I don't know where she's gone?'

'How bad is Petros?'

'He is resting now. A better colour. I thought he was having a heart attack,' she wept.

'Now, now Christina. Have you called a doctor?'

'No. He insists he will be all right. But Carrie has gone, they have been arguing. I mean really shouting at each other, Alexis.'

'Don't you know where she has gone?'

'I think she's coming to the mainland. She seemed frantic,' Christina whispered urgently. 'Please find her, Alexis. I will never rest until I know she's safe.'

The breath that was expelled from Alexis's lungs came as a huge relief. Was she on her way to him? Hell, was she considering having his baby?

'Christina, don't worry. I have a feeling Carrie is coming to see me. I will make sure she is safe,' he assured her. 'Now go and relax for a while. I'll call as soon as I hear anything.'

Pushing the button down, he sat back. So they'd argued. Petros had been so sure he could get Carrie to see things his way. What verbal tool of persuasion had he used to force her to come rushing out? Still, with Petros collapsing like that it would have placed a heavy load of guilt on anyone's shoulders, especially anyone who had a conscience, and he knew Carrie cared more than most.

'Mr Stephanides.' Nina had come back into the office. 'Shall I take your letters now?'

'Yes, but firstly would you check on the hydrofoil from Poros? I want to know its arrival time. Then I think we can cancel some of my morning appointments, or give them to Stephan, and I will then take you out for a working breakfast. You can bring your notepad. I think we both need some fresh air. Would breakfast by the harbour suit you?' He was beaming a smile, his eyes alight with a devilment Nina had not seen before.

'That would be lovely. Who's coming on the hydrofoil, sir?' she added as an afterthought.

Alexis smiled and touched his nose. 'That's for me to know and you to find out.'

She laughed. 'I just love intrigue.'

As she went out, Alexis sat back. Carrie couldn't be going anywhere else? Petros had been right. She would do almost anything for him.

The temperature was already soaring. Today, the weather reporters had forecast, would be the hottest this year.

Alexis sat back in the comfortable chair, pleased with himself. He knew the taxi was waiting for them and had paid him handsomely to make the journey back. But for now he could relax. The hydrofoil was late setting off from Poros and they had plenty of time.

Placing his sunglasses on, he looked out at the flat sea. It was truly beautiful today, but far too hot. As they'd reached the cool reception area before setting off, Stephan had called to Alexis.

'Why am I taking these meetings?'

Alexis raised his sunglasses, saying softly, 'Because I'm paying you to do so.'

Stephan shuffled about, uncomfortable, his gaze washing over Nina. 'Where are you going?'

'To have breakfast, Stephan!'

With that he had taken Nina's arm and marched her out of the building. He'd not missed the forlorn look which had passed across her face. Poor Nina.

Looking out at the boats, he accepted the cool fruit-juice from the waiter.

'Now Nina? What shall we eat?'

As he suggested their breakfast she'd laughed. 'Food is the last thing on my mind. I want to know who is on the hydrofoil?' She threw a look to her boss that made him laugh. 'But I reckon I know. It's Miss O'Riordan, isn't it?'

'And tell me, what makes you think it is that nasty tempered Irish woman?'

Nina thought about the best way to answer this one. 'Because I can't imagine any other woman tackling a man like you. You're a rare breed, Mr Stephanides.' She shook her head. 'I couldn't handle you, but she just might.'

'No she can't,' came the soft reply as he beckoned to the waiter to take their breakfast order.

Alexis had discarded his jacket and tie by the time they saw the hydrofoil arrive. The heat was oppressive, dry, with shimmering waves of vapour above the water line. Nina and Alexis were both sitting in the taxi when they saw a frazzled Carrie run off the hydrofoil at the harbour front. Picking up his tie, Alexis called for the driver to make haste.

Looking out of the taxi, Carrie could see the offices looming closer, but was still not near enough to jump out. As she stared blankly at the traffic hold-up, she reflected on the awful moments the morning had already brought.

It had been almost time to get up, and still Carrie had tossed and turned, unable to rest. The deadline was looming closer, she knew, but she'd already made up her mind to refuse Alexis's ludicrous suggestion. There simply must be an alternative. Knowing she couldn't try to sleep any longer, Carrie jumped up out of bed.

As she entered the dining room Petros gravely interrupted her thoughts. 'I take it your argument yesterday evening with Alexis was a serious one.'

Carrie looked shocked; she'd not realized that from the terrace Petros could hear her shouting on the beach. Alexis had angered her once again. Not being able to deny it, she nodded her head.

Petros sighed heavily, his breath shortening in frightening gasps as he said, 'That being the case you leave me no other alternative but to arrange a marriage for you. If Alexis has argued with you I cannot see him buying into the fleet, and I must assure your future.'

The coffee cup that Carrie had just filled fell to the floor, its contents staining the beautiful Italian rug. She stood there open-mouthed in shock.

'Petros! How many times have I told you? I will marry whom I want to marry. I am not a Greek girl!' cried Carrie in utter confusion.

She stared at Petros; she just couldn't believe she was hearing him say this.

Petros's eyes glazed in stubborn intent, 'You became my ward at the age of fifteen. I believe you have to obey my wishes.'

'I will not!'

'You will, Carrie!'

Wrapped up in her angry outburst, Carrie failed to see Petros's face turn bluish in colour. He held onto his chest, raking his breath harshly inward. 'Carrie, quickly get my tablets,' he groaned as he slid to the floor.

Luckily the hydrofoil had been delayed long enough for her to catch it. Seeing Petros lying helpless on the floor had pressed the heavy burden of guilt even further down onto her shoulders.

Crying, she had helped him to put the tablet under his tongue, assuring him that her argument with Alexis was merely a lovers' tiff and one that she would mend immediately.

With the hydrofoil being late and her taxi ride through Athens a long one, the deadline was looming close, and another hold-up seemingly inevitable.

'I need to be there for twelve, please hurry,' she begged the taxi driver, but the man confirmed her worst nightmare; it was already past twelve. Under normal circumstances being late for Alexis would not have bothered her, but there had been something in those dark, secretive eyes that had warned her to do so at her peril!

'*Efharisto,*' she mumbled to the driver as she threw him plenty of drachmas. Then she fled as fast as her feet would carry her, the silver mane of her hair flowing behind her like liquid white gold in the midday sun.

She reached the third floor breathless and pale as the reality of what she was about to do hit her square in the face.

Alexis was bent over his secretary's desk and he turned sharply on hearing his name, though Carrie didn't realize she'd even uttered it. Her voice came over mechanically, her excuse thin and rasped out from the small shaking frame, 'Hydrofoil was late.'

He studied her, shaking his head in disbelief, 'You always like to push me. Well, this time you've . . .' He never finished, his frown spoke volumes as he assessed her quickly.

This was all too much, surely he wasn't going to stick to his stupid deadline. Her head throbbed heavily. She held her temple to ease the pain as nausea washed over her like a swift punching wave, taking her breath with it.

'Please, Alexis, I tell you it was late.' Like a limp rag doll she collapsed to the floor.

CHAPTER 6

Alexis rushed to her, barking out orders for his secretary to get a doctor. Lifting Carrie easily, he carried her to his couch, and laid her softly against the pale cream leather of the settee. He studied her complexion, at the same time noticing just how frail she was. Gently he began brushing her hair back from her hot cheeks. He shook his head, scowling at his own thoughts.

Quickly he found a cloth and a bowl of water. If nothing else he could keep her cool. As carefully as he could he wiped her face, her neck.

Carrie felt the blessed coolness on her forehead. It pressed gently down her neck into the hollow of her throat, then back once more to her face.

'Carrie. Can you hear me, Carrie?'

Weak blue eyes opened to see Alexis wetting the cloth once again.

'How do you feel?'

Their eyes met. Carrie had been expecting to see triumph in his gaze, not this soul-searching concern.

She swallowed uneasily, unable to cope with the look of compassion in his eyes. It was much easier when he was bad tempered with her.

'Better for the coolness against my skin.' She reached to take the cloth from him but he pushed her hand aside. 'I can do it, Alexis,' she moaned bitterly.

Amusement crossed his face, laughter lines making grooves in his cheeks as he carried on his ministrations, 'And stop all my fun? I think not.'

Sighing softly, she couldn't fight him, nor did she want to. Giving in to him like this, to his demands, had taken its toll. Carrie just didn't want to fight at all, at least not for the moment.

Nausea washed through her again.

'Carrie, are you all right?'

'I feel sick,' she muttered, weakly.

With no effort at all Alexis scooped her into his arms.

'Bed-rest, the doctor said, so bed-rest it is. That has been one vicious virus,' he declared with a slight tinge of guilt colouring his cheeks. He hadn't believed her excuse in London, now he felt ashamed about it.

'I'll be fine, Alexis, please don't fuss. It's not as if I have any work to do. I can just take it easy for a few days,' she whispered in hope, and yet all along she knew he was about to refuse her.

'On the contrary – ' his gaze dropped to her lips – 'we have a baby to conceive and the sooner you're better, the quicker we can get started.' He brushed the blonde tendrils out of her eyes, then smiled, as a kind of wicked amusement lifted the corners of his mouth when he saw the colour rush deeply into her cheeks. 'I want you, Carrie.'

Carrie searched his face; if ever she'd thought he was doing this for revenge, she realized now that she was wrong. It was lust. He wanted her because she was obviously a woman he lusted after. That was why he had been so angry that morning in London when she'd insulted him. He'd been expecting sex, and instead received verbal abuse.

Of course, it fit into place well. Alexis Stephanides didn't like to fail. He would get his child, he would get Carrie for a while. And, once he'd had her, that was it, she'd be on the Stephanides scrap heap.

Carrie shook her head. 'This is all too quick, Alexis. I mean, how do I know that you won't betray me? Why, we could do it now, right here on the couch, you could make me pregnant and then not help Petros.'

Flint seeped slowly into the dark eyes. 'I could, but unlike you, Carrie *I* keep my word. However, if you like we'll get all the agreements drawn up before I . . .'

He spread his hands in a gesture of annoyance, and turned to look out of the window. 'Before I *what*? Jump your bones? Have rampaging sex with you? It's obvious you're not going to consider this as making love, this making of something so special. A new life.'

Tears filled Carrie's eyes, 'Why, are you? How can

it be special to you when you want me to have no more to do with our child than give birth to it?' Carrie struggled to a sitting position on the couch as Alexis turned once more to look at her. 'I think you're going to treat me like some kind of . . .'

'Don't insult my intelligence. I'm every bit as capable at fulfilling your sexual fantasies as those youngsters you were dating, probably more so. Sex between us will be good, I can assure you of that, and besides, we will have a contract. You've agreed to have my child . . .'

'*Our* child,' Carrie butted in, her icy stare leaving him in no doubt he was fuelling her anger.

'OK, *our* child, in return for me saving Petros's and your own delectable neck, because if he goes down, you go down with him. At least this way you keep your allowance. I'll make sure that . . .'

'No! You just help Petros. I'll make other arrangements for my life after the child is born. I want no allowance from you. All I ask is that I will be allowed to see our baby, to be somehow instrumental in its upbringing.'

'We can discuss those details later when the child is here. Firstly we have to conceive the baby, something I am going to thoroughly enjoy,' he declared dangerously.

'Why?' she demanded, 'because I will be some kind of a conquest? Some kind of invisible trophy to sit in your study?'

Carrie once again sank back into the cushions as if the conversation was exhausting her.

Walking back toward her, Alexis took her breath away. The mere thought of his darkly tanned fingers touching her intimately, drove all thoughts of him being a first-class bastard completely out of her mind.

He was standing, looking down at her with a grave expression on his face, then he nodded almost to himself. 'I can think of better things to do in the study. I'm going to enjoy making you scream out in pleasure, and you're going to hate me even more than you do now, because every time I touch you you'll want me more. You'll never be able to resist me once I've had you. I'll be like magnet to you. You'll always come back for more.'

'Bastard,' she whispered, then held her breath.

He was tracing his finger over her lips, slowly down her neck, resting temporarily on her pulse and all the while holding her eyes with his. He moved his finger lower, ever so slowly circling the already proud nipple until he held it between finger and thumb.

'I could take you right now if I wanted, and what's more we both know it. As a matter of fact I don't know why I'm waiting.' He saw and enjoyed the panic in her eyes and nodded. 'Yes. Of course I forgot, the doctor said you should take it easy for a few days.'

Carrie closed her eyes; she was fighting within herself for all she was worth. She was hot, flushed and it wasn't with the illness. Unless of course you called wanting sex with this man an illness?

She wanted him, desperately, and with each roll of his finger and thumb over her nipple she wanted to hate him too. Why did he have this power over her? She mustn't lose herself totally to him, at any cost.

The soft knock against the door saved her any further embarrassment, 'Mr Stephanides, Mr Kouras is waiting outside for you.'

The young secretary spared a look for Carrie, her little grin affectionate as she mouthed silently, 'Are you OK?'

'No, she's not,' interrupted Alexis. 'The doctor says she has to rest and eat plenty of good food. It's a good thing I'm to join my sister for a while on the yacht. She can recuperate there.' He indicated to the other room. 'Tell him I'll be out in a minute, will you?' Turning to Carrie he waited until his secretary had left the room. 'We'll talk later, you try and rest while I'm out.'

Reaching for the blind at the window he shut out the sun. It seemed he could even dictate to the sun these days!

'Alexis, I can go and wait out there. I won't take up residence in your office. I promise I won't go away,' she said as he threw her a guarded look. As she watched him move over toward her, the pulse in her veins skipped precariously.

'Carrie, for once listen to the doctor. I won't be too long. I can conduct my business in the board room. You try and rest. You're still too warm. I'll get a fan sent in; maybe that will bring your temperature down.'

Carrie couldn't help a small smile. He actually sounded quite genuine in his concern.

'I would have thought the hotter my temperature the better you'd like it,' she taunted in a voice *so* velvety soft. If this was what life was offering she may as well make the most of him.

A smile spread broadly across his lips. God, but he was so good-looking when he smiled, which was rare.

'I want to be the one who raises your temperature. Not a virus. Try and sleep.' He ran his thumb over her lips, shook his head slightly then left the room.

Carrie watched him retreat. As soon as he had closed the door, she moved gingerly to her feet. She'd never collapsed before like this and it had been as much of a shock to herself as it had to Alexis.

Moving slowly over to his desk she sat in his chair with an exhausted sigh. She could still smell the essence of him, that subtle cologne that went everywhere with him. She wondered if he ever smelt sweaty. He must, she knew, work out at something. He was too physically fit not to.

His desk, like everything about him, was orderly. The big leather-bound blotting pad had his name imprinted in several places. She scanned the sheet some more. It was like delving into a part of his soul, intriguing her to move on.

She lifted the blotting paper out, turning it over. Why she'd done that she couldn't explain but what she saw shocked her.

The word *baby* had been circled several times, an arrow slashed right across the page to another word which had been obliterated by ink. Licking her dry lips, she touched the word *baby* again. It seemed to sing a song in the depths of her being, and the more she looked at the jotter, the more she knew the word obliterated was her name. Was he having second thoughts?

On hearing the door open, she looked up guiltily.

'Oh. I'm sorry to disturb you. Mr Stephanides said you were resting.' The girl moved further into the room, her curious eyes straying to the blotting pad. 'I think perhaps Mr Stephanides would be angry if he knew you were looking at his personal things.'

Carrie smiled, placing the blotter back the way it was. 'He won't know.' She sat back in the chair; it certainly had an aura of authority about it. 'Will he? What's your name?'

A small smile appeared on the Greek girl's face as she placed the fan down on the desk. 'I'm Nina.' She wrung her hands. 'Maybe you would like coffee or tea?'

'Yes. I do feel a little better. A cup of tea would be very nice, and I'd also like you to share it with me,' she said sweetly, feeling a kind of warmth for the girl. It was obvious Alexis intimidated her.

Nina didn't look too perturbed as she left. She returned with tea and coffee and a small plate of Greek delicacies.

'Do you ever have coffee with Alexis?'

Nina shook her head. 'Not really. I'm not his full-time secretary. Anthea has broken her ankle in a water skiing accident. I'm from the admin office.' She moved closer to Carrie, handing her the cup of tea. 'He scares me a bit.'

'You too?'

Nina giggled. 'He scowls a lot, but then at times he can be so sweet.' She handed Carrie a biscuit but Carrie shook her head.

'Sweet? What? Alexis, can be sweet?'

'Oh yes. I came into work crying last week because my old cat CoCo had died. I was inconsolable for days. Eventually Mr Stephanides took the problem into his own hands and brought me a beautiful ginger kitten. She's lovely. I've called her . . .'

'Don't tell me you've called her "the red devil"!' Carrie laughed when she saw the horror in the girl's face 'I'm sorry. It's just I thought you were going to say you'd called the cat after Alexis, and I think of him as a devil.'

Nina laughed too. 'He can be a nice devil.'

'Who can be a nice devil?'

Both girls looked guiltily at the man standing in the doorway, leaning casually against the dark wood.

'Not you, that's for sure,' Carrie laughed, trying to feign a calmness she knew was not there. With remarkably steady fingers she lifted the tea to her lips in a mocking salute. 'We were talking about Mr Kouras.'

He straightened himself and Nina shot immediately to her feet. 'Sorry, Mr Stephanides, I was just keeping Miss O'Riordan company.'

Alexis waved her back down. 'You two carry on. I've just come in for a file. I thought I'd check and see if Carrie was doing as the doctor told her.' His eyes narrowed as he observed Carrie's blatant look of rebellion. 'Instead I find her up and about. Disobeying everything he said.'

'Oh don't be such an old woman, Alexis. I feel fine now; in fact, I'm quite hungry. How long will it take you to finish your business? We could go to lunch.' Carrie met his long hard stare. 'I realize of course I'll have to buy something to wear. These shorts are crumpled, and my T-shirt is . . .'

'Maybe Nina will pop down to the stores and buy you a sundress. It's far too hot for you to go,' he announced in a voice that brooked no argument.

Carrie smiled stiffly. 'I think you are over-reacting, Alexis. I fainted, nothing more!'

Reaching into the filing cabinet he located the file he'd come back for before turning his head towards her and answering.

'Over-reacting or not, Carrie – you are not to leave this building without me by your side. Is that understood?' He strode across to the big armchair.

Carrie raised her chin. 'I do what I want!'

'You do as you're told!'

'I do . . .'

Spinning the huge chair around to the side, he rested both arms threateningly either side of her, reiterating softly, 'You do as you are told, and if you don't . . .'

'If I don't, what? What is the powerful man going

to do? Throw his weight about, smack me around? *What*?' she demanded, her blue eyes flashing angrily.

'I ignore the doctor's orders.' He grabbed her chin, pushing her face up to meet his scowl.

Carrie pulled away only to be caught again, his hand not being quite as gentle this time.

'You will stay here!' He turned to Nina. 'Go to Echos, get something on my account.' As the girl scooted quickly out of the office without a backward glance, he confirmed, 'I'll arrange for Christina to pack for you. The sooner you recuperate a little, the quicker I can start taming this wild streak in you'

Tears sparkled brightly in Carrie's eyes. 'You'll never tame me. This is just a deal we have. I won't enjoy any of it!'

'No, you won't enjoy it! You'll revel in it, in each touch, each movement. When I make you mine I'll spoil you for any other man. You'll only ever want me!'

Turning, he strode angrily out of the room.

Carrie was asleep on the couch when Alexis returned to the office. Her pale face was softened by sleep, her lips full and damp. Running his gaze down further he could feast on the swell of her breasts beneath the thin T-shirt without so much as a derogatory word from her now silent lips.

He'd love to trace his tongue over the edges of her low-cut bra and nibble his way to her nipples, each in turn. He was no fool; he knew the sparks of lust had only to be ignited and he'd known that for a long time. Even in her teenage years she'd flirted with him, her stunning eyes and body telling him one thing, her unruly mouth biting out another.

He'd wanted her for a long time too, much *too* long, he laughed bitterly to himself. Instead of courting her in the proper way, he'd left it all too late. Time was running out. Now he was making all kinds of demands he knew he shouldn't have to make. Yes, a child was needed, their child, but was forcing her hand like this the only way he could have her and a baby?

She stretched her legs in sleep, then dropped her knee crookedly over the edge of the couch. Her position as she lay there, legs apart, made his blood boil. He was like a youngster wanting to rip her clothes off and let his passion awaken her.

Alexis tore his gaze away, then pulling uncomfortably on his tie he sat down in the chair, rocking it backwards with the force of his anger.

He had to admit it, she aroused him in a way no other woman ever had, and Lord knew he'd been no angel over the years. He'd had his share of affairs, but there was something different about Carrie and until he had her, he would never be able to get her out of his system.

As for the baby, well, he needed an heir and he could think of no finer combination than the two of them. She could be quite icy, whereas he was like a furnace always ready and prepared for the big melt-down. Amalgamating their two bloodlines should have dynamic results.

'Don't look so down in the mouth. It's me who's getting the short end of the deal,' came her sleepy voice. Sitting up was no easy task for Carrie.

Alexis was at her side immediately, scolding, 'I told you not to try and overdo things. What did the doctor say? The words *you must take it easy* come to mind.'

Carrie scowled at him, or was it the feeling rushing through her veins and cascading to the core of her being that she was really scowling at? 'I know. He said I should rest, and I shall on board the yacht.'

Alexis nodded. 'Yes. But maybe we should start now. I'll get food brought to us. You look far too weak now to walk anywhere.'

She knew before he bent his head that he was going to kiss her, but when the kiss came, she was unprepared for his gentleness. His cool lips covered hers, and the kiss deepened as his tongue stole through into her mouth with velvet softness.

Someone moaned, and Carrie realized it was her. Her hands moved automatically to his shirt buttons. She needed to feel his skin under her fingers.

A knock came on the door which neither heard, 'I've got the dress and Mr Simari is on the telephone.' When Nina saw Alexis she froze, 'Oh I'm really sorry, Mr Stephanides.'

Carrie closed her eyes, a groan escaping her lips as Alexis pulled away, 'Your godfather has a way of getting his timing all wrong, and I shall tell him so. This will be finished later.' He promised, touching her nose with his forefinger.

Moving over to the desk he picked up the receiver of the telephone, 'Petros, your timing is getting better, old man. I'd almost got your god-daughter to succumb to my manly charms right here on the couch. I was just about to take her to bed for a siesta with a difference.'

Carrie's eyes flew open. Petros would be astounded!

'Oh, *that's* what you wanted to talk to me about. Then talk, Petros, I have an urgent matter to attend to.' He listened. Carrie could see a frown appearing on his brow.

'You did what?' Alexis expelled a breath. Carrie could see he was furious. 'You want what?' He shot her a look that could kill. 'I don't like being blackmailed like this, Petros. Yes, that's true she will have my child, and I shall have her, that doesn't mean to say . . .'

'Alexis, what is he saying? Let me talk to him.' Carrie tried to take the telephone receiver from Alexis's fingers but he pushed her gently, but firmly away.

'Carrie, keep out of this. This is between Petros and myself. The man's crazy. He wants me to marry you, and if I don't he will arrange a marriage with Theo.'

'What?'

It was all he could do, in spite of his anger, not to laugh at the outraged look on her face. Perhaps a marriage with Theo would teach her a well deserved lesson.

'Well, I've a good mind to let him go ahead. If you married Theo you'd realize I'm not too old to be your lover.'

'You can't do that, Alexis!'

'Can't I?'

CHAPTER 7

Carrie turned away in disgust. These two men were treating her like some kind of bargaining tool, a chattel. They *couldn't* treat her like this. This was the nineties, for God's sake; she didn't *have* to marry anyone. Unless they were using blackmail against her, and Alexis was!

When Alexis slammed the receiver down he stared angrily out of the window. The old man had gone too damn far this time.

Only as his raging blood cooled did he look over to the couch where Carrie was curled up, hugging herself like a small helpless child, having heard everything he'd said.

Hell! He had cheapened her, had said he didn't want to marry her, but just wanted an affair as he always did with his women. If only the old man hadn't interfered by making ludicrous suggestions about marriage. If only he hadn't phoned at all.

For the first time she'd been kissing him back, returning his embrace with enthusiasm and Petros had spoiled it. Just when he was finally getting somewhere!

'Carrie.' Alexis moved forward. 'Carrie, I didn't exactly mean it, like you heard. I think . . .'

'Go away!' she screamed into her fists.

It was then he realized she was crying. He could see the tears coursing down her cheeks, her shoulders shaking with heaving sobs. He'd done this with his thoughtless words.

'Listen to me, Carrie,' he said gently, hating that his outburst with Petros had caused such pain.

'Go away, I said.' She sobbed again and hit out as his fingers touched her cheeks. 'How can you let Theo marry me? How can it be possible? I'm Irish, not Greek. I don't have to do this. I'd rather die than marry him. I hate Theo.'

Alexis looked down at her, and as if seeing her for the very first time he touched his hands over her golden hair. He shouldn't have threatened her with Theo, just as Petros shouldn't have either.

As he drew her up into his arms, she fought, but only for a short while before she collapsed against him in a new fit of tears. 'I can't marry Theo. I *won't* marry him. Do you hear me, Alexis!' She looked at him, pleading, for she was unsure how far Petros would take this ridiculous idea. Alexis was one thing, Theo was a nightmare!

He held her until her sobs completely stopped, then pulled her onto his knees in the big chair. Pushing the hair away from her wet face he looked down into her eyes.

'Oh, Carrie, little one. You're right, you're not a gift-wrapped present for me or Theo, and Petros has no right to do this.' He hugged her a little more. 'Just as I have no right to ask you to bear our child without a wedding ring.' He kissed the top of her head, then reached for the telephone.

'Petros, Alexis here. Carrie and I have discussed your proposition. We were going to be married anyway, I just don't know why you had to interfere. No! Absolutely not.' Alexis exhaled deeply. 'There would be no point in a chaperone. Carrie slept with me in London *and* it was only by the grace of God that she didn't become pregnant then.'

Petros must have been angry, because Alexis snorted, saying, 'We all have secrets, Petros. Now you just arrange for Carrie's things to be ready. Isn't it enough that she is having to sell her soul to keep you happy?'

Carrie caught and held her breath. Did Alexis want a baby way back then? In London? Is that why he had come looking for her? To take her to bed, to get her pregnant?

Reluctantly she untangled herself from his hold, but his arm clamped her safely to his side. He replaced the receiver. 'Not so fast. We have to talk.'

Carrie wiped her hands over her face; she knew she must look a mess. She sniffed in an unladylike fashion and met the simmering anger in his dark eyes.

'You knew he would insist I take your hand in marriage. Didn't you, Carrie? Is that what happened this morning?' Alexis asked with distaste.

Carrie's lips trembled. 'No, it wasn't like that at all.' She spread her hands in futile gesture. 'I had made my mind up to tell you to jump off the nearest cliff, if you must know.'

A harsh laugh escaped his lips. 'That's honest of you. So what changed your mind?'

Again she met his eyes, then dropped her lashes to cover her shame. 'Petros and I argued. He told me he would arrange another marriage for me. Then he collapsed, he was ill.' The look he saw in her eyes was unfathomable. 'I panicked. I swear I'd do almost anything for Petros, but I can't marry Theo. I just can't, Alexis.'

Alexis regarded her through eyes that were mere slits of revenge. 'Ah. I see.'

'No you don't.'

'Oh but I do. I am obviously a far better catch than Theo, am I not?'

'He didn't mention Theo when we argued. I would have drowned myself if he had,' she said with vehemence, then grimaced at her own vision of what even being kissed by that sweaty . . . old man would be like.

Alexis suddenly burst out laughing. 'Imagine what it would be like with old Theo.'

'You're disgusting!' Carrie struck out at him in horror.

'Realistic, Carrie. Theo would expect exactly the same rewards as I in exchange for a life free from financial worry. He's the next richest man I know.' He laughed again as the thought tickled him.

'Don't, don't laugh at my expense. I tell you I would kill myself first.' Carrie scrambled off his knee, hurt by the truth in his words. For a moment she held onto his shoulder, knowing he'd seen her tremble violently as she'd stood up. She was asking too much of herself, and had been since her play had so miserably flopped, taking with it a large chunk of her ambition, her goal. Or had that been Petros's ambition for her? She was so confused.

When she finally managed to move, she sat opposite Alexis and felt a little more in control. Now she could question him while he was safely at arm's length.

He was regarding her through lazy, half-closed eyes, when she attacked breathlessly, 'Why did you tell Petros I'd slept with you?'

He shrugged, throwing an approving glance over the length of leg she was revealing. 'You did sleep with me. I held you safely in my arms for most of the night. As for having sex, that will be remedied shortly.' He raised his brow, his voice soft, suggestive. 'I insist we sleep together even before we are married. That's all part of the bargain, Carrie. I don't care whether you have a child in or out of wedlock. I want you, full stop.'

Alexis watched her, fascinated as she quietly weighed up the pros and cons. Petros had obviously frightened the hell out of her with his threat of Theo and, what's more, had infuriated Alexis, though perhaps he was right and marriage to this short-tempered little hellcat would be fun. Most of his other affairs, or liaisons as he liked to call them, had been engineered to keep his mother off his back. He'd never allowed any of them too close, but Carrie was different. He wanted Carrie any way he could get her; he always had. But marriage . . . he was still unsure.

Pressing a button on the telephone, he said softly, 'Nina, would you like to bring us more coffee, and maybe arrange for a light lunch to be brought in.'

'Yes, Mr Stephanides.'

Alexis then made arrangements for Stephan to take over while he was having a break.

Stephan, Alexis's cousin, had been worth his weight in gold over the past ten years. He was charming, polite, had boyish good looks and was everything Alexis professed not to be. He'd always been a perfect gentleman, in Carrie's eyes, and that was something she suspected was alien to this tall athletic Greek businessman. Sadly, Stephan was going through rather a trying divorce at the moment and was still hurting over it, so Petros had informed her.

A little knock came on the door.

'Come in, Nina.'

Nina, whose face was suffused with colour under her olive skin, trotted in with coffee. She looked up sheepishly at Alexis. 'I'm sorry about earlier, Mr Stephanides. I should have . . .'

Alexis waved her excuse away. 'Don't be silly, Nina. I'm the one to blame. I initiated it.' He smiled warmly. 'Have you ordered lunch?'

'Yes. I'll have it sent in as soon as it arrives.' Nina turned to Carrie who was sitting with her legs now curled tightly under her as she silently pondered the events of the past week.

Nina said, 'I've brought you a lovely dress.'

'Thank you. What about shoes, underwear? I have nothing at all with me,' Carrie asked.

Nina was rooted to the spot. 'Oh Lord. I never thought, of course you will need . . .'

'Maybe shoes. I don't think she'll need underwear, certainly not with what I have in mind for her,' intervened Alexis with a grin.

Nina laughed uncertainly. 'No, of course not,' she said, before making a quiet exit.

Carrie's blue eyes danced with shock, dilated with unknowing passion. She bit her tongue before a grunt of disgust escaped her lips.

Mischief whirled through Alexis's eyes, inviting Carrie to do combat. A half-smile appeared on his lips. *Come on, retaliate*, were his unspoken words.

'I can't wait. I hope your efforts will be better than Theo's.' She smiled sweetly at him. 'Sex doesn't interest me one bit, my darling. You'll have to be a master at it.'

'Touche,' Alexis said softly, 'and I *am* a master at it.'

Carrie's glance flew to his as excitement whirled through her. His voice had held a promise, a promise of something special. But even so Carrie wasn't convinced. Too many times she'd heard of disappointing encounters from women expecting too much of their men.

Alexis was *her* man now, just as she was *his* woman.

Once outside the office Nina sat down with a thump in her chair just before Stephan came marching through the outer office. With a big sigh she looked up at him. Not being satisfied with making a fool of herself in front of Alexis, she felt she was about to become an even bigger fool for this man. Simply because she was in love with him.

'Clever, aren't you?' he accused.

'Stephan, I don't know what you mean?'

Eyes so like Alexis's burnt into the young girl's face. 'No? He's taking you with him, on the yacht. Tell me you didn't know that little gem!'

Nina looked astounded; she shook her head.

'I don't understand. He's said nothing.' Nina jumped up as she realized his intention was to go in and see Alexis. 'I wouldn't do that if I were you. He has Miss O'Riordan in with him, and by the looks of things it could be getting pretty intimate in there.'

'Intimate with Carrie? Never! They've had a hate thing going for years. They just love to hate each other,' he said with disdain as if the subject bored him.

'Precisely, they *love* to hate . . .' She stopped, pondering on his earlier words and said, 'I wonder why he wants me to go with him?'

'Probably heard you'll take your knickers off for anyone. Maybe that's what you did this morning?'

'That's not true!' she defended herself. Whoever said loving someone was easy? Since their disagreement he had been intolerable.

'It's common knowledge that my dear cousin likes a diversion when on the yacht. Could he have been trying out the merchandise?' His look showered her with disgust. 'Maybe you'd like to try for the biggest fish of all. I doubt even he could resist some the things you have on offer. Horizontal gymnastics have nothing on your moves.'

A loud clap echoed around the outer office as Nina's small hand contacted with Stephan's face.

'Why you . . .!'

'What in hell's happening here?' demanded Alexis as he witnessed Stephan about to grab Nina. 'I wouldn't if I were you Stephan. Your private life should be dealt with outside this office.'

Stephan reddened. 'You know then. I suppose she's told you all the fascinating details.'

Nina's face dropped. The hurt was obvious.

'That you've both been using my office as . . .' He sighed heavily. 'I think the whole of Athens knows. You could have been more discreet. No wonder Caroline found out. It was Caroline who told me, if you must know. After she found you on *my* couch.'

'Oh and what about your little fiasco? Nina tells me you have Carrie in there begging for it,' Stephan continued, ignoring the deep frown which appeared on Alexis's face. 'To be honest I thought Nina would suit your needs much better. The love 'em and leave 'em type. I can recommend her talents between the sheets.'

'Enough!'

'And she's quite a jockey . . .'

'I said *enough*! Don't cheapen my secretary any more. You just take over for me without another word if you cherish your position in this company,' said Alexis soberly. He'd got Stephan's full attention. 'And if you must know, I'm taking Nina out of your way because she's had enough of your childish attitude. You don't deserve any woman.'

Stephan looked like he'd been slapped again. 'My job?'

'Is on the line, Stephan, and has been for the last year. Now do what you're best at and organize a reception for my official engagement. I'll talk to my mother and ask her to furnish you with the details. No doubt *Mama* will want to sort out the finer details with you,' he said, his voice sounding rather bored now.

'Who are you betrothed to?'

'Me,' came the soft feminine voice from the doorway.

'Carrie? How lovely to see you. It's been too long.' Stephan went to her, kissing her gently on the cheek. He liked Carrie, 'I'd like to say you look wonderful, but you don't look very well at all.'

'She's not. The doctor says she needs rest and plenty of good food. Which reminds me, Nina, give the chef a call and ask him where our lunch is?'

'Speak of the devil,' said Nina as she saw one of the company's kitchen staff wheel in a trolley.

'Maybe you two would like to join us? Stephan, Nina, please say you'll join us for lunch?' implored Carrie to a smiling Stephan.

He inclined his head, 'If Alexis agrees I'd love to.'

'Nina?' Carrie saw doubt in the young girl's face. 'Don't let me be outnumbered. I have a lot of trouble putting a feminine point of view across here. I need your support. Two against two,' said Carrie, her look imploring Nina to agree.

'Sounds like a war,' Alexis murmured softly, his look connecting momentarily with his fiancee's.

'Exactly,' replied Carrie.

There was laughter in his voice, amusement written over his face. 'Then I insist you both stay.'

Stephan inclined his head in acknowledgement then turned to Carrie. 'Petros told me you were thinking of coming home for the Easter Mass this year. He was disappointed you could not make it.'

Carrie felt a surge of guilt. She had promised Petros, but then Peter, her friend's son, who suffered a mild form of Down's syndrome, had been rushed into hospital with appendicitis. He'd been crying for Carrie and in the end she'd stayed at the hospital, her flight bag at her side.

The look in Carrie's eyes softened; she missed Peter dearly.

'Yes,' she said thoughtfully, 'I couldn't leave Peter, he's my friend, you understand. We've been through a lot together,' she explained when all three pairs of eyes searched her face. 'He was in hospital, and he was asking for me, and I love him so much I couldn't refuse.'

Alexis tutted, but before he turned away Carrie swore she saw the green-eyed devil rise to the surface threatening to shake his habitual cool demeanour.

That thought gave her the strength to carry on. If Alexis was jealous he must have more feelings for her than he let on. But the question she couldn't answer was, why did he insist there be a child? Yes, she wanted children, but he was forcing her hand, and all because she'd spurned him in London.

'So who's Peter?' asked Stephan.

Carrie shot a look at Alexis and saw his shoulders stiffen. This man needs teaching a lesson.

'He's someone I love very much. I would have brought him with me but it was impossible.' She turned to Alexis, her blue eyes sparkling with mischief. 'Darling, would you put some fruit on my plate? I think I'll sit a while, I do feel rather "flimsy", as if the slightest exertion will do me no good at all.'

Petros sat drinking his brandy. Plan A had gone better than he'd at first anticipated. His accomplice had said it would and she knew Alexis Stephanides of old. Petros could only bow to her superior knowledge.

Whilst Alexis and Carrie were sailing around the islands, Petros and his accomplice would be visiting the heart specialist in New York; she had convinced him it was the only way.

Taking another drink of his beloved, yet forbidden brandy he sighed softly. Things were now starting to take shape. He looked at the dark rich liquid swirling about in the glass as he twirled the stem through his fingers.

Pouring out another measure, he picked up the telephone. 'It's me. Plan A went perfectly. Alexis went into a rage, but he's agreed.' He sipped his drink. 'He mustn't know – neither of them must know.'

The woman on the other end of the line tutted, her refined voice just a little too sharp. '*I* told you they mustn't know. And by the way, Petros, that consultant told you to stop drinking brandy. I suggest you do it now.'

The line went dead. Petros afforded himself a big grin. What a woman she was. Raising his glass, he downed the brandy. Soon, soon he would have to stop drinking the stuff.

Carrie looked around the half-finished room. It was huge, airy and at one time she knew, had been desolate. She'd expected to see a very expensive apartment by the sea and had been quite shocked when Alexis had helped her into the former bakery by the small Tourkolimano harbour.

'Does it surprise you, my love?' came a voice very close to her ear, whispering a potent and powerful message.

Carrie jumped at his nearness, at the hidden depths beneath that dark mahogany voice. His intent had been obvious all through lunch; he was about to start his quest for a child. The more Carrie had looked at him, the more she'd begun to see him in an entirely different light. He'd cajoled her, been attentive, even good fun, and she had to admit to herself that she was extremely attracted to him. Losing her virginity to him was something she had long taken for granted. But she mustn't lose her heart to him.

She nodded, surprised again as his arms slid around the flatness of her belly, gently pulling her back against him. The feel of his rock-hard body excited her.

Oh Lord, he's aroused, thought Carrie as she tried to concentrate on the sandblaster which stood in the corner of the room. He must have felt her stiffen because he backed off just a little.

'Are you having it decorated? It looks like some major changes have taken place.' Her pulse raced mercilessly as he nibbled the side of her neck.

'You could say it's my hobby. I'm trying to restore the old stonework to its former glory. Unfortunately I don't get much time, and only this half of the room is decent.' He indicated the far wall which could only be partially seen through the temporary dividing screens. 'Someone has painted over it, as you can see, and not with whitewash.' He nuzzled close to her ear whispering, 'I want you out of that dress, as nice as it is.'

'I know,' came the soft affirmation. She wanted the dress off too!

Light, caressing fingers moved from the flat of her tummy upwards gently moulding over her breasts. She heard his sigh as he stilled for one timeless moment over her nipples.

She held her breath as everything within her being erupted. Excitement such as she'd never felt bombarded her veins, her senses, her body.

Then, his hands were gone from her covered breasts and he was reaching for the delicate shoulder-straps of the blue sundress. When the dress dropped like a feather to the floor, Carrie was pleased he'd sent out for some underwear for her after all, as basic as it might be. She only wore minute blue lace panties but they afforded her some modesty and a little comfort. When she would have covered her breasts with her hands he caught them and held them captive at her side, as if he'd been reading her mind.

From his superior height he could see her full breasts standing proud. He watched, fascinated as they trembled when she shuddered with desire. He could no longer keep his hands off them; her erect rosy nipples were just screaming to be touched.

Carrie was not only breathless, she was almost begging him to dampen the fire he'd evoked inside of her merely by undressing her. The fire that had been smouldering for years deep inside her.

She swallowed hard, then swayed against him as his fingers circled each nipple, seductively slowing when he reached their centre. He scoured each in turn with his fingertips, then held each nub between finger and thumb.

'Alex,' she gasped.

'Tell me what you want.'

'You. I want you.'

He chuckled, satisfied that she'd at last admitted the attraction. 'How shall I take you, and where?'

Carrie shook nervously. She had to tell him. Carefully, she turned in his arms, and looked up at him with uncertain eyes, unsure of how he would take the news. Bracing herself against him she held onto his broad shoulders. His hands had obediently stilled and clutched her waist.

'What is it, Carrie? Don't tell me you're nervous?' His voice was incredulously calm.

She could see passion in eyes as deep and mysterious as the ocean itself.

'Where, Carrie, and how?' his deadly soft voice reminded her. 'Do you want to be like most and have sex in the bedroom. Or would you like to be bold and have me take you on this beautiful Italian rug, coloured with the birds of paradise.'

Carrie glanced the rug. She was throbbing with desire and had been all through lunch. She didn't know what on earth had come over her. She was scared, and yet excited beyond her wildest dreams. But she was hurt too. Hurt that the two men she cared for most were treating her like this.

'It's just . . . I don't know how . . .' She looked up at him, desperate for some help.

'How? What? Where is this all leading?' He frowned then grabbed her chin, his eyes half-serious. 'Are you trying to tell me what I think you are?' He kissed her softly. 'I don't believe you're frigid, not in a million years, and I'll prove it.' Covering her mouth with his own he kissed her softly and thoroughly, until she responded wildly, grabbing his hair, pulling his head down so she could reach inside his mouth with her tongue. Her eyes were tightly shut now, her little moans delighting him. 'And definitely not gay, the way you respond to my kisses.'

'I'm not frigid or gay. I'm a virgin, you fool.' She met his eyes, saw a flicker of surprise, then warmth before she carried on with her explanation. 'Well . . . It's just that I've never got around to it. The thought of sex has always seemed to . . .'

'That sounds challenging. I think the birds of paradise will be an apt place to deflower you, my darling.'

With a quick movement he'd up-ended her, laying her softly against the rug. As she leaned her head back, he hooked his fingers into her panties and whipped them off.

She was totally naked. Her only saving grace was the shadows in the room, cast by the blinds which were still slightly closed on the evening sun.

He looked down at her, a muscle twitching slightly in his darkly tanned cheek.

'Take *your* clothes off,' she said as he dropped to his knees, but he shook his head.

'Not until I've finished with you,' he groaned as he parted her trembling legs with his hands.

'I thought all this usually started with a kiss,' she said, her breathing becoming more rapid by the second as he leant nearer to her core.

He raised his head slightly. 'It does, but there are no rules to say where that kiss should be.'

She was wet through with perspiration, her cheeks hot and flushed by the time he moved over her. She couldn't even remember when he'd shed his clothes.

'This,' he said roughly, 'is going to hurt a bit. I'll be as gentle as I can, but I'm no saint.'

She gasped, even before he partially entered her. Having caught a glimpse of him earlier she closed her eyes, wondering *how on earth it would fit.* But the thought excited her. As she felt him enter her, she saw him bite his lip as he urged himself forward steadily. It was obvious he wanted nothing more than to join them swiftly together. He'd been so good up to now, so kind, so gentle. She'd never read about this in the magazines. The uncomfortable pressure, the stretching and aching of muscles she'd never used. Shifting slightly, she allowed him further access.

She saw him frown again, beads of fine perspiration on his brow as a slight tremor took hold of him. *Oh hell,* she thought viciously, *he's frightened of hurting me*! Grabbing his buttocks she pulled at him and surged her hips forward, wrapping her legs about him in the same movement. She caught her breath as something gave way. Damn! That did hurt!

He opened his eyes, frowning a little as he settled himself deeply inside her. She never failed to surprise him.

She pulled his head down to her waiting lips. 'Thought I'd take the onus off you. And you were right. It did hurt.'

He kissed her and shaking his head and grunting in disapproval, he ground out, 'Serves you right. I was taking it gently.'

'Gently! We'd be here until Christmas waiting for you.' She laughed and then gasped as he withdrew and penetrated her properly. It was a good way of getting her attention. 'In retrospect,' she mumbled, 'maybe I *would* have liked that.'

From then on, they stopped talking, stopped teasing and both became very serious, their goals solitary, yet mutually entwined. With every rise and fall of his muscular body Carrie heard enchanted birds singing, felt excitement racing through her. When she began to climax she cried his name so loud and clung to him so much, that he just had to spill himself into her, unable to wait a moment longer.

Alexis looked down at her asleep on the rug. This had surpassed even *his* expectations. He'd never made love to a woman quite like this and she'd been a virgin too. A pure, white flower, opening from a bud into a beautiful bloom in front of his very eyes.

He'd believed her boasts that she'd bedded all those men in London because she was so beautiful, and so beautiful a flower is usually picked in bud; he was enthralled this flower had been left.

It was a good thing she'd told him in time of her innocence; at least he'd taken it a bit slower. He smiled as he remembered how she'd given him that tug of his hips to take him over the last hurdle, the last barrier before he'd felt her body surrender completely. He would always treasure that memory.

She'd have been astounded if she could have read his thoughts over lunch. He'd been insanely jealous of this man she called Peter. Damn it, he'd almost lost control and gone into a major rage. He frowned. The reason he hadn't gone into a rage had been simple. There had been this look in her eyes, as if somewhere, lifetimes before now she had shared something just as deeply with Peter. He'd felt he'd been punched in the gut, the feeling had been so strong. At least now, he was one step ahead of Peter and always would be; she could give her virginity to no other man.

She stirred beside him, her almond-shaped eyes opening slowly. She shivered; the violet hue in her eyes darkened momentarily as she surveyed the shadowed room.

It was cooler now with the evening breeze coming in from the sea stronger. She threw Alexis a shy look from beneath her lashes, a smile appearing on her full pink lips.

'Why the smile? Are you happy?'

Her smile broadened. She was throbbing, her whole body was throbbing, she needed to take part in the act of love once more.

'I didn't think your performance was entirely up to scratch. I could be happier.' She heard Alexis's indrawn breath as she dared herself to raise her cheeky face to his. For there was no mistake what message it would relay to the man at her side.

He sat up on the rug, his strong forearms resting on his knees, his chin on his hands. He met that look. 'Cheeky baggage, the doctor said you should rest.' His eyes connecting with hers, he whispered, 'You're jesting, right?'

'Hell no.' Carrie held her breath, hoping wildly that he would take the hidden challenge.

He frowned, drew his breath slowly in again. Expanding his powerful chest he unfolded his arms, then dropped slowly onto his side, his face dangerously close to Carrie's breast.

Her heart skipped, her lips twitched with anticipation as he looked sedately down her length, his eyes lingering until the tips of her breasts formed into hard buttons and her womanhood shivered beneath his gaze.

'Not happy, eh?' His face darkened as she shook her head. She knew she was playing a dangerous game, that he could demand far more than she knew how to give, but she wanted to experiment with her soon-to-be husband.

A lazy finger circled her nipple, then pinched as he watched for the emotion in her eyes. Carrie bit her lip; she must not give herself away. The torture of his fingers was exactly that, only this time he was less gentle.

Her shining eyes challenged him, the subtle movement of her body excited him.

'So you're impervious to my advances, are you?'

Closing her eyes she nodded. 'I think you should try harder . . . I didn't feel a thing last time . . . I . . .'

His mouth came crashing down on her lips, wiping away the words before she could utter any more. All along he'd thought she was with him. Now he became the aggressor, taking her with such passion, such force.

Carrie cried out as he pushed her legs apart and entered her swiftly. To see Alexis lose his cool in such a situation thrilled her. She'd always, always pictured him as a mechanical lover. She should have known better. She should have listened to her own body, for that had always said they shared something special.

'I'm going to plaster the birds of paradise on your backside for that comment, *agapi mou*,' he muttered with an upward thrust of his hips.

'No! Alexis, let *me* do that to *you*,' Carrie stilled, as did Alexis. What had she said? Oh, lord! Whatever it was he was obeying her. Flipping her over with ease, he left her for one moment. Then he was lifting her on top of him, lowering her down on the hard shaft of his desire.

'Oh. Oh . . . oh. Oh Alexis,' she moaned softly, closing her eyes tightly, for the feeling which filled her was truly beautiful. Instinctively she began to move above him.

A rumble of laughter erupted from him. 'I've been had. You minx, I've been had.'

Opening her misty blue eyes she nodded, her hips moving rhythmically. 'Never believe a woman who's got lust on her mind.'

CHAPTER 8

The first light of early morning filtered through the arched bedroom window. This room too was bare but for a tall lamp, a rug, the antique set of drawers and the big bed they had shared all night long. The room itself had been a storeroom at the top of the building, Alexis had told her over their simple supper of cheese and bread with a good bottle of wine to wash it down, and the flickering of the single rose red candle.

Carrie opened her eyes. Alexis was already out of bed. Shrugging into his discarded shirt, still littering the floor from the previous evening, she made her way to the stairs. With every step she ached. A small smile etched her face with a profound contentment. He'd lost control last night, and what's more she'd encouraged him to.

Standing on the second step, she could see him working below with a sandblaster. His muscles bulged, beads of perspiration rolled down his arms, his back, his legs. Oh, but he was beautiful. Why had she only just realized this? And why did the whole episode have to be about 'owning her'? First Petros, when he officially adopted her at fifteen and now Alexis. To be fair to Alexis though, he didn't want to marry her. He wanted a child from her. He'd always been truthful about that.

'I wondered how you kept fit. This must be it,' she said as the machine came to a grinding halt.

Brushing the perspiration from his face, Alexis turned. 'Nice shirt. I prefer it on you than myself.' He studied her. 'On second thoughts maybe I prefer you naked.'

Carrie smiled. 'That being the case why didn't you wait for me to wake up? We could have had round six up against that wall! You seemed insatiable last night.'

Alexis turned fully towards her, hands on his hips. 'Carrie, what's got into you? It was *you* who suggested to me to, to . . .'

Carrie blushed. Making love on the veranda at midnight had been her idea, even down to the adventurous position. 'I know. I know.'

Alexis saw the way she was chewing at her bottom lip, the sweet way she was colouring. He'd thought at the time it was all too soon, but Carrie had been so persuasive. 'Carrie, most married couples do exactly the same thing.'

'We're not married.'

'We will be.'

Carrie shook her head. 'I never agreed to this. We will have a child, but I never agreed to marriage,' she said adamantly.

'Have you forgotten Theo? Petros means every

word. It's me or Theo, the choice is yours. And, if I remember rightly, you did agree.'

'Theo?' Carrie nodded. 'How could I forget Theo?' Only she *had* forgotten. The man standing across the room looking like *Adonis* had hardly left room in her thoughts for anyone else, least of all Theo!

Thumping herself down onto the bottom step, she held her head in her hands. 'How could I forget the threat of Theo? Have you two planned all this?'

Alexis moved swiftly toward her. Guilt surged through him like a raging tornado. He didn't like himself right this minute, the lies he'd told. 'Carrie, don't be ridiculous. You know my reasons.'

'Do I?' She shrugged her shoulders, the movement allowing him a tantalizing glimpse of her breast. 'I suppose you think you'll have me popping kids out like puppies, by the dozen. Well, you're a one-off, matey. One child is my quota, you hear me?'

When she would have turned and dashed from the room, he caught her to him, laughter deep in his eyes. 'Carrie, let's just take it as it comes. Anyway I doubt I'd cope with a dozen little Carries. Now let's find you something to wear. I need to wash and we both need feeding.'

From then on, they settled into a comfortable routine. They shared breakfast in a taverna overlooking the small harbour, both dressed in cycling shorts and shirts, sunglasses and bandannas. Carrie had never seen this side of him, and she knew most other people hadn't either.

'So come on, lover, what are we eating?' he whispered softly.

She couldn't see his expression behind the glasses but knew it would be beautifully wicked. Reaching her leg across to his she ran her foot delicately over his muscular calf.

She giggled. 'Poor Petros, had he known I was still a virgin he would have put a bodyguard outside my room. Then you, you sex maniac, you'd have got nothing last night.'

Slowly Alexis took his glasses off. 'You call me a sex maniac ever again and I'll . . .' He moved forward and whispered something in her ear.

'You sex maniac, you,' she screeched as he made to stand up. The scream that came from her mouth was quickly hushed with a kiss. Minutes later he raised his head and a broad smile which couldn't be stopped curved his lips upwards. He'd never known a woman who could be so much fun.

Sitting back in his seat, he hailed the waiter. 'We'll have bacon and eggs twice, two coffees and plenty of bread.'

Carrie was still pulling herself together after his tormenting kiss. Why on earth had he ordered all that, when all she wanted to do was take him back to the old bakery and devour *him* for breakfast. He didn't like fried eggs anyway, she was sure.

Alexis sat back, once again hiding behind the tinted lenses. He'd always tried to please his lovers, but pleasing Carrie was taking on a different meaning altogether. Yes, he'd been prepared to make love to her, even to get her pregnant for the old man. Petros had desperately wanted a grandchild before his fight for life was over. Like a fool, Alexis had agreed, though he had not liked all the conditions. But now the old man insisted he marry her? The urge to haul Petros over the coals had been paramount after that phonecall. Then, when he'd seen Carrie's reaction to Petros's ultimatum, all he'd wanted to do was to love her till she felt better, to hold her. When he'd held her in his arms he wanted to protect her, but he knew that protecting Carrie wasn't an option one considered lightly. It was clearly more like a full-time job. He shook his head in denial then slowly he came out of his reverie.

'Alexis. I said why bacon and eggs?'

'What?'

'You've ordered bacon and eggs, twice,' she muttered again. Removing her sunglasses she placed them on the table.

He laughed. 'I know, Carrie. I also know you love to make Petros bacon and eggs for days in succession, so I thought I'd get used to it *now*.'

She laughed; he couldn't possibly want her to make him bacon and eggs every day.

'Peter loves them too,' she said, her eyes misting with affection at the thought of Peter. Oh how she missed the sound of him chattering away to her.

'Peter. Who the hell is this Peter?' Alexis asked sharply, at the same time removing his own sunglasses and slamming them down on the table.

'Are you jealous, Alexis?'

Alexis grunted something at the waiter as he placed bacon and eggs in front of them. As soon as he had gone, Alexis retaliated. 'In your own words, Carrie, *you have to care for someone to be jealous*. We just have an arrangement to be married under the old Greek custom.'

Had someone sliced her down the middle it would have been less painful. She looked out at the water, and quickly reached for her sunglasses. She would hate for him to see the trace of tears.

She broke into the bread, scattering a few crumbs on the surface of the shimmering clear water. Fish below the surface made bubbles as they nibbled the fresh crumbly bread.

The waiter came out, waving his fishing net in his hand. 'You keep doing that, lady, and I catch the fish for your lunch. Yes?'

'No!' Carrie looked beseechingly at Alexis. 'I don't want them caught. Tell him, Alexis.'

'Tell him yourself. You speak Greek adequately enough for him to comprehend.'

Carefully she explained to the waiter her reasons why the fish shouldn't be caught, before wading her way through her breakfast and ignoring the man opposite. The latter part of the meal was eaten in complete silence.

When she'd finished Carrie threw the remaining crumbs from her plate into the sea, where the fish soon demolished every morsel.

'Oh Christina, stop fussing,' muttered Petros irritably. 'I have everything I need, *everything*, I tell you.'

'Yes, including the brandy. This is going back in the cabinet.' She confiscated the brandy, putting it in her apron pocket and stubbornly raising her chin in defiance.

'You're a hard woman, Christina, a hard woman,' said Petros. 'Now be off with you. Alexis is sending over his man for Carrie's luggage.'

Turning her larger frame away from her employer she sighed. 'And that's another person in this family I worry about. She's not been herself since the play, and all this plotting against her. I don't agree with this forcing her into a marriage that won't last. She's not a Greek girl, Petros. This will all end in trouble. Trouble, I tell you.'

Christina didn't often cry, but Petros knew the signs well. Her head would loll to one side, her shoulders would hunch and shake.

'Christina, don't, *please*.'

Petros laid a hand against her shoulder in comfort. 'Both Carrie and I will be fine. I am just going for a check-up because of that last attack, surely you know that, and Carrie can look after herself.'

'Surely you know that!' mocked Christina. 'A check-up, my foot. We both know it is more serious.'

'No. No.'

Christina turned on Petros. 'Oh, I *know* it's far worse than you tell me. I am no fool, Petros.' She shook her head. 'And my poor baby, my Carrie is no match for Alexis. Yes to that too,' she said to his surprised look. 'I heard you, threatening my poor baby with Theo if she didn't marry Alexis. The thought makes me sick.'

'Carrie and Alexis will sort out their own destiny, they just need a helping hand. You know, to push them in the right direction. And for your information I was threatening Alexis with that offer, not Carrie,' he confirmed with a slight smile.

'Same difference. Alexis will have told her. You just remember, old man, that the gods will never forgive you for interfering like this,' reminded Christina with a bustling force.

Petros looked solemnly at the housekeeper for several minutes before reaching across to kiss her. 'I am going to America, where I hope they can perform miracles. Wish me luck and stop worrying about Carrie. She's her own person, even if you don't realize it.'

'Humph,' she retorted, then mumbled, 'I will light a candle for you, not that you deserve it.'

Petros smiled. His housekeeper was a good woman.

'Would you like a taste of luxury this evening?' asked Alexis as he moved towards Carrie who was sitting cross-legged on the rug she'd dragged to the balcony of the bedroom window. She'd been sitting overlooking the harbour for what seemed like hours.

'Luxury?' She shrugged, asking acidly, 'Why? Are you talking to me now? Have you got over your fit of jealousy or whatever you'd like to call it.'

Alexis frowned. 'Be careful, Carrie.' He pushed a hand through his dark hair, 'I have been working and letting you rest. I won't have much time for the next few weeks so I thought I'd catch up.'

'I didn't mind that. What I do mind is that you have been sulking like a little boy since this morning when I mentioned Peter. I hate silences like that. If there's something bothering you, then tell me.' She turned from the panoramic view back to Alexis. 'Which reminds me, I must ring him before we go out. I presume I can use that antiquated phone you've got connected up?'

She looked at him with a defiant stare. A muscle twitched in his cheek. Insolent baggage, she was now throwing the man in his face. Well he'd see what kind of a game she was playing with him, and in the meantime he would drag her defences down so low she'd never think of Peter again once he'd finished with her.

He inclined his head. 'Of course you can, but just remember – ' he pulled her up into his arms – 'you share my bed.'

After his lips had reduced her to a shaking mass of jelly, he'd put her away from him slowly, dragging in his breath as if it were to save his life.

When he became as possessive as this she could secretly imagine that he cared for her, even if that wasn't true.

She looked up at him, 'If by luxury you mean a decent restaurant for this evening, you can forget it. I still don't have my clothes.'

Alexis was still watching her, that strange look on his face. 'Didn't I tell you, your clothes arrived about an hour ago. I came up, but you were asleep.' He didn't want to say, I couldn't bear to wake you, you looked so peaceful, so I just watched you, and I imagined . . .

She smiled. 'In that case I'd like to walk around the national gardens, then maybe walk through the fleamarket. We can eat in the *plaka*. If that's all to your liking.'

Grabbing her chin, he frowned slightly. 'You're up to something. I know when you're up to something, Carrie. You never agree without a fight.'

Her smile broadened as she shook her head and locks of white gold hair cascaded around his fingers. 'I'm just enjoying myself. I have to make the most of a . . .'

'A bad situation,' he broke in, watching the colour of her eyes change with mood and thought.

'A promise,' she replied softly. 'Now if we are to stroll around the gardens, we must go soon. I believe you'll have to practise the art of wooing me amongst the bushes where all the other lovers meet. That is the man's job, isn't it? I don't believe in the woman having to do the chasing.'

'You want romance?' His eyebrows shot up in query.

She nodded, a soft smile playing on her lips. 'I want romance. I want you to *make love* to me – ' she saw his frown 'I don't want sex. If we are to make a baby this evening, it has to be a beautiful moment, one we can share. One I can remember as romantic.'

'You'll have romance,' he assured her before dragging himself away from her.

Slamming the shower door, he switched on the water. To his utter disgust it came out cold, in short bursts. The groans that came from the pipes only echoed in his brain that he needed to sort this problem out too. All at once there seemed to be too many problems.

Carrie sat in the taxi only inches away from Alexis. He looked so handsome and dashing in the pale green shirt of soft silk, with the even darker green slacks. He'd smiled at her, held her hand, kissed it softly before handing her into the taxi. He was keeping his promise, so far it had been a romantic evening.

As she sat there in the warm taxi she was pleased the weather had cooled down. A hot, blistering taxi was definitely a no-no. She pondered silently, knowing that as soon as she could get a free hour she would visit Petros's shipping office, here in Ormonia Square, in Athens. She'd like to know exactly how much he did owe to debtors and exactly how much Alexis was going to have to pay out. It must be well into the millions by all accounts.

'What are you thinking?'

The deep resonant voice vibrated through her brain, breaking into her innermost thoughts.

'I beg your pardon?'

Blue eyes he could swim in looked innocently back at him, a soft inviting smile played on her lips, teasing, tormenting, for she knew he couldn't read her mind.

'I asked what are you thinking? And why is your beautiful hair tied back in that, that *thing*?'

Her laughter fluttered around the taxi like a beautiful butterfly. 'It's called a snood, and I find it cooler, and my thoughts, Alexis, belong to me.'

Again the frown, then a tender smile. 'Of course your thoughts belong to you.' He reached out and touched the delicate lace edge of her white dress. The low-cut front seemed too inviting for him to resist. With a sigh he tore his fingers away and let his gaze do the touching. 'You're always so feminine, even in shorts. Do you ever wear jeans and things?'

She'd closed her eyes once his fingers had touched the edges of her dress. Didn't he realize she'd worn this dress for him; with its clingy material at the bodice; the neat little belt and the swirling folds of the short flouncy skirt, she'd known it would entice him.

'I wore nothing else when we were rehearsing the play but jeans and jumper, and I can assure you I looked rough. We worked so hard on that play I still don't know what went wrong,' she confessed softly as she remembered all the pain of being involved in the biggest flop London had seen in years.

'Your review was good. I read it in one of the papers.' His hand covered hers. 'If it will help we can talk about it.'

Carrie glared at him. 'Why, so you can gloat? So you can tell me everything you touch turns to gold and everything I touch puts me further into debt.' She shook her head. 'No thanks. I think we'll talk about Petros; at least that subject is nearer to my heart at the moment.'

'Alexis felt his heartbeat increase. 'What about Petros? I've contacted my solicitor, everything is under control.'

'Is it? Then tell me what is wrong with him. Every time I ask, I get a non-committal reply, an evasive retort to *stop worrying*. But I do worry. He's all the family I've got.'

Alexis contemplated her words. Reaching for her hand he linked his fingers with hers. 'I know as little as you do. He has seen a consultant, a heart consultant who told him to stop drinking brandy so heavily, to ease up on his cigars, to watch his diet.' He squeezed her fingers. 'I think for a man of seventy-two he doesn't do badly.'

The taxi driver pulled up outside the national gardens. Once they'd both alighted they began strolling hand in hand, the long silence evidence of the fact that they were both deep in thought.

It was Carrie who broke the silence.

'What are the tablets for? Do you know?'

Alexis shook his head. Why the hell had he promised Petros? Why? Carrie deserved to know the true state of Petros's illness.

'I know one thing for sure, he should let Raymon do much more. God knows he gets paid for it.' He squeezed her hand once again and turned her to him. 'Smell the delicate scents, they remind me of you.'

The roses, the oriental lilies, the sub-tropical trees whispered as their delightful scent wafted across the gardens. A peacock fanned his tail feathers in the distance, his cry a high-pitched warning to another male. Carrie inhaled the delicate perfumes, smiling.

'Maybe I should take over the running of it. You know, his business. Once you've paid everything off, I should look after it. This way at least he can rest more,' she suggested. 'He was all for it a few years ago. He didn't want me to leave the island the first time. University was a pure waste of time in his eyes. Then, suddenly, he changed and virtually pushed dance school into my face.'

Alexis shook his head. 'You're right, at one time, he would have pooh-poohed anything that took you away from the island.' He frowned darkly. 'I find it odd he should send you away so quickly. Nevertheless, I believe Raymon can do the job. Besides, you'll be busy looking after our children.'

Carrie frowned and corrected, 'Child.'

'Okay. Child. You'll still be busy, you'll be keeping my bed warm too.'

'Stop right there, buster. Marriage or not, I won't be blackmailed like this. I will need to work,' she assured him, staring rebelliously up into his dark bitter-chocolate eyes.

Alexis touched her cheek with the back of his hand, and said, 'Then we can discuss the finer details of your career later. This evening is for romance.' He touched the nape of neck, running his finger down and over her collarbone, the hidden promise filtering through his rich deep voice. 'Or had you forgotten?'

With each touch it seemed he was going to turn her to jelly. Had she really agreed to marriage, and why was he suddenly all for the idea? Isn't it obvious, you fool, she thought. Oh you utter fool, wasn't all this about sex? His libido, his manhood, his *perifania*. Most of his friends were already married with children. Most Greek men of his age had at least one heir.

Cupping her face in the soft evening light, he wished he could capture this moment forever. She stirred him like no other woman and the thought of marriage was ever more attractive. Petros certainly knew what he was doing.

'Alexis. How good to see you,' came the American voice across the walkway. 'And with one so beautiful.'

After Alexis had made the introduction, Senator Walker and his wife, plus several bodyguards walked through the gardens with them. Carrie was aware of the huge walls of muscle either side of her.

'I see business is going well. The new hotel in Palm Beach is sensational. Thanks for the *gratis* weekend, it was so relaxing,' the senator commented with a smile.

'Yes. It's a worthy investment.'

'I hear your friend, what's-his-name . . . the one we met you with not long ago, Petros, that's it, I hear he is going to see a heart consultant in New York this week. That's my home town honey,' he said for Carrie's benefit.

Carrie felt she'd been thumped in the chest. She could hear the surprise in Alexis's voice as his fingers tightened around hers.

'A consultant?'

'Yep. The best in New York by all accounts.' The senator slapped Alexis on the back. 'He'll be all right. If any man can help him, John Steiger can. He kept my old man going for years. Put a new battery in, kept him ticking like a quartz clock.'

After what seemed like an endless walk through the gardens, a walk where everything seemed to have blurred edges, the ponds, the water fowl, even the proud magnificent peacocks, the senator and his group left. Alexis invited them to spend time on the yacht whenever they wished.

Carrie was speechless, tears blurring her vision.

'You didn't know, did you?' She looked up in earnest at Alexis's ashen face.

He shook his head, taking her gently in his arms. He hated lying. 'Oh Carrie, I'm so sorry. I didn't know it was this bad. He never said how bad his illness was. He only told me that he'd consulted a specialist in London.'

It would have been so easy to fold up there and then into the safety of his arms, so easy. But she couldn't; she had to stand up and face whatever the truth might be. Her life seemed to have been marred by one tragedy after another. She was determined not to let Petros be the next.

'Did the senator say he'd already gone?'

'No.' He could read her thoughts this time. 'Come on. We'll charter a boat, go to the island if that pleases you. You need to see him, right?'

She drew in a nervous breath and nodded. 'You're so thoughtful. It will spoil our romantic evening.'

'No, it won't. We can assure ourselves he is all right, and then maybe we should sail alone for a few days. We can always join up with *Challenger* one day next week. Besides, I cramp my little sister's style if I'm on the yacht too much,' he declared with a laugh.

'Come, let's go and get ready. It's a long time since I sailed, and the wind is about perfect now.'

'Petros. Petros. George has seen lights coming from the jetty. He says there is a small yacht berthing.' Christina looked worried. 'Who could be visiting so late?'

Petros sat in his favourite chair. He was irritable, nervous that soon he would be on his way to New York where he would most definitely learn what his future held, if there was to be one.

'Shall I send George down to look?' Christina urged him.

He shook his head, his tired face resigned. 'It can only be Alexis and Carrie. Only Alexis would try and dock here at night when he knows how dangerous it can be!'

'And you know all about danger, don't you, old man? You play with it often enough!' Christina said, concerned, before she turned towards the front door.

CHAPTER 9

Alexis's voice came from the darkened doorway: 'If it hadn't been for us learning about your visit to New York, believe me, Carrie and I would be tucked up in bed. As it is, I've left her asleep on the yacht.' He moved further into the room, his commanding, angry figure sending even Christina a few steps back. 'And while she's out of earshot maybe you'll enlighten me about this marriage, and your possible operation, Petros.' He pushed his fingers through his dark wet hair. The spray from the sea had been heavy, the sailing tougher than he had anticipated.

Petros turned to Christina. 'Get Alexis a drink . . .'

'Coffee will be just fine, Christina,' Alexis cut in.

Christina nodded and left the room quietly.

Alexis turned to Petros. 'It's not that I want you dead, my friend, but you told me the doctors had given you five years at the most to live, and there was no suitable operation. Do I take it there is some miracle cure? Quite convenient, wouldn't you say?'

'Alexis, please. I am visiting New York to see a friend and was merely advised to see this particular consultant while I was there. I'd never heard of the man until last week when my friend called me,' whispered Petros his voice thin and pained.

'Then why not tell your god-daughter? She is sick with worry about you, and she doesn't deserve all this. I agree, that when she was a child, she could be a disobedient, rude, little madam, but she doesn't deserve all this secrecy now. She loves you, Petros; she's selling her soul for you! Goddamn it, man! She needs the truth and by heaven she's old enough to know.' He ran his other hand through his hair whilst pacing about. 'And what is all this farce about Theo? Theo, I ask you? The man's an imbecile.'

In a quiet distinctive voice Petros said, 'It is no joke. Theo would gladly take her hand in marriage, and if you're not careful, young man, that's exactly what will be happening.'

Alexis lowered over Petros, his height, his strength intimidating the older man. 'Don't threaten me! Carrie will become *my* wife, because *I* say so and for no other reason. Is that understood?'

Petros shrank back in his chair, back-tracking a little. 'Alexis, my friend, Carrie is yours, just as long as you want her.' Petros shrugged. 'If not, Theo is next in line.'

'You old fool, you're almost as bad as Theo himself,' Alexis claimed fiercely with a low, low growl. 'I don't like all this, *this* subterfuge. I want to come clean with her. I should never have agreed to this.'

'Oh and you want to be vindicated, I suppose? Exonerated of any involvement in this charade. Well

I won't allow you to do that. I know for a fact you've waited years to get Carrie into your bed. And you've already admitted she's been there! You either marry her and keep quiet or Theo does the job for you.'

Christina walked into the room with coffee on a tray. 'Christina, make Carrie's bed up. Alexis and Carrie will be staying the night.'

Christina smiled. 'I'll make up the guest room too.'

Alexis raised his eyebrows, his face suddenly drawn and pale. 'Carrie and I will be sleeping together, Christina.' He turned to Petros, who didn't even blink.

'Yes, Petros, my *friend*, your plan is going according to schedule.'

Petros looked lazily at Alexis. *Better than you imagine my boy*, *better than you imagine*, he thought to himself.

Carrie woke up to semi-darkness. She knew they'd berthed the yacht by the steady sway and the silent engine. Most of the way Alexis had sailed, but the last mile or so he'd used the engines for safety. It had been the gentle thrumming which had finally rocked her off to sleep.

She smiled. Alexis had placed a blanket over her sometime during the journey. He could be very gentle and thoughtful when he wanted, it seemed.

'Carrie!' Alexis's voice boomed down the deck.

'OK, I'm awake. You don't have to wake the dead,' she muttered wondering why he sounded angry when only hours earlier he'd been so wonderful.

The look on his face confirmed to Carrie that someone had ruffled his feathers. 'You're wanted up at the house. Now!'

'Hi, yourself,' she replied, 'Nice to see, you my darling girl. I've missed you so much whilst you were asleep my heart is actually broken . . . or, at least, very sore.'

Alexis smiled; she could nearly always lift his mood. 'If you don't get up to the house a certain part of your anatomy will be sore too.' He bent to kiss her lips. 'I'm sorry I barked at you but Petros wants to tell you about the consultant.'

Reading his anger as worry, she burst out nervously, 'He's really ill, isn't he?'

Alexis nodded, and said solemnly, 'Yes he is. It could mean a heart transplant. I'm not sure and neither is he, not yet.'

Carrie bit her lip. 'Isn't he too old for that?' She hugged herself. 'I've wasted so much time in England. I just assumed he would live forever.' With uncertain eyes she searched his face for encouragement before throwing herself into his arms. She didn't cry; she just clung to him like a frightened little rabbit.

'He's not going to live forever, is he?'

Tugging at her hand, he gently led her off the boat. She would have no one if Petros died, acknowledged Alexis, absolutely no one. True, Christina had been like a mother to her, but the headstrong Carrie had been looking decidedly vulnerable since Senator Walker had dropped his bombshell. All this, and she was still feeling the effects of the virus she'd had back in England.

As they walked into the *sala*, Carrie went over to Petros and kissed him soundly on the cheek. 'Why ever didn't you tell us? You're a stubborn man, Petros,' she chastened softly.

'Now, now, Carrie, I didn't want to frighten anyone. I fly to New York tomorrow. The doctor there will tell me my fate.' He saw the look in her eyes. 'And before you ask, I *am* going alone! I am meeting a friend and I will have neither of you with me.'

She wanted to protest, but all the fight had drained out of her. 'As you wish, but when you come back you must join us on the yacht.'

'Yes, Petros. I believe my mother is coming to spend a few days on the yacht. You can relax with someone nearer your own age for a change.' Alexis grinned, but Petros could still see his anger shimmering below the surface.

'Humph,' he grunted. 'All she ever does is complain at me. "Put your tie on. Smile, Petros, you look miserable. Stuff your shirt in your trousers." That's great fun!'

Alexis bit his lip to stop from laughing. He knew all about his mother.

'Maybe Helena Stephanides knows how to handle you, Petros,' came Christina's comment as she joined them. 'Since her operation she has become a more assertive, formidable woman. She knows how to handle you men, *all of you*!'

Carrie smiled; she loved Christina so much.

As if reading her thoughts, Christina turned to Carrie and held out her arms. 'You look as though you need a cuddle, my girl. All these men think of is themselves. Come with me, I've put on some cocoa for you. Leave them to their talk.

Carrie followed Christina into the kitchen. 'Have you eaten?' Christina asked, concerned.

'Yes. Alexis made me an omelette earlier.'

'Alexis? Well, I *am* surprised.'

Carrie nodded, and smiled.

'Are you happy? With this arranged marriage that they've set up? I think it's all wrong myself.'

Carrie couldn't let Christina know the finer details; she'd be appalled. 'Yes. I'm happy.'

Christina stuffed her hands in her apron pockets. 'He says he's sleeping with you in your room. I didn't know what you would think to that. What I mean is . . .'

'That's fine, Christina.'

'Is he? What I mean is, well, I know I shouldn't be asking this . . .' She paused.

'Ask anything, Christina.'

Christina dived in. 'Is he gentle? If he hurts you I'll kill him.'

Carrie placed a soft hand over Christina's in reassurance. 'He's a very thoughtful lover. And he's soon to be my husband. Don't worry, Christina, deep down, he's a very good man.' She laughed. 'All the cool sophistication, growling and barking out orders, they're all a front, I'm sure.'

'Deep down? I suppose you mean fathoms deep,' said Christina sarcastically.

'Yes. Fathoms deep just about describes him, but when you reach that point . . .' She stopped, unable to explain this feeling.

Christina put the cocoa in front of her as Carrie sat at the table. 'I'm sorry I couldn't tell you about Petros. I didn't know exactly what was going on until tonight. Not everything, you understand.'

'I understand. Petros is too proud to ask for help. We just have to be here for him.'

Christina sat too, her tired brown eyes watery, and would have cried, but heard the *sala* door close. She quickly composed herself. 'You do understand, don't you? You both mean so much to me, and I could love Alexis easily too. He's always been so polite to me. Like a son, you understand?'

The following morning they were sailing away from the island and out to sea on the yacht *Adonia*. Alexis explained the origin of the name: the beautiful goddess of the resurrection, of eternal youth. Their eyes had held for a moment that was solely theirs. Was he trying to tell her something?

The day was invigorating, the breeze swept through Carrie's hair, the wind cooled her face as they left the craggy islands behind with their bald skulls of rock jutting out into the sea, and they sailed in the expanse of the Aegean. There were blue skies and even bluer seas, and the fact she'd got Alexis all to herself made it all so worthwhile, even if it was for only a few hours until they met up with his friends.

He was a good sailor, relaxed and confident in almost anything he undertook. Of course, Carrie had sailed with her father and Petros when she was younger, so she was no novice.

'I thought we were meeting friends of yours? Where will they be?' called Carrie from the cabin below as she busied herself making coffee.

'Not sure yet, just be patient. You'll like my friends, Carrie, they're wonderful souls,' he returned with a smile as she peered up from below. 'Come and help me, let me see if you remember what I taught you last night.'

He looked so at ease with life, so boyish. Who would ever think him the chairman of a shipping line, the owner of several successful hotels? A ruthless contender in the game of big business. He'd dropped his guard now and they worked well together as they manned the *Adonia*.

Carrie watched him closely, caressed each sinewy muscle of him with her eyes. A hard shaft of desire hit her again and again as he moved about, this way and that, keeping the vessel on course.

'Carrie, stop daydreaming, woman, and take the wheel.' He snapped out his order and she obeyed, but questioned him with a look. 'Okay, Carrie, just hold her steady. I'm taking down the sail and then we'll anchor her.'

'Then what?'

'Then, we wait.' His eyes shone mischievously as he flashed her a brilliant white smile. A smile that spoke a million words, if she only knew the language.

Carrie's eyes widened as she looked around her; there was nothing but sky and sea. 'Is this our rendezvous point, here in the middle of nowhere?'

Alexis nodded as he dropped anchor. 'Come on, let's have some breakfast. I don't know about you but I find sailing hungry work. You keep telling me about these Irish tatties. I'll have some of those.'

'Petros will be surprised when I tell him I had breakfast in the middle of the Aegean Sea. If I cook the tatties, you cook the bacon and eggs.' She let him help her down the steps into the cabin.

'To be honest with you, I was hoping *you'd* cook everything. I've brought all the ingredients. It's hard work, being a captain and having an insubordinate and thoroughly beautiful sailor to look after,' he pleaded so sexily that Carrie was loath to deny him anything.

True enough he had brought along lots of fresh fruit, eggs, cheese, bacon, crusty bread and potatoes. It didn't take long before she had him almost drooling with anticipation at the food she was preparing.

'Can I do anything for you?' he asked as he watched her skilfully crack eggs into the pan.

She shook her head, aware of his intense gaze as his eyes blazed a lingering trail from the unruly blonde tendrils of hair to her hot cheeks. They moved slowly downward to the line of that very feminine throat, where her fast-beating pulse raced frantically out of control. Then to the vee of her cleavage, where he halted for a while, as if thinking.

Then on to the knot of her soft blue muslin blouse tied up against her midriff. He stopped there and made to stand up.

'For goodness' sake, woman, either feed me, or let me feast myself on you,' he ground out as he moved towards her, sounding like a hero from a classical play.

Carrie had seen that look before and was unsure she could contend with him right now, especially after yesterday evening's fiasco in her room. She'd felt rejected when he turned away from her and had immediately fallen asleep.

Quickly she tossed his bacon, eggs and potatoes onto a plate and pushed it into his hands before he could get closer. Her voice was a little too sensitive, a little too shaky; 'Eat your breakfast.'

Alexis looked from Carrie to the plate of food scowling at having to choose, but then his hunger temporarily won the day as he leant forward and whispered, 'Maybe I'll have you for dessert.'

Carrie smiled. Promises, promises, that wasn't how he had felt last night. Perhaps the magazine statistics of 2.3 times a week were true and men couldn't generally perform more than twice a week?

Sitting opposite him, she passed him fresh bread and butter and settled herself with a cup of steaming black coffee.

Alexis looked across at her and scanned the cabin for her plate. A frown appeared on his brow. 'Where the hell is your breakfast?'

'I was going to share yours.' She grinned playfully.

He tore a chunk of the bread off and dipped it into his eggs and handed it to her, before his face took on a serious scowl. 'I'll make sure you do. I've told you before, and so has the doctor, you're too thin.'

Carrie refused to get into an argument, but to console him she took the bread offered and dipped it in his eggs again. If he'd known the truth, she was sure he would have scoffed at her weakness. He'd be surprised that her loss of appetite was solely down to the profound effect his muscular body was having on her. It felt as if even her bones were liquefying at his nearness. But she could never tell him that. She mustn't tell him that!

Satisfied that she'd eaten her share of his breakfast, Alexis made them fresh coffee and sat opposite her once again. The silence seemed endless, until she filled it with her words of query.

'Who are we waiting for?'

Looking down that aristocratic Greek nose, he tapped it and said, 'Wait and see. It's a surprise.'

'Huh. I'm not sure anyone is coming, and to think we had to forego our night of romance yesterday evening,' she complained, pouting just a touch, then adding, 'But I'm glad you understood that we had to see Petros.'

Alexis smiled and admitted, 'Last night was not a good night for romance, after all. You're looking tired and I think it's time we took the doctor's advice and let you rest. However, while we're on the subject of romance maybe you'd enlighten me about Peter. Who is he and why do you have to phone him?'

Carrie nodded her head and forced a smile; so, there was some kind of interest in Peter. If only he would try and care for her feelings, maybe she could give her love unconditionally. *Love*? Was that a word she would associate with Alexis? She looked across at him.

'I told you. Peter is someone I love. He won't cause problems with this arrangement we have, but don't expect me to stop loving him, because I can't!' There, let him think on that for a while.

He held out his hand a little stiffly, nodding his reluctant acceptance with a frown. 'Come back on deck, we might see them coming.'

Carrie cautiously slid her fingers into his, and he lowered his head close to her ear. 'Don't look so worried, my friends won't bite you.'

It's not your friends I'm worried about. It's you, she silently screamed. It was impossible. She wanted him, and yet she was still so afraid. She must forget about the word *love* for the moment.

'Are they Greeks?' she asked out of curiosity as she pulled at his hand to stop his ascent.

Alexis smiled warmly, but shook his head, pulling her with him as he led her up the steps. 'You ask too many questions. Wait and see, some of them may well be Greek.'

They did wait, for almost four hours, during which time Alexis smoothed suncream onto her shoulders and back, the backs of her legs and up to her thighs to keep her from burning too much. The rhythmic movements were relaxing yet drove her almost to a point of no return. She lay quietly on her stomach wanting him more with every passing second.

As he massaged the cream into her shoulders, he thought about this Peter. The conversation she'd had yesterday with him had only added fuel to the fire. She was right, he could never stop her loving him, but he could stop him getting in touch, stop the calls. He'd already made approaches to a private investigator to check Carrie out when he had been in London but he'd changed his mind. Now Peter had raised his ugly head, he needed to know the extent of her love for this man. All it would take was a phonecall. He'd find out exactly what this Peter meant to her.

'We're in luck, Carrie, my friends are on their way. Don't make too much noise, you'll frighten them.' His whisper sent shivers down her spine.

'Inquisitiveness drove her into a sitting position and she gasped when she saw them cutting through the water. Dolphins by the dozen were swimming towards the yacht, some just below the surface, others jumping slightly above the foam. Never had she seen them this close, and they were coming nearer. Tears of happiness suddenly welled in her eyes at the sheer beauty, their gracefulness, and their trusting souls as they neared the starboard side of *Adonia*.

She watched in fascination. They seemed happy to swim and perform for their human friends. Turning back to Alexis she caught him watching her, a strangely sad look in his eyes, though he masked it quickly and sent her a reassuring smile.

'Pleased I brought you?'

'Oh yes, thank you so much – ' she reached out to touch his face with the softness of her palm – 'I'll never forget this moment. Never.' Turning back to the dolphins she moved nearer the side and was rewarded as one bravely allowed her to lightly touch its silvery-blue mottled skin.

'How did you know I loved them?' she asked turning to him again. The joy was evident in her eyes, her love for the beautiful creatures emanating from deep within her soul.

If only she could look that way for me, he thought suddenly, but he was no fool, he knew she was here only because of a so-called debt.

He looked surprised at her question and shrugged his large tanned shoulders. 'I didn't. I know that for me seeing them is a very wonderful experience, as is swimming with them – ' his eyes darkened as he moved closer to her – 'an experience I wanted to share with you.'

She looked up into his face as she knelt on the deck. 'Thank you.' Her words seemed insufficient, but he silenced her with his finger across her lips as she sought for something more appropriate to say.

He was shaking his head. 'No, don't say any more. Just enjoy.'

She did with all her heart. As she cut through the water, a mother and baby dolphin alongside skirted her movements. She could almost feel the wave-lengths of communication between the two, could see the body language of the mother warning the youngster not to get too close to the human female. It touched her, like no other moment in her life ever had.

Eventually they set sail again. The dolphins followed them for a while in the glistening sunlit water. All too soon they headed off, leaving Carrie and Alexis alone with their thoughts and memories.

Looking across at her Greek lover three days later, tears gathered in Carrie's eyes. She was so, so relaxed and in many ways quite happy. Since the very first time they had made love in the old bakery overlooking the harbour, she had felt this way. Then, when he had rejected her at Petros's the other evening, turning over without saying a word, she knew Petros and he must have had harsh words. At some point during last night she had felt his arms embrace her. He'd dragged her so close and just held her to him. For days he had simply laughed with her, talked with her, reminded her of their sometimes painful memories. He'd been himself with her and she had loved that. He'd pulled her defences so far down that she couldn't do anything else but fall deeply in love. The only thing he hadn't done lately was make love to her, something that was beginning to worry her.

She was such a fool to let all this happen, but what choice had she? With Petros so ill, there seemed no other way. But wouldn't it be nice, if Alexis had wanted her just because he loved her?

Noticing that Alexis was dropping the sails, her time and thoughts were taken up with helping him, and it was only as they chugged slowly into the harbour at Alonnissos did she realize what had been nagging her all morning. It was when he had been lowering the sail, just as he had done in the harbour at Skiathos. Yes, that was it. There had been a small uniformed man, a man who'd greeted him softly and spoken quickly in their own language, their words hushed when they saw her coming. That moment had triggered off a thousand questions she urgently needed to ask him. Did the man have anything to do with the *Aphrodite* fleet or the beautiful new liner at anchor in the bay? Suddenly Carrie smelt a big, fat, rat. A rat she would check up on once they were back in Athens.

As Alexis tied the yacht securely to the side of the harbour wall Carrie stared at him, unable to believe that he would be involved in any scams, though she felt suddenly suspicious of both Alexis and Petros. Alexis looked up, caught the frown on her pretty brow and saw her teeth sink into her bottom lip.

'Hey, why the frown?' he asked, laughter echoing in his voice. His eyebrow rose as he noted the gleam of anger in those beautiful blue lagoons she called eyes. The renowned Irish temper looked about ready to blow!

Alexis assisted her off the yacht, but Carrie snatched her hand away and stomped ahead of him. She heard his indrawn breath, and chose to ignore it, until he spun her around to face him on the quiet harbour front.

'What the hell's got into you?' he bit out, angry with her display of temper and confused by the change. She'd been so lovely these past few days.

Carrie would have run like a rabbit, but she was being held tight by two strong, imprisoning hands. She inhaled, drew a deep breath before she attacked him verbally. 'As if you didn't know!'

She received a quick, hard look, 'I *don't* know, so I suggest you tell me, while I still have a modicom of good temper left!'

Biting her lip, she struggled with the words. Damn it, what was the use? If she had rumbled some devious plan and then let him know, she would be lost.

'I'm waiting.'

'If you must know the truth, it's about last night, and the night before that.' She fumbled with her words, her thoughts. It was the only way out, so she flared up at him, 'You – you devil. You men have the cheek to call women teases! Isn't it enough you reject me in my own home after telling everyone we were sleeping together? Then last night you cuddle close to me, and what? I ask you what? Nothing, zilch.'

Carrie stiffened at her own words, his grip tightening on her upper arms at her futile effort to escape. 'Come with me, back to the yacht. I think we need to talk. In private!'

Carrie struggled, 'What good's talking going to do?' Digging in her rubber-soled canvas shoes as he pulled her along, she yet again ended up the loser to his superior strength.

One second she was dragging her feet, the next she was fireman-lifted over his bare shoulders and told in no uncertain terms to behave, as he strode purposefully back to the boat.

They stood assessing each other in the darkened cabin, like two beautiful wild animals about to embark on a fight to the death.

Alexis took his stance with hands firmly on his hips as he ground out, 'Are you telling me you're fit for sex? All you've done on this voyage is sleep. You're exhausted, woman!' He looked down his perfect nose and sneered, 'I told you we would be lovers, we would conceive a baby. But look at yourself, Carrie. You've done nothing but sleep. You are *ill*.'

Carrie was quick to retaliate. 'Oh, that's right, blame me! Turn it all around so that I'm the guilty one. Typical Alexis, a man who can do no wrong!'

Fury blazed in his dark eyes like a comet shooting through the midnight sky. 'Be careful, Carrie!'

'No, Alexis, it's you who should have been careful. You who should, should . . . I mean have you really thought this thing out? I mean do you really want a baby?' Carrie moved around the cabin liked a caged animal. 'Well, what I mean is, we should – '

'Should what?' His low voice vibrated with the distinct warning that she was going too far. He was certainly in a filthy mood.

If only she'd seen the signs then – the way his intense gaze was raking her body. The way his deep voice vibrated around the cabin. But she didn't. Blindly she continued her attack, regardless of the consequences. 'We need to *talk* about it – !' she shot him a look – 'I mean *I* need to!' she said adamantly, disregarding his swift intake of breath.

His smile was twisted, distorting his handsome looks, 'You do?' he asked quietly.

Carrie nodded her head and said in clarification, 'Yes, I do,' and then she stared at him. Really stared, square in the eyes, gasping as she saw the raw emotion of passion. Passion that was teetering on the very edge of his control. Any moment that control could snap!

He shook his head in disbelief and took a step nearer, his stance threatening. 'We've done all our talking. I think *you* want action.'

'No!'

Suddenly the cabin was too small, too cramped to escape. Carrie backed away at the sudden feeling of *deja vu*. Hadn't this happened in the bakery? Yet, this was different, she was challenging his masculinity, his power to seduce her. Now he was definitely the aggressor.

'Are you saying "no" to me?'

Carrie began to shake, with nerves or excitement, she couldn't be sure. Did he mean to take her here, *now*? Oh why had she tried to put controls upon him? People in love didn't put limits on their affections, but then Alexis wasn't in love! This was just an agreement, a marriage of convenience for him, she thought angrily.

Even though her hormones were raging through her body, screaming for fulfilment, she knew she mustn't give in. If she did he would win this battle, and indeed, their own particular war. Licking her lips, she stood her ground, 'I don't want to make love now.'

'Liar!'

'I'm not!'

'You want me to rip your clothes from you now. This minute!' He moved nearer, a fraction away from her. Not touching her and yet drowning her in her need to have him take her here in the cabin. He circled her slowly, a whisper away and still not touching her.

Her mind was screaming out, 'I can't,' as he teased her senses merely by being there. Taunting her with the thought he could take her to heaven and back and the knowledge that reality would be so much better.

'Still no? You know damn well I wouldn't even dream of forcing you,' he whispered seductively against her neck. She shivered as he urged, 'Give yourself to me.'

'I can't,' she moaned, closing her eyes so she didn't have to look at him. This was a barbaric way to bring her to her knees, and yet he was still tempting her with his primitive suggestions.

'All you have to do is nod your head and I'll take you to a pleasure land no one else can find,' he taunted, his breath feather-soft on her face.

Torn – she was torn between two worlds, between

two choices. Heaven or hell! If only she hadn't swayed against him and felt his hot tanned body ready to exert its potent effect on her. If only her disobedient head hadn't nodded fractionally, for that was all he wanted. Her permission!

CHAPTER 10

The water was clearer than she'd ever seen, her thoughts more tranquil but not with the clarity she would have liked. Although this place was a paradise, so calm and peaceful, she never went out of her depth willingly, always waiting, until Alexis was by her side. He'd already warned her about the dangers of being too far away from the shoreline. Cramp, he had said, could attack anyone, at any time.

They'd soaked up the sun, walked the length of the small beach and then swam again. Later they'd dined under the shade of the blossom trees amidst the gentle, serenading music of the *bouzouki*. Neither of them mentioned their earlier argument as they ate and drank their fill, laughing and teasing whilst they shared each other's meals.

'This is the most beautiful place on earth,' sighed Carrie, happy as she looked out across the beach to the enclosed cove where the harbour lay.

Alexis took her hand and squeezed it gently as he linked her fingers with his. 'I'm pleased you like it.'

She searched his face, but he gave nothing away. 'I love it.' Her mind was screaming 'I love you too', but she dare not voice her words for fear of rejection. Eventually she dragged her eyes away because she was afraid he would read her soul. She looked back out to sea. A sea so tranquil, yet a sea with hidden depths and hidden dangers, so like the man at her side.

'We must make the most of the next few days. Soon we join up with the *Challenger*,' said Alexis softly, waiting for her response.

Huge blue eyes widened like saucers in surprise. 'So soon?' Her heart slammed in panic against her ribs, her frown reflecting her concern that Petros would be back from New York with the results of his tests. Helena, Alexis's mother, was joining the yacht too, at Skiathos.

Grabbing both her hands Alexis pulled Carrie towards him, having paid the bill only minutes earlier. 'Let's take a walk on the beach. I do realize why you don't want to return to the yacht. I'm not *so* insensitive, you know,' He linked her fingers in his once again. 'Putting it off won't help Petros. You have to be strong, Carrie.'

Like a zombie facing hell, Carrie walked alongside him, her mind in turmoil. What was he saying? Of course she would be strong!

'I will be strong. Of course we must join the yacht.

He coughed. 'I think you ought to know now that we will not be sharing a room on the yacht. My mother will insist otherwise.'

Carrie almost smiled to herself. Greek mothers were certainly well up in the ranks of liberated women. They were always telling the men what to do, and the men just had to do it.

Carrie turned to him, despatching the breath she had held for so long. 'She dictates to *you*, on your yacht?' she questioned him quietly.

Alexis smiled down at her, shaking his head. 'No one *dictates* to me.' He dropped a quick kiss to her lips.

Carrie laughed up into his face, 'Is that so?'

'That is so.'

'And pigs might fly.' She pulled away from him, only to be pulled back. Her laughter filled the air as she asked breathlessly, 'So who else will be there? Your sister Maria? Nina?'

Alexis framed her face with his hands, lowering his mouth over hers, kissing her thoroughly, until she moaned against his teeth. He drew back, his voice laboured, 'There will be other guests on the yacht, yes.'

Carrie shrugged and then saw the glitter in his eyes. She knew what he was about to say.

'Marsha and her father will be joining us, plus a few other friends of Maria's,' he told her softly. All the time he was watching her, studying her as she fought with her emotions.

'Marsha?'

She'd heard all about Marsha over the years. Helena had once been a fan of the famous Greek model.

'Yes. I invited them a while ago and you might as well know, Marsha and I had a thing together. We had an overrated affair.'

'Overrated by whom?'

'Marsha thought we had a permanent thing going. I kept on telling her it was just an affair, but she refused to face reality. I just thought you ought to know. I don't want to keep anything from you.'

'So what? She will hardly pounce on you, and I'll be there all day and all night, guarding you!' As the words left her lips she remembered his words about the rooms. Her heart fell to her feet, plummeted to the floor to smash into pieces, though she consoled herself quickly. What on earth could Marsha do anyway? She was married herself.

'Sweetheart, we will have our own rooms. You know my mother well enough. She is very, very old-fashioned,' he offered gently. 'I suggest we make the most of the next few days.'

His intense gaze dropped to her covered breasts, her small, sand-covered feet, and back to her full pink lips. His examination was leisurely but very deliberate and her nipples tightened in response.

'I don't want separate rooms,' she complained honestly, searching his face for confirmation that he didn't mean what he said. 'We'll never make babies with separate rooms!'

A wild look of passion entered his eyes, his lips lifting sexily at the corners. 'Then maybe we will have to sneak you to my room after dark, and deliver you back to yours before dawn. Our affair will be that much more exciting.'

'*My* room!'

He smiled, nodding. '*Your* room then, but I'm afraid we do have to respect her wishes in front of our guests.'

Carrie knew she would have to be satisfied with that; he would never upset his mother willingly, and she couldn't blame him. Mothers were a precious gift, as she knew to her cost.

'Why are you frowning?'

'It's nothing! Race you back to the yacht.' She took off across the beach at lightning speed, excited because he was hot on her heels, and yet sad that she was having to share him so soon. The next few days she vowed he would come to love her. If only for the time they spent together, he *would* love her.

Breathless and panting she collapsed on the harbour in front of their yacht. He had allowed her to beat him, but he'd made the chase exciting, reaching for her and grabbing for her blouse as they ran. She'd yelped and laughed and pulled away, still at speed.

Alexis collapsed beside her and she was sure his look held a loving light, some spark of raw emotion, just before he dragged her to him and kissed her senseless.

It was like no other kiss they had shared. Almost as if they'd just found each other, just discovered their mutual passion. Together they were special, alone they were just that – alone.

* * *

The next four days were spent in heaven. Sailing the islands, discovering caves, meeting up with the dolphins again, snorkelling under the expert guidance of her lover. It was idyllic, a time which blotted out any life before. They swam naked in the sea and sun-bathed on deserted islands, finding shells together as they walked hand in hand through hidden, secret coves. They played ball on soft sandy beaches and barbecued fresh fish under the moonlit skies. She was in love with the most wonderful man in the world, until he spoilt it all with a few careless words.

'Carrie, I want you to know how special these past few days have been for me.' He'd been sitting by the fire, cooking fish.

'Me too.' The look she'd received was full of warmth, but his next words had cut right through her like a sabre, slicing into her heart with a powerful force.

'Good! and with any luck you may be pregnant,' he'd said arrogantly, with a supremely confident smile.

Carrie's heart sank, leaving her unable to answer. Foolishly she had thought he was falling in love with her too, but now his intention was clearer than the whispering, moonlit sea behind her. He wanted her child, and nothing else.

This couldn't be happening. Surely he could see she was in love with him? But then he *had* warned her, had been above board all the way. He wanted a child, he never got in too deep. He never fell in love!

Is this what lust was like? thought Carrie in the darkening light as the yacht chugged slowly back towards the jetty. Would it take you out to sea on a mystery tour? Fill your heart full of promises, of dreamy nights and magical days, and then drop you to the sharks when it had taken its fill? Would she find the promises were empty, the mystery tour nothing more than a nightmare voyage?

She looked at Alexis and knew without a shadow of doubt that she was deeply and irreversibly in love with him and that was why these past few days had been so special. Could it ever be possible he would come to love her too?

They drank wine that night in Skiathos. In a candlelit room which smelt of pines and echoed with crickets she spent her last night alone with him. He'd booked them into a hotel, even though the *Challenger* was berthed in the harbour.

'You're frowning again, what's the matter?' asked Alexis, his voice softly concerned. He moved nearer to her this time, pinching her chin gently in his fingers.

Carrie glanced quickly up into his face and avoiding the penetrating, probing look in his eyes, she lowered her long lashes.

'The truth is I'm afraid of being pregnant,' she revealed quietly. Oh why couldn't she explain what she meant? What was really tearing her apart?

Alexis dropped his fingers from her face as if he'd been burnt. The look of pain shadowed his eyes, but he turned away. 'I see.'

'No you don't see,' she cried, imploring him to listen. 'You don't see at all.'

Getting to his feet, Alexis slowly moved towards the veranda doors, a frown marring his brow. He waited there for several silent minutes. When he turned back to her, he was obviously livid, the contours of his face white with anger.

'There will be no abortion!' He was striding across the room, dragging her to her feet. 'Do you hear me, there will be no abortion! We have an agreement!'

Bruising fingers gripped her upper arms. Her senses swam. Why was he angry? That was what she wanted to hear. If he couldn't give *her* his love, maybe he could offer their child his love? For she was sure of one thing: she was having his baby.

'So you still want to go through with this farce of a marriage, all because Petros says so?' Carrie cried, desperately. 'Petros would not insist I marry you. All I need to know is that you'll care for our child.'

He was shaking his head. 'You're a fool if you think you can change Petros's mind. If you don't marry me it will be Theo! There is no way out of that.'

Nina had done the polite thing and arranged for tea to be made for Helena Stephanides.

'Oh *Mama,* don't fuss so,' said Maria, sulking.

'I don't know what has come over your brother, allowing you free rein of the *Challenger*. If your father had been alive you'd be holed up in a convent and not running around England or the Greek islands as if you were a hippie,' said Helena with disdain, her glance going to the cut-off Levi's and short-cropped top that her daughter was wearing.

'They're not hippies any more. They're . . .'

'Don't interrupt me!'

'Sorry, *Mama*, but you must understand the world has moved on. You're almost sixty years old,' Maria whispered softly but not softly enough.

'Lord, that's ancient!' Garry shouted with a grin from the deck.

Helena lifted her stick. 'Who is that?'

Maria looked lost for words. 'Garry is . . . Garry is . . .' How could she tell her that Garry was an out-of-work lecturer?

'Garry is a friend of your son's, *Kiria* Stephanides,' replied Nina quickly, saving the younger girl.

'My son knows this boy?' She raised a questioning eyebrow.

'Yes. Yes, he knows Garry.'

'Then I shall have a word with my son as soon as he boards the yacht.' She yawned behind a perfectly starched handkerchief. 'I will go and lie down. You, young lady – ' Helena pointed to Maria – 'you will dress for dinner this evening.'

'Yes, *Mama*.' Maria stamped her foot once Helena was out of earshot. 'I hate this obedience rubbish. *Mama* never did as she was told, not once, from all I can gather.'

'Then why do you put up with it?' asked Nina with a smile. She was so lucky; her own mother was very soft and understanding. She looked across at Maria, a dark-haired nymph with bright shining eyes. She was lounging on the cushions of the pink sofa, looking very young, very beautiful.

'I don't know why. Maybe because she's a ruthless woman. Who knows?' Maria watched Nina. She'd heard all about Nina's affair with Stephan. 'You're the one who's having a fling with Stephan, aren't you?'

Nina smiled. She could get all upset about the comment, but no matter, it was yesterday's news.

'We *were* having an affair, yes!'

'Oops. Sorry, I didn't know he dumped you. What happened?' Maria bent forward. 'By all accounts Caroline found you *at it* in brother dear's office, spread-eagled over the desk. Is it true?'

Nina laughed this time. 'I don't know who told you that, but it is not quite accurate. We were kissing on the couch when Caroline came in.'

'She socked you in the jaw, didn't she?' Maria asked in a soft husky whisper.

Nina shook her head. 'No, she did *not*. Your cousin's wife is nothing but a gossip-monger. If she can't keep her husband happy that's hardly my fault.'

'Oh no, Nina, I don't blame you. I'm all for you having an affair with Stephan. All for it. I wish I could pluck up the courage to sleep with Garry, but then he's always drunk.'

Nina looked shocked. Maria and Garry; they weren't a match. Never in this world!

'Maria, don't do anything in haste. I wish I hadn't.'

'You do?'

'If I hadn't been quite so eager, maybe Stephan would have held me in greater esteem. Now he thinks I'm a trollop.'

'A trollop. Really? Why, Nina? You're one of the most sensible girls I know. I wish I could be more like you.' Maria pondered over Nina's words, then added, 'Why did you sleep with him then?'

What was the use in lying. When the heart is involved it seems a futile exercise. 'Because I love him.' She reached for a peppermint from the gold-leafed dish on the onyx coffee table. 'You do crazy things when you're in love. You agree to stupid conditions just to be with someone.'

'Wow! I guess I've never been in love.'

'Who's never been in love?' The small figure loomed out of the darkened shadows of the lower deck.

'Petros!' Maria went to him and kissed him soundly on both cheeks. 'Am I glad you're here!'

Petros sat down and patted the seat next to him for Maria. 'And why is that?'

Maria smiled. 'You can keep an eye on the dragon. She's here, you know, checking up on Alexis and me.'

Petros shook his head. 'She's here because Alexis has announced his engagement to Carrie.'

'To Carrie? Beautiful Carrie and *my* brother? She must have lost her marbles! She never said anything to me when I saw her in London.'

Petros coloured under his tan. 'No? Well she has to marry under the old Greek custom.'

Maria gasped. 'You mean an *arranged* marriage? Oh Lord, Petros, surely she hasn't agreed! Carrie is Irish!'

'She has no choice,' Petros said with a note of finality in his voice that stopped Maria from commenting further.

'Who has no choice?' The dark elegant features of Marsha came into view as she stepped down onto the lounging deck, her impeccable entrance obviously a result of her former modelling career.

'Marsha, I didn't know you were invited?' Petros's face contorted with suppressed anger. Why had Alexis invited her?

'Yes. Alexis himself invited me.' She ran her hand down the brass railing onto the highly polished wood and smirked. 'I seem to have interrupted a private conversation. I'm sorry, I'll go and make myself comfortable in my room.'

'Oh, it wasn't private,' said Maria. 'Alexis and Carrie are to be married. Isn't that lovely news?'

Nina gasped, as did Petros, for they both knew of Marsha's recent involvement with Alexis. Marsha frowned; the only indication that the news had shocked her was her iron grip on the brass balustrade. Her knuckles paled with the force.

With the air of royalty, she looked around the deck and asked, 'Is your brother not here?' She plastered a smile on her face. 'I must congratulate him.'

'He arrives in the morning.' Maria stood up, slipping into her sandals she turned to Petros. 'I must go and freshen up for dinner. *Mama* has insisted that I look my best, and I suppose I had better sort Garry out. Poor Garry won't know what's hit him if *Mama* singles him out.'

'Well, if you'll excuse me too, I have a rather important call to make.' Petros said, making a quick exit. He moved along the corridor on the starboard side of the yacht, presuming he'd be in his usual room. Alexis always gave him the room next to the dragon lady. He grinned; poor Helena, if only she knew what they called her.

Carrie lay on the bed after her shower wondering how on earth she had managed to let herself fall in love with the naked man she could glimpse through the open bathroom door, whistling as he shaved. He had no shame standing like that, no shame at all, but he did look . . . magnificent!

Brushing her hair absently as she watched him, she felt a sudden tingling in her nipples. She frowned; she would have to find a chemist and buy a pregnancy testing kit just to check. She had no real proof that she was pregnant, only a feeling. It had to be confirmed, and to be honest she was amazed at how quickly she had become pregnant, if indeed she was.

Poor Alexis *had* flown into a rage last night when he thought she didn't want a child. She shook her head; if only he knew how much the opposite was true. She was afraid as well, though. Her own mother had died in childbirth.

But she didn't want to think sad thoughts. In the last few days Alexis had dispelled her theory of lovemaking 2.3 times a week. He hadn't left her alone since she'd challenged him that day in Alonnissos! Not that she was complaining. She just wished things could be different.

'What's funny?'

She looked up. Alexis had a towel wrapped around his lower half, and still he could turn her limbs to jelly just by standing there.

'Nothing. I was just thinking.'

'He frowned. 'Of Peter?'

'Nooo . . . I was actually thinking about us. Do arranged marriages really work?'

'They do!'

'What about love?'

'No such emotion – which is why arranged marriages work so well.'

'Then why haven't you been snapped up before now? If you've had a thing going with Marsha, why not her?'

His frown deepened. 'Marsha is married and bored; she threw herself at me.'

'Marsha is rich, she could get divorced. You could have waited for her,' she reminded him softly.

He moved further into the room. '*I* am rich. I need no one's money and as I say, Marsha is married. What is this, Carrie, *Question Time*?'

'No, it's not. I was just thinking how shocked she will be if she hasn't heard of our engagement.'

He brushed a hand through his dark hair. 'Yes, it will be a shock, but it won't matter to me.'

Carrie sat there open-mouthed, wondering if he would be so flippant should the time come to get rid of *her*.

'You're really heartless, aren't you?'

'Maybe.' He regarded her coolly. What would be the point in explaining to her? She'd never believe him. Not in a million years. He moved over to the bed, hands on hips, looking down at her. 'Are you going to get ready or am I going to join you on that bed?'

Carrie grinned affectionately at him. Heartless or not, she loved him. She wriggled out of the towel, absolutely loving the way his eyes darkened with desire. 'I don't know where they get 2.3 times a week. You must be going for the *Guinness Book of Records*. Come here!'

With a hoot of laughter he joined her on the bed.

'I thought you were joining us for breakfast,' came the caustic comment from the bespectacled woman lounging under one of the ten umbrellas.

'*Mama*, I apologize. We went looking for our wedding rings.' Alexis shrugged his large shoulders before bending over and kissing his mother's cheek.

'Carrie, my child. It is so good to see you.' Helena took off her sunglasses to look more closely at Carrie's simple attire. Simple yet elegant. 'What a lovely dress.'

'Thank you.' Carrie bent to kiss Helena on the cheek. 'By the way, *Kiria* Stephanides, we didn't find a wedding ring. Alexis says you know an excellent jeweller. We know exactly what we want.'

Helena nodded. 'Of course, my child. Once we reach Athens we will arrange for him to visit us.'

Carrie smiled, then froze as she saw Alexis taking Marsha into his arms. She heard a strangled cry of, 'Oh, Alexis, why didn't you tell me? I was so near to my divorce. I wanted to surprise you, my love.'

His whispered reply was muffled as Petros bustled onto the sundeck.

'Petros.' She kissed her godfather, her eyes still fastened on Alexis and Marsha as she watched them over his shoulder. 'How are you?'

'Carrie, I must tell you. I have had news from the doctor in New York. He wants to operate, do some kind of a bypass.' Petros smiled. 'I have told him, only after the engagement.' He patted his rotund belly. 'I've to lose a few kilos first.'

'And the chances of a successful operation?' she asked, concerned.

'Are good.'

'Petros.' Alexis moved forward and shook hands. Carrie noticed he was tense again. Something had obviously upset him.

Helena watched them thoughtfully over the top of her sunglasses as Maria made her noisy entrance. 'Listen up. Captain Savidis says we're setting sail now.'

Carrie saw Alexis smile, ready to catch his little sister to him as she threw her arms about his neck. At eighteen she was still a baby to him.

'Congrats, brother mine. I think she must be crazy but I wish you the best of luck.' She untangled herself from Alexis and smiled at Carrie. 'My brother needs someone to love him. I'm so glad it's you.' She leaned forward and kissed Carrie on the cheek.

'*Congrats, brother mine*,' scoffed Helena. 'If this is what my money is paying for at university, I want a refund.' She waved away Maria's excuse. 'I know, don't tell me. I'm ancient. Things have changed.' She scowled at her son. 'By the way, who is this Garry fellow that seems to be forever drunk, Alexis? And forever fawning all over your sister.'

'*Mama*, he does not!' Maria defended hotly.

Marsha frowned. 'Who's Garry?'

'My question, I believe, Marsha,' came Helena's authoritative voice. Marsha smiled, inclining her head to Helena, and Nina covered her eyes with her hands and cringed. Maria looked dumbfounded, her expression pleading with her brother to cover for them.

'Garry?'

'Yes, Garry. Nina says he is a good friend of yours.'

'She does, does she?' Alexis cast a glance at Nina who was still bowing her head.

'Well, no matter. Whoever he is, please tell him to stop mauling your sister. She's far too young.' Sighing, she went on: 'I'm rather disappointed with you, Alexis, for inviting him. The man has no manners at all. He seems a shady character.'

Alexis shifted his head to one side. 'And where is my friend Garry now?'

Maria was the one to answer. 'He's having a drink down on the lounge deck.'

Alexis smiled tolerantly at Maria, 'Then perhaps Maria will come with me and we can talk to him together!'

'Come, Carrie, sit with me a while,' said Helen, softly patting the seat beside her, whilst watching her son and daughter. 'And rub some suncream onto your exposed shoulders. We don't want to spoil your beautiful soft skin.'

'Thank you, *Kiria* Stephanides.'

'Call me Helena. We will become even better friends now, you and I. I can feel it in my bones,' she declared. Helena passed Carrie the lotion. 'Come. Tell me about this musical play you did.'

Petros had stripped himself of his robe and carefully lowered himself into the small swimming pool. Carrie watched him, not wanting to meet Helena's eyes. Who had told her about the play?

'It was a flop. There's nothing more to say.'

'But the dancing I saw was beautiful, almost as beautiful as the choreographer. A choreographer that should not have given up as she did,' she said pointedly.

Carrie met Helena's look. 'You saw the dancing?'

'Alexis and I saw the whole play as did Petros, Christina and George. Petros was so proud of you he flew us all over. And yet you insisted we should not see it. Did you know it was going to flop?'

Carrie sighed; this was almost too much to take in, tears glistened in her eyes. 'I knew I'd done my job well. What I didn't know was that my money had been spent on other things, squandered. What should have been spent on top quality props had been drunk away, and not by me.' She shrugged. 'It was also bad timing, the wrong venue.'

'And in spite all of that, you had a good critique in one of the top papers, no less.' Helena patted the younger girl's hand. 'You should stop blaming yourself, you know! I hope when you marry my son you will think about going back to your work,' Helena said, looking over her glasses again, 'Once you're better. He tells me you've not been too well. He's been rather concerned for you.'

Carrie nodded her surprise. 'It is my intention to work at something. I don't know if it will be within the dancing world though. You need money to invest in your ideas unless you're really lucky and get seen and noticed as new talent. And to be honest, I don't want work in Hollywood or London. Greece is my home.'

'Then work in Greece. We need new talent in Athens too. As for the money, your future husband could finance you. But then you wouldn't take his help for yourself, would you?' said Helena softly, before she added, 'I think I shall sleep now.'

Carrie went to stand by the rail. No, she wouldn't be using Alexis's money. Not now, or in the future.

From Skiathos they set sail to Skopelos. Carrie went down into her cabin. The yacht had plenty of cabin space, with 'en suite' facilities for everyone, including the crew.

Sitting on the double bed, she leaned back against the many pillows. Why had he invited Marsha? Was it just to rub her nose in the fact that he'd had her too? It was sickening the way she was canoodling with him, reaching up to plant pink lipstick marks against his cheek. True, Carrie had seen him wince, but there was something other than indifference in his eyes when he looked at Marsha's more shapely figure, her bigger breasts, her larger thighs. Marsha had grown since her modelling career had ceased five years ago.

A little knock on her door surprised her. 'Can I come in, Carrie?'

Carrie smiled, 'Yes, Maria, of course.' She stretched back on the cushions, making herself comfortable.

As Maria walked in she beamed a smile. 'You couldn't stand the smarmy bitch sucking up to him either. Makes me feel like I want to vomit.' She sat on the bed leafing through one of Carrie's *Vogue* magazines. 'I was surprised you'd agreed to this . . . this marriage thing, knowing of his recent involvement with her.'

'Yes. So was I. I surprised myself too,' she replied coolly. 'Last month I was in London with not a care in the world. Now I'm almost married.' Her voice was incredulous.

'Ah, but London wasn't good for you, was it? What with the play and the loneliness,' Maria stretched herself across the other side of the bed, knocking the magazine to the floor. 'The only thing in London that you would ever have to go back for is Peter and his family. They're wonderful people, and little Pete. God, he's adorable.'

Carrie's eyes misted over. 'Yes, Peter, I do miss him. I'd love to have him over here.'

'Do you remember when you took me with you to that zoo? We laughed and laughed about everything.' Maria was grinning now. 'You've been so good to me, Carrie. The first three months were horrendous at uni. I would have gone insane had you not let me visit, and you taught me so much about dancing. I told *Mama* you'd been good to me.'

Carrie shook her head admonishingingly, 'You don't have to thank me. I can score my own brownie points with Helena,' They both laughed. 'And I hope you mother doesn't think your penchant for slang comes from me?'

'Never. She thinks you're quite, quite sweet, a lady in fact. She loves your beauty, the way you dress. And – ' Maria leaned closer to Carrie – 'I heard her saying your temper was a match for Alexis any day!'

'Who was she telling that to?'

Maria shrugged. 'Who knows. Couldn't see so I just crept away in case she saw me.' She looked over the bed whilst reaching for the magazine once again. 'Aren't those Alexis's shoes?'

'Yes.' The girls looked at each other, 'Are you going to tell on me?'

Maria looked at the shoes and shook her head. 'Nope. But I have to be honest I can't imagine you two doing it, or you even sleeping in the same bed.'

Carrie laughed, 'Why ever not?'

'Now me and Garry on the other hand I could imagine. But Alexis seems to do everything in a strait-jacket. You never know what he's thinking, unless he's angry. His anger I CAN predict. I just can't imagine him being sensitive, or – or sexy.'

Carrie smiled. 'I refuse to go into detail about our relationship, but I will tell you he's *very* sexy in bed, and he doesn't ever use a strait-jacket!'

'Wow!' Maria screamed with laughter. 'That's why Mauling Marsha is still after him. It's got to be.'

They giggled together. 'Come on, let's go out to the sundeck and spoil her fun.'

Maria bounced off the bed. 'You put your sexiest bikini on. I'll just be a mo.'

Carrie sighed; she looked down the side of the bed at Alexis's shoes. Would his shoes always be under her bed? Shrugging herself into a pink bikini, she picked her sunbag, her floppy hat and went to the sundeck.

Alexis sat with the kitten on his knee, stroking it from head to tail as it purred happily. The day he'd been to fetch it from the sanctuary, it had looked like a lost soul. The only surviving kitten of four, Jonathan had said. Alexis hadn't wanted him to furnish him with the cruel details of how it ended up at the sanctuary, he was just pleased he could find the little lady a home, and Nina had needed something to love after her old cat had died. Especially now since her affair with Stephan had been blown out of the water.

'Is this the red devil?' Carrie smiled, stroking the kitty, cooing at it when it raised its tiny head into her palm for more.

'Red devil?' Alexis scowled. 'This is Saffy, she belongs to Nina.'

'I know who she belongs to,' Carrie bit out trying not to sound bad-tempered.

Alexis raised his eyes to hers, but said nothing.

'Where's Marsha? I thought she was keeping you busy, what with her size 40 double dees, you can hardly lose interest now can you?' Carrie knew she sounded like a jealous feline herself. The kitten looked up, stopped purring and meowed. 'Sorry, Saffy, some things just have to be said.'

Alexis smiled passively. 'She's actually 36DD.'

'You were still fraternizing with her,' she accused, the Irish acid now apparent in her voice.

'Are you jealous?' Alexis pushed the sunglasses up onto his forehead. 'If you're jealous, I'll tell you what we were discussing in some detail; if not, I won't!'

Carrie scoffed, 'Jealous? Never. I keep telling you that . . .'

'I know. Spare me the lecture,' he butted in, his eyes now roving over her skimpy attire. 'Turn around.'

'What?'

'I said turn around.' She yelped with the sudden shock as his fingers slid under the panties to pull the material straight. 'You were showing off your assets to the crew.'

His fingers lingered, and as they did she felt that same fire begin to ignite. She throbbed with desire and Alexis knew it. 'Maybe I should help you out of these?' he said softly. 'How about it?'

Carrie shook her head, squeaking incoherently, 'I can't. I promised I'd sunbathe with Maria.'

'Until tonight then,' his voice whispered, and with a playful slap to her bottom he gave her a little push towards his sister who had just arrived on deck.

Carrie turned hissing, 'I'll get you for that, Stephanides.'

Alexis dropped his sunglasses back over his eyes and taunted, 'I'll look forward to it.'

With as much dignity as possible she walked away, leaving him with just the purring kitten and his thoughts.

'Nice to see such lovely girls enjoying themselves,' choked Garry as he took a big mouthful of Ouzo, although he was oblivious to anyone but Maria. Maria was the one he was after, Carrie felt sure. If they weren't lovers yet, they soon would be!

'Oh Garry, shut up. Stop ogling us and stop drinking so much,' said Maria stiffly. 'You're supposed to be a fun person. You told me you'd liven up the party for me on this dull yacht. I haven't had any evidence of that yet.'

Carrie looked at him from the shade of her sunglasses. He was pouring something from a small bottle into his drink. She'd been watching him most of the afternoon and his eyes had never left Maria. Whenever she moved, he watched, whenever she swam, his eyes followed her. If Carrie hadn't been so sure he was just an island hopper she would have thought he'd appointed himself Maria's personal bodyguard, or even her avenging angel!

And yet she couldn't understand why Helena was concerned. He was a little scruffy, yes, but attractive too, in a rugged, outdoorsy, sort of way. Unshaven, he wore the same tatty cut-offs he'd probably worn all week. Maybe she *could* understand Helena's concern after all, but she still liked him.

'You want fun?' he said softly, luring Maria to his side. 'Then meet me in my cabin in an hour,' he whispered, his eyes lingering on the other woman, apparently asleep on the ajoining lounger. No way could she hear him, thank heavens.

Maria's eyes widened. She looked around to see if anyone was close. She nodded, her pulse accelerating beyond control. The reason she'd let him accompany her on the yacht was because she was absolutely lost when she looked into those delicious green eyes. Could love at first sight be on the menu here?

Lord! She just couldn't wait! She'd been angling for this from their first meeting. 'Why not now?'

Garry's eyebrows rose in question, a smile hovered about his lips. His bosses would have his guts for garters if they knew his intentions were to guard her quite this closely. But what the hell? She was beautiful beyond words, and the one place she was really safe was here, on this yacht! So why not indulge himself? She was obviously more than willing, and the idea of playing a few games with little Miss Heiress was delightful.

'Ten minutes,' he said softly. 'Now cool off with a swim.'

Maria laughed, diving into the pool. Funny, she thought after three lengths of the small pool, he doesn't seem as drunk now.

She watched as Garry got up and staggered slightly on his way to the steps. Everyone else seemed to be oblivious to him. Maria wasn't fooled by his drunken act. She knew differently now.

Swallowing air, she dived under the blue surface. This was so exciting, to think she could soon be making love right under her mother's nose. Now that *was* exciting – especially when her mother disapproved so much.

As Maria climbed out of the pool, Carrie got up from her lounger. 'Maria,' she said quietly so no one else would hear, 'You do know what you are doing, don't you?'

Maria's eyes widened. 'Yes, I'm fraternizing with the enemy.' She tried to qualify her reasons, 'I really like him, Carrie. In fact it could be love.'

Carrie sighed, 'Like the one in London? You really liked him, *and* the one that broke your heart at university. Just be careful, Garry doesn't seem like the boys you're used to. A kiss will be a signal that you'll go all the way with Garry.'

'That's what I'm hoping for, especially since *Mama* dislikes him so. That makes it all the more exciting.' Maria grinned devilishly.

Carrie reached for her arm, 'Is that fair to Garry?' She shook her head, blonde wisps dancing in the soft, caressing breeze 'You may think he's a drunken low-life, but it's no reason to use him.'

Maria stared at Carrie, her bottom lip pouting as she said waspishly, 'He'll be using me too!'

Carrie backed off, 'Sorry, I didn't mean to overstep the mark as a friend.' She watched Maria walk away, then turned and went back to her lounger. Alexis was nowhere to be seen. Neither was Marsha!

Sneaking down the corridor at the starboard side had an accelerating effect on Maria's pulse. Looking round, she knocked on the door and entered Garry's cabin. He was standing, looking out of the small porthole, his back to her. Her dark eyes ran longingly over his entire length. In this confined space, he was much, much bigger than she'd anticipated. Taller, his muscles more pronounced, his rich blond hair longer, his tan . . . Well what could one say? He was gorgeous. If she could have been his student at uni, she wouldn't have missed a class!

'I'm here,' she babbled foolishly, all of a sudden feeling just as Carrie had said, unworldly. She was used to boys. Garry was no boy.

He turned, his green eyes encompassing the contents of her skimpy red bikini. She was small in height as were many Greek girls, but her hips and breasts were more than generously proportioned without her being fat.

'You still want fun?' His deep voice was deliberately scary, his eyes like slits. 'Fun with a capital F?'

She hesitated, she wasn't sure she liked the sound of his voice when he spoke to her like this. The connotation was quite derogatory, and yet, quite shockingly exciting.

She shook her long, wet dark hair out of her eyes. 'I want fun, yes, but I don't want force.' She licked her lips.

'You get what I give you, lady, and believe me you'll have fun. So much fun you'll never want to be a boring, spoilt little girl ever again!'

'I'm not!'

'Oh but you are!'

As Maria turned for the door, he beat her to it, locking it, pocketing the key and looking down at her with a smile.

'Isn't this fun, Maria, to be doing it with someone Mummy doesn't approve of? A drunken low-life?' He gloated at her surprised look. 'Oh yes. I heard you, both of you.'

'You heard?'

'Yes. I heard and I'm just deciding whether or not I do want to *use* you. One so young without any scruples? I wouldn't want to catch anything!'

She tried to hit him, but he caught her hand.

Pushing her back on the bed, he pinned and held her wrists above her, easily capturing them in one of his hands.

'You won't catch anything off me, and I'm almost twenty-two for your information,' she lied breathlessly, and as he lowered himself down over her, her eyes widened to huge saucers 'And I've changed my mind. I don't want to be used.'

His voice softened. 'In that case I'll make love to you,' he whispered seductively with the smile to kill all smiles.

'Make love?' she whispered, her heart hammering relentlessly against her chest.

'I never force women, and never one so beautiful as you.' He lifted a brow. 'Do I proceed? Or do I throw you out on your bottom into the corridor just when your brother is about to pass?'

He meant it too. She could see he would carry out his threat. Closing her eyes she shifted her position underneath him, enticing him, giving him his answer without words.

Unclipping the front-fastening of her bikini top, he swiftly pushed the offending material away so that he could feast his eyes on her dark, tempting nipples.

'Fun starts with kissing you.' He looked at her lips, and smiled. 'Like this.'

He was so gentle, she was left begging for more. Her eyes were tightly closed until he moved downwards, taking her nipple in his teeth and she cried out, her body writhing. She tasted so sweet. Reaching over, he switched on the radio and came back down beside her.

Eyes wide, she questioned breathlessly, 'What are you doing?'

'I wouldn't want anyone to hear your screams, now, would I?'

She smiled, sexual excitement enthralling her. The two other men in her life had left her so bored. This one was different. What was that saying? Third-time lucky? Leaning across him she turned the radio up another notch, her smile one of pure impudence.

'Nor I yours.'

CHAPTER 11

'Has anyone seen Maria?' asked Alexis, his haughty glance encompassing the inhabitants of the sundeck Helena shrugged lazily, Petros shook his head.

'I have,' replied a stiff-voiced Carrie. Alexis had been missing for two whole hours, and so had Marsha. 'I think she's gone for a shower. She came on deck not long ago. If you'd been around you would have noticed. Funny – both you and Marsha have been missing all afternoon.'

'Marsha has a headache,' he hissed softly. '*I* have been working in the office; ask Nina if you don't believe me. She's been taking shorthand.'

Helena raised a brow when she saw Carrie's eyes flashing at Alexis and she intervened. 'Now, now, you two. You should be making love not war. You're betrothed.' She pulled her sunglasses back down. 'And you should be allowing your *Mama* a siesta.'

The look Alexis threw her was one of tolerance.

'Yes. We mustn't forget that.' Carrie raised her eyes to his. 'Is it important, with Maria? I believe she is going to lie down for a while after her shower.'

That wasn't a lie either; she would definitely be lying down at some point if Carrie knew Maria!

'No, it's not that important.' He held out his hand, 'Come, I want to talk to you, in the office.'

Carrie refused to take his hand and reached for her shirt, slipping into the cool confines of the white cotton.

'Haven't you forgiven me yet?' His voice was teasing now, his hand on her arm gentle, and warm.

'For what?'

'For leaving you to your own devices. I *am* sorry. There have been things to sort out, accounts to set up, transport to arrange. I don't want you to feel that I'm smothering you. You should still have your freedom, if you want that.' He took her hand this time, guiding her into the office. 'If you feel you need to look after Petros's business, then that's fine with me. I shouldn't have interfered.'

Carrie sat in the chair opposite his, her forehead creasing. 'But you should feel free to interfere, seeing as you're investing a large amount. Why, it must be millions.'

Alexis disguised the guilt he felt and agreed, 'Yes. A huge amount.'

'Then we should do it together. Didn't you say that most of his ships needed renovations?'

He nodded, gave a cautious, 'Yes?'

'In that case I'll arrange to have an expert look over them, get reports done on the major problems. You *did* say some of the ships were hardly sea-worthy, didn't you?'

Alexis looked her straight in the eye, his slight flinch enough to tell her she was on the right track. He and Petros were up to something.

'Yes. I did say that.'

She settled herself in the chair. 'Then that's settled.' With a quick bright smile she questioned, 'Could we have something cold to drink?'

Alexis rang through for a brandy sour for himself and a fresh orange juice for Carrie.

'I'd like to discuss your finances. By the time we get back from our cruise, you will have bank accounts, credit cards and account cards set up – ' Alexis watched her lips compress – 'As my future wife, I will expect you to use them.'

She inclined her head, her eyes like ice. 'That's really not necessary, I do have some money of my own.'

He ignored her remark, saying firmly, 'Should you require more money, you only have to ask.'

Temper simmering, her eyes turned colder than ever. 'I don't ask for money, nor do I want your credit cards. You seem to be forgetting that this is a business arrangement. Petros is going to be free from financial worry, that's all the repayment I ask.'

'Use the credit cards, Carrie! Your money won't last forever!'

Carrie was saved from making a reply when a sharp knock came on the door and their drinks were placed on the desk in front of them. She looked at Alexis's brandy sour, the tall frosted glass with the sugar-rimmed top, and wished for her own.

'May I taste your drink?' She took Alexis's glass,

sipping the contents. Divine recall; she closed her eyes, for the taste brought back memories of a holiday in Cyprus with her parents. Her mother had been drinking brandy sours by the dozen, or so it seemed, and every time she looked away Carrie would sip the cool liquid, gasp and pull a face. She could hear her parents giggle as they watched her face, as sour as the brandy drink itself.

'I don't mind sharing, but why not just order one?' asked Alexis as she handed him the glass with hardly any of the liquid drunk.

She smiled sweetly at him. 'You know how alcohol affects me. Besides I wanted orange. It just reminds me of Cyprus, of the last holiday I shared with mum and dad.'

Alexis studied her for a while, fascinated as always when he watched the anger simmer in her eyes; the blue always turned violet before it turned back to blue. It was those eyes that haunted his dreams, his thoughts. 'It must have been so hard, to lose your family like that. You were so young.'

'You must know how I felt, you lost your father too.'

'Ah yes, but I lost only my father. You lost your whole family in the space of what, six months?'

A sad mist covered the blueness in her eyes, but she swiftly blinked away the tears. 'My mother died in childbirth; they could save neither her nor my baby brother. My father died of a heart attack several months later.'

He looked suddenly shocked, realization of her words sinking in. 'In childbirth you say?'

She nodded, lowering her eyes. 'I know it seems silly

but that's why I am afraid of having children.' She smiled at him, nervous and suddenly very shy. 'I've always wanted them, children, that is, but I've often been so afraid that I would die too. Because of that, I never gave the thought much time, always spurning men's advances, never wanting to get involved.'

The sadness in his eyes was profound. 'And here am I forcing your hand.' He clenched his fingers as if his hand were hurting. 'Why didn't you tell me, Carrie?'

She reached across to him, touching his tense arm. 'You wouldn't have listened. If it's any consolation, I'd rather have your child than Theo's any day.'

Happiness lit his face, but there was still that something she could not define as he whispered the only words that seemed appropriate; 'Thank you.'

Maria lay spent on the bed, one long-nailed finger running down Garry's bronzed hairy chest as she lifted herself on her elbow and leaned over him, the underside of her breast just touching his forearm. She'd lost all reason when he'd touched her like he had, everything washing away on a sea of delight, including the thought that this was a means to get her own back on her strict mother.

'Why do you pretend to be drunk?' She looked closely at him, as he opened one delicious cool green eye. 'I'm not a fool. Your breath doesn't reek of alcohol, and it should, the amount of Ouzo you've consumed.'

'You're cleverer than I first thought. You tell me.' He threw the gauntlet down at her feet.

'OK.' She circled his nipple. 'I think my brother has hired you.' He opened both eyes and really looked at her. 'I'll grant you, I really thought you were an out-of-work lecturer on an island-hopping holiday.'

'And what destroyed that notion?'

'You did!' she retorted.

Pushing his hands behind his head he hoisted himself up slightly to look at her more closely. 'I did? How?'

Dark shining eyes were laughing at him. Dare she tell him she'd been through his things? Dare she reveal she knew of his dangerous weapon, and it wasn't the one that now lay limply just inches away from her fingers? It was the one in his shoe in the closet, the revolver.

She shrugged, knowing instinctively he'd be angry if she told him she'd been in here this morning looking through his things. That was indeed a little rich girl's pastime.

'I heard Nina saying something to Alexis.' She smiled. 'Does it matter? I don't mind protection. Alexis is always cautious, he has to be. I've been threatened with numerous kidnappings.'

He nodded. 'Really, what makes you think I'm here to protect you. It could be his future wife, Carrie. Now there's a fiery creature if ever I saw one. I heard her biting his head off as they came onto the yacht. Something to do with that Marsha woman.'

She shook her head. 'You'd still be on deck if it was Carrie. I'm the one you can't stop looking at. You're here to protect me, Garry.'

'So what happens now? Do you tell everyone why I'm here, frighten them all? It's a precautionary measure only, and if your brother knows that you've blown my cover, I'll be out of a job.'

Her lips lifted at the corner, her hand drifted down the flat expanse of his belly. 'As long as I get your individual attention, I can see no reason to alert everyone. You can stay in your drunken stupor providing we can still have fun – ' she felt the movement under her fingers and played to it – 'with a capital F.'

Garry studied her for a long moment. He nodded, feeling the ache in his groin come alive. He didn't know what the hell was coming over him. He'd never played like this when he should have been working, but this time he couldn't help himself.

'Fun, that's all it is.' He had to spell it out; once this was all over he was going back home like a flash.

'We'll see,' chuckled Maria.

Garry was hauling her to him, in a split second looking threateningly down into her face. 'We won't *see*! This is fun or I don't play the game, little rich girl.'

Maria was quite breathless. Lord, he was *all* man and if that meant only for this cruise then she'd take it; she had to. Things this good didn't come round twice in a lifetime.

'What is there to do on Skopelos?' cried Maria as the group moved up from the harbour to wander around the town's shops, good exercise for walking off their lunch.

'How about we go and see some of the churches? We have nearly four hundred to choose from. I could do with lighting a few candles,' said Nina, truly enjoying herself.

Alexis smiled as he silently predicted Maria's reaction.

'Oh no, no more churches, please! Locals don't count sheep here when they can't sleep, they count churches! I'll go shopping with Garry.' She turned to Garry, quick enough to see the exchange of looks between him and Alexis.

'Actually I'd like to see the churches,' he agreed, knowing the silent order was to keep her in the group.

Reaching for her arm, he ignored Helena's look of distaste. He couldn't care less whether the dragon lady liked him; he had a job to do.

'Carrie, what about you? How about hiring a motorbike?' asked Alexis, his hand at her elbow. He remembered she'd had an accident with a motorbike, as he saw her gaze flickering over the harbour side, where the pavement was strewn with the blue and red machines.

'No. Motorbikes and me hardly mix, as well you know. I think I'll stick to lighting a candle or two myself.' Looking up at the nearest church she sighed.

'We could shop first,' moaned Maria.

'Yes. I'd like to shop,' added Marsha, her heavily made-up eyes sweeping across Alexis's broad back.

'Really, Marsha, didn't you get enough clothes and things when you were last in America?' Helena asked as if she were bored with the whole situation.

'Why don't we walk around the shops this evening? It will be cooler and most will be open. Then we can have dinner overlooking the sea,' suggested Carrie, wishing they would move on, it was so blisteringly hot now.

'We're going inland for dinner. A friend of the captain's by all accounts,' said Helena, linking arms with her daughter and dragging her away from Garry. Carrie looked up, 'Wherever we're going, can we go now? It's far too hot to stand and chatter.'

'Hear, hear,' Alexis said, motioning everyone towards the town and the cool confines of the nearest church. He looked eastward. 'We'll visit the monastery on the hill when we're done here.' The monastery hugged the hillside, built within the rock with many flights of steps to climb.

Petros took Helena's arm. One look at the steps had put both him and Helena off. 'We'll wait in the shade. I'm not fit enough for those steps.'

Alexis took Carrie's arm and then Nina's leaving Maria and Marsha to Garry as they visited the churches. He could no more touch Marsha than look at her.

Later as they sat under the striped canopied roof of the seafront taverna, Garry suggested they all went for a powerboat ride.

Maria gave an ecstatic whoop of joy, 'At last some real fun.'

Carrie touched the cacti plants littering the ground between the different waterfront restaurants, while Alexis watched from behind his sunglasses. She was thinking about something, touching things while they waited for their coffee. At first her slim fingers touched the plants, the trunk of the tree which sprouted between each different canopy. Each canopy signified change of ownership, a different eating house. The condiments rack was next; her fingers felt the shape, the size and then she ran her hands over the wicker chair Alexis was lounging in. When he linked fingers with hers under the cushion she looked up, startled, but smiled.

'Would you like a powerboat ride?' He was talking to Carrie. The others could have been a million miles away. She nodded, her lips breaking into a sweet smile.

At the water's edge Garry, Nina, Maria, Marsha and Helena went into the first boat. Petros had refused, and Alexis had insisted he and Carrie use the smaller one made for two. He had bartered with the owner of the two boats before leaving the harbour. Their destination, he told Carrie, was the caves around the headland which jutted out to the left of the island.

'But that's the other direction to where Garry is going,' she stated.

Alexis grinned wickledly. 'I know. But I couldn't wait a moment longer to have you to myself.'

Woman overboard was hardly the term she would have used, thought Carrie two days later when Saffy, teetering playfully on the rails at the portside of the yacht like a young ballerina, had been cruelly swept over and into the sea by the careless hand of Marsha.

'Woman overboard!' Marsha shrieked pathetically. 'Carrie – help the cat! I'm not a good swimmer.'

Carrie was the first into the water, diving smoothly off the side. Good thing they'd anchored in the secluded bay, Carrie thought as she surfaced.

Maria followed with Garry right behind her. The poor kitten was swimming in the wrong direction.

Nina was crying, '*Ela, ela, Saffy.*'

Alexis had watched unconcerned as Carrie reached the kitten first, directing it towards the arms of her owner. The poor feline was looking all forlorn and scared, its pathetic feet striking out as best it could.

Suddenly Alexis frowned. Had he seen the dorsal fin of a shark in the sparkling waters or was it a dolphin? He put a hand to his brow to try and look more closely, but the reflection on the water was terrible. The feeling of dread rushed through him. Feelings like this were never to be ignored.

Both Carrie and Saffy were safe. Or so he thought. Carrie was already reaching up out of the water with the kitten to Nina's waiting arms. Maria and Garry were still on their turnabout, splashing playfully when the horn sounded.

The captain had seen it too, so was it a shark? Deadly or not, one had learnt to take such sightings seriously.

'Maria, Garry, out of there fast,' cried Alexis, reaching down to haul his sister out of the water. His attention had been so taken up by the shark, he'd not realized that Carrie was in trouble. She clung to the side of the yacht. Cramp was attacking her legs again.

Panic surged through, her; she'd seen the shark and knew what to do, but the cramps were crippling her.

'Carrie, for God's sake, give me your hand,' cried Alexis. 'Now, darling, *now*!'

He reached down, but the cramp had got her again. Alongside him, Garry slid quietly into the water. He reached her in the nick of time.

The shark swam in circles some twenty feet away, not a huge one but big enough. Alexis held Carrie to him, then bent to massage her cramped muscles.

The atmosphere was tense, almost electric, until everyone was back on the lounging deck. Still the shark circled, its dull lifeless eyes watching them all on board, as though the creature was thinking, *Next time I'll get you.*

'Everyone OK? We don't usually see them here at this time. Usually bottom feeders,' said the captain, counting all heads. 'What happened?'

'The kitten fell overboard,' said Marsha, still manicuring her nails.

'More like was pushed,' attacked Nina, tears surfacing as she dried Saffy off with a towel.

'It was not pushed!'

Carrie towelled herself dry, listening to Alexis as he said, 'It doesn't matter. Everyone is safe.'

A knowing look passed between Garry and Alexis; it was obvious they both thought it had been a deliberate act of menace. I bet Marsha wants me out of the way, thought Carrie as she went to change.

They were setting sail for Skyros soon; maybe life would be less dangerous there.

Carrie couldn't sleep that night, however much she tried. They'd anchored out of Skyros harbour as the weather report was fine for the next week or so. Pushing her thongs onto her feet, stepping into cycling shorts and dragging a T-shirt over her damp body, she went out on deck.

The quietness was broken only by the gentle lapping of the tide against the yacht, the moonlight's pattern only chequered and broken on deck by the shadow of a stray, listless cloud.

The air was not much cooler on deck but it certainly afforded her a little more comfort. It had been two hours since Alexis had left her and even a cold shower had not cooled her down sufficiently. He did something special to her and she was sure it was much more than sex! He was so thoughtful, so tender, and yet sometimes he became all possessive with her. He kept on telling her she belonged to him, almost as if he were convincing himself.

Sitting back against the coolness of the seat, she sighed to herself, unaware of the diver bobbing about beneath the yacht, unaware of what he was looking for as he skimmed his hands over the yacht's propellers and down the belly of the vessel.

Looking at his watch with the underwater torch, he knew he must surface soon, his air almost out.

A cool drink, that was what Carrie wanted; something refreshing, something tangy, preferably with lime. Getting up, she went to the refrigerator. A cool drink of five fruits mixed with crushed ice in a tall glass was soon by her side, as she leant with her arm hanging over the side.

As she sat there listening to the quietness she heard the faint sound of bubbles. She frowned: bubbles from someone's air tank? She'd recognize that noise anywhere. Leaning over she saw the reflection of the torch, her audible gasp enough to wake the ghosts. A shiver of dread ran through her veins. Who was down there? And *what* were they doing? Leaning over, she realized that the diver, whoever he or she was, was surfacing near the steps.

Taking her drink with her, she rushed headlong towards Alexis's room, her pulse hammering loudly in her ears, her heart drumming fast. She stopped, waited as she saw the black figure hauling himself up on deck, then yelped loudly, dropping her glass as he came in her direction.

She was scared, almost petrified. Who could it be? Garry? There was something definitely not right about Garry. But it wasn't Garry or Marsha moving towards her. Marsha had said she was a poor swimmer with no head for heights and scuba diving definitely required that, the way some underwater ravines dropped a hundred feet or more.

Fleeing, she almost cried as she heard a noise behind her. It would have been easy to go into her room, but Alexis must know of this!

As quickly as her trembling legs would carry her she fled to the other end of the yacht and quietly entered his cabin.

'Alexis! Alexis, it's me, Carrie,' she whispered urgently, her breath hurting her with the panic she felt. There was no sound, but as she reached for the light switch she was caught from behind, pulled against the wet rubber suit, a hand swiftly placed over her mouth to stifle her scream.

Fear rocked her back against the diver's body, but as swiftly as the fear stilled her, her survival instincts came into play almost automatically.

Fight rushed back into her body.

She struggled hard and landed a kick which connected with *something*, from the sound of her attacker's grunt. Leaning back she caught hold of his wet hair, pulled like crazy and heard another muffled hiss before she bit into his hand.

'Witch!'

She would have bitten him again, but she was dumped on the bed stomach first, her head held against the pillow so her screams couldn't be heard. She still fought on as he held her face down, his knee on the middle of her back, her hands cruelly captured.

Then suddenly she was free and the light was on and a very angry Alexis was looking down at her, at the same time as checking the blood and teeth marks on his hand.

'What the hell's going on here?'

She was speechless!

Breathless. It had been Alexis under the yacht!

He was furious, she could see. But why?

Swallowing hard, she found her voice. 'I thought, I thought you were asleep. I thought . . .'

'You thought what?'

Her breathing shallowed. 'I couldn't sleep, I went out on deck and saw . . .'

There was stiff tolerance written upon his dark face. 'You saw what, Carrie?'

'I was scared. *You* scared me!' She scrambled up to sit on the bed, still aware of how angry he was with her.

'What did you see, Carrie?'

She swallowed again. 'Look Alexis, I saw what I thought was a diver. A diver who could have been planting a bomb, or, or . . . Well I don't know,' she hissed, suddenly exasperated.

A smile transformed his face, the devil sparkling in his eyes. 'You've got a vivid imagination, Carrie O'Riordan, absolutely vivid. I was down there checking the propeller for Captain Savidis.'

'At this time of night?' She moved to get off the bed, but Alexis pushed her back, lifting her up against the pillow.

'I, too, couldn't sleep.' He looked at the blood on his hand and shook his head. 'You certainly know how to look after yourself.' Unzipping the black rubber wetsuit he dragged it off, leaving himself naked.

'I'd better let you get a shower,' she said shakily, wanting him and yet hating herself for being so weak.

'The shower will wait. You have to kiss my hand better; in fact, you have to kiss *me* better, full stop. Here was I checking the propeller for Captain Savidis, and what do I get? A good kicking, bitten and hurt. A woman around here who bites could get more than she bargains for.' He saw her eyes widen and almost, almost couldn't stop himself from laughing. 'I'll tell you what. The reason we were both on deck is because we couldn't sleep.' He looked her straight in the eye. 'I amused you earlier, maybe you'd like to trade a forfeit. Amuse me, Carrie, I'm an injured soul and I need you.'

He could see the light of passion in her eyes as they greedily feasted upon his body, upon a straining part of his anatomy that had sprung into life. Pulling him down beside her, she grazed his entire damp length with taunting fingers.

Alexis gasped. 'I thought it started with a kiss?' He gasped again as her fingers closed around him.

She smiled, reciting his words from their first night: 'There are no rules to say where that kiss should be.' Then she dipped her head, and he was lost!

A week later, they all sat at a taverna on the edge of the harbour.

'I'll have brandy,' said Petros to the waiter hovering just at the edge of the table.

'No, he won't. He'll have an orange juice,' Carrie told the waiter, staring adamantly at Petros. She could see the approval of her actions in Helena's face. Helena rarely approved of anything. And lately, she'd noticed Helena's constant agitation.

The taverna was lit by coloured bulbs shining from the many trees around it.

'This is so nice,' said Nina to Carrie. 'I think Mr Stephanides is very kind to let me have a working holiday like this, and especially kind to let me bring Saffy. The crew say she's become the mascot. Although she didn't like being left on the yacht tonight.'

'Yes, it *was* nice of Alexis. He seems to be quite a nice man,' Carrie whispered almost to herself. If only he would stop encouraging Marsha. She was like a leech, forever reaching up to kiss him when Carrie was about.

She looked across at him and even though he was next to Marsha he had not taken his eyes off Carrie all night. Carrie could feel the sexual tension between them, but there was another tension there too – anger! She'd managed to anger him five times or more on this voyage so far and they'd only been cruising for just over a week!

Each and every time he was in her bathroom, which he used frequently, she would phone Peter. This evening's conversation had been sensational and now it had Alexis scowling intently.

'Peter, my darling,' Carrie had said loudly, 'Of course. I love you with all my heart, you know that. Yes, I'm sure you could visit. What, maybe next summer, during the school holidays?' Carrie cringed to herself; she'd almost let herself down when Alexis had said, '*School holidays? What does Peter do?*'

Carrie had to think quickly. 'He's the head teacher. He can only have school holidays off.'

Whether or not he'd believed her she wasn't sure; what she did know was he asked her specifically if she could phone Peter once a week only. Carrie had refused, declaring that she would phone him whenever she wanted to.

Looking at him now, Carrie began to realize just how nice Alexis could be. She would have fallen in love with him had he courted her the conventional way, she was sure of that. So why had they forced her into an arranged marriage? She now suspected that Petros's shipping fleet was intact, as was his money. As soon as they got back to Athens she would investigate the books and accounts, and confirm her suspicious.

'Isn't that so, Carrie?'

'What?' Carrie looked blankly at everyone.

'We were saying you do the best Irish jig in the Greek islands,' beamed Petros proudly.

She smiled. 'Yes, Petros, I do.'

'Then why don't you do it for us?' Marsha's tone was strangely vehement. This was only the second time she'd addressed Carrie directly. Obviously she thought: *ignore and the enemy will go away*, but Carrie wasn't going anywhere.

'Of course.'

'You will need music?'

'No. Alexis, Petros, will you clap your hands as I taught you?'

If Marsha had hoped Carrie would show herself up, she was wrong. To be a good choreographer you have to be at least a decent dancer. Carrie was excellent at this type of dance, her mother had taught her so well! With clicks of her heels she danced in time to the clapping, along the cobbled floor of the harbour-front taverna, making one of the most physical of dances look easy. To the shouts of *Oria*, *Bravo* and *Wunderbar* from some of the other visitors, Carrie showed them what Irish dancing was all about. The last dance was of course her favourite, her very own creation. It was a sensual routine where she twirled and clicked her heels, then almost poetically slowed, dancing for herself, dancing for her man.

Breathless and panting, she was about to sit when Alexis caught her by the hand. He asked for some slow music. Pulling her to him, he caressed her pale flowing hair, held her head in his hands and kissed her.

'When you dance like that, I forget about your Irish temper. I forget about arranged marriages and babies. You *almost* make me believe there is such a thing as love,' he whispered softly in her ear.

Carrie's heart lurched, speeding out of control as his hand moved sensitively up and down her spine. And she would have fallen for his sweet words had Petros and Marsha not been dancing within earshot. It was obvious he wanted Marsha to be jealous.

Carrie pulled slightly away. '*Almost*? Maybe you were right when you said there is no such thing as love. It is an overrated feeling connected with sexual compatibility. One thing you have in your favour though, if I get tired of sex, maybe Marsha will oblige!'

It had started out as a romantic conversation, but now Carrie felt Alexis stiffen.

'Tell me, Alexis, why didn't Marsha's father arrive with her? Who put her in the cabin next to yours? And why, for heaven's sake, do you put up with her kissing you all the time? Unless of course you enjoy it?' Carrie queried softly, but with venom. This thing had to be sorted out once and for all!

His dark eyes sparkled like angry jewels, his lips tightened. 'You dare accuse me of flirting when *you* openly flirted on the telephone this evening? Peter must get pretty sick of listening to you vowing your neverending love, when every night you sleep with me!'

'Oh I do, do I?'

'Yes, you do!'

Carrie stabbed him in the chest with her finger. 'Not tonight, buster. There is no way I'll be sleeping with you tonight!'

'Great! That sounds just great to me – it leaves me free to sleep with who the hell I like. Until we are betrothed we are both free agents,' he announced, still watching her as the reality of his words sunk home.

Carrie pulled out of his arms, and felt sick knowing that Marsha was within easy reach of him. 'At least I know the score. Now if you don't mind, I'll go back to the yacht. I have a blinding headache.'

It was no lie. She did have a throbbing headache, which wasn't eased by her slow walk back, nor by the beauty of the moon lying on its back against a midnight-blue sky. She stood looking over the port rail for what seemed like an age. She could see the taverna, could see Alexis dancing with Marsha, see them laughing together. Turning away, she went back to her cabin and wept.

Sleep didn't come easily. Someone disturbed her in the early hours of the morning whispering outside her cabin. Was it Marsha? There was a man, but it wasn't Alexis. Slowly, the voices drifted away, and closing her eyes she fell into a fitful sleep. Who had she heard? She was certain that she had heard that voice before, that urgent whisper.

'So dance with me. It seems your betrothed has left you to your own devices, and I'm here just ripe for the picking,' cooed Marsha to Alexis.

Alexis had looked down at the woman whom he had once bedded, or was it the other way around? She had bedded him! He laughed bitterly.

'Sure. Let's dance. Why not?' He took her in his arms, resting his cheek lightly on hers. He was cruel, using her like this, for he knew that Carrie was watching, he could see the white-gold of her hair in the lamplight from the yacht.

'Why didn't you tell me?'

'Tell you? Tell you what, Marsha?' He looked down at her and laughed harshly. 'Surely you knew I wouldn't have an affair with you!'

'But you did!' she protested.

Alexis laughed out loud, cruelly stating, 'I had sex with you. Men do that on occasion. You really left me no choice. What I want to know is how on earth you got a key to my room that night.'

Marsha shrugged. 'Oh that was easy. The bellboy was easily pleased.'

'You mean . . .?'

'Yes. I mean I'll do anything to be with you, Alexis. I bribed him. It was 30,000 drachmas for a room key. Rather expensive, don't you think?' She sidled closer. 'But it was worth it.'

'You got what you wanted.' Alexis breathed deeply; for one awful moment he'd thought she'd bedded the bellboy too! He knew that would be exactly the kind of thing Marsha would do.

'But darling, I didn't get half of what I wanted. Not at all, and then when you phoned the other day and asked me to join the yacht party, I knew that you'd changed your mind. It's always been you.' She stretched up and kissed his cheek.

Alexis laughed down into her face. 'You thought I'd changed my mind? About what? There is no *us*, Marsha! You live in a dream world. How many times do I have to tell you? We had sex. For God's sake, woman, you crept into my bed, trussed up in your . . .'

'It's called a body.'

Alexis sighed. 'Try and let her down gently,' a voice cut into his thoughts. 'A body then. Well, I'm not a machine, you know. You're a very attractive lady, and maybe if things had been different, we could have had a real affair. But that's all it would have been. An affair.'

'Things will be different.'

'Oh Lord.' He took Marsha by the shoulders, shaking her. 'Marsha, listen to me. I am betrothed to Carrie under the old Greek custom. I will be married to her!' He really sounded convinced, and yet in his heart of hearts he knew anything was possible where Carrie O'Riordan was concerned.

'If you say so, darling.' Marsha rested her head lightly against his shoulder. 'If you say so.'

Catching the captain's eye, Alexis implored him with a silent plea. The other man cut in immediately and Alexis left Marsha in his capable hands.

'*Mama*, isn't it about time I danced with you?' Alexis smiled as his mother walked quietly into the circle of his arms. She wasn't normally this meek and mild.

'Tell me, son, what have you done to Carrie?'

'To Carrie? Nothing, she's just feeling a little out of sorts. She's not used to being the centre of attention like this.'

'Plus . . .?' encouraged Helena, having seen the display of temper flare in Carrie's eyes not ten minutes earlier.

'Plus we had an argument about nothing.'

'She's not pregnant, is she?'

Alexis stopped moving. 'Did I hear you correctly?'

'Yes. I know you've slept with her. Petros gave me a lecture on the morals of my son. I told him not to be an old fool and realize that we are living in the nineties. Helena smiled up at her son. 'Don't look so shocked. I was pregnant with you when I married your father, but we were clever and I got away with it. We told most people you were premature, and we kept you hidden for weeks from the outside world.'

As they danced Alexis smiled to himself. All these years and she'd kept that little gem safe and sound.

'By the way, darling, I don't want to be a stick in the mud on this vacation, but will you please talk to Maria? I'm not very fond of her friend Garry. And yes, I know he's *her* friend. I'm no fool.'

He sighed. '*Mama*, Maria is old enough to look after herself. You've trusted her in England, trust her now.'

Helena was shaking her head. 'Wrong answer. She is very young, too young for the likes of him. I want him off the yacht or a promise from her that she'll keep herself intact. If we're not already too late for that.'

Alexis scowled. 'You mean she's slept with him?'

'Not yet, I hope. Talk to her, please, Alexis,' urged Helena. 'I'm worried that he'll hurt her, and God knows she has never listened to me.'

'I'll go and talk to her, but he must stay on the yacht, *Mama*, at least for the moment,' said Alexis, leaving his mother to Petros, who looked somewhat baffled.

'Maria, a dance I think.' Alexis could hardly soften his strong tone as he took his sister in his arms.

'Oh Lord, you have that, "I'm going to give you a lecture" look again.' Maria accused, then yipped as her brother's hand tapped her knuckles lightly.

'Ouch, Alexis!'

'Don't look so hurt, Maria. It could be worse. I could take you across my knee in a taverna full of people.'

'Alexis, you wouldn't! Besides, I'm too old for that!'

'You think so? *Papa* wouldn't think so if he were here and you know it. So think again, Maria. Now tell me why did you lie to *Mama*? Why did you make out that Garry was a friend of mine? And where the hell did you pick him up?'

Maria looked up at her brother. She'd like to say '*I know your game, Alexis*', but she couldn't. Besides, she was having way too much fun with Garry, and she wasn't about to drop Nina in it. Instead she went along with the gameplan. 'I'm sorry, I shouldn't have done it. *Mama* wanted to know who he was. If I'd told her he was an out-of-work lecturer she'd have gone spare.'

'Gone spare?'

'Yep. You know, *loopy*.' Maria shook her head. 'You think he's not right for me, huh?'

Alexis spared a look for Garry who was pretending to be drunk again. '*Mama* thinks he wants to get you into bed. I'm wondering if he is capable.'

Maria nodded emphatically. 'He's good at heavy petting. We've not really got around to the rest.'

'Geez, Maria – ' his exasperated breath rushed out – 'I thought Nina was looking after you?'

'She is, and I'm joking.' She shrugged her shoulders. 'He's always quite, quite drunk and always asleep. But have no fear, brother mine. The fact that he falls asleep puts me off him. My virginity is intact. I was just experimenting.' She leaned forward. 'Actually I prefer James. He joins the yacht in four days' time.'

'I forbid you!'

Maria smiled broadly. 'Look, all I can promise is that if I do, I'll be careful.' She leaned up and kissed his cheek. 'I decided last night that when I give myself to a man we must love each other. Just as you and Carrie do.' Maria saw by Alexis' softened expression that her ploy had worked, and thanked heaven!

'It had better be for that reason too. If I find out otherwise there will be trouble. Big trouble.' Alexis's arms tightened around his sister. She was thin, much the same shape as Carrie had been in her teens. He'd danced with Carrie at a party some years ago, holding her as close as he dare until she'd objected.

She'd pushed him slightly away. 'Alexis, I need to breathe. Don't hold me so tightly!'

'Why not?'

'Because I'll sock you in the jaw. I'm not afraid of you now.' Carrie had struggled as his arms grew ever tighter.

He'd pulled her closer, ignoring her remarks. 'Well, you should be.'

'Alexis!'

'Alexis!' Maria complained, breaking into his thoughts. 'Take that frown off your face and let go. You're like a boa constrictor.'

Alexis came out of his reverie. Lifting his hand through his sister's long dark hair, he said, 'You're a very pretty girl and I love you very much. I'd be very, very annoyed with you if you did something so stupid as to go to bed with just anyone.' He kissed her cheek. 'Very annoyed,' he reiterated softly.

Maria caught her brother's dark look. He was hardly ever dictatorial with her, but there was a subtle warning there somewhere.

She nodded. 'I understand,' she reassured him, but added silently, *It's too late, I've had him every night since we left Skiathos*!

'Make sure you do. Now tell me where did you pick up Garry? Tell me the circumstances,' he said softly.

As Maria enlightened him as to how Garry had chatted her up, Alexis watched Garry through half-closed eyes. A check with the agency would do no harm. He'd said he wanted a discreet bodyguard and he'd got exactly that. Garry had more or less flirted his way into his sister's heart, and boy, was she gullible! Feeling agitated, Alexis excused himself.

'Excuse me now, I should dance with my secretary and give her a telling off too for involving me as a friend of this fellow Garry,' he murmured quietly.

'You knew?'

He laughed at the ease with which she fell into his trap. She definitely had a little more growing up to do. 'I do now! You've just confirmed my suspicions.'

Maria stamped her foot in mock disgust as he moved away. 'Alexis, how could you? That's called trickery.'

He saluted, walking over to the table where Nina and Garry sat. 'I'd like a word, Garry: I will tell you this only once! If you intend to complete your holiday without injury then leave my sister alone. Do we understand each other?'

Garry's eyes were crossed. He pretended he couldn't understand what Alexis was talking about, so he smiled and saluted with his glass whilst slurring, '*Efharisto. Parakalo.*'

'Mr Stephanides?' choked Nina, eyes wider than normal. Nina knew something was wrong, simply by the firm tone of her employer's voice.

'Young lady. I thought we'd agreed that you would chaperone my sister to the best of your ability. That ability seems to be lacking. Not only are you sharing a twin room with her, you should know her exact movements day and night!' he said roughly. 'My sister was in Garry's room last night. Where the hell were you?'

Nina coughed, dropping her face to hide the look in her eyes.

'Look at me!' Alexis burst out. 'You knew, didn't you?'

Nina turned away only to be brought sharply back. Alexis was smouldering with anger. 'I said, *look at me*! I want an answer. Did you or did you not know Maria had gone to Garry's room?'

'I did. I told her not to. I'd told her earlier this week she shouldn't be such a fool as I was. That jumping into bed doesn't resolve anything, but she waited until I'd actually gone to bed.' Nina sniffed.

'She crept out while I was asleep. I woke up, as luck would have it. I normally sleep soundly but as soon as I realized I went after her. I guess I got there just in time.'

Alexis scowled. 'What do you mean just in time? What the hell was happening?'

'You know.' Nina blushed. 'You know, I stopped them. They hadn't quite got undressed. He was still getting his pants off. I dragged Maria out of the room,' said Nina proudly, thinking she'd saved Maria's innocence.

'Why the lying little . . .' grated Alexis, his eyes on the guilty face of his sister. 'You mean Garry was about to . . .'

'To do it. Oh yes, without a doubt. Didn't seem to be drunk out of his skull then. Had the same thing on his mind as most men. Sex! Well, we don't need them! We could do without the lot of you.' She looked at Alexis who was staring down at her. 'Present company excepted, of course.'

Alexis merely glanced down at his secretary. His attention was on Maria, who was looking worried. She was now dancing with Petros but her eyes never left the stark angry face of her brother. He looked livid!

'Nina, if you will excuse me, I have some unfinished business to attend to.' Alexis left as quickly as he had come to stride across the paved dance floor.

Maria flew out of Petros's arms, up the steep cobbled street with Alexis in hot pursuit.

'What was that all about?' Petros took Helena into his arms to dance.

'I think my daughter has been lying to her brother. Looks to me as if she's in for a telling off. It will do her good. All I seem to get is cheek from her,' said Helena, totally unconcerned about the fate of her daughter. It was about time her son took his sister in hand.

By the time everyone had arrived back to the yacht, a tearful Maria had departed to her room. A drunken Garry had been ordered to sleep it off. Helena had gone to bed, as had Nina, and only Petros, Marsha and Alexis joined their captain for a nightcap.

'Glad you've given that Garry fellow a telling off. Something not quite right about him. I can't explain it but there is definitely something, Alexis,' said Petros thoughtfully.

Marsha frowned. 'I feel sorry for him. He wasn't hurting anyone. I think you should let up on him.'

Alexis said nothing.

'He wasn't really Maria's friend, you know. He just arrived at the yacht asking for a ride. I told him to leave. The next I knew Maria had him in tow, and when I tackled her she told me she had your blessing,' said the captain. 'I agree with Petros. He's not altogether plausible.'

Alexis frowned as he watched Marsha tucking something into her bag.

'I think he's harmless. I don't know why he can't continue on the voyage,' said Marsha.

'He can,' grated Alexis, his eyes deliberately holding Petros's. 'And it's what I think around here that matters.'

Over an hour later Alexis stood near the bow of the yacht looking over the harbour of Alonnissos. He remembered just a few days ago he'd looked at Carrie's face and her eyes had sparkled with tears at the realization that they would be joining up with the *Challenger*.

That was such a happy memory. They were both relaxed, both themselves, talking, laughing, just enjoying life to the full. He thought about the other side of the coin. Would they always argue like this? If Petros wasn't holding a gun to his head, he would be giving the girl her freedom back. He would at least give her the choice.

He pushed a hand through his hair and laughed harshly to himself. The choice! Carrie would never choose him willingly, and yet she *gave* herself so willingly. Sadly he knew that was all part of the agreement. If only he could believe she cared.

Hell, why did he have to be involved in all this mess? Why on earth had he agreed to go along with this stupid plan of Petros's? Why? The answer was staring him in the face, but he wouldn't give it room to flower. Yes, he agreed he cared for her, always had, from the day when she had had the guts to disobey Petros and a room full of grey-bearded, boring men, barring himself. She'd had the devilment to disfigure the beautiful polished table, one that still bore the scars. Oh yes, he would always care for her. Always.

And if he let her go now, where would she end up? She'd be straight back to London, to her safe little Peter. The head of an infants' school, she'd said. God help him but he hated Peter, a man he didn't even know. Yet he hated the very thought of him, the very sound of his name.

He should go and sort out this mess with Carrie. Go to her, wake her and apologize for making such an ass of himself. He would demand an answer about Peter, not the evasive words she'd been fobbing him off with . . .

'Alexis.' His stomach curled with distaste at the sound of Marsha's voice.

'Marsha. It's late. I thought you would be asleep by now?' Alexis said, his eyes watching her every move as he turned towards her. There was something about Marsha that he didn't like. Oh yes, he'd gone to bed with her, but only because she'd crept in beside him when he was feeling vulnerable.

'I couldn't sleep. I thought maybe we could share a little . . .'

'We could share nothing!' Alexis bit out harshly. 'I don't know how many times I've told you. It's over. I thought that by seeing me with Carrie you would understand. I have never loved you. *You* came to *me*, remember.'

'Make love to me again,' she whispered hoarsely. 'You wouldn't want it to be over then. We'd rekindle everything.'

Alexis closed his eyes, pleased that the breeze was

whipping around his face, cooling him down. His temper was still hot from dealing with his irresponsible sister. He couldn't cope with this too!

'I know your game, Marsha. Sorry I can't oblige,' he growled, his eyes glittering. 'Maybe you should return to your husband. Maybe one of the other men on board can help you out, if you're that desperate.' He caught the upswing of her hand. 'Oh no! There isn't a woman alive that would get away with that, unless I actually deserved it, of course.'

'You do, you bastard! You let me believe I was coming on this yacht for a reconciliation.'

He shook his head. 'Oh no, honey. We both know you're out for something else. Maybe my money. Whatever it is, I haven't quite figured it out yet, but I will.'

He looked across at her as she shivered.

'My husband has lots of money.'

'Your husband is divorcing you, Marsha, and if I know him, I'll bet he had a prenuptial agreement drawn up as soon as he laid eyes on you.' He saw the look on her face. 'Look, why don't you go in and pack? I'm not playing ball ever again. We'll drop you off tomorrow. I suggest you go home to hubby and salvage what's left of your marriage,' he said in a harsh, metallic voice that made Marsha shiver even more.

As she left, Alexis sighed, looking down at his wristwatch. Soon he would be able to watch the sun rise, to see the shimmering mist of early morning over the harbour. Maybe he would swim before the dawn. Stripping down to his shorts, he jumped over the yacht side, cutting through the cool waters around him.

This was what he needed to sort out this mess with Carrie, a clear mind. With each strong stroke he went further out into the deeper waters. He trod water and turned. The yacht was a good distance away; he'd swum harder than he'd thought. From there he witnessed the dawn, the breathtaking sunrise, as the light hit and rebounded off the shimmering silver water beneath him. He swam slowly back and hauled himself up the steps of the *Challenger*.

'Alexis. We have bad news, I'm afraid. Stephan is on his way over in a powerboat. There has been an accident on one of your tankers,' said a tired looking Captain Savidis as he met his employer, towel in hand.

Alexis took the towel, drying himself briskly. 'Yet another accident?' He shook his head. 'Do we know any of the details?'

'Not until Stephan arrives, which shouldn't be too long. I believe there has been a fire,' explained the captain.

'Any casualties?'

The captain nodded. 'I'm not sure of the numbers but not many.'

'One man is *too* many.'

'Yes, sir.'

Alexis walked across to his clothes. 'I'll get changed. Fetch me as soon as you see Stephan's boat, and make them wait. I may have to leave with them.'

'Yes, of course.'

Alexis turned back to the captain. 'By the way, I'll be in Carrie's cabin when you need me.'

The captain nodded as he watched Alexis go down below deck. He knew this was the second time a ship had been damaged. Such losses were devastating.

Carrie's cabin was at the other end of the yacht to his own. Alexis frowned; who the hell had swapped rooms? Carrie was right. Marsha had been put in the cabin next to him, when his orders had been just the opposite! Nina had been in charge of that too. Was she so in love with that cousin of his she couldn't think straight?

Silently he opened the cabin door. Carrie was asleep, her tousled hair stretched out over her pillows, her cheek to the side. She was lying flat on her stomach, naked but for a thin sheet covering part of her pert bottom. He smiled. He'd love to sneak into bed with her, but he knew the reception would probably be a frosty one. She had been very angry last night. They both had!

Stepping through to the shower, he stripped off and switched on the water. Standing under it he began rinsing the salt water away from his olive skin. He knew he would have to leave because he still had obligations that he must meet. People were depending on him and damn it, *he*, too, wanted it all sorted out. He just couldn't think which of his crew, if any, could be trafficking the stuff.

When he returned to the bedroom, Carrie had flipped over but was still soundly asleep. He was going to miss her like crazy, that was one thing he was sure of. Putting his lips softly to hers, he just couldn't resist kissing her. Just one kiss, that is all he would take.

Her lips were so soft as he explored them gently, he lowered himself down on the bed. He kissed her again and again, softly, gently. She moaned, opened her mouth and began kissing him back. He knew he shouldn't do this with her still half asleep. He just had to drag himself away.

Luckily the soft knock on the door brought him swiftly to his senses. She moaned as he left her, but he slipped quietly out to find Stephan on the deck looking particularly harassed.

'From the look on your face it's bad news.' Alexis went to sit next to his cousin.

Stephan leaned forward, whispering, 'The authorities need our help again. It looks like arson.' He threw his hands into the air. 'We've lost three men in all of this, Alexis. Something must be done!'

Alexis nodded. 'Give me the details. I'll get out there as soon as I can. The motor launch is still here?' Stephan nodded. 'Good! I'll take that. You must make the necessary arrangements to escort and make sure the people on this yacht remain safe. If you think we need extra bodyguards, then get them.'

Stephan handed Alexis a file, explaining, 'James Franklyn will be waiting for you. They're still busy trying to kill the fire. You were right by the way. They've found the stash.'

Alexis rose to his feet. 'I'll go and pack a few things. Send Nina to me immediately, there are some things I need her to do.' Alexis sighed when he saw Stephan grimace. 'Look, Stephan, this is work. Just do it. She's bunking in with Maria, and make sure the guy called Garry is given a free hand in ensuring Maria's safety!'

Stephan grabbed Alexis by the shoulder, stopping him from going anywhere. 'What do I tell Carrie? And what do you mean, Maria's safety?'

Alexis looked at him with a frown. 'You tell her nothing, nothing at all. I don't want anyone frightened, especially Carrie. She has enough to contend with, what with Petros's illness. I'll tell Nina what to say to her. As for Maria, I'm just being ultra careful. Garry is actually called Tate Johnson, and he's here to keep a watching brief. Tell him everything.'

'I still think Carrie should know that you could be in danger,' remarked Stephan, but Alexis waved him away.

'Say nothing!'

CHAPTER 12

As the early morning light filtered through the porthole, Carrie put her hands to her lips. She looked around; had she dreamt those soft, enticing lips moving over her own? Had she?

Lifting her head she felt sickness wash over her. As soon as she moved, she knew she was going to be ill. Morning sickness had caught her in its grip.

'Carrie, are you awake?' called Nina some thirty minutes later. 'I have a message from Alexis. Carrie?'

Carrie opened the door, clinging onto her soft towelling dressing-gown, her hand resting heavily on the brass door handle.

'Carrie, are you all right? I'll get a doctor!' Nina panicked as she saw Carrie's drawn, white face.

Carrie shook her head. 'No! I don't want a doctor. Come in, please. Tell me what Alexis said.'

'Oh, it's so awful. There has been a tragedy: one of our oil tankers is on fire, we've lost men, Mr Stephanides left early this morning, said to tell you he may be gone weeks! He gave me this key to give you.' Nina held out the key. 'He said you'd know what it's for. He's going to phone as soon as he can but he wants you to enjoy the rest of the voyage and not worry too much.'

Carrie accepted the heavy iron key for the bakery. It felt as cold as her heart. Raising hurt blue eyes to Nina she said, 'And Marsha? Is Marsha still here?'

Nina shook her head. 'She left the same time as Mr Stephanides. He took her to the airport with him.'

'I see.'

Nina lowered her eyes to the floor, but she had to say it. 'He doesn't love Marsha. He told me that this morning before he left. From what I could gather they were talking most of the night. Marsha *did* want a reconciliation. I know I shouldn't be telling you this, him being my employer. But I guess you need someone on your side.'

Carrie couldn't help her sneer. 'Alexis loves no one but himself.' She didn't believe a word of it. They were *talking* all night indeed!

Nina smiled softly. 'It may look that way, but I think he is a good man. By the way Carrie, what are you doing in this cabin? I had you down for the other, the one next to Alexis.'

Carrie shook her head. 'When I looked at the plan, I was down for this one.'

'I'm sorry. I'm sure I had you down for . . .'

'It doesn't matter, Nina. Look, when did the news of the tanker come in?'

'Stephan flew in himself early this morning.'

'Stephan?'

'Yes. He is to accompany us for the remainder of the holiday.'

'Where is he now?'

Nina shrugged. 'I believe he's with his aunt having breakfast in the state rooms.'

She had that soft hurt look. Poor Nina! They were both in the same boat.

'Ask him to come and see me when he appears on deck, will you? I think I'll rest now,' Carrie said, giving the Greek girl her cue to leave.

An hour later there was a sharp knock on the door, and Carrie let Stephan in.

'I've ordered you some mineral water. Nina said the meal from last night made you ill.' Stephan looked her over dubiously.

'I ate too much and then danced too much,' confirmed Carrie, ruefully.

'Ah yes. Alexis did mention your dancing,' he whispered softly. 'You wanted to talk to me about the disaster. Yes?'

Carrie nodded. 'What happened?'

'Who knows? Some kind of a storm threw the tanker onto rocks. How the blaze started we don't know, which is why Alexis wants to lead the investigation himself.'

'So why did Marsha go with him?'

Stephan looked surprised. 'Who told you she'd gone with him?'

'It doesn't matter, does it? I know.'

'Beats me why she left. All I know is they travelled to the airfield on Skiathos together. Alexis went by helicopter after that to Athens, where he would have taken the jet.' Stephan laughed. 'You're jealous, aren't you? Well, well. The ice maiden has melted after a bit of old-fashioned Greek charm. Maybe I should have got in first. Would *I* have stood a chance?'

Carrie laughed off his comment. 'You couldn't handle me, Stephan.'

Stephan sat down in the dusky pink armchair. 'No? I thought you two spent all your time hating each other? Now I find the opposite. Mmm-m, this is very intriguing. My dear cousin to be married, no less!'

Turning the key in the bakery door some six weeks later Carrie stood back and stared at the large downstairs room. In the three weeks since she had finished her holiday on the yacht, she'd completed the sanding in this room. The floorboards were still to be polished a second time, but at least now she had more furniture in the place. It was taking shape as a home now. A home Alexis had not shared with her since that first weekend. He was still sorting out the details of the accident in which four crew members died.

Carrie made herself a cup of coffee and went back into the lounge. She looked approvingly at the new blinds she'd had fitted. At least now she could open them wide and see the harbour at any time of the day or night. The only thing that could relax her was watching the yachts sail in and out the harbour, or listening late at night to the musical tinkling of the boats moored close by, as they whispered enchanting stories in a language of their own.

She sighed when she saw the coffee table strewn with paperwork. She had only just picked up the accounting books for the past six years from Petros's office and that had a been a feat in itself.

She had had to persuade the head of accounts that there was some information Petros urgently needed and that *she* alone was to look for it – she had shown him a letter confirming this, on which she had most convincingly forged Petros's signature!

Having pored through everything with painstaking patience, she was back almost five years before she spotted it – a huge deposit in 1991–2 by Sealings Inc. Since then it appeared everything had run smoothly: no glitches, no shortfalls.

The question was, did she try to unravel the truth when Alexis returned this evening for their engagement party, or did she dig deeper by herself? The amount deposited was the only anomaly she could find, and she had spent almost three days searching.

She took a large gulp of coffee, sat cross-legged on the sofa and sighed. Their engagement! Huh, what a farce. He'd phoned twice in six weeks, twice! Looking at her tummy she rubbed her hands over the small bump, still hardly even noticeable. She hadn't consulted a doctor either. Alexis, she felt sure, would be livid. If he cared enough to be livid?

Remembering their first telephone conversation almost made her blood boil. Why wouldn't he let her go to him? When she'd asked him, he'd gone crazy.

If she so much as dared come out to him, he said, he would drag her straight back. The punishments he threatened if she disobeyed him were almost the very thing to tempt her into going despite his orders! In the end, however, it had been simpler to stay at the bakery. To sandblast the stone walls until her frustrations had petered out. To work.

Their second call, however, brought tears to her eyes. He was really upset, telling her that a fourth man had died in the blaze. Carrie had listened, had tried to comfort him. Telling him it wasn't his fault. She was sure he'd shed tears, emotion had travelled down the line like a separate connection. Carrie had never heard him sound so down, so vulnerable.

They'd talked for over an hour, in which time she told him about their wedding rings and of course how much she missed him. If only he'd told her the same.

The telephone rang, interrupting her thoughts. Carrie stretched across to reach it. 'Hello.'

'So you think you can take him away from me that easily, do you? Well, I'm warning you, you leave him alone. He's mine, do you hear?'

It was Marsha again, and the fifth time she'd rung. She was drunk, or high, or something. How on earth had she ever got this phone number?

Unless, of course, Alexis had brought *her* here. The thought sickened her.

'Take *whom* away from *whom*?'

Marsha's cruel laughter rang out down the line. 'Don't play with me, little girl. He loves me! He told me so only last week. Last week when we were in New York. When I was running around half-naked in his hotel room, and he was chasing me. The only reason he is marrying you is because of this stupid Greek custom! He feels bound by it!'

'Look, I don't know why you are calling again, but let me give you some advice! I've known Alexis a long time. If he told you he loved you, then he's lying. Alexis loves only himself!'

'He does not, he loves me!'

'And as for running half-naked around his room, he must be getting slack. He always makes sure the woman he's making love to is completely naked!'

With that she slammed the receiver down. Damn the woman!

Picking up the receiver she phoned Peter; she needed comfort from that gentle little voice that would tell her he loved her, simply because he did.

'Hello, Audrey, how are you?' she said, making herself more comfortable, with her legs stretched out on the sofa.

'Oh Carrie, he's been ever so poorly,' cried Audrey.

'What? Peter has been ill? He's still in bed?' Carrie frowned.

She listened to how Peter had been ill with a severe bout of bronchitis, and was still suffering the after-effects. He'd been camping with his dad, had been caught out in the rain last weekend and got wet through.

'Look, Audrey, I'll try and sort out a holiday for you all. Lord knows you deserve one.'

'If only Graham would accept. You know how proud he is, and we just can't afford the airfare. The boiler burst not long ago and we had to pay out for another,' wailed Audrey, who was clearly feeling a little sorry for herself, and rightly so, thought Carrie.

'I know you can't afford the airfare and that hubby dear doesn't like taking charity, but this isn't charity, is it? This is called friendship.' Carrie sighed. 'We'll sort something out. Give Peter my love. I miss you all very much.' Staring at the telephone she caught her breath. Oh Peter, please be all right.

When she reached the villa where the party was being held, Carrie went straight to her room to get ready, having been informed that Helena was resting and that Alexis had still not arrived. From her balcony she could see the sea below. She held onto the railing as she looked out over the bay, and wondered what the future held in store for her.

Feeling drowsy, she undressed and lay on the bed for a while before it was time to get ready for the party. The heat had been affecting her for days. She felt heady with tiredness and soon her lids were so heavy, she drifted off to sleep.

In her dream she could see Alexis kissing Marsha, dazzling her, putting a spell over her, like he did most women. He looked so arrogant, so potently male. As he put her from him, Marsha scowled, then sensuously rubbed her body against his, but he pushed her away. Carrie wanted to scream as he then turned to her, pointing at her with his finger, indicating she should come to him. She went. Fighting her instinct to stay away, she moved grudgingly forward, her unwilling limbs carrying her ever closer.

'Dance,' he said and she did. It felt so good to be back in his arms, within the safety of that strong grip. He danced expertly, but now his grip became stronger; she looked up and saw the red eyes of the devil. *She was dancing with the devil.*

Her eyes flew open. She gasped for air. Moisture beaded her brow. She looked at the bedside clock, it was 7.30 p.m. Her breathing gradually slowed, but she dared not close her eyes again for fear the devil would return.

The hot jets of water dashed against her sleepy body, refreshing both mind and spirit. Whenever she closed her eyes however, Alexis was there, laughing down into her face.

By the time she had finished and was towelling herself dry, she felt much better. She'd barred the images successfully. The dream had frightened her but she knew she was getting nervous because she'd not seen Alexis for six whole weeks.

The memory of their last conversation had been replayed over and over in her mind. She'd thought constantly of Alexis the whole time she'd been sandblasting, polishing and arranging furniture. He was dominating her thoughts and she knew her resolve against him was weakening. A part of her didn't want to love a man who could change women as if they were shirts, but she couldn't help herself. The time they'd spent together on board the *Adonis* had been so special to her. They'd talked, *really* talked, and laughed so much. She had been so sexually aware of him and that had taken its toll. Sighing, she turned her thoughts to the evening ahead.

'Look sexy,' he had said on the telephone the last time they had spoken. Those had been his last words to her, and that was exactly what she planned to do. She would show him exactly *how* sexy she could look! Her black silk dress would be just the thing. Before the night was over, she would have him panting for her, body and soul!

Applying her make-up with a less than steady hand she studied her bruises, now barely visible down her cheek and across her collar-bone. He would be livid to know she had fallen while using the sandblaster. A dash of make-up would soon hide them, but the short skirt of her dress left her still-healing cut uncovered, and there was no way she could hide that from view.

Shrugging into the bodice, she pulled the dress down over her thighs and flattened the soft material over her tummy. At that moment she caught sight of herself. The woman looking back at her from the full-length mirror was stunningly beautiful, her mass of blonde hair tucked up into a loose chignon, leaving her shoulders bare but for thin shoelace straps and a delicate gold chain.

The bodice hugged her high perfect breasts, clinging to her like a glove, accentuating her neat waist. The skirt of the dress was short, tight and sensual, leaving a good proportion of her shapely legs bare to the eye. She looked sophisticated, if not downright sexy, but what the hell! He wants sexy, he's got it, she thought wildly, unconcerned about the consequences.

Her black and gold silk bag, wrap and shoes completed the outfit. Now she was ready to go down into the *sala* and face Alexis.

A low whistle made Carrie spin around. She wondered just long had Stephan been standing in the doorway.

'Stunning, sweetheart. Absolutely stunning,' he declared with a crooked grin. Carrie could see what Nina found so attractive in him.

'You think? One has to make an effort for one's engagement.' She looked at Stephan. 'Did you want something?'

'Wondered why you had invited Nina, that's all.'

Carrie shook her head and laughed. 'You really want to know?'

Stephan nodded.

'I don't think so.'

'Oh but I do. Come on, Carrie, tell all.'

'Well, if you must know – ' she rounded on him – 'I thought you might finally realize that girl is the best thing that could happen to you. She loves you. God knows you don't deserve it with the things you say to her, but nevertheless, she loves you.'

Stephan looked suddenly grey. 'She told me . . .'

'She told you what Caroline wanted her to tell you! You see Caroline has been very unfair, very devious as per usual. She told Nina she was pregnant and that you are the father of the child,' said Carrie, not caring now. It had to come out, and besides, in her opinion Stephan was arrogant. He always seemed to use people and in a way he'd used Caroline too, so one could hardly blame her for getting her own back.

'I was the father? I haven't slept with my wife in over a year!'

'Nina won't know that unless you tell her. It's called communication, something you're supposed to be good at. That's why I invited her, but I haven't mentioned anything to her. If you love her, then you'll do the right thing. You should have listened to Alexis; he told you not to marry Caroline in the first instance.' She shrugged, looking down at her gold watch. 'Look, I'm sorry but I have to go downstairs. Is Alexis here yet?'

'He's on his way by helicopter. Called not so long ago.' Stephan smiled, his eyes gleaming now. 'He likes to cut things fine, doesn't he? He won't be told. Had some business, apparently, that took longer than he thought. I wonder if she's worth it?'

'No, he won't be told,' she said, totally ignoring his final sarcasm, but still wondering what kind of business could keep Alexis from his own engagement party. 'Look, Stephan, maybe I should mind my own business, but I think you have feelings for

Nina. If you have, take it from there. And don't tell her I've told you.'

He snorted, looking across at her with disdain. 'Oh I won't, but tell me one thing? When does a woman mind her own business? To be honest, a lecture coming from you I find a bit hard to swallow. It's you who needs the lecture.'

Carrie laughed softly. 'Me?'

'Yes, you. You're the one who's getting yourself into a big, big mess. Marsha will not allow you to stand in her way. She wants Alexis *and his money*. I've seen her in action before. I think you should do yourself a favour and get out now. Don't think he hasn't been with Marsha, since you two got together. I know he has. As for your heart, it will heal, as will your wounded pride.'

He smiled at her gasp. 'Oh yes, I know you love him too. I can see it in your eyes. Maybe we should console each other?'

Carrie went to Stephan and kissed his cheek. 'Thanks for the warning, and the offer. But if I choose to *dance with the devil* I shall fight for him too!'

CHAPTER 13

The flight had been the only relaxing time Alexis had had in weeks. He'd worked so damned hard until his accident. He brushed the burn on his cheek and forehead which was healing now, as was the one to his back. Whoever had set the *Grecian Summer* on fire the first time had struck again once it had been towed back to port.

He'd worked diligently with the police, but although they now had four suspects for the haul of cocaine they'd found, there was still no definite evidence, just as in the previous cases.

As they circled he could see the shimmering lights of the island come into view. The helipad was lit up, the wind marker blowing out towards the sea as they made a good descent.

He smiled. What kind of reception would he get from his fiancee? Probably a sock in the jaw, but perhaps Carrie was too ladylike to resort to violence. He was expecting at least some kind of retribution for not letting her join him in the States. A frosty reception perhaps? He could cope with that; he could melt the ice, he knew that now, and how to achieve it. Grinning to himself, he brushed his chin with his palm. He felt like a boy coming home for his birthday party. Life had never seemed so precious before his accident.

He frowned. At least Marsha wouldn't be here to interfere. He'd forbidden her to come, especially after the episode in the hotel lobby in America. He grimaced as he remembered the scene. Seems the woman didn't like taking no for an answer. His thoughts flipped back to Carrie. As for his fiancee, hell, he couldn't wait to get her alone.

A short, sharp laugh emerged from him. He'd never been in this much of a hurry to jump into bed before, but Carrie did things to him that no other woman ever had. She stirred the elemental male in him, and that primitive man was well and truly evident this evening!

Entering the reception hall, he first encountered his mother and was pleased he'd already showered and changed into his evening clothes. Her critical eye was forever vigilant. Even when she'd been blind, she had touched his suit, put her hands to his face just to check he was cleanly shaven. And now was no exception.

'Darling, where an earth have you been? I was beginning to think you'd got lost,' Helena said, accepting the kiss from her son, shrewdly assessing whether he was dressed for the occasion. She slid her palms over his cheek, her face showing concern at his injury.

'*Mama*, I'm sorry I'm late. Things got rather

hectic.' He looked around the huge hallway full of people, waving at some of them. 'Where's Carrie?'

'Last I saw she was on the balcony,' said Helena.

'I'll go and find her. I have something for her,' he said, and his mother did not miss the twinkle in his eyes.

Carrie was just coming out of the first-floor guest bathroom when he saw her. He caught his breath; she was more beautiful than he remembered, and well worth the long flight back.

Carrie felt a strange sense, as if someone was watching her. When the prickly sensation tripped down her spine she knew he was here. She looked about the first floor, nothing there, then as she looked between the marble spindles of the banister she caught him staring up at her.

All day she had been practising her scowl, rehearsing her cutting words. Mesmerized, she watched him climb the stairs.

Biting back a retort she couldn't remember, she looked him slowly up and down as he neared her, accepting that arrogant smile flashing across his face for what it was. Of course, he was dressed in a black dinner suit and looked every inch a movie star. Carrie swallowed hard, gulping as her heart thumped savagely against her ribs.

Her pagan god, with his impeccable breeding, his extreme good looks, and the audacity to dress in an Armani suit and become every woman's fantasy man.

Carrie forgot the scowl, the caustic comment. He looked dangerously sexy from the top of his head down to his highly polished leather shoes. His eyes glistened as she watched him, his lips twitched in quiet amusement as she took in every detail. He was far too hot for her to handle! She was in a volatile state of mind already and she knew damn well she couldn't cope with him looking this good!

The spell was enhanced as he moved forward, pushing her gently through the doors behind her which led out onto a small vine-covered terrace, his words delighting her ears. 'You are so beautiful, *agapi mou.* However, I fear there is one thing missing.' He stepped nearer, a blue velvet box in his hands. 'May I?' He indicated her necklace. Carrie nodded in a daze as she watched him bring out the most exquisite diamond necklace she had ever seen. Matching earrings lay cushioned in the box.

His fingers brushed the nape of her neck in a feather-like touch. So light was his touch she shivered under his expert ministrations as he carefully removed the gold necklace and replaced it with the glittering diamonds. Turning her to him with a solemn smile, he held out the earrings to complete her appearance.

'You are the most beautiful woman at the party.' He studied her for what seemed like a neverending moment. She had thought for one single, solitary, breathtaking second that he was going to kiss her, and her heart stopped in anticipation. But he didn't.

'These diamonds are yours. I have just collected them, which is why I'm late. I'm sorry,' he said softly, his eyes lingering as they travelled all over her beautiful figure.

'Are you sure you want me to wear them? They must be worth a bomb,' she declared, fingering the delicate necklace. All the while she was asking herself the question: had he been with Marsha?

'Oh yes, I am very sure. Come, let us make our way to the party. It is going to be a grand affair. There will be many people here, including my grandparents. Have you met them yet?' he murmured as he took her hand.

Carrie stopped dead in her tracks and looked up into his mischievous face. 'You didn't tell me you had grandparents still alive.'

Alexis smiled down at her. 'You never asked me, now come on.' He pulled gently on her fingers. 'My grandparents do not like to be kept waiting, my darling.'

Carrie pulled her hand away from him, suddenly hurt by all the secrets he had. 'You don't have to call me that, we don't have an audience yet, you know.'

'Why do I need an audience?' he soothed. He determinedly grabbed her hand a second time and refused to let her go, in spite of her struggles, until she was safely sitting out on the lower terrace.

Carrie looked around properly for the first time.

The villa was huge, and had the usual white painted stonework with a red tiled roof which blended superbly with the town's houses. It stood back amongst the rolling hills way above the harbour of Poros. She'd always wondered who this place belonged to. Now she knew! She gasped at the unashamed luxury of it as she stepped down from the terrace. Tonight she was getting engaged to Alexis. She was sealing her future. Nerves caught her in a storm of sudden emotion.

'Alexis, I can't cope with a party of this scale. I'm not a social butterfly, I'm more at home in shorts and a T-shirt. I *can't* – ' She was interrupted as he put a finger under her chin, forcing her to look into those unreadable depths.

'You can and will, Carrie. You've always been able to cope with anything I throw at you. Just relax, and for this evening let us truly believe we are betrothed and in love. Come, my grandmother will be waiting,' he said before planting a brief, thrilling kiss on her argumentative lips.

His grandmother scolded Alexis for being late before turning to Carrie to greet her. She didn't look her eighty-two years. Her keen dark eyes inspected his escort with obvious interest nodding her approval as she murmured something to Alexis in their native tongue. She nodded her head again, her inspection thorough. Taking a hold of Carrie's hands she pulled her towards her and accepted the girl's kiss on her cheeks.

'Come, Carrie, Helena says you have not seen the whole of the villa,' she said kindly as she led her away from a smiling Alexis.

The villa was beautiful. No, more than beautiful, thought Carrie. It was out of this world. Mosaic tiles covered most of the ground-floor rooms, with richly coloured Oriental rugs thrown down. The effect was simple but elegant.

Marble fireplaces dominated the larger rooms, and the furnishings were from the finest French and Italian craftsmen. The original sculptured cornices and ceiling paintings left Carrie breathless with wonder. There were many Grecian artifacts, French statuettes, original paintings. So much, she hardly dared touch a thing for fear of knocking something over.

'Call me Alicia, my dear,' said Alexis's grandmother, breaking into her thoughts as they walked around the huge interior. As she showed Carrie the rooms, she opened her heart to her. 'I'm Alexis's mother's mother. Helena, my daughter, was a beautiful, untouched flower when she met Spiro. Alas, I fear he was a bad influence on her. She married him against our will and the only good thing to come of their marriage was my grandchildren.'

Carrie stared into space, wondering if history was about to repeat itself. Would the only good thing from this marriage be children?

Alicia went on regardless, telling Carrie all about her family as if she had known her for years. 'Spiro died in a tragic accident soon after Maria was born, an accident which could have been prevented but for his own foolishness. Children need their parents. Both parents!'

Carrie took the older woman's hands and squeezed them, unaware that her sensitivity and empathy were a part of her charm. 'I'm so sorry. You must love your grandchildren very much, you must have felt their pain.'

Alicia smiled. The years had taught her to hold back her tears. Her grandson especially had been her salvation, her hope for the future. 'Spiro died after falling overboard from his yacht. He was drunk, and foolish.'

'I'm sorry.'

A haunted look passed through her eyes. 'What hurts me is how it affected Alexis. Children need their fathers, just as surely as they need their mothers.'

Carrie looked uncomfortable as they stood looking down over the balcony. In the distance they could see the hydrofoil returning to harbour. Eventually Carrie admitted softly, 'Alexis never speaks of his father.'

'I know.' Alicia smiled and continued. 'Unlike *your* father. He was a dear man, I knew him well, but I fear he was a little browbeaten by Petros.' Her brutally honest statement had a ring of truth to it.

Carrie smiled. 'If it's any consolation to you, although I know that Petros is an organizer and I don't agree with any of his principles, I still love him.'

Alicia patted Carrie's hand. 'I'm sure you do. You'll make my Alexis a lovely wife and I'm also very sure you'll give him plenty of healthy children, and I hope before not too long. I'm getting old, I'd like to see my great-grandchild before I depart from this world.' She arched one eyebrow at Carrie and smiled.

Carrie almost choked under her smile. If only they knew.

After their brief tour Alicia insisted they go back to the party. 'This is, after all, your engagement party, my dear. We mustn't let our guests miss the match of the year, and of course you must a set a date for your wedding. I hear it is to be soon?'

Carrie sucked in her breath. Alexis had some explaining to do! This was totally ridiculous and getting more out of hand by the minute, and boy, would she tell him so! Soon? Huh!

Following Alicia down the marble staircase she could see Alexis talking to a petite Greek woman. She was very beautiful dressed in a long flowing red dress. A woman who was leaning sexily against one of the two huge white pillars in the hallway, moving ever nearer to Alexis. She was openly flirting with him. Carrie gasped in horror!

They were laughing, both relaxed, both having fun. A surge of something so strong and yet so uncommon to Carrie went pulsing through her veins. How dare the witch lean against him in that suggestive way? How dare she laugh up into his handsome face?

'Don't look so worried, Carrie. That is Marianne Stethandros, and as much as she would like to have my grandson back, having once been his escort, there is no room in his life for her. You are the only one Alexis has ever loved,' said Alicia as she watched Carrie's eyes take in the scene below, and smiled in her wisdom at the jealousy she saw there.

Carrie shook her head, not believing the older woman's words. 'That's impossible for me to believe. For many years when I was a teenager your grandson hated me. He thought I was a spoilt brat.' Carrie laughed bitterly.

'You probably *were* spoilt; he's rarely wrong about naughty young things.'

Carrie blushed, agreeing. 'I suppose I was.'

'I may be an old woman, and he hasn't always told me his feelings, but I do know that my grandson cares for you, and has always cared. He just doesn't know it himself, that's all. Hasn't recognized the feeling for what it is, and besides, hate is very much akin to love. Remember that when you fight.' Alicia shook her head as she saw the disbelief in Carrie's eyes. 'Go to him, go and ask him if he cares. Maybe then he will admit it to himself. Why are you afraid? You are to be married, are you not? I know you love him dearly, it is written in your face and there is no escaping a love like that, Carrie.'

Carrie merely nodded, accepting her own fate, yet knowing Alicia had got it wrong about Alexis's feelings. Whatever he had told her, he'd just done it very convincingly. That was all.

Smiling at the older woman she said, 'Yes, I will, Alicia. After I've powdered my nose, I will go and challenge him.'

Fixing her make-up didn't take long and as she looked at her slim shape in the long gilt-edged mirror she saw Marsha enter the room, her eyes like burning coals. Marsha didn't have an invitation!

Looking at her now Carrie realized Marsha was less slender than in her younger years but nevertheless was still a beautiful woman, with her long flowing black hair bouncing as she jerked her head back angrily in Carrie's direction.

'You think you can take Alexis away from me, you smutty little Irish girl. Then think again! Alexis will always love me and I will stop at nothing to make sure he marries me. So be warned!' Her voice was low and held a warning most women would cower from.

Carrie smiled, though she was astonished that Marsha was attacking her this open way. 'You know, I always thought Alexis was a man who made up his own mind. He won't be manipulated by a woman; neither you, nor I. You may think you know him very well and if that's the case, please enlighten me and tell me why I'll be wearing his ring and not you.'

Marsha snorted and moved towards Carrie. 'He is just using you, you imbecile! The man wants nothing more than sex from you. Do yourself a favour and leave the island before you get hurt!'

As Marsha stormed out of the bathroom Carrie sighed, knowing that the Greek woman was actually less than correct in her assumption. He was using her, but for much more than sex.

'If it *is* only sex, Marsha, then why isn't he marrying you!' she said into the mirror. Somehow she knew Marsha hadn't been with Alexis for a while.

The woman was a fool if she thought Carrie would back down from a challenge such as this. Smiling at her reflection in the mirror once again, she turned.

She always loved a challenge and Marsha had just thrown down the gauntlet. Time for round two. She would successfully take Alexis away from the glamorous Marianne! Any way she could!

Sweeping past admiring glances from several of the male guests, Carrie made her way to Alexis. He watched her advance towards him, keeping a critical eye on the men around her, and their approving stares.

His eyes followed every sensual curve of her body, his concentration wholly centred on her approach, so much so that the dark exquisite Marianne turned her head to see what had caught his undivided attention and frowned. It seemed yet another beautiful woman was interested in Alexis.

'Darling! I thought I'd better get back to your side, as Alicia explained the sole purpose of the party is for us to celebrate our engagement and fix a date for our wedding. It is to be soon? Fancy you not telling me, you naughty man. Was this one of your little surprises?' she admonished as she slipped a hand inside his jacket to cling to his steely muscular frame. Then she raised her mocking lips to receive his kiss.

Alexis didn't like being scolded in front of Marianne and Carrie knew it. However, he did respond to her little invitation by crushing her lips roughly with his, and the feeling was wonderful, like a first morsel of food after six weeks' starvation.

Rather stiffly he pulled away from her to bow slightly at Marianne and introduce her to his fiancee. A fiancee who just might feel the roughness of his hand against that sexy little bottom she was wiggling if she didn't behave. Silently he watched the two women size each other up. What was this, a fight to the death?

'Pleased to meet you,' said Carrie politely, her blue eyes flashing a warning to the other girl to leave her man alone.

Marianne merely inclined her head, an insincere smile etched across her face

'Have you two met before?' asked Alexis, his eyes searching their faces in turn, but neither answered him. He frowned. 'Come, Carrie, we must circulate. I have a surprise for you.'

Turning to the Greek girl who stood fuming in the background, Carrie said sweetly, 'I just love surprises, don't you? But then you'll know how Alexis surprises people. After all, you were once his lover, I believe?' Carrie leant forward. 'And obviously not up to scratch, my dear, as I've taken your place.'

Several people gasped!

Carrie knew she was playing a dangerous game, but for once she didn't care. She knew Alexis was barely keeping his temper in check but he could hardly berate her in a room full of people, could he?

Alexis grunted something inaudible in Greek and both girls stared at him. His face was red and angry under the dark tan, and his hands were knotting into fists at his side. Marianne launched harsh words in her own language at him, before she reached forward and slapped him hard on that arrogant face!

The room hushed. Marianne turned and ran from them, almost tripping before she reached the sweeping staircase. There were concerned murmurs and all eyes were transferred back to the betrothed couple.

Immediately Carrie regretted her words. Now she was scared, but it was too late. Alexis was livid, his temper tiptoeing on a tightrope. Of course she'd seen this kind of anger in his eyes before and felt almost sick as she remembered who had been the loser that time!

Alexis gripped her arm ruthlessly and marched her away from the curious onlookers into a quieter part of the house. Briefly she caught Alicia's wicked grin. 'Hate is very much akin to love, remember that when you are fighting,' came flooding back into her mind.

Bundling her into a room that resembled a study, Alexis pushed her forward before turning and locking the door behind them. He pocketed the key.

Carrie's heart bumped and raced as she stood stock-still in front of him, afraid to move lest he retaliate. He was in a filthy mood now and Carrie couldn't really blame him. What an earth had come over her? Biting her bottom lip she looked appealingly at him . . . beseechingly, but she saw no mercy in his eyes.

She was like a scared little rabbit who'd been caught in a snare. 'What, what are you doing, Alexis?' She dared to meet his eyes, taking a step backwards as she caught the glitter of rage.

'I'm going to do what I should have done a long time ago, and teach you just who is in charge in this relationship. Your time just ran out, Carrie O'Riordan,' he said dangerously before sweeping closed the blinds at the only window in the room.

Carrie licked her lips in a very nervous gesture. She backed up slowly, but halted against the desk as he stealthily advanced on her.

'Alexis, I want to explain,' she begged him, but he was angrier than she'd ever seen him.

'Explain what? How you embarrassed our guest?'

'A guest who's been your lover!'

Alexis laughed harshly. 'A lady whom I once had a fling with when I was twenty-three years old. She is now married with three children!'

'Oh,' mumbled Carrie weakly.

'I'll give you *Oh*!'

His breathing was laboured, a muscle dancing in his cheek revealing the true extent of his anger. It was only when she met his dark gaze again, that she saw the light of fevered passion in his eyes, the wicked curve of his mouth. Only when she felt the roughness of his hands against her skin did she realize what he intended to do; and she revelled in it. Her pagan lover had lost control!

She'd brought it on herself with such bitter jealousy, had shamefully embarrassed him in front of his ex-lover, and now, well now she was about to suffer the consequences. Rage had transformed itself to ardour in the blink of an eye. He was about to take her, here!

Only as his lips came down hard on hers did she cry out, not with fright, but with excitement. Exhilaration. This was what she really wanted, all of it, all of him. Could it be that he truly cared for her as Alicia had said? His hands were hot, and hard, and hungry.

'God, I've missed you so much,' he muttered against her lips.

Hallelujah! He'd missed her!

He pulled the chignon loose, and ran his fingers like a comb through the mass of blonde hair before kissing her again, his kiss proof that on this level at least, he *had* missed her.

'Six weeks I've waited for this,' he ground out.

She could tell that he was still annoyed at her outburst. Full of anger, and yet all the energy, all the force, was redirected to the uncontrolled passionate creature before him. He lifted her easily whilst still ravaging her mouth and carried her to the gold striped *chaise longue* where he dropped her to her feet.

Now she was kissing him back, ripping at his clothes, losing herself in her own desire as he swiftly stripped her naked, leaving only the shimmering diamonds next to her skin. In the minutes that followed he kissed every part of her pliant body. Her nipples responded long before he reached for them, long before his teeth had clasped around each button and he had sucked them, leaving her panting and crying for more. Lowering her to the *chaise*, he parted her legs. A wicked smile was etched upon his lips as she responded so willingly to his unspoken demands. His eyes inspected every inch of her honey tanned skin before he shifted above her, his powerful, body moving to cover her.

'Six whole weeks. It was worth being celibate.' He laughed, whispering, 'I should have let you come to me. I wouldn't be so damned desperate!'

Within a moment's breath he was astride her, naked, his hard golden body a fraction from her own. He was holding himself back, teasing her, delighting her with teeth and tongue until she begged him again and again for fulfilment.

Reaching for him, she explored his hardened flesh with a shy inquisitiveness that drove him insane. Her ministrations were almost too much for him to bear as he growled her name seconds before he pulled away from her teasing fingers and thrust himself forward into her hot, tight body.

Carrie gasped against his lips as he lifted her hips to take him deeper, her warmth shrouding his desire. He filled her completely, urgently, stilled there for seconds, his breathing heavy as he waited. His dark eyes were watchful as he drew his head back to inspect the depth of passion in those exquisite blue eyes. The sight of the hunger of her love written on her soft face spurred him on.

It was then he pushed himself into a rhythm that sent them both almost mindless. She kissed him with a feverish passion, dragged her fingernails up the side of his bare torso and heard him cry her name out loud. He retaliated by grabbing both her hands to still her tormenting touch and pushed them above her head where he held them easily in his, even though she fought the tormenting restraint. Again he propelled his frenzied body into her with renewed but tender force. With each thrust, her laboured breathing and muffled cries became faster. She threw her head back wildly and choked back her voiceless screams as wave after wave of ecstasy washed over her. She wanted to hold him close but Alexis refused to let go of her hands until he was ready. He was in control, mastering her, until she clenched her thighs together and she heard his growling moans; for now he knew *he* was *her* captive.

Alexis pushed himself faster, harder, filling her completely as she screamed out one last time against his lips. Moments later he released her hands so that he could pull her tight against him whilst he poured the very essence of him deep inside her. Six weeks had seemed like a lifetime to him.

Minutes ticked by when only their ragged breathing could be heard as it slowed. Alexis raised himself on his arms, his deep brown eyes scrutinizing her expression as he dropped his head once again and kissed her gently on her lips. Tears pricked the back of her eyes at the tenderness of his touch.

Pushing himself up, he sat with his head in his hands and smiled to himself. He sat there for several seconds before turning to her. 'Come, we have to get back to the party.'

She nodded, not daring to utter a word for fear she would spoil this precious moment. He continued to stare at her, as if seeing her for the very first time. His lips twisted in humour as he expelled a long low breath.

'Witch, when are you going to learn that I will only be pushed so far. *This* wasn't meant to happen here!'

'Where was it supposed to happen?'

He laughed. 'Not on a *chaise longue* in the study.'

Carrie stood, naked in the semi-darkness of the room and was aware of his intent gaze upon her breasts, she smiled, murmuring softly as she bent her lips to his, 'I liked it in the study.' Then she laughed wickedly, and rekindling a special time when he'd embarrassed her, she said, 'Mr Stephanides did it in the study, with his lead pipe!'

'Why, you cheeky little baggage.' He leant forward and caught her nipple in his teeth, making her breath catch in her throat. 'So you do remember playing Cluedo with me?'

'Maybe we should play it in the ballroom?' she asked with an arch of her brow.

He shook his head. 'Dress, now! Ple-a-se!'

They returned to the party, hand in hand. Alexis left her in the hallway for mere seconds to retrieve two glasses of pink champagne. He handed her one, and clinked her glass in a toast.

'To my beautiful, outspoken fiancee.' He studied her for a moment and whispered softly, 'You realize, now, Carrie, there is no turning back?' He watched her possessively over the rim of his champagne glass.

His eyes shining in triumph, he pushed the exquisite diamond ring onto her engagement finger.

'I know,' came her shaky reply. Now she was truly resigned to her fate, her future. But what did it hold? He had never promised her anything other than a marriage of convenience!

CHAPTER 14

Quietly Carrie and Alexis mingled amongst the dancing couples. She was still in heaven, revelling in the power she had over this man. Even if it was only sexual power, she conceded, even if he didn't love her, at least *he'd missed her*! She felt sure now that she had the right elements to make him fall in love.

'And what are you mulling over in that busy mind of yours?' His hand rested lightly on the slight swell of her covered bottom, his lips a breath away from her ear.

She shivered delightfully, her laughter intriguing. 'That would be telling, Mr Stephanides.'

'You do realize I ought to make you apologize for your rudeness back there. Poor Marianne, she didn't deserve that,' he went on, then inclined his head to look into those sultry blue eyes. Eyes that were still dilated with passion from the shocking way he had taken her. Or was it the other way around? It seemed she'd not only taken him into her, she'd held him captive.

Carrie's heart thumped unsteadily. If she were truthful the thought excited her, the thought of another clash of wills, as Alexis 'encouraged' her to apologize!

'But you won't.'

'No I won't,' he replied tauntingly. 'Maybe next time if you're lucky.' He abruptly stopped dancing as his mother came to his side.

'Excuse me, Alexis, Carrie, it will soon be time to eat.' Helena said a hand on Alexis's arm. 'Time to introduce your fiancee to your grandfather.'

Alexis nodded and led Carrie through the room to an old man sitting in a wheelchair. He was watching the dancing couples, happy to be in attendance. His eyes swept over Carrie as she came forward to clasp his hands. His grin was one of welcoming warmth though he looked frail. Her heart went out to him.

Carrie stooped down to kiss the old man, and then knelt by his side to hold his hand in hers for a while.

Alexis spoke in Greek to his grandfather and then turned to Carrie, explaining that his grandfather spoke no English at all, but wished to welcome her to his homeland.

'Like you said, Alexis, I know enough Greek to get me by. I understand perfectly well,' she said solemnly, and then stood next to the old man trying to explain.

Alexis stared at her in disbelief, and nodded. Grandpa Costas smiled, inclining his head, patting Carrie's arm with his frail hand.

Helena came to his side. 'Come, Alexis, we must start the meal. Our guests will be hungry. And then you should announce your wedding day. There will be so much to arrange.' She caught his arm, whispering, 'By the way, did you invite Marsha?'

Alexis stared at his mother, 'No! I told her not to come at all.'

Carrie watched his expression, he looked livid.

'Where is she?'

'Oh, she's drunk as a lord. Unconscious by now, I should think,' retorted Helena with disgust. 'But you shouldn't waste your time on her. You have Carrie to think of.'

'Don't think you can give me a lecture on how I run my life, *Mama*. Marsha chased *me* across the world to America, *Not* the other way round,' he bit out softly, noticing Carrie's expression.

Carrie turned her head away. So she *had* gone out to be with him.

His voice at her ear made her jump, 'It's not what you think.'

She turned. 'Isn't it?'

'Carrie, we will talk about this later. I've done nothing with Marsha, I promise.' He looked her straight in the eye, waiting for a response. Carrie shrugged, leaving the matter until later. Why the hell should it bother her?

Alexis announced that their wedding was to be in six weeks' time. Carrie just managed to stop her mouth dropping open. No one had consulted her. No one!

Petros looked across the table at the beautiful woman opposite, the slight incline of her head said it all. Plan B was well under way now.

'Petros,' said Carrie minutes later, 'Did you have something to do with the suddeness of this wedding?'

Petros nodded. 'If things were to go wrong with my operation which is due the week after, at least, my child, I would know you are settled with a good man – your *husband* Alexis.'

What could she say to that? These men were very good at blackmail.

'But Petros, he's hardly out of a relationship with Marsha. I think rushing things like this is wrong. Can't we wait a bit longer?' urged Carrie.

Petros hated himself for what he had to say. 'It is that or Theo. Theo is here tonight, *I* can approach him if you prefer. But no, I think we both know Alexis fulfils your needs. He had no shame when he told me you'd slept with him. As I suppose you have no shame too?'

Carrie blushed fiercely, marching off after grating out her departing words, 'Petros, I am a woman of the nineties. I have no shame over my actions!'

Petros closed his eyes. He hoped this charade was worth it, for if the truth ever came out, he knew Carrie and Alexis would be livid!

'A dance, Carrie?'

Carrie squirmed when she heard the voice behind her. Theo was hovering dangerously close by.

'Sorry, Theo, I did promise Jonathan one. Oh look, he's over there. Ouch,' cried Carrie as the huge man pulled her into his arms with little effort, even though she'd pulled back.

'I think you owe me a dance.' His watery brown eyes looked insolently down the front of her dress. 'At least one dance!'

'Look, Theo, it's very nice of you, but I really must insist you let go!'

His laugh was insolent. 'I haven't really got hold of you yet. Maybe on the terrace.'

The next thing she knew she was out on the terrace. Her breathing was laboured, her hands pushing him away.

'So what did he do to you in there? But then I know, I was outside the door.'

Carrie's eyes opened wide, she felt sick.

'Oh yes, little Miss Irish. I heard him walloping you. I wouldn't have done that. I would have been kind, and kissed you like I am going to do now!'

Her knee came up just as Jonathan stepped out onto the terrace. 'Carrie, you're here. I've been looking for you all over. I believe you owe me a dance.'

Carrie pushed past the hard wall of Theo's frame. She hated him! Ever since he'd tried to kiss her when she'd been fourteen at one of Petros's parties. Luckily her mother had come to her room, to check on her.

'Jonathan, nothing would please me more.'

* * *

'Carrie, are you all right?' The soft voice of Nina could be heard through the bathroom door. Carrie wiped away the stray tears. These men weren't worth it.

She opened the door and said, 'Come in, Nina. I need to talk to you.'

Nina sat on the edge of the vanity unit whilst Carrie sat on the cream stool. 'Stephan sent me.' Nina blushed. 'I didn't realize that Petros had upset you. Stephan saw you leave the table, and then we saw Theo drag you out onto the terrace. You were struggling, so we sent Jonathan out to you.'

'Thanks. Theo is a letch!' Carrie smiled. 'Enough of me. Are you talking to Stephan yet?'

Nina shrugged. 'Who knows? He says I've to reserve the last dance for him. Maria says I should tell him to *shove it*!'

Carrie laughed, her tears all dried now. Maria would say that. University in England had taught her some wonderfully expressive language, if nothing else.

'I'd reserve it if I were you.'

Nina raised her dark brows. 'Look, I came to see if you were all right? Stephan and Alexis have just bundled Marsha back to her hotel in a taxi. That's goods news, isn't it? Stephan said to Alexis that she was out looking for trouble. I heard Alexis saying she was going to get it, if she didn't watch out. Boy, was he mad! Scared me to death. I'm just glad I'm not Marsha.'

'Poor Marsha,' murmured Carrie. 'Poor thing is getting the rough end of the deal! I'm sure she desperately loves Alexis.'

Nina was shaking her head. 'No, Carrie, that's all wrong. She loves only herself.'

'Does she? She was in America with him. Maybe he wants me *and* a mistress.'

'No! He was telling Stephan yesterday on the phone . . .' Nina looked at the ceiling, 'I shouldn't be telling you this, he'll fire me if he finds out I was listening.'

'Tell me what?'

Nina smiled doubtfully at Carrie. 'When he was in America, someone tried to kill him. He was on the tanker with another man, and they were both knocked unconscious. Alexis was injured, he was in hospital most of his stay. The other man was murdered. Marsha, from all accounts, turned up in America like a bad penny. I think that's how you English say it! But I'm not supposed to know this. I only listened in because . . .'

Carrie thought back and heard no more of Nina's conversation. Alexis injured! The graze on his head was evidence enough so it was true. The second telephone call, when he'd said the fourth man had died? He'd sounded so desperate, so down.

'Why would someone want to kill Alexis?' The thought petrified her!

'I don't know.'

Nina jumped when a sharp knock came on the door.

'Nina! Carrie!' Stephan called.

'Yes, we won't be a minute,' cried Nina, 'Do you think he heard? They'll finish me, I'm sure. I'll never get another job.'

'Nina, shut up. I won't tell them. I need someone on my side,' said Carrie urgently.

'You mean the women against the men?'

'Something like that. There is definitely something going on here and we need to get to the truth.'

'What the hell took you so long?' an irate Stephan asked Nina.

Carrie answered quickly for both of them. 'Just comparing notes on how you two perform.' She saw Alexis frown, then he smiled broadly.

'Women do that, Stephan,' Alexis said softly.

Stephan's lips twitched. 'Compare notes on how we perform?' He grabbed Nina's arm. 'You will come with me. I won't have you discussing me like this!'

Nina was marched off, a sly grin thrown in Carrie's direction.

'Oops. Maybe I said the wrong thing.'

Alexis was looking at her, still smiling and shaking his head. 'Oh no. I think you said exactly the right thing. Stephan told me of your conversation earlier.'

Carrie's heart sank. 'He did?'

'Yes. You were trying to bring them back together. That's very sweet of you.'

She looked at Alexis. Thank God he hasn't told you how I feel about you, Carrie thought, the idea of his knowing, and not loving her in return would destroy her. At least now she could have him love her in her fantasies. If he ever said '*I don't love you*' that would be the end for them.

'Sweet or not, it's what was needed. Caroline has used Stephan for far too long. Nina, well, she loves him,' defended Carrie in deep earnest, all the while moving back toward the door as Alexis shuffled her into the bathroom. 'What? . . .'

He smiled down at her, his hands on her waist. 'We said we were going to be lovers tonight.' He looked at his watch. 'I think the night should start now!'

'Here in the bathroom?'

'No.' He closed the bathroom door, taking her slowly into his arms. 'I just want to kiss you senseless, here in the bathroom.'

And he did just that.

'Ouch. Do you have to be so rough,' complained Alexis as Carrie scrubbed the graze on his cheek with antiseptic.

'You were rough with my wounds,' she chimed with a laugh. 'Tit for tat.'

'Tit for tat. What kind of language is this?' He frowned. He could have fallen head first into her laugh and lost himself there, but he knew it was a ploy to put him off track. 'Speaking of your wounds, how on earth did you get them?'

Carrie licked her lips nervously. 'I fell. I hurt my knee too.'

He'd noticed the graze to her knee, and the one on her hip last night when he'd been loving her. So she'd fallen, had she?

'Fell? Where?'

'What do you mean, *where*?' she said crossly. 'At home! In the bakery, that's where.'

At home! In the bakery. What more beautiful words could come from her lips? To class that ramshackle old building he was doing up as 'home' made him smile.

'And what made you fall I wonder?' His dark eyes surveyed her. She was hiding something and he knew it.

Carrie moved away, only to be brought back sharply to his side. She stared up at him, knowing that only the truth would do. He had that no-nonsense look in his eyes.

'I had a go with the sandblaster.' His grip tightened. 'I was bored. B.O.R.E.D! Bored! You wouldn't let me come to you. I was going crazy, Alexis.'

His grip slackened. 'Come here and sit on the bed. We need to talk.'

They sat down on the bed, facing each other. 'Firstly, the sandblaster is too heavy for you.'

Carrie boiled inside. What did he think she was, some weak little waif? 'Too heavy? The sandblaster is *not* too heavy for me.'

'Not even if you're pregnant?'

Large blue eyes shot to his. He raised his dark eyebrows. 'I heard you this morning in the bathroom. If I'm not mistaken I think this is morning sickness?'

'Yes, well,' she coloured. 'So what if it is!'

'If it is?' he said slowly, 'I think the sandblaster is too heavy.' Then he grinned, boyishly. 'Just how much of the bakery have you done?'

Carrie relaxed; he wasn't going to make an issue of her not telling him about her pregnancy. 'Not much. Just finished the downstairs room.' She clasped her hands in her lap. 'Look, it's only just been confirmed that I'm pregnant. I was going to tell you.'

Taking her chin in his fingers he raised her face to his. 'I was hoping your outburst in the taverna that night was due to hormone changes.'

She grinned, 'That seems like a lifetime away. And what was yours due to?'

He frowned. 'Jealousy, and frustration. I realized what a bad idea it had been inviting Marsha. I'm sorry, and I'm sorry about last night. Whatever Marsha has said to you, I swear I have not slept with her since before I saw you in London.' He watched her lick her lips. 'I took Marsha off the yacht. It was my idea she should leave. I just didn't want her poisoning your mind. We seemed to be getting along just fine.'

'And America?'

'America?'

'Yes, what did she do in America?'

Anger swept across his face. Just what had Marsha said? 'She came into the hotel lobby threatening to strip off if I didn't take her to my room and . . . make love to her. I ignored her for so long and then when she started to strip. I – ' he looked at Carrie expecting to see anger in her eyes but her look was soft and full of compassion – 'I didn't know what the hell to do. Yes, I took her to my room.' He saw Carrie's face. 'But I did not touch her. I told her that I was marrying you and there was no hope. That she should give it all up. She went crazy.'

Carrie brushed his hair away from his face as it fell forward, her voice soft in answer. 'Thank you for telling me the truth.' She looked at her hands. 'She told me that you loved her. I told her that you only loved yourself. Did I do right?'

Alexis winced. What the hell did he expect; he was always telling her he didn't believe in love. 'Yes. You did right.'

Petros sat on the edge of the bed looking at the indentation on the other pillow. Reaching for it, he could smell the expensive perfume and cuddled the pillow to his face. His accomplice was some lady and far too young for him, he was sure. Take it easy, the consultant had said. Ha! This was by far the fastest his heart had beaten in months. Who would have expected her to come to him, *in this house*, and when several guests had stayed over. If anyone had seen them, heard them? The smile that tickled his lips turned into a frown. Women like her were always dangerous.

Picking up the glass of water, he tossed two tablets onto his palm before taking them. He'd hurt Carrie last night with his cruel words, hurt the nearest thing he'd ever have to his own child. All for a selfish cause, for his own foolhardiness. If only he hadn't got involved all those years ago. Too late. It had all got too complicated and now he was deceiving almost everyone.

A sharp knock came at the door. 'Petros! I want a word!'

Alexis pushed past Petros once he'd opened the door. Petros's eyes flew to the bed. Thankfully, the pillow had dropped to the floor.

'What is it, Alex?'

Alexis scornfully threw back his head. 'Don't take me for a fool, my friend. I want this to stop. Right now! We must tell Carrie the truth. For God's sake, she knows you are ill now. Why not tell her the whole truth?'

Petros shook his head, his eyes bitter.

'Don't tell me what to do. I can have my goddaughter married to Theo just like that.' He snapped his fingers. 'And we both know you wouldn't want that. You are besotted with her, and have been for years. Oh yes! I've seen you watch her. You couldn't wait to get her into your bed.' He saw Alexis flinch and knew then his accomplice had done her job well. This man did love Carrie. Petros was astounded that Alexis was capable of such affection! 'The time to tell Carrie will come soon enough. I must have her produce an heir. That is the only thing I want before I die!'

Alexis thumped the chair. 'You may not die, you old fool. The operation may be a success! Have you thought of that?'

Petros shook his head. 'Operation or not. If Carrie doesn't have a child, I will die!'

Alexis pushed a hand through his hair, pacing about the room. It was then he caught the lingering softness of the perfume. A perfume he knew well. He scanned the room quickly, the idea was absurd, surely? There was nothing to indicate that *she* had been here.

'How will you die?' Alexis attacked scornfully, dismissing the scent that had rung definite bells in his brain.

Petros was very serious. 'Just believe me, my friend. I will and that, Alexis, will cause my Carrie great grief.'

Alexis closed his eyes. Carrie had enough to contend with, knowing she was pregnant, knowing that Petros was to undergo a huge operation, she could do without any more heartache. Slowly Alexis nodded his head.

'You don't deserve the love she has for you,' Alexis growled.

'Nor do you,' muttered Petros.

'A few more weeks, then I tell all I know!' Alexis stormed out of the room.

'And you know so little, my friend, so little,' whispered Petros as he watched Alexis march past his mother and his grandmother without a word.

'And what are you doing with my son, Petros? He looked ready to choke you,' said Helena with a hint of sarcasm as they stopped adjacent to his bedroom door.

Alicia hissed softly for Helena's ears only. 'He *should* choke him! The man interferes in everyone's business.'

Helena laughed, her voice like the tinkling of Christmas bells. 'Hush, *Mama*.' She looked pointedly at Petros. 'Are you going to join us for lunch on the terrace before you leave, Petros?'

Petros grunted and then nodded. This wasn't exactly what he had in mind!

'If you insist!'

'Oh we do. Don't we *Mama*?' Helena said sweetly with a smile. 'You're going to be Alexis's godfather. Of course you must lunch with us.'

'He ought to stop interfering in their lives,' said Alicia with obvious disdain. 'This would have sorted itself out.'

'*Mama*!' scolded Helena. 'Alexis and Carrie are both stubborn. They needed a push.'

Alicia marched on in front of the other two; she knew she shouldn't condemn Greek marriages, hers had worked out just fine, after the first three years. It had taken her three years to train her husband. She afforded herself a sweet selfish smile. Men thought they were the bosses. Women *knew* they were!

'Do we have to have lunch with them?' Carrie asked a brooding Alexis.

'I'm afraid so,' His frown lifted slightly. Slowly he walked across to her, out on the balcony of their room. 'I think we owe *Mama* at least that. She has relaxed her rules by letting us sleep together.'

Carrie laughed huskily in remembrance of their sleepless night. 'I don't remember sleeping very much' She got up and moved towards him, her hands going around his waist. 'Did you mean it when you told me you had missed me?'

He looked down into her upturned face, his gruff reply warm and tender. 'Of course I meant it.' He pulled her hand. 'Come, we must go and have lunch.'

Walking hand in hand, they made their way to the terrace where dishes were laden with food. Cheeses, meats, salads, fresh crusty bread with mouthwatering fruits for dessert.

'Carrie, how do you feel this morning?' asked Helena with a smile.

Carrie shot a glance to Alexis who shook his head.

'I'm fine, Helena,' replied Carrie affectionately. 'It was a good party.'

It was Alicia who answered rapidly, 'Yes, we had a wonderful party, for two wonderful people. People who shouldn't be coerced into a marriage by bumbling old fools. They should be allowed to find their own destiny.'

'*Mama!*'

'Don't you *Mama* me!' she shot to Helena, 'Petros knows how I feel about all this. His interference has been despicable.'

Carrie moved forward, placing her arm round Alicia's shoulders. 'Please, don't upset yourself. I am happy with this arrangement. Alexis will be a good husband and father to our children.'

Reluctantly Alicia agreed, her eyes meeting those of her grandson. He winked, his devilish smile too irresistible for her not to respond, 'Yes, my child, I'm sure he will be just wonderful.' Then she added lightly, 'But he won't be a perfect partner. No man can live up to that!'

Carrie chuckled, her expression changing when she met her godfather's eyes. 'How are you, Petros?'

He inclined his head stiffly, his wince obvious when he saw the hurt still lingering on her face. Helena intervened as she felt the atmosphere crackle with tension.

'Let us forget about all this. Shall we tell you about the cruise, Alexis? I was disappointed when you disappeared that morning. Stephan was hardly a good replacement for you, you know how we clash.' Helena looked down at her nails. 'Where is Stephan? He was staying overnight, wasn't he, *Mama?*'

Alicia swallowed her iced water before replying. 'Yes. I have an idea he has company; he certainly took a young lady out on the terrace yesterday evening. And I must say they looked quite a match.'

Alexis and Carrie exchanged looks, both absorbing Alicia's words. He turned to his mother.

'So tell me, *Mama*. What happened on the cruise? Did I miss anything of interest. Did Stephan look after my friend Garry as I asked him to?' Alexis asked.

'He did, but why *he* had to stay I'll never know. Then again, he knows how to handle a powerboat really well. I suppose I could get to like him, but I'm sure he's not who he says he is?' Helena reached for a slice of cheese. Her expressive grin brought a smile to her son's lips. She loved him so much when he smiled like that. But Alexis was frowning now. 'What do you mean?'

Mother looked at son. 'I didn't trust him. I asked a friend of mine to check him out. Maria told Nina he was an out-of-work lecturer. That's not what I found out.' She picked up a grape and began to peel it carefully.

'I've also had him checked out,' admitted Petros soberly. 'I *know* he is not an out-of-work lecturer! And I know I didn't like him.'

'Then what is he and who is he?' asked Alicia.

Carrie sighed with relief, she wanted to know, but she hadn't wanted to ask the question. Things were getting more and more complicated.

'He's a professional diver.'

'He's a scientist.'

Petros and Helena spoke simultaneously, then stared at each other aghast that *their* opinion might be wrong.

In soft quiet tones Alexis said, 'He is a bodyguard! He's visiting Greece, island hopping, so I hired him to look after you all, discreetly.'

'A what?' Helena's mouth dropped open.

Alexis assured her, 'There is no need to worry.'

Carrie felt quite lightheaded. Did she tell everyone now or did she tell Alexis when they were alone about seeing Maria and Garry hand in hand, walking past the bakery. One thing was for sure, Maria was not telling him about their holiday affair. So what should she do? Maybe she should talk to Maria herself.

Helena let out a deep breath. She was normally so composed, so in charge of herself and the situation. All of a sudden she seemed fragile and weak, as if life was taking its toll.

Petros was watching Carrie. 'And what did you think of our friend Garry? Did you suspect something?'

'Long before all of you. The drunken man was drinking mainly water with his water, one Ouzo all afternoon, the rest was just water with aniseed flavourings. I watched him at the taverna, I saw him on the yacht,' she said with a smile as everyone looked at her aghast, including Alexis. She coloured. 'And the reason I know is because I used to buy the same aniseed flavouring when I was younger.' Everyone was staring, so she scowled then qualified her statement, 'I used to pretend. You know, pretend I was drinking, when I was fifteen I used to . . .'

It was Alexis who broke the silence first. He started to laugh and then he just couldn't stop. Everyone else then began to laugh, including Alicia, even Carrie herself. The raucous noise brought Maria, Stephan and Nina out onto the terrace.

Tears were streaming down Petros's face, as they were Helena's. Alexis was hugging Carrie to him.

'You are so precious, my darling. 'Here they are, all budding Miss Marples and you beat them hands down. If you knew who G . . .'

Carrie kissed Alexis to stop his words then whispered. 'Don't let Maria know. She'll tell him and it will spoil everything for her.'

Alexis drew slightly back, looking down into her eyes for the silent message he found there. He nodded, putting a warning finger to his lips to silence their companions

'What is all the noise about?' demanded Maria as she marched up onto the terrace still dressed in short silk pyjamas. 'Why, it's the middle of the night. I need my sleep after such a party!' Stephan and Nina followed Maria up the terrace steps.

'Any lunch left?' asked Stephan.

'I hope so, we haven't really started,' said Carrie with a smile. 'And I am starving.'

'The question is, do we go to my villa and be pampered by the staff?' He watched as she grimaced. 'Or do we go to the bakery where we can talk in private and I can see what wonders you've performed?' asked Alexis after a delightful lunch.

'Talk?'

'Yes, I believe we need to talk. Really talk. Firstly, there is a matter of my sister, and then who knows? Maybe we could discuss the question of us,' he said solemnly, his eyes shrouded by the shadow of the blossom tree which overhung two small tables and several chairs.

'We go home,' she said simply. She frowned. His voice sounded so serious. Was he regretting their engagement? If only she could see inside his soul, just once would be wonderful, but his eyes never revealed any of his secrets.

He acknowledged Stephan as he walked towards them.

'Where is Nina?' Alexis asked, pushing his shirt sleeves further up his strong tanned arms.

'She's getting changed. We wondered if you would need her again? She's so damn serious about her job with you she sent me to ask you,' said Stephan sitting opposite Alexis. 'Too serious I believe.'

Alexis shook his head. 'I don't own the girl, Stephan, I merely employ her. And yes, the next time I want to see her is in the office on Monday.' He glanced at Carrie, deep in thought. 'Tell me, cousin, did my fiancee's pep-talk do any good at all?'

Stephan smiled with disdain.

'Women! Huh. I can never figure them out. I offer her marriage, once I've been granted my divorce that is' – he threw his hands in the air – 'And what does she tell me? *She* tells me we should live together for a while, even though her parents don't agree with it.'

'What's wrong with that, Stephan?' Carrie interrupted, suddenly infuriated by the man's attitude.

'Wrong, why – why it's immoral,' he cried outraged at the idea of living together.

Carrie sighed, the deep scepticism visible in her voice. 'Oh here we go. It's OK to have an affair with her, but then when it suits you, *you* want marriage. Typical man!'

'Of course I want marriage, especially before we have children. I can't see what's wrong with that!'

'You can't?'

'No! This is entirely different, and I can see nothing wrong with it.'

'You men never can!' Carrie abruptly shot out of the chair, throwing a look which could have killed at Alexis. 'And you've no need to look so pleased with yourself. You're all the same. When it suits you, that's when things should happen. When it suits the darned men!' With the last remark she marched off in search of solitude.

Stephan looked astounded. 'Her too! It seems the whole female force have it in for us today. What with Maria in a foul mood this morning and now these two.'

Alexis smiled tolerantly. 'Women are very temperamental, Stephan. I always thought I could live without them but I'm afraid I can't.'

'It's nice to know that you've finally succumbed! It seemed so unfair that you always remained immune Stephan acknowledged with an atom of satisfaction.

Alexis found Carrie on the beach some thirty minutes later. 'Hi. Mind if I sit with you?'

Carrie wiped away the last tear and looked up at him. She noticed he'd changed into an Armani suit. 'You'll dirty your suit if you sit in the sand.'

He shrugged, 'So what? Who cares?'

Dropping down beside her, he reached for her hand. 'How do you feel now? Are you any better?' He smiled gently, compassionately at her. 'I fear Stephan was the victim of overwrought nerves, what with you and Nina. He was absolutely shocked rigid by your outburst.'

A short disbelieving gasp emerged from Carrie. 'He shouldn't be so . . . Male chauvinist!' She pulled a face, the kind he loved so much. 'He makes me cross!'

'Do I make you cross too?'

She looked at him, really looked at him. Would she ever be able to feel her love returned? Surely he could sense this special feeling, surely it affected him too?

Carrie grinned. 'You always make me cross. I was cross with you when you told me to stay at home when all I wanted to do was join you in America.'

'Ah. Well that was difficult.' Squeezing her hand, he looked out to the tranquil sea. 'For two years now I've been helping the authorities investigate several high-profile drug barons.'

'Drugs?'

He nodded. 'About a year ago my company employed a Captain Marretti. His references were excellent. I found out later they were forged.' Alexis shrugged his shoulders. 'That was when I also discovered he'd had the gall to use *my* ship to smuggle drugs from South America to Europe.'

'Have they caught him?'

Alexis shook his head. 'Marretti was murdered when I was in America. His boss, whoever he is, knows we're getting close. Much *too* close.'

'That's why they . . .' Carrie stopped herself before she blew it all. 'What I mean is that's why you've been helping them. To sort it all out.'

He nodded, brushing a tendril of Carrie's hair out of her face and behind her ear, 'Yes. They tried to kill me too while I was out there, which is why you couldn't come.'

'How?' Putting a hand on his knee she repeated. 'How did they try to kill you?'

'I was knocked unconscious. I was lucky; one of the crew members died,' he said sadly.

'Would my life have been threatened too?'

They were now looking into each other's eyes. 'Who knows? What I do know is I would have loved you to be there with me but it was too dangerous. I missed you.'

'Loved?' she questioned thoughtfully.

'Metaphorically speaking,' he amended quickly. Why the hell couldn't he just tell her he loved her? Maybe Petros was right and he'd always loved her. There had never been anyone else that he truly loved. But the knowledge was new to him and he had to come to terms with that feeling himself.

'Yes, of course.' She frowned, repeating softly, 'Metaphorically speaking.'

'I still missed you, Carrie.' He looked at her bottom lip tremble. 'Surely missing you is a start in the right direction? Love seems to me to be a word that has a thousand different meanings. Surely it's feelings that matter? As man and wife, knowing we care will help our children.'

Leaning forward she kissed him, feeling the roughness of stubble, the fresh scent of cologne and man all intermingled. 'Of course it is feelings that matter.' As she held him her heart cried and one solitary tear fell down her cheek.

'Come. We should be making our way to the bakery.' He squeezed her shoulders. 'We'll have to think up a more appropriate name for the place.'

Pulling herself together, she smiled. 'How about *The Hideaway*?'

Alexis grinned. 'More than you'll ever know. Only you and I know the address. No one else needs to know. My mobile telephone number is all I tell people when I'm there.'

They walked up the beach hand in hand and up the winding track which led to the back of the villa.

'Your mother owns a lot of this land, doesn't she?' Carrie remarked.

'She does. *Mama* has money in her own right and my father left her well provided for. I don't meddle in her affairs unless she asks my advice. My father was one of the richest men in Greece,' he said soberly, as if money were irrelevant. To him, it probably was. 'Now I am.'

They'd almost reached the wrought-iron gate which led onto the terrace when Carrie stopped.

'And that's why you need an heir? To leave your money to him?' asked Carrie, already knowing the answer. He'd gone through this more times than she cared to remember. It was part of the bargain but what she needed to know was – why? It certainly wasn't his reward for getting Petros out of financial difficulty. Petros *wasn't* in difficulty, she knew.

'No. It's not just to provide an heir, not any more.'

Carrie stared at Alexis who was looking down the path towards the beach. He looked tired, and strangely vulnerable.

'Then why?' came her tentative question.

CHAPTER 15

Just as Alexis was about to answer, Maria came running down the terrace interrupting both with bad news.

'Carrie, thank God I've found you. Audrey has rung, she wants you to fly over to England. Peter has got pneumonia, he's terribly ill in hospital, and he's asking for you,' cried Maria, not sparing a look for her brother.

'Oh no! Not my Peter!' She turned to Alexis and her breath caught in her throat. He was livid. Quietly livid!

'Don't tell me – you have to go.' Sarcasm shot through the air like a bullet ripping its target in half.

Maria turned on him, counter-attacking in Carrie's defence. 'You don't understand! Peter is crazy about Carrie. If he asks, she has to go, she just has to. Their love is a special one. I've never seen anything like it before. And besides, you can't stop her.'

Carrie saw his face distort. She felt sick at the thought, but she had to go as soon as possible and only one man could get her there quickly. He was standing in front of her.

Touching his arm, she felt him recoil from her. 'I need your help. Please, Alexis. I need to get there quickly. Come with me? Come and see Peter for yourself, please. You'll understand then.'

Blankness fell over his face, like shutters closing everything out. In a voice that Carrie barely recognized, he told her he would have the jet fuelled and ready to leave for London late this evening. With that he walked away.

'What on earth is he so mad about? He was livid! Surely he understands about little Petie?' asked Maria, outraged by her brother's behaviour for the second time that day. Was he turning into some kind of a tyrant?

Carrie shook her head. 'He thinks Peter's a man. I've told him Peter is the person I love.' Carrie threw her hands up in the air. She was tired of all this pretence. 'I needed to know he cared for me. This marriage would mean nothing to me if he didn't care!'

Maria's mouth dropped open as she interrupted, 'You lied to my big brother, and got away with it? Carrie, that's a sin.' She grinned. 'But one that I like.'

'I didn't lie to him. I just didn't tell him the pertinent facts about Peter, that's all. I let him assume what he wanted. I let him think Peter was the man I loved.' She paused briefly as a wave of panic rushed through her. 'Oh God, Maria, is Peter really bad?'

Maria winced. 'I've written down the name of the hospital. It sounds as if he's pretty rough. Audrey wouldn't ask you to go back to London if he wasn't bad, would she?'

Carrie shook her head. 'No, but I was only talking to her yesterday. He'd been ill, but not too desperate, I'm sure.'

Maria shrugged. 'Have you thought she may not have wanted to spoil your engagement?'

Carrie smiled, knowing only too well Maria was trying to ease her worry. 'She doesn't even know. I could hardly burden her with my problems when she has enough with Peter. It's not easy looking after a Down's syndrome child. The last thing she needs is someone else's worries. Peter has lots of energy normally and he can be really tiring.' Fresh tears sparkled in her eyes, but she blinked them back. 'He also has a lot of love.'

'Let me help you pack,' Maria suggested.

Carrie waved her away. 'If Alexis is in there I'd rather not cause a scene.'

Maria shook her head. 'You're joking! He'll go out now to let his temper cool down. Are you going to tell him? About Peter?'

'Yes. I'm sorry I ever let him think otherwise. That was so unfair using Peter's love like that.' Reaching the main veranda door, she stopped.

The car that sped out of the driveway was skidding on the dusty surface and Carrie was in no doubt who was driving that car!

'Look – he's gone. I thought he would. I can help you pack now, if you like,' said Maria softly, noting the strained look upon Carrie's pale face. Reaching out she put her arm around Carrie's shoulders. 'Don't worry, he'll be back to you in a flash. I've never seen him quite like this with a woman. The man's well and truly attached to you, Carrie.'

Carrie sighed; she'd give all the world for him to be with her just because he wanted to, not because he was forced.

Alexis looked at his watch. The gold hands were at 7.00 p.m. and her flight was due at approximately eight depending on flight conditions. How dare she use *his* jet to run after her love! And yet he'd given the all-clear for its use. When he'd seen the love for Peter in her eyes, he'd been blindly jealous, insane for a moment. If he hadn't walked away he'd have blown a fuse. Maybe even blown ten!

He sighed. The folder lay unopened on the desk, and had been there for days according to Nina. The seal was unbroken. So what was he waiting for? The dossier on one Peter Burnley was right there in front of him. Part of him didn't want to open it, simply because he was scared of what he might find.

Carefully he unfolded the file. The picture that fell out was that of a child. A child with huge green eyes, a simply beautiful smile, and a face that had his condition written all over it. Quickly he read the report until he knew everything about Peter Burnley.

Why, the conniving, deceiving little witch! He'd been held to ransom over a child! Driven half-crazy at the thought of her loving someone else. Oh what a fool he'd been. He began to laugh again for the second time that day. She'd had him well and truly fooled, dancing to her tune, and now she was off to England to escape the consequences. He looked down at his watch again. He would allow her to use his jet – but at a price. Even Carrie didn't deserve to get away with this!

Reaching for the telephone receiver, he barked his orders down the phone. Picking up the report, he placed it carefully in his briefcase, grabbed his car keys and made his way down to the car.

So, Carrie had known Peter for quite some time. She had obviously built up a special relationship with the little boy, if the loving look in her eyes earlier was anything to go by.

Annoyance surged through him; the cheeky little baggage had used a child to make him jealous, and what rattled was the fact that it had worked. He'd fallen for it hook, line and sinker. Now was the time for retribution!

The jet's engines slowed again and looking out of one of the small windows Carrie could see the captain running over the tarmac towards the jet. He'd left alone, just minutes earlier, and was now returning, accompanied. Carrie turned away, only to swing her head back, her eyes disbelieving, noting the movements, noting the way the newcomer moved, as he ran toward the plane. The man who accompanied the captain was Alexis!

As he walked into the cabin, Carrie just stared, and he stared back at her before he moved silently across the floor to stand near her.

'What are you doing here?' Her voice was a little whisper. Deep inside she was pleased to see him; she needed his support right now, but the expression which passed across his face was disconcerting her somewhat.

'I thought you could hardly run away from my questions at thirty thousand feet,' he said, sitting down beside her, giving her no opportunity to flee. Raising his brow in query, he assessed her silently; he knew she was fraught simply by the way her fingers were fidgeting in her lap.

She stuttered slightly, the Irish accent very strong. 'Why would I do that? I have nothing to run away from.'

'Oh you haven't? Well think again. I think you'd love to cut and run from me.' His voice held a note of cynicism, his words a tiny hint of threat. 'But there would be no point. If you run I will catch you. I'm very angry with you, Carrie.'

Carrie held her hands in her lap, stilled now by his words. 'Has Maria told you about Peter?'

He shook his head. 'Oh, so she knows too, does she? It's only me – ' he stabbed his chest – 'who knew so little.'

Her heart began to palpitate. 'Knew? As in the past tense?'

He agreed softly, all the time watching her response. 'As in the past tense, Carrie, and now I want to know why?'

The stewardess smiled down at her employer and his fiancee. 'Mr Stephanides, your seatbelts, please.'

Once off the ground she would be back to ask them if they would like refreshments but for now she left them quietly to resume their conversation.

Alexis handed Carrie the folder from his briefcase. 'I'm disappointed in you, Carrie. You were using this child to do what? Make me angry? Get your revenge because I forced your hand? I expected so much more of you.'

'I never intended getting revenge. I didn't do it for that. I did it to try, to try . . .' Her voice trailed away into silence.

'Yes, to try what?' He turned her face around to him. 'I want no more lies, Carrie.'

'I didn't lie to you. I do love Peter.'

'Stop procrastinating, just tell me why?'

Carrie looked out at the darkened sky, at the lights flickering on the wings against the blackness of the Grecian night as they taxied towards the runway.

'I wanted a reaction. You'd always been in such control until I mentioned Peter, and then later when we, we made love . . . You lost it . . .'

'Lost what?'

'Your control! I realized then that you might care about me. So I let you believe Peter was a man. I never actually lied to you. I just wanted you to care, not just for the body that's carrying your child, but for *me*, Carrie O'Riordan.' She pulled herself free of his touch. 'I just needed to know you were jealous. The mention of Peter has a way of getting a response out of you, a reaction.'

'It does?'

'Oh yes, your face contorts, like this . . .' As she copied his face for one illuminating second he nearly succumbed to laughter. As it was, he suppressed the urge, he was still angry with her. Wasn't he? Well maybe not.

'Just like that?'

'Yes, and when you're angry, like this . . .' She pulled another face, this one quite frightening.

He pushed an irritable hand through his hair, relaxing a little. 'I guess I've been pretty tough on you. Demanding that you marry me, forcing you to have my baby all in the name of a shipping fleet.'

The jet engines revved loudly, they were now on the runway getting clearance ready for take-off.

'Oh, don't give me that! I know all about Petros's finances. I know he's not near to bankruptcy; in fact, on paper his business is quite healthy, so don't give me that rubbish!'

The stewardess quietly coughed. 'Would you like coffee, sir, madame?'

Carrie nodded as did Alexis and they both watched the stewardess retreat into the galley area of the jet before they continued talking.

'And yet you're still going through with this. Why?' Alexis asked, intrigued to know the answer to his question. He'd known she was no fool, known

Petros's little plan would never hold water. There had been too many holes, just as Alexis had predicted.

'Have you forgotten our child? Not only are we good in bed together, it would seem we are an excellent match in the act of conceiving.' She was tired of this, so tired. OK, so she would have liked the full fairy-tale, the romance, the kisses, but the voice of reality told her it wasn't to be. She would marry him for their child's sake and for herself she would have to make do with loving a man who didn't really love her in return.

'Any other reason?' he enquired softly.

'Two more reasons,' she shot at him.

He lifted a brow in query. 'Only two? Then tell me them.'

For a fleeting moment she was so scared she wanted to run away. Fear gripped her by the throat, in the heart, the lungs. She could scarcely breathe let alone speak to him. As long as he cared she would cope, just as long as he cared. She was wise enough to realize that this strong proud man didn't often vow love, just loyalty and commitment

'I'm waiting.'

'Theo. I can't stand the idea of him . . .' She'd been going to say what Alexis was thinking, but she couldn't bring herself to utter the words '*bouncing up and down*'. 'Well I'd leave the island, leave my home rather than marry Theo – even to give Petros the grandchild he longs for.'

She looked at him in earnest.

'And the second?'

'The second – ' she laughed – 'you won't believe the second at all, so I may as well not mention it.'

'And the second?' he reiterated, his dark eyes searching her face.

Could she say it? She must, she'd come this far.

'The second reason is because I care very deeply for you.' She allowed herself to look at his reaction from under her lashes. Damn! Why had she messed it up, why not just say it?

'What?' His face was a picture, obviously her reply was not what he had anticipated. It spurred her on.

'In other words . . . I mean – I love you! I did all this, even involving Peter, because I LOVE YOU,' she repeated a second time, watching him frown.

The coffee arrived and was drunk in silence. He was acting as if she hadn't said anything!

'Alexis! Don't leave me out in the cold. I've been honest with you, my heart has been on display for weeks. I just need to know you care.' She hated herself for being so weak; she was almost begging him to give her a reply, almost begging for his approval, his respect. Whatever he could offer her.

'Yes, Carrie, I too, care very much,' he said and pulling her within the circle of his arms he rested his chin on her hair, her words resonating within his head. Resting like this, they slept the remainder of their flight in sweet, relaxed contentment.

'Carrie, let me,' said Alexis, frowning as she tried to lift her cabin luggage down. She was standing on the seat reaching for a bag as Alexis came back from the cockpit.

Just as she said, 'I'm fine,' her foot slipped and she crashed to the floor, banging her hip and her head, crying out with pain.

Running to her, Alexis handed the stewardess the bag, instantly alert to Carrie's distressed condition.

'Are you all right, Carrie? Here, let me take a look at your bruises,' said Alexis softly as he removed the smaller bag from her shaking hands. She winced as his thumb traced the edges of the pink abrasion on her face, whilst he studied her pallor beneath. He swore in Greek and looked into her deep confused blue eyes.

Carrie swallowed; she wished with all her heart he would stop touching her. She ached so much, and it wasn't from pain.

'Do you feel faint? Are you feeling sick?' came his concerned questions.

Carrie shook her head and licked her lips, not knowing which question she should answer first. In truth, she felt terrible! Her lips were dry and her throat was parched, but it was her stomach that was heaving. Perhaps it was the flying. They had certainly come across several bouts of turbulence, or maybe it was the worry about Peter.

Alexis immediately took charge. He ordered the stewardess to bring a glass of mineral water and told Carrie to sit with her head between her knees as he massaged her neck.

Thankfully, the water and biscuits he handed her to nibble on took away the queasy feeling in her stomach.

'I need to freshen up, Alexis,' she said, when she was able to stand steadily again.

Carrie retied her hair off her face and refreshed herself with the wonderfully warm water. Splashing it on her face and around the back of her neck made her feel much better. Now she would go out and face the man she loved. She hadn't really had the answer she truly wanted earlier; she just hoped it would be enough knowing that he cared.

Unlocking the bolt Carrie escaped the confines of the powder room only to find Alexis just outside. He didn't look tender and concerned any more, just tall and remote. He raised his arm and blocked her entry to the cabin. Carrie jumped back as if he'd struck her, not daring to meet his eyes for fear of rejection.

'Look at me,' he said softly, and although his words were deceptively soft, it was clearly an order.

An order she couldn't comply with. She shook her head, her eyes examining the carpet beneath her feet. Her emotions were shot to pieces: she'd revealed her love to him, and he had not returned his. That took some coming to terms with.

'I said look at me, Carrie.' This time, the casual sexy tone of his voice made her shudder inside. This time he brought his hand to her unresisting chin and raised her face, and she had no alternative but to lose herself in the river of his warm chocolate eyes.

'So. What do you want?'

'How do you feel now? I thought I heard you being sick?' he questioned, then added, 'I also feared you were running away from me because I can't return your love. It's not that I don't want to love you, it's that I don't understand the word. Or the big deal it is in relationships. I'm sorry – ' the words seemed to be coming straight from his heart – 'All I know right now is that I care for you very much. I need time to assess this thing you call love. And I don't know just how much time I'll need.' His concerned voice and the searching look that seemed to delve deep inside her did something to her, weakened her resolve to stay annoyed with him.

She smiled tentatively. Her voice came out wobbly and unsure; 'I'll give you that time.' He lifted her hair, checking for more damage from her fall. 'I'm all right now. I will be all right, Alexis, I promise. I only went in there to brush my hair and straighten myself up.'

Again he was massaging his thumb over the slightly bruised area of her cheek. She felt hot, and weak, and wished with all her heart she could fall into his arms. Closing her eyes in an effort to blot out the pain, she sighed. Opening her mouth ever so slightly she released her soft breath in a rush as his thumb massaged further down her neck and over a very definite erogenous zone. With gentle fingers he pushed the cotton blouse to one side. His inspection of her neck and shoulders went unnoticed by her as tender hands caressed her warm, satin skin. He framed her face with his strong tanned hands and bent his head to claim her parted lips. Yes, she knew he cared.

The hospital smelt clean, the damp morning air rushing swiftly through the doors as they opened.

They were told that the Intensive Care unit for children was on the first floor. Visiting was any time day and night.

Their journey to the first floor seemed to take an eternity. She wanted to get there but in another way she didn't. She was scared. The kindly nurse on the desk in her starched white uniform enquired who they were visiting.

'Peter Burnley,' confirmed Carrie.

'Ah yes. You must be his Carrie.' The nurse smiled warmly throwing an appreciative eye over Alexis. 'He asks for you every hour on the hour. I'm afraid he is very poorly though. I'll take you through. His parents are with him and I believe the priest is on his way.'

Alexis immediately put a supporting arm around Carrie; she'd lost so much colour.

'He's not going to die, is he?'

The nurse didn't answer, her. She said softly, 'If you come this way, you can talk with his mother.'

The small woman who looked round to see Carrie and Alexis enter the room let out a cry and ran into the younger girl's arms.

'Oh Carrie. I'm so sorry to drag you here like this. He's been asking for you, he's really ill,' cried Audrey, her tired eyes full of pain.

'It's OK. You know I want to be here. But how did it happen? You said he'd had bronchitis,' whispered Carrie, her searching look encompassing the youngster in the bed.

'As you know, he's always been weak from his asthma, but he has so much energy when he's well.' She sniffed and wiped her tears with a sodden hanky. 'The school arranged a camping weekend for the children. We took him along, and several of them got caught out in the weather. Peter came down with bronchitis. When I spoke to you he was on the mend, but then this happened. Oh, Carrie, he's so poorly. Bless him, he's not even had his orange juice this evening and he loves his orange juice.' She broke down again. 'The priest is coming to see him. That means they think he's going to die, doesn't it?' she wept.

'No. Don't say that. He won't. What he needs is a warmer climate. When he's well he can come on holiday with us, can't he, Alexis?' Carrie looked for the confirmation she knew instinctively she would get.

'Of course he can, you *all* can.'

Graham Burnley was a man of few words, but now he was sitting by his son's bedside praying. He looked up at Carrie with tears in his eyes. 'Thanks for coming, love. You know how special you are to him.'

'As he is to me,' whispered Carrie.

Alexis looked down at the child, his breathing helped by the oxygen tent. His chubby little face looked warm, his cheeks rosy in spite of his condition. His button nose which was turned up at the end was cute, but as his eyes flickered and the long sweeping eyelashes swung up Alexis saw a light that no one could resist. The light which had so obviously dimmed now shone in his eyes when he saw Carrie. Now he understood their bond.

'Cawwie,' the thin voice whispered, the chubby little hand reached out.

Alexis watched a gowned Carrie reach for Peter's hand. Graham moved so that she could sit with him.

'Petie, what are you doing in here?' Carrie looked around the room, her eyes raising to the ceiling in mock disgust.

His lips, thinned with the pain of breathing, broke into a smile. 'Cawwie. I love you. Gweek, Cawwie, say it in Gweek.'

'*Sagapo*,' she said softly, meaning every word, every syllable.

'*Saggipoo*,' he repeated with a little grin. His pronunciation was obviously their joke and one that brought a smile to Alexis's lips too.

Carrie closed her eyes momentarily to compose herself. 'I love you too, my darling. I want to kiss you but I can't.' She indicated the oxygen tent.

As carefully as he could, little Peter pushed his mouth towards her. They kissed through the tent, a tender and touching expression of hope.

Alexis was standing motionless, emotion such as he'd never felt surged through him. It hit him like ten thousand volts running through his veins. Peter had confirmed something for him just now. Carrie was special, she cared more passionately than any other person he knew, and not only for Peter.

'Who dat?' Peter's chubby finger pointed to Alexis as he gave him the once-over. Alexis smiled, giving the child a wink.

Carrie took Alexis's hand.

Carefully she said, 'This is Al-ex-is.'

'Aw-ex-ees,' repeated Peter.

'That's it, he's my fiance. We are going to be married soon and I want you to be there, to be my pageboy. You will come?' asked Carrie, the dread in her heart lifting when he smiled. His breathing was thin again, but he nodded. Audrey watched on with tears in her eyes when the priest arrived.

Alexis, Carrie and Peter all held hands. The oxygen tent had been lifted for a few precious minutes as the priest talked and prayed. He'd been in every day for the past week. Carrie and Alexis, Graham and Audrey and the nurse who was monitoring Peter's progress kissed Peter goodnight. It was a simple ceremony, but one that always sent the child into a deep and satisfying sleep.

Carrie and Alexis walked out of the hospital into a bright summer's evening. The birds were singing, the odd cloud skimmed in slow motion through the sky, a vapour trail lay still against the pale blue background as they walked around the hospital gardens for several precious minutes.

Alexis himself had sat by Peter's bed for several hours each day, hoping to give Carrie and her friends some time alone. Time to talk. That was something *he* wanted to do, sort out this whole business about Petros, especially now.

'Thank you,' said Carrie with a pleased smile upon her face. She touched the diamond engagement ring. It felt so right somehow, so perfect now Peter had blessed her relationship with Alexis.

'For what?' He smiled. 'I didn't want to disappoint you or Peter. He's all you said he is; he's a terrific little guy, and he certainly brightened up a lot when he saw you.'

She bent to touch a rose petal, inhaling the sweet perfume as if it were the breath of life.

'Do you understand now why I had to come?'

Alexis pulled her towards the seat in the small garden. 'I do now. I do now, Carrie. Audrey tells me you've been an angel with him. You've taught him much more than they could get through at school.'

Carrie looked across at her man. Why had she never admitted to herself just how good-looking he was? There had been a moment of jealousy, a flash, streaking through her like lightning when Peter's nurse had given him the once-over.

Thoughtfully she said, 'It was a two-way street. I never really settled in London.' He raised his eyebrow in question, as she qualified: 'Oh I know I used to tell Petros that London was outrageous, that I loved the fast living. It was all a lie. I lived that lie for quite a few years until Peter came along.' She sneaked a look at his frowning face. 'He gave me something, gave me a reason for continuing to live there. Then, when I saw you in London, when we . . .'

'You mean when I tried to seduce you, and failed?' He laughed harshly. 'That really dented my ego. I thought you'd had the hots for me all these years only to find out suddenly you were immune. So what happened that night?'

'The next morning I realized I was deluding myself. Greece had become my home. I never truly wanted to be a choreographer in London, I did it all for Petros.' Again he threw her a critical look. 'Oh I'm not saying I don't enjoy dance, I do. But I just don't feel it's the direction I should be going in. I need something more.'

'So why didn't you return to Greece immediately?'

'I couldn't. I was torn, Peter needed my help, as I did his, and then I'd lied to you about those men at the nightclub. You thought I'd bedded each and every one. I was so ashamed that you actually believed me, when I could force myself to think about it, that is,' she said in a soft voice, remembering how bad she'd felt the next morning.

Alexis reached for her hand. 'That's all in the past. You really don't know what you gave me that first afternoon at the bakery.'

'I know what you gave me,' she said with a grin.

'What?'

'Birds of paradise plastered to my behind!'

He laughed so loudly that several hospital visitors and nurses turned their heads to look in their direction.

'Come, let's go back to the hotel. Peter looks better now than he did this morning.' He pulled her into his arms, sneaking a hand around her waist.

'Yes. The doctor has given him a bit more of a chance.'

'He looks heaps better, as I keep hearing everyone say,' he whispered as they walked along.

'Audrey and Graham have been warned that he could go any minute. Peter has a heart disease too, so that doesn't make it any easier.' They'd reached the taxi rank when she looked up at him. 'I want to stay in London a while longer, until he's out of danger . . .'

He put his finger against her lips. 'In that case I think we should have our romantic evening tonight, the one I didn't give you in Athens. And what night could be more appropriate?' he suggested, the smile etched upon his face.

Carrie got into the taxi. 'Just as long as I can keep ringing the hospital.' She patted her stomach. 'Besides, I think I've had enough romantic evenings with you, Mr Stephanides to last me a lifetime.'

He laughed. 'They haven't yet begun.' He told the taxi driver the name of a small private hotel then he took her hand. 'After visiting Peter tomorrow we'll have to fit you in with a consultant. I need to know you're all right and all is well with the baby.'

Carrie scoffed teasingly, her bright blue eyes suddenly alight with torment. 'Bit late now, isn't it?'

He shook his head. 'I don't think so. I have to make sure you're going to be just fine.'

The evening had been romantic in its own special way. Firstly, they showered together, then Carrie sat watching Alexis shave, in his usual stance, unselfconsciously naked and presenting her with his magnificent back view. She loved the way he stood when he was shaving. Words seemed irrelevant while they were getting changed, each look was charged with something good, something special.

The short pale blue dress with the white linen jacket and matching shoes had been a present from Alexis together with a jade brooch in the shape of dolphin. She'd insisted on buying something in return and he'd settled for a gold money clip, engraved with a crab representing his birth sign, Cancer.

Looking at him, she knew he was a typical Cancerian. At the first sign of real commitment he'd rushed back into his shell and she could never predict the moves he made, maybe because like a crab he sidled in from the perimeter. She could never read him, principally because he was as deep as the ocean was blue. Yes, he was a true Cancerian.

Once in the dining room of the hotel, they cleared the air first about things that needed to be said.

'You must obviously know why Petros put you up to this?' asked Carrie as she delicately forked fresh prawns with the smooth rich flesh of the avocado into her mouth.

Alexis had always used this private hotel when he was in London, and it so near to Carrie's place that a taxi or his chauffeur-driven car would have to go past the street where she lived. Not that she'd questioned him, when he'd asked her to stay with him. He'd never really questioned his own reasons either, but now he was, those reasons were panicking him.

After a long while he spoke. 'He asked me to go along with this ludicrous suggestion because he said he was a dying man. You're the nearest thing he has to a daughter and I reckon he wanted to see at least one of your children,' replied Alexis, dropping the napkin into his lap. He was now wearing a classic charcoal coloured suit, a white shirt and plum tie. The tie was obviously irritating because he loosened it, before he looked up to meet her soft blue eyes.

'Children?' she enquired, then qualified, 'I thought our bargain was *A* child.'

He sat back in the chair, surveying her, leaving the pate and toast to stand for a moment. 'My father was one of twins. His brother died at a very young age. There is a memorial on the road where he was killed in Poros.'

'So what?'

'So, little Carrie, twins usually miss a generation and go from there,' he informed her, the amusement written deep in his face. He pointed to her barely altered tummy. 'There could be two already in there.'

'Oh that's very funny.' She spooned more prawns into her mouth. 'If I'm eating for the five thousand I may as well eat my dinner.'

He laughed, agreeing, 'You may as well. Would you like one glass of wine?'

She shook her head. 'No, but I would like to know why you agreed with Petros's plans. I need to know this, Alexis.'

Alexis bit into his last piece of toast. 'I felt sorry for him, at first.' He rushed in, seeing her outraged reaction; 'To be honest, I didn't think you'd fall for it. As far as I knew, I had to put this preposterous proposition to you and that was it. Petros needed a grandchild.' He threw the napkin on the table. 'And I'll be honest, I wanted you, full stop. Any way I could get you.'

Carrie swallowed her prawns, staring at him. She felt like a piece of precious jewellery. Something that someone *owned*.

'I see.' Her voice was tight, her face angered.

'I'm telling the truth. I didn't think you'd agree to it, certainly not the Carrie I knew. In a way I hoped you wouldn't, which was why I was particularly horrible to you.' He took another sip of wine, 'When you agreed then fell headlong into my arms I knew even more I had to have you, but I guess I've wanted you for so long I decided to play ball.' He sighed, smiling at her. 'Only then he went too far when he brought Theo and marriage into it. He knows I hate Theo; he also knows I wouldn't deliberately hurt you. The only reason I said I'd marry you was for your sake. Had I wanted to hurt you, you'd be going down the aisle with . . .' He looked at her long and hard.

'Don't put me off my food. The deed is done. I'm having your baby and whether you like it or not, buster, you have a responsibility to this child.' She watched as he covered her hand with his.

'Don't let's argue. Tonight we are to be romantics.' He let go of her hand. 'Talking about romance, what do you know about Maria and Tate?'

She shrugged, wishing he hadn't digressed. 'I saw them only last week hand in hand. They must be having an affair, but she's old enough, Alexis.'

Placing his hand on his chin he rubbed his clean-shaven skin, 'You knew, didn't you?'

'That she was having an affair?' She nodded. 'Yes, but I also think she could be in love with him. I've never seen her like this.'

Alexis grunted, pulling a face, 'That's a road to nowhere, Carrie. He's from the States, you know, too far to carry on a relationship, besides which Tate and Maria are as different as chalk and cheese. He won't take her on permanently.'

Carrie loved him when he copied her expressions. 'He might. Alexis, you of all people should know that opposites attract.'

Their plates were taken away and their main meals placed in front of them, as he replied:

'Rubbish!'

'But we're opposites.'

'Are we? I'm not so sure. We are not opposite in bed. And, when we go back to Greece there is something I want to show you that will prove we have something in common. Now eat your dinner, woman. I want to dance with you.' He picked up his knife and fork.

Carrie looked at him and all her insecurities came rushing back to her. 'You're a very successful business man. Me, well the only project I've worked on was the play, and I failed miserably.'

'That's not true and you know it!' His eyes narrowed. 'Your biggest failing is that you're too gullible. You should have kept hold of the reins, not let them go after you'd ploughed money into the project. No, Carrie, your biggest failing is that you are too trusting.' He inclined his head. 'Having said that, it's one of the things I find so enchanting about you. The reason why I . . .' He paused. It just wasn't right to tell her he loved her, he just couldn't do it. Love had never been an issue for him before. He truly didn't believe in it and he wouldn't do it just to make her happy. 'The reason why I care so much. Don't lose that trust, Carrie.'

Carrie stared at him. 'I guess I should never have gone into dancing. I was always too big to be a ballet dancer, and as a choreographer, I was hopeless. A failure.'

'You didn't *fail*! Like you said, it was bad timing. You had a damn good review for a lousy musical. I was there, I saw it, and the choreography was good. Damn good! Now if you don't mind we'll have no more of this self-deprecation. Whether you go back to dancing or not you're a wonderful passionate person. You haven't failed in life, so let's not look back now. The future is ours, Carrie. Now please have just one small glass of wine, and then once we've had a dance we'll ring the hospital.'

How could he preach about her being a wonderful passionate person when he was doing a sterling job himself? Carrie was so proud he was defending her like this. She'd never seen him quite this involved.

The dancing was the slow smoochy kind, but Alexis was obviously not in that kind of a mood. He argued with her, teased her, made her laugh, whispered rude suggestions in her ears. He also persistently kept on trying to pinch an inch on her waist and when that failed he bit her chin, her neck, all the time teasing.

When the faster music came back on, Carrie begged him to let her sit down, but her request fell on deaf ears as he twirled her round to the sounds of the sixties.

Much, much later, laughing and breathless, she ran off the dance floor, collapsing into her chair.

'Lord. I don't know where you get your energy from!' She drank the half glass of wine. 'Come on, let's ring the hospital.' She held out her hand, her short worried frown soon dissolving when he winked at her.

'He'll be OK, he's a fighter,' comforted Alexis. 'And besides, I promised to let him steer the *Challenger* with the captain's hat on.'

She smiled. 'You did?'

He grinned. 'And much, much more.' He held his hand out. 'Come, I'll tell you all about it in the privacy of our room.'

CHAPTER 16

'What I can't understand is that Petros won't even discuss this with me. He knows that I know about this farce, and he won't even acknowledge the fact,' commented Carrie as they took breakfast on the terrace.

Carrie looked cautiously at Alexis. Over the past ten weeks they had hardly spoken of what they had secretly entered into in London. Their child had grown inside of her, their relationship a steady progressive wonder. But always she was waiting for the bubble of happiness to burst.

'Maybe he's waiting until he's had the operation. We know that he lied about that. He's waiting for a heart transplant, not some kind of bypass. If it's any consolation he lied to me too,' he returned unsmilingly. He picked up the coffee pot, poured two cups then asked, 'And what, might I ask, are you doing today?'

'Jonathan has asked me to help with the new donkey. It needs to swim in the sea to strengthen its muscles. Jonathan, Andreas and myself are going to take him out in the boat and swim him back.'

Alexis threw her a worried look; he knew his insisting she be careful would get him nowhere. Since he'd shown her the sanctuary she'd never been away. All her efforts, all her time was spent with the animals. She now led the project team from his office, and gave them a new direction, different goals each week. They'd even adopted a puppy found scrounging for food in the streets of Athens, the same one that was at his feet now, staring up lovingly into his eyes. He'd accepted that soon his villa would be full of strays. A menagerie, Carrie called it. All of this had their housekeeper Kiki's blessing. She too loved animals.

'You will be careful?' he asked with a smile. Before she could answer he went on, 'By the way, my mother has been ranting over the cancellation of our wedding. I did tell her it was a mutual decision.'

Carrie grinned affectionately. In London they had reached a mutual understanding that their wedding would be when they were ready and not for any other reason. 'As soon as Peter is fully recovered we'll rearrange a ceremony. He's come on so well since we stayed at the hospital with him, and if you remember, we promised.'

He touched her hand. 'I remember as if it were yesterday.'

Rani trotted happily over to greet Kiki, wrapping herself around the woman's legs.

'I have brought some lunch for your team of helpers today, Carrie.' She looked at Alexis, her employer for the past six years, and smiled warmly. 'Mr Stephanides, will you be home this evening?'

He looked across at Carrie. 'Are we going to stay in Athens this evening?'

Carrie shook her head. 'No! You've forgotten, haven't you? I invited Garry to come and see us. I told you I saw him near the sanctuary.' She frowned. 'I think he's missing Maria, and besides he'll be going back to the States soon.'

Alexis's lips compressed in anger. 'How can a man miss someone when his whole intention was to use her?'

Carrie turned to Kiki. 'We'll be in for dinner. Just three of us and you can cook whatever you want.'

Kiki smiled. 'Come, Rani, you have to stay with me. Soon you will have a friend. The one you rescued, Carrie, the one from the beach. Yes?'

Carrie nodded.

When Kiki was out of earshot Alexis snorted. 'How the hell can you have him here to dinner? He's hurt Maria.'

Carrie shook her head. 'Not intentionally. He told her things wouldn't last, and still she wanted to carry on. Alexis, she has to make her own mistakes.

Alexis thumped his hand on the white metal table.

'The man was in my employ! I was paying him to protect her, nothing more.'

'I'd say that was an added bonus, her having his body. He's ever so cute.' Her voice tinkled with laughter.

'What did you say?' This kind of frown would have

frightened her before she'd lived with him but not any more, she was used to him now.

'Credit where credit is due, Alexis, the man *is* attractive,' she answered lightly.

'And I suppose *you* are attracted to him too?'

Carrie listened to his dark voice getting lower and lower. Could he be jealous of Garry too? Things were looking up.

'He's cute, but no, I think I'd leave him to Maria. Besides, I quite like you,' she admitted, hoping to soothe him, but to no avail.

'He'll not protect her again,' he said adamantly.

'That is presuming he did protect her!'

Alexis looked at Carrie as recognition dawned. 'You mean? You mean they didn't use . . .'

Carrie shrugged. 'I don't know, I'm just saying they may not have. You didn't. You wanted me pregnant!'

'That's entirely different. And just for the record, it was Petros who wanted you pregnant. It didn't matter to him if I was the father or Theo was! Your godfather simply wanted you to have a child.' The tone of his voice was hurtful.

Carrie winced as his remarks landed home with a directness that sent pain lancing through her heart. 'I see. I didn't realize you felt that way. I thought this child was for you too.' Tears stung in her eyes. 'Had I known I was being tricked into all of this, I would have stayed in London. You said you wanted me, but it's not true, is it? You no more want a wife than you do a ten-ton weight around your neck.'

Alexis tried to backtrack as he saw the damage those few words had caused. 'Carrie, I didn't mean . . .'

'Oh, but I think you did!'

'Carrie, listen to me.' He moved forward.

'No! Don't touch me!' She stepped back, faltering slightly, her eyes wild with fury, her hurt camouflaged. 'I realize now what a fool I've been, what an utterly stupid fool I've been to trust you.'

'That's not true, and you know it. Haven't these last few weeks meant anything to you?'

'They have to me, but obviously not to you!'

She marched off towards her car. Alexis left her, hoping she'd cool down once she had time to think. He watched her marching round the corner, her pretty shape a tiny bit fuller in her candy-striped shorts with bib and braces and her strawberry-pink vest clinging to her curves. She looked so pretty today and he'd not even told her so. Cursing himself, he knew he shouldn't have said what he had; he certainly *did* want her to have their child and not for Petros, but for himself. But he still couldn't admit that to her.

Sighing, he pushed away the remnants of his breakfast, all appetite suddenly gone. Looking down at his watch, he got to his feet; half a day in the office would do him good. He'd take an early trip back on the hydrofoil and go and bring her back from her swim with the donkey, then he'd explain. If she wished, he would be cordially polite to Garry through dinner just as long as they could get rid of him early.

'Adro,' called Alexis. 'Get the car. We need to get an earlier sailing.'

Adro smiled, inclining his head. Kiki was still trying to teach her Spanish husband English but he and Alexis seemed to get on fine without many words.

Carrie arrived at the sanctuary with time to spare. The queasy feeling had left her but still she felt dull, listless. Life seemed only half as exciting, half as promising since her argument with Alexis.

What she wouldn't do was mope about; she would help the staff feed the donkeys whilst they waited for Jonathan and Andreas to arrive.

Tiny, as she called him, was waiting patiently with his head over the stable door, as was Dooly.

'Today we're going swimming. We need to get those legs muscled up,' she told him as she put the small amount of food into the trough. He was only allowed a little snack before swimming, unlike Dooly, whose greedy eyes lit up at the sight of his large feed.

'Hello,' came the deep voice behind her.

Carrie spun around. 'Garry. Hi!' She turned back to the donkeys, listening to their munching as she talked. 'I was expecting you for dinner this evening.'

He shrugged nonchalantly. 'I thought, seeing I was at a loose end, I would come here and give you a hand.'

Carrie frowned. He'd been around a bit too much for her liking. It was almost as if he was protecting *her* now.

'Garry – ' she looked him straight in the eye – 'what's going on? And don't tell me Alexis sent you because I know different! You're not exactly his favourite person right now.'

She stopped stroking the donkey's neck, waiting for an answer.

'I can't tell you! I just need your co-operation.'

'Then I don't co-operate. I'm not a fool, I know something is going on,' she insisted. 'For God's sake, what is it? Is it Alexis?' Her heart flipped sickeningly.

'No! Don't worry about Alexis.'

'Then what is it?'

'What the hell, it's going to come out anyhow.' He guided her out of the stable into the feed room, making sure no one was about. 'I have orders to protect you.'

'From who?' She saw the look on his face. 'And don't lie to me Garry. It's got something to do with this drug thing hasn't it?'

He laughed. 'I knew you were a clever little thing. Yes it has, and even Alexis knows nothing about this.'

'Exactly which side are you on?'

Garry raised his brow. 'The good side. If not, you'd be dead by now, believe me.' He took his ID from his back pocket. 'It's authentic, I promise.'

Carrie nodded; her gut instinct was to trust him. 'So what happens now?'

'We just carry on as normal. I'm here merely as a precaution,' he said softly with a smile.

'But Alexis doesn't know?'

Garry looked at his watch. 'He will, in about one hour. James flew in last night and he'll be seeing Alexis this morning. My orders are to carry on as normal. I've just got to watch you, that's all.'

'Am I allowed to know *who* you suspect?'

He shrugged his large shoulders. 'Marsha is heavily involved.'

'What?' Carrie looked astounded. 'I just thought she was after Alexis, for other things.'

'We believe the reason she made a play for Alexis is because her present marriage is failing, and she needs money. Big money.'

Carrie sat on the old wooden seat, her mind mulling over his words. 'Who else? She must have an accomplice in all this?'

'She's does but we're not sure who yet. That's why James is over in Athens; we've heard that something is going down on board one of the Stephanides ships. We've been tracking the handling ship which is due in Piraeus tomorrow afternoon.'

'Have you NO idea?' Carrie got up to make him a coffee, 'I mean no idea at all?'

'I have my own personal ideas. I've done some digging but I'm just not sure. Whoever they are they've certainly covered their tracks well.'

Stirring the coffee, she handed him a cup. 'I'm afraid there is no Greek coffee left. I know how partial you are to it. Gets rid of all those pretend hangovers.'

Garry smiled. 'So you knew too, or did Maria tell you?'

'I knew, but you were quite convincing, honestly,' she confessed, then went on: 'Have you heard from Maria?'

'No.' He shook his head. The sadness in his green eyes was replaced quickly with a look of indifference. 'It was something that shouldn't have happened.' He put both hands around the cup as if he was cold, and yet it was just heating up outside in the sunlight. 'She's the only woman I've ever ignored my duty for. It's sacrilege what that woman made me do but I just had to have her.'

Where had she heard those words before? Was it a line with all men? Did they all think women were fools?

'So you don't love her?'

She'd obviously got close to a nerve because she saw him wince.

'No.'

Carrie almost choked on her coffee. 'Then may I ask why you crossed your fingers behind your back?'

'Lord, woman, but you're nosy.' He paced the room. 'Are you some super-sleuth or what? I told her that things just couldn't work out. I warned her of this.'

'Of what?'

'That we'd get too attached!'

'We?' asked Carrie softly, her grin of triumph lighting her face up.

He stared at her. 'OK, so I care for her.'

Carrie moved to put the empty coffee cup in the

sink. 'So tell me, you being a man, that is: why is it so hard for you to tell someone you love them?'

'I don't know.' He pushed a hand through his hair. 'But it's hard. And what's more she's so young, Carrie, and, and so damn rich!'

Carrie was shaking her head. 'She isn't rich. Alexis is rich, her mother is rich and her grandparents are rich too, but Maria is not rich. She's comfortably off with an allowance which is adequate for her lifestyle.'

'And she'll inherit a fortune one day!' For the first time a look of almost despair seemed to cross his face. He moved towards the door and looked out. 'The vet is here. If you don't mind I don't want to talk about Maria any more.'

She reached up and put a casual arm around his shoulder. 'If it's any consolation I'm in the same boat, only you have an added advantage.'

'What's that?'

'Maria loves you; she told me before she left for England.'

He looked at the floor, awkwardly answering, 'She told me too. It still doesn't change a thing. The whole thing is impossible. Now, if you don't mind I would rather leave the subject well alone!'

Alexis pressed the intercom. 'Yes! I thought I told you not to disturb me, Nina?'

'You did, sir, but I have a gentleman out here who says you'll see him any time of night or day.' Nina sounded vaguely annoyed herself. In the background

Alexis could hear a familiar American drawl. He frowned, something was wrong.

'I'm coming through,' muttered Alexis, striding through to the other office. 'James, what brings you here?'

'Alexis, my friend, we have movement. Is there anywhere we can talk privately?'

Alexis nodded. 'Nina, all my calls, unless they are urgent, give to Stephan. If Carrie calls tell her I'm out and I'll call her later. You know the number to get in touch with me?'

Nina nodded. 'Yes. I understand.'

'Good girl,' said Alexis, then using Carrie's phrase he said, 'Expect me when you see me.'

James was a smaller man than Alexis, smaller but powerfully built, fit looking, with dark brown hair and grey eyes. It was hard to guess his age, which was probably around the late-thirties. Alexis knew he was a good man and good at his job.

'I'm sorry I have to drop this on you, Alexis.'

They were walking towards the car. 'That's OK. You say that something is about to happen?'

'Yes. I've made progress. I've found out that your friend Marsha is definitely involved. She has been all along: she got into drugs when she was modelling. Not in a big way then, but she knew all the contacts. She knew a few of the high society pimps, they're all in it too. We're arresting most of them as soon as we have this side of the operation in the bag. I'm gonna need all your help here, Alexis.'

He nodded. 'It's yours. I just need to make sure that Carrie is safe.'

They got in the Mercedes. 'Don't worry, Alexis. I've got my best man looking after her this very minute. You know Tate. I put you onto him. He's my man.'

Alexis stared. 'You mean that son of a bitch who bedded my sister whilst he was working for me? The same one is looking after Carrie?' He shook his head. 'Oh no. That is simply not on. I want Carrie at the bakery with me.'

'It could be dangerous, Alexis. This is a very dangerous matter,' James soothed, 'And what do you mean Tate bedded your sister? He was on duty.'

'Oh yes, he was on duty all right. Both day and *night*! But I'm afraid he took it all too seriously.' It suddenly dawned on him what James had said. 'He's *your* man?'

James had the decency to look ashamed. 'I couldn't tell you. I couldn't risk blowing his cover. He's a good man in spite of this little hitch. When I phoned in that time I planted that little idea about Maria's safety into your head. I also gave you the solution.'

'So just who was he supposed to be watching?'

'We believe Marsha had a contact on your yacht.'

'What?'

'We've still to decide who that contact was.' James sat back as Alexis drove deftly through the busy streets of Athens. 'So exactly what did Tate do?'

Alexis grunted. 'He had an affair with my sister though I suppose she did ask for it. Carrie told me she chased him. I guess she was infatuated with all that bronze muscle.' He frowned. 'I still don't like the idea of him looking after Carrie. If he beds one woman he can bed them all.'

'He's not like that, man. Anyhow I thought you said Carrie was pregnant – she must love you,' he encouraged with a smile. 'Come on, the guy had the hots for your sister. He's not about to take your woman too.'

'I know he's not!' Alexis smiled cruelly. 'Do you know why? When we get to the bakery we're going to phone your man and tell him I'll break his neck if he hurts one hair on Carrie's head.'

James grinned. 'That's OK. I agree with you there.'

Tiny was revelling in the water, his legs treading rhythmically in the clear blue sea, sparkling in the heat of the afternoon sun. One more swim, Jonathan had said.

Carrie looked over to Garry: he'd never taken his eyes off her. He watched everyone in sight with suspicion, but that obvious fact didn't bother Carrie. What did bother her was Alexis. How did she know he was safe? Garry had forbidden her to go to Alexis. When she'd phoned the office Nina had said Alexis would ring her; he hadn't.

'Once more around the bay?' asked Andreas.

Jonathan nodded. 'Once more.'

'We can go home then,' she said to Garry. 'We can wait for Alexis at home.'

Garry nodded, not guessing Carrie's little plan. She wasn't sure it was the right thing to do, but what the hell, this was the most exciting time in her life. To have that woman, that blood-sucking Marsha out of her life, now *that* would be satisfying.

Carrie checked her pocket, the drachma was wrapped in cellophane to keep it dry, along with a note for Spiro, the boat man. She almost felt sorry for Garry, for if her plan worked, he would definitely be in trouble.

Tiny worked hard, his short legs thrusting down into the forty feet of water, his neck outstretched to keep the water from his nostrils.

Now – she would do it now – she had to. The powerboats were not far away, near enough for her to swim to.

'Jonathan, Tiny has got something wrapped around his feet. It's hampering him. I'll just slip in and see if I can release him,' said Carrie quite calmly, although inside she was a bundle of nerves.

Jonathan frowned. 'Be careful, watch his feet don't hit you.'

Garry was at the top end of the boat. His eyes widened as she swiftly dived and disappeared under the crystal blue surface of what seemed like a beautiful mill pond. Several seconds slipped by.

'Damn! Where the hell is she?' exclaimed Garry, expecting her to come up at the side of Tiny. The little donkey swam on.

Andreas laughed, waving Garry down. 'She does

this all the time. It is her joke,' he said in broken English. 'Carrie is an excellent swimmer.'

'Carrie sometimes gets cramp!' bellowed Garry, feeling suddenly sick.

Jonathan looked over the side. 'I can't see her. For God's sake, someone go in after her. She's pregnant.'

Garry did, going down as far as he dare. He couldn't think, he just couldn't imagine, if anything went wrong . . . Surfacing to the offside of the boat, he heard Andreas, heard his laughter and looked in the direction he was pointing.

'Witch!' He struck out towards the powerboats, leaving Andreas and Jonathan in a daze, his thoughts on exactly what he was going to do to her once he caught up!

'Lord, this is so relaxing.' James was looking out onto the small harbour – the tranquillity of this place was amazing. 'No wonder you don't tell anyone where this joint is. Peaceful, it's so darn peaceful.'

Alexis smiled. He hunched his shoulders then stretched and relaxed, but it was hard. 'Maybe we should call them again. I'm getting worried. Even if she took the donkey swimming she should be back by now.'

'The donkey swimming?'

Alexis nodded. 'Yes, but don't ask. I wouldn't know where to start . . .'

Just then the door flew open, and Carrie rudely interrupted their conversation. 'Maybe I would!

Firstly, however, I think you should start by telling me what the hell is going on!' Icy blue eyes stared at Alexis and then James. Her hair was tangled from the wind, her cheeks flushed, her lips compressed. She looked wild!

James took a step back, stunned by Carrie's dramatic entrance. Her eyes were boring holes into him. By God, he could see why Alexis wanted to keep this one to himself.

Garry rushed in breathlessly only one minute behind.

'Nice you could join me,' she cooed sarcastically, 'You should never underestimate the powers of a woman when you tell her lies. Now, can we all sit down and find out what's going on?'

'I tried to keep her away, James, but she gave me the slip. She said she was going over the side into the sea to help the donkey, and then she was gone. I thought she'd drowned, got cramps or something.' He laughed harshly, 'Hell, was I fooled! She came to the surface near to where they hire the powerboats. I chased her, I did, boss. But the lady got away.' He moved forward to reach her but James indicated he should back off. Silently Garry wished he could break her pretty little neck, or at the very least shake her senseless.

'Come on, Garry, give me a break. I swam what? A few feet under water?'

He shook his head. 'Let's put it this way, lady, in your condition you shouldn't be holding your breath that long.'

Alexis stared at her. He wanted to shake her for being so reckless, and with the next breath he wanted to crush her to him because she'd beaten the man at his own game, and Garry was a professional.

James offered Carrie a seat on one of the two sofas.

'At least we have one gentleman present. Thank you. Maybe you can enlighten me as to what our next plan of action is.'

All three men stared. 'Our?' they said in unison.

'I see we're in agreement. Tell me everything, please,' she added. 'Then I'll tell you what I know. It came to me on my way here. You were right Alexis, teaching me how to steer that powerboat came in handy. I don't know who'll take it back, but I did explain to Spiro via a note.' She smiled smugly. 'I just followed the hydrofoil if you're wondering how I got here.'

Alexis felt as if he'd been hit over the head with a hammer. 'Carrie, I want you out of here now. I want you back at the villa where you are safe.'

'What? So looney Marsha can take a pot-shot at me! We all know that shark business was no mistake, and we all know she'll stop at nothing to get me out of her way. Oh no, Alexis, I stay here! This is not about what you want any more!'

It was Garry who answered, the atmosphere between these two people so combustible that even he was afraid to get caught in the crossfire. 'At least she's safe here. I made sure nobody followed me. She's safe here all right.'

James nodded. 'Well until we get our call, I suggest we eat. Do you cook, Carrie?'

'No. The kitchen isn't quite finished yet, and besides I don't feel like cooking for a tribe who try and keep me out of things. There is a nice taverna down the road where we could all go, where we'd be quite safe, If not, we can send out. Garry can wait by the harbour wall for the food to arrive. Junior and I are hungry.' She stretched out, patting the obvious little lump.

'Carrie,' warned Alexis, but in spite of himself he wanted to laugh.

'Maybe you'll tell us what you know?' interrupted James as he sat down by her side.

She shrugged, ignoring Alexis. 'It may be nothing at all. On the night I danced at the taverna, I came back to the yacht early, for reasons I won't go into.'

'We had an argument,' supplied Alexis in a droll voice, suddenly seeing her in a new light. Miss Marple eat your heart out! he thought with great interest.

'Oh yeah. I remember,' said Garry.

'Well, I couldn't get to sleep at first and I heard voices. I knew one was Marsha's and I couldn't identify the other voice at first, not at all.' Alexis was looking intrigued now. 'A week later when Alexis had gone to America, we had the fishing party on board the yacht. You remember Garry?' She put a hand to her windswept hair. 'I heard the same voice again, it was just outside my cabin. So I checked. It was Captain Savidis.'

'Captain Savidis, you say?' asked Garry with obvious interest. He pondered a while.

'Yes,' confirmed Carrie as she watched Alexis.

'Oh that's impossible!' Alexis argued. He was strongly in favour of the captain's innocence. He moved to stand up, stock still on the central rug, his powerful body hidden beneath the expert cut of the tailored grey suit. 'The man's worked for me for five years now.'

'And then,' she said softly, not perturbed at all by Alexis's interruption, 'I found him in my cabin. Didn't I, Garry?' She looked at Garry to corroborate her story. He nodded.

'What the hell was he doing in your cabin?' growled Alexis, trying hard to keep the green-eyed devil under control.

'That's what I asked. He told me some cock and bull story about the porthole window needing repairs.' Carrie smiled proudly. 'When he'd left I checked the window, it's fine. I think he's your man.'

'Cock and bull story?' enquired James with a laugh.

Carrie scowled at him with disdain; he was mocking her. 'This is a serious business, if you did but know it.'

'Precisely, which is why you are out of here in the morning,' interrupted Alexis softly. Now he was serious. 'I've had enough of Miss Marple for one day, Carrie.'

Carrie sighed, 'Alexis, I can help.'

'I said enough.'

It wasn't the words, nor the tone of his voice, it was the look in his eye. He meant every word. Sadly, she nodded. Her love for him wouldn't allow her to let others think he was weak, because he wasn't. He was the only man who could handle her because she loved him.

'I'll put the kettle on,' she said without further ado, then added, 'We can make coffee, but the kitchen is being replaced so we can't cook yet. And I can't make Greek coffee, Garry, so it'll have to be instant. Sorry.'

Alexis let out a breath as she left to go into the kitchen. He frowned; her clothes still looked damp. He sighed heavily. He was so mixed up. He couldn't even think straight. Her actions had been precisely what he expected, and yet why had she come here, after this morning's argument?

'Some lady, Alexis. I like her very much,' commented James with a rueful smile.

Alexis smiled. 'So do I. So do I, my friend.'

As Carrie prepared the coffee she didn't bother to turn around; she knew Alexis was standing in the doorway. 'What do you want?'

He raised an eyebrow at her tone. So she *was* still angry from this morning. He could cope.

'I think you should leave the coffee to me, and you should go and change; you'll feel better once you've changed. Your clothes are still damp. Neither you nor the baby need a chill,' he remarked considerately.

'It was red-hot out there, I'll be fine.'

'I still think you should . . .'

Carrie turned on him, her blood boiling, her pain obvious. 'Don't you dare tell me what I should do!

You don't care, if you remember rightly. Anyone could have given me this child for all you care, so what does it matter if I get a cold? For all you care I could have had sex with any Tom, Dick or, or . . .' She grabbed a breath of air, anger stopping her vicious attack.

'Carrie, I was angry. I shouldn't have said those things, but you do infuriate me with this taunting. You hurt me, simply by telling me how attractive Garry is.'

'And you hurt me!' Holding her head high, she left the room, finding momentary solace and peace up in their bedroom.

'Carrie, are you awake?' Alexis called from the door. When there was no reply he went into their bedroom. He loved the soft colours she'd decorated it with, the pine furniture, the cream throw, he loved it all.

She was sitting by the window, her bare feet on the cool tiled floor. She did not acknowledge him.

'I've brought you coffee.' He moved further into the room. 'Carrie, let's talk.'

Carrie shook her head. 'I can't at the moment. I just want you to leave me alone. Please, Alexis.'

She couldn't explain how she felt, it was impossible. Part of her wanted to run to him, the part that usually gave in when he smiled at her, the part that usually surrendered. But today had changed things; his words had hurt her deeply.

She could almost see him recoil inside his shell at her words. Well, it would make a change for him to be rejected. This whole damn affair seemed to be futile now. There seemed to be no future for them together.

He was at her shoulder, not touching her but near enough for her senses to pick up the unique vibrations which always passed between them, 'I don't want to leave you alone. I was wrong this morning. I was hurt and I struck out at you, and Theo is always the perfect bait. I went too far. I'm sorry.'

Don't do this to me, her heart cried, please don't say you're sorry. You hardly ever say you're sorry. I need to stay angry with you.

He touched her shoulder. 'Come to bed. Let me hold you.' She shrugged away from his touch. 'For heaven's sake, Carrie, I only want to hold you.'

Tears dropped one by one down her face. Dragging in her breath, she shook her head. 'Please just leave me alone. I need time to think.'

Reluctantly, he left the room, muttering something to James about needing a walk. Much later, when everything was quiet and the only sound was the nightlife, insects and mosquitos, the boats bobbing on the gentle sway of the water as it lapped the edges of the wall, he returned from his walk.

Now was not the right time. He needed time to really talk to her, really sit down at length and make her understand. Their future needed sorting out. He didn't want to keep her within a marriage that was bound to fail. He loved her too much for that. He smiled as he opened the back door; now he knew what love was. He knew he'd been in love with idea of loving Carrie for years, but reality was far different from his daydreams, and in truth, he'd been scared when she'd accepted that stupid deal of Petros's. So why had he gone along with it?

Love didn't mean getting together because of a child, it meant sharing life with someone you wanted to be with, someone who cared, someone who felt the same about the fundamental things. Tonight she'd been so near and yet so far. He'd wanted to hug her to him, but he wasn't sure she felt the same. Could he salvage the love she had for him? He wasn't sure, and he hated this vulnerable feeling.

If she loved him would she forgive him?

He heard a cough from the other doorway and saw James smiling at him, but there was a look of concern there too. 'The meal was wonderful, thanks. Pity you and Carrie didn't share it with us.'

He threw his hands up in a helpless gesture. 'I couldn't eat.' Sadness passed through his soul like a slow moving cloud. 'I said things yesterday to her that I didn't mean. I was angry.' He looked James in the eye. 'That's no excuse though. I hurt her, James, I hurt the woman I love.'

James grabbed him by the elbow, steering him into the lounge. 'Sit there while I get you a brandy.'

He managed a small smile. 'Drowning my sorrows won't help any.'

James passed him a glass. 'This is medicinal. Drink it!' He sat opposite him, relaxing back in the comfortable sofa. 'If you need to talk, I'm here. I don't sleep before a showdown, I can't.'

'James, I'm afraid I've blown it with her.' Slowly, Alexis related the whole story of Carrie and himself.

James sat back in the cushions; he'd known this man a while. They'd been through dangers in the past few years that lesser men would have shied away from. So he knew the glisten of tears in Alexis's eyes was for real.

'That sweet honeypie lying in your bed didn't fob my man off for nothing. She loves you, and if you can't see that, you're a bigger fool than I thought,' he pronounced to a guilty Alexis. 'And what's more, you grab her with both hands, my man, and don't let her run away because that sweet thing is worth all your millions. Believe me, take it from a man who's lost his love.'

Carrie woke up with a start. As soon as she realized where she was, she began to hurt. Unrequited love had a pain all of its own. The sickness that came was not from her growing baby but from the knowledge that Alexis really didn't care whether he'd fathered their child or not. That meant he didn't care for her!

Pulling on a clean T-shirt and shorts she brushed her hair and tied it back, dragging it back off her gaunt and worried face. Sure, he'd tried to say he was sorry yesterday, but there hadn't been a trace of regret in his voice, not even an atom.

Slipping her feet into soft white pumps, she looked at herself, really looked. All her life she'd been pushed into things. Had she been strong enough to stand against Petros she would have gone to university, not for dance as her mother had, but for business studies or animal husbandry, something she was really interested in. Her mother had often told her how her grandfather had been animal mad. Carrie believed she took after him. Strong? Huh, she didn't feel strong, she felt tired of all the pretence. She was going to live life truthfully, no matter what the cost.

The knock at the door made her jump. She watched through the mirror as Alexis moved into the room. He looked shocking, the stubble around his chin was dark, his eyes looked almost lifeless.

'I'm taking a shower. James has my personnel files on the computer he wants to show you something about Captain Savidis. I think you could be right,' he said, moving over to her.

She flinched as he put his hands on her shoulder, and as soon as she flinched he dropped his hands.

'Thanks. I'll go and see him,' she muttered, her voice husky with emotion. He blocked her exit as she made her way to the door.

'When this is all over, we need to talk,' he reiterated. As their eyes met, Carrie winced; she'd never seen a look like this in his eyes. Not in all the time she'd known him.

She nodded, her reply just as sad. 'I know.'

James was leaning over the computer, his eyes scanning the screen with great concentration. 'Hi sweetie. Had a good sleep?'

Carrie smiled. She'd been rather rude yesterday evening, leaving the men to their own devices.

'I'm better than I was. I'm sorry we couldn't have met under different circumstances; it's been hard for me.' In the past twenty-four hours her life had been turned upside-down. Automatically she sat next to him at the computer.

'If it's any consolation, Alexis is hurting too,' said James without compunction. Someone had to say it. The man was too proud to say it himself.

Carrie nodded. 'I know. We'll sort something out.'

'He cares for you,' he said suddenly, as the screen switched to show data on Captain Savidis.

'I know that too,' she confirmed with a finality that told him she wasn't prepared to talk about it now.

He coughed, clearing his throat. 'Right, you look at this. Captain Savidis has worked for Alexis for five years now. Before that he worked for a shipping line, called Sealings, now defunct. Before that he . . .'

Sealings? That was the company the paid cash into Petros's accounts. Could Petros have been involved? Panic surged through her when she realized James was talking to her again. She must concentrate.

'Sorry, James,' she apologized. 'Who owned Sealings?'

He shook his head. 'We're not sure yet. We're going to look into it. But our friendly Captain also worked for your godfather before he went to Sealings.'

'Surely that doesn't mean . . . You don't think that Petros is involved?'

'We're not sure yet.

'That's impossible! He's a lovely man he – why he – '

Carrie sat and thought about Petros, about all the wonderful things he'd done for her. So what if she had gone into university for the wrong reasons? That was her fault; he'd not exactly forced her. It was her guilt that had sent her running to London.

'Here, have a coffee.' James looked worriedly across at her. 'Are you OK? Look; this is all circumstantial, evidence about Petros. We're not sure he is involved, only that he may be.'

He's not! I know he's not!'

'Carrie,' Alexis's concerned voice came across the room. He was standing at the bottom of the stairs, looking fresher than he had minutes ago. 'Don't worry about it now. There is no evidence. He's just a link, that's all, and may not be the missing one.'

Alexis moved over to her and this time she didn't flinch when he took her shoulders. Not at all. She moved into the caress. She owed him the truth. He was trying to stop this drug racket. 'What if he is though? What if?'

He didn't get the time to answer. Garry barged through the front door. 'We're on. This afternoon.' He looked at Alexis. 'Where should your yacht be?'

Alexis shrugged. 'I charter it out sometimes. Senator Walker has it.'

James looked up in recognition of the name. 'Who?'

'I'll confirm. I'm sure it was Senator Walker.' He picked up the phone. 'Stephan, who has my yacht and what is its destination?' He nodded. 'I thought as much. Thanks.'

'Who, Alexis?' asked James, his mind working well into overdrive.

'Senator Walker.' Alexis put the receiver down. 'He should be on his way to Santorini.'

'He's not!' confirmed Garry. 'He's anchored off the coast two miles away from Piraeus. Coastguard confirmed it for me. And another yacht is anchored close by, *The Pearl of Aphrodite*.'

'That's Theo's yacht!' cried Carrie.

'It would seem the exchange will take place this afternoon,' Garry said. 'I'm just waiting for confirmation.'

Just then the phone rang. It was for James.

'Did you get the information about Sealings Shipping Line?' asked James as he momentarily put his call on hold

'Yes.' He threw a glance at Carrie, 'It was owned by Petros. We're checking it out.'

'Petros! Oh thank God.' Carrie sank back on the chair as all eyes turned to her.

'Carrie?' questioned Alexis with a frown.

She looked like a guilty child caught stealing sweets. Should she tell them? A shudder ran the full length of her body, but she had to tell them, so with a sigh she began. 'Petros had a large amount of money paid into his accounts about five years ago. I thought, at first when you mentioned Sealings, that maybe he was involved. But if you say the company ceased to exist then maybe *he* transferred the money across himself.'

'Well actually it didn't cease,' said Garry swiftly. 'It was sold on, then the name changed and the shipping fleet was disbanded for a time.'

Alexis jumped in before anyone else could. 'So who was it sold to?'

Garry raised a brow, looked at James for confirmation and received the nod. He looked awkward for a moment before he answered, 'Your mother!'

CHAPTER 17

'My mother? Are you sure?'

'Yes. What we are not so sure about is why it now belongs to Theo Aristotelous, when no payments have been made into your mother's accounts.' Garry cringed on the inside; he could see that Alexis's temper was ready to blow.

Just then James put the receiver down and shook his head.

'You've checked my mother's accounts?' Fury welled up inside him, but he tried to keep his anger under control.

'With her blessing, Alexis. It is all with her blessing. She's being very helpful,' explained James. 'I couldn't tell you about the leads immediately because I had to check out Carrie here too. Everyone has been checked.'

Carrie lifted her head swiftly to attack but Alexis caught her before she lashed out. 'Of all the nerve!'

'Carrie,' Alexis had calmed as quickly as he had become angry.' James has his reasons.'

He turned to James. 'My mother and Petros, have they been vindicated of all this?'

James nodded. 'More or less. There are a few things that need sorting out but I believe they are both completely innocent of any involvement. I think you should ask your mother about why the fleet now belongs to Theo though. It may help you both out.'

'What are you hinting at, James?' Alexis asked, the dark frown covering his brow deep and harrowed.

'Ask your mother. I think before you two plan playing any more games of cops and robbers you should know Petros is ill.' James winced as Carrie looked up, her eyes wide with shock. He continued gently, 'When Petros heard the news I'm afraid he had a heart attack. A *mild one*, Carrie.' He touched Carrie's arm. 'He'll be OK.' He turned to Alexis. 'By the way, that was your mother on the phone, Alexis. She just wanted me to pass the message on. She says she'll talk to you both when you arrive at the clinic but needs your jet ready to leave this afternoon. They're flying him to New York for an operation.' James moved around the desk. 'Move it, Alexis, this is no time to stand around. Don't worry about this mess, I'll let you know the outcome. We've almost got it in the bag.'

Carrie looked up at Alexis. In a daze she walked into the kitchen. Petros had had a heart attack. Numbly she let him usher her through the back door to his car, where Garry had taken the driver's seat.

* * *

When Alexis and Carrie arrived at the clinic, Helena was nowhere to be seen. Petros explained weakly that she was with the doctors, finalizing details for the flight.

As Petros looked across at Carrie pain grew within him. He'd done more to hurt her than he'd ever thought possible. All he had wanted was to ensure her future happiness.

'Carrie, my child,' he began tears rolling down his face. He knew it could be the last time he held her in his arms, the last time he kissed her beautiful face. She'd been his daughter in more ways than he deserved. She would have married Alexis for no other reason than to save his business, that's how much she loved him.

'Petros, don't cry. I'll come with you to America,' she said lovingly.

Petros shook his head. 'No, Carrie, my lovely, lovely girl, you mustn't. I don't deserve having you for a god-daughter. I just don't deserve it. And it's all my fault. My fault.'

'Petros what are you saying?'

'I'm saying I let you down.' His thin voice was tearful, full of emotion. He looked across at Alexis. 'I'm sorry, Alexis, I let you down too.'

'What are you talking about, you old fool?' he said. But his voice was gentle.

'You must know the truth, both of you.' He looked to the ceiling, holding Carrie's hand. 'When I officially had you in my care, I promised Theo he could have your hand in marriage. I promised him, because I owed him money from way back!' He met her outraged look. 'You were such a handful, Carrie, and he – he was a little younger then.'

Carrie's chest was heaving. 'You promised Theo he could marry me?'

Alexis turned to look out of the window, into the garden of the clinic, to gaze at the flowers, if only to stop himself from screaming at Petros. Petros had never mentioned any of this!

Petros nodded. 'If you remember I sent you to university very quickly, in spite of your tantrums. I got you on the dancing course – anything would have done, anything to get you away from the island.' Tears still ran down his cheeks. 'I had to stop him . . .'

'No Petros, you don't have to go on.'

He nodded. 'I do. I want you to know what an utter fool I've been.' He coughed, accepting help to sit up. 'There was no way out. Five years ago he called that debt in. He wanted me to arrange your marriage, he's always had a thing about you.'

Carrie grimaced; she felt ill, and completely alone, and utterly used.

'Go on.'

'I refused him. Point-blank. I refused your hand in marriage. I realized what an old fool I was and I decided to declare bankruptcy first rather than see you unhappy.' He looked at her again. 'Then someone came up with the perfect solution.'

'Don't tell me – my mother!' said Alexis without moving.

'Yes. Your mother said she would buy one of my companies, the one he wanted, which would then leave me the one shipping line, and of course she would pay him off.'

Alexis turned around. 'My mother doesn't do anything for nothing. What was her price?'

Petros couldn't think straight. It was all too much of a mess. 'What do you mean?'

'I mean what does she get back in return?'

'That I go along with her plan. It is she who wants to see her grandchild, and she who wants to see you married.'

Alexis could have been breathing fire as he demanded, 'Where is she?'

'Two doors along on the right. She's expecting you, Alexis. Go gently with her, she loves you very much.' He reached forward as Alexis was about to leave the room. 'If I don't make it through this operation, you promise you'll marry Carrie. Promise me you'll take care of her.'

'Tell him,' Alexis said to Carrie. 'You tell him.'

Carrie looked across at Petros with tears in her eyes. Although he'd used her like a pawn, she loved him. He'd obviously thought she needed his help in finding a husband.

Squeezing his hand she said with a smile, 'Alexis and I were married over ten weeks ago, in London. It was what we wanted.'

'I don't just walk away from that kind of commitment Petros.' Alexis's words had a ring of truth about them. Carrie turned to look at him, questions rushing about in her head, but they would have to wait.

'Ha! You two have had the last laugh. Ha, that'll teach your mother!' he scoffed, all at once looking sleepy. He waved Alexis away with his hand. 'Go and see Helena, and don't be too hard, she's suffering too.' He held onto Carrie's hand. 'Forgive me.'

'Of course I forgive. I love you, don't I? I just wish you could have told me about all this. Trying to run other people's lives, Petros, is a foolish thing. Interfering with destiny is wrong.'

Helena was standing facing the gardens when she heard Alexis behind her. Deep red flowers adorned the bushes against a backdrop of well watered lawns with carved seats to sit on. It was a very nice clinic, and one she had made donations to many times.

'So, you know all about it?' She turned, her eyes hidden by the dark glasses, her concerns expertly disguised by her nonchalant expression.

At first Alexis couldn't speak, his chest was so tight with rage. How dare she try to run his life for him? How dare she?

When eventually he found his voice it held a dark and sinister note. He would not be held to ransom by his mother. 'I know you've manipulated both Carrie and me, even Petros. I should imagine Theo was running scared too when you'd finished with him. What exactly did you *pay* for Carrie? Because that's what you effectively did, you *bought* her for me.'

'Alexis, it wasn't like that. It wasn't, I promise. I merely paid a debt off for Petros. It really wasn't like that.'

'No?' he snorted angrily. 'Are you saying you didn't manipulate us?'

'Of course I didn't. I just gave destiny a helping hand, that's all,' she said softly, raising the white lace handkerchief to her eyes. For once her tears were real; her guilt was a heavy burden, but she had a right to this last wish before . . . Oh God, was it really going to happen?

'Destiny, my foot! And tears won't help you get out of this.' He paced aggressively round the room. 'I won't have this interference. I just won't have you telling me what I should be doing with my life. Do you realize you've successfully taken the choice away from us? And as to whether Carrie and I should have been together at all is a question I often ask myself. For all you know we could be hating each other for the rest of our lives.'

'Are you saying that you and Carrie are not made for each other, my son?' She raised one dark perfectly shaped brow in horror.

'Yes, I suppose I am! Carrie is having a baby. I would not have had it happen this way. Not at all!' He paused for a while, then turned to look at the door which was ajar. He thought he'd heard someone running down the corridor.

'Which way *would* you have had it?'

'Oh no! You first, *Mama*. I want to know *why*?' He moved towards the window, almost standing next to her, his big body overwhelming even while he was so still.

'I'd have thought that was obvious, my son. All the men your age have families, someone to hand their fortunes to. You need an heir, you need a child, and only one woman is good enough for you!'

'That woman being Carrie?'

'Yes. She has the most beautiful blue eyes I've ever seen. I hope my grandchild has blue eyes like that,' she said, sitting down at the desk in the centre of the room.

'No go, *Mama*. I know there is a reason other than her beautiful blue eyes and believe me if I have to shake it out of you I will!'

'Then shake it out of me,' she dared, disregarding the folly of her matchmaking. 'And just for your information she *was* very expensive. You only have the best, that's what you deserve, the best. You're a good man.'

'*Mama*,' he warned darkly.

Helena looked at her son. If only he knew what she'd gone through these last few years. OK, so she was being selfish, but she wanted him to marry the love of his life and she wasn't blind to the way he looked at the girl.

She also wanted to be able to see her son's child, to look into his or her eyes. And if it took helping Cupid or destiny along the road, then so be it. Proudly, she told him her reasons.

Still standing at the window, his mind racked with his own guilt, Alexis saw his wife running out of the clinic grounds. She was distressed, hurting, panicking, he could see that.

Helena looked at him. 'Oh my God! Is it Petros?' They both rushed into his room.

'Petros my love,' cried Helena, for he was crying.

'What have you said?' Petros attacked Alexis. 'She heard you. What on earth have you said?'

Alexis turned on his heel shouting, 'The jet is ready. Good luck, Petros. I have to go and save my marriage.'

'Marriage? What on earth is he talking about?' he heard his mother say to Petros. He ran then as fast as his feet would carry him after his wife.

In a state that could only be described as a hypnotic trance Carrie managed to reach the park seat. She was breathless, agitated, and heartbroken. Quickly she looked around her and realized she was in the National Gardens.

Words were swimming about in her head. '*Are you saying that you and Carrie are not made for each other, my son*?' Then Alexis: '*Carrie is having a baby. I would not have had it happen this way*.'

This was the reason he had wanted to talk to her. Obviously he couldn't face marriage to her a moment longer. Another voice in her head told her that he did care, but that wasn't enough now, not by a long shot.

Oh God, why couldn't the earth swallow her up? Why did she have to feel this way? The bottom had fallen out of her world, just as, foolishly she'd begun to believe in that world.

Getting up, she wondered around again, aimlessly mulling over what had happened in the past day, the words that were a haunting reminder he didn't love her.

She went through the Plaka, aimlessly wandering. Had she got his words wrong? Petros said Alexis was besotted with her but she was sure now he wasn't!

She roamed around the town under the hot afternoon sun, oblivious to anything but her thoughts. Eventually she spotted something she wanted, a Grecian urn for the window. She bought many things, all in a daze. Paying for this, paying for that, it was all done on automatic pilot. She was numb, her heart was dying from the grief. Just when she had believed he could be falling in love with her, she found she had lost it all.

A dry sob caught in her throat as she gathered her handkerchief from her bag. Tears swamped her eyes. It was his handkerchief, the one he'd given her in his office not so long ago. Everything was a constant reminder of how much she really loved him.

Walking towards the harbour minutes later, Carrie sat outside one of the tavernas. She could hear the clinking of the boats as they rocked about. The wind was getting up, the boats moving restlessly against each other, unsettled on the water. She waited for the cup of tea she'd ordered, not knowing how long she'd been there.

How would she cope without him? She knew now that she could settle for nothing less than his eternal love. How had her life started and ended within the space of a few months? The thought worried her, but she didn't want to think at this moment. All she wanted to do was sit and not be noticed by the passers-by, all in blissful ignorance of her pain.

'*Thespinnis*, are you OK?' asked the waiter, obviously concerned.

Carrie forced herself to smile and reassure the small man. 'Thank you, I'm fine. I must get a taxi, can you help me?'

The waiter nodded. When the taxi arrived she did not go to Alexis's office, nor to the bakery; she needed to think some more, needed the space. She needed the islands, the peace and tranquillity of the place she'd always called home, *her* Greece.

Once he'd left the clinic, Alexis had followed the taxi she'd caught but then he'd lost her in the crowds of Athens, just below the Parthenon. He searched for hours, eventually making his way back to the bakery.

Opening the door, the silence that met him was a lonely one. Darkness had descended on the city, and now all he could do was wait. He'd phoned the villa and the office but no one had seen her.

He sat on one of the two sofas and looked around at the work she'd done. How could he have ever thought there was no such thing as love? Holding his head in his hands he almost cried for only the second time in his adult life.

What a fool he'd been! Why hadn't he just said he loved her. He knew she must have only heard half of his conversation with his mother at the clinic. She wouldn't have run away if she'd heard all of it.

On hearing the back door open, Alexis looked up. Disappointment must have been evident on his face as James and Garry walked in.

'Alexis?' said James. 'What is it? You have nothing to be glum about, do you? Is Petros OK?'

'Petros is fine. It's Carrie – she is missing.' He stood up and began pacing the large room. He moved the blinds so that he could see the harbour. 'She overheard a conversation with my mother, or at least half a conversation. Now she must finally believe I don't love her.'

'And do you?' The deep tones in Garry's voice held suspicion.

Alexis glared at him. 'Yes. Unlike you I stick by my woman.'

'Oh give me a break, man. Your sister instigated the affair – and just for the record, my terminating the relationship was mainly because of my job. Not because I didn't care.'

'Hey, you two. Let's get this conversation back to Carrie. When did you last see her?' asked James, holding Garry by the shoulder and pulling him slightly away from Alexis.

Alexis looked ready to hit out at anything in his path, including his colleague.

'Outside the Parthenon. I lost her in the crowds.' He pushed a hand through his dark hair. 'I've lost her, James.'

James shook his head. 'Don't give me that rubbish, Alexis. Let's get out there and look for her. Do you have a photo of her?'

Alexis grabbed his wallet. 'This photo is no good, she was only sixteen when I took it, but I can get hold of one.'

'No time. I'll radio the men. We can all search for her.' James looked at Garry. 'So can you, Tate, or should I call you Garry?'

The big built American smiled stiffly at his partner's sense of humour. He hated the name Garry. 'I'll help, she's a nice kid, certainly beat me at my own game.'

Their search of Athens was extensive. Alexis had recruited several Greek police officers, and one holidaying police officer from Britain, who was a friend of Garry's.

They all met outside the bakery to be briefed as to the last time Carrie been seen. They tracked her down to the taverna just up the harbour where the waiter told them about her taxi.

'She was not very well, I think,' said the waiter to James.

'Alexis. Over here. She got in a taxi, he believes it was to the harbour front where they hire the boats. He said she looked shocking, and very tired.'

Alexis was at the end of his tether, tormenting himself with guilt. 'If anything has happened to her . . .'

'Come on, she's a sensible girl. I know she'll be all right,' commented James without a frown. Inside he wasn't feeling quite that confident. He wondered why she had gone to the harbour front.

Garry came running up, a strange sadness engulfing him as he looked at Alexis. The hard-headed Greek wasn't his favourite man, but he still didn't wish to hurt him. How did he say this?

'The coastguard – they've just picked a woman out of the water; she's dead. I just heard it over the radio. She has no ID, Alexis, and the police think it could be Carrie. They think she might have drowned' He met the Greek's look and winced: this man looked completely broken.

Alexis bit his bottom lip with strong white teeth. 'It can't be Carrie, she's a good swimmer.' He looked at the rolling sea, at the waves tripping furiously over each other. The best swimmers could die in this, a summer storm, but he refused to believe the sea had taken her life. Her father had called her child of the sea for a damn good reason.

In a mute silence the three men walked solemnly over to the harbour wall where the body of a woman lay covered by a white sheet, lifting slightly in the wind. Passers-by were staring as if at a peep show, until officers pushed them back.

Alexis felt sick. 'I can't do it.' He looked at James, his sadness reaching out to his friend.

James put his arm around Alexis, his sigh one of great relief. 'If Carrie is a heroin addict with dark hair and not pregnant, she may be under that sheet. If not . . .' James pulled the sheet back. He nodded, he'd suspected as much when he'd seen the needle marks on the soles of the woman's feet, revealed when the sheet had lifted in the wind. 'I knew it wasn't Carrie.'

Alexis's relief was so real he wanted to smile until he looked at the woman lying dead. His heart went out to her; no one deserved such an end.

'Sir,' interrupted an officer, 'We've just found out that a lady who fits the description perfectly has hired a boat.'

'Which boat – was it a yacht?' asked Alexis his hopes a little higher.

The officer looked down at his notebook, 'The *Adonia*. She took it out some time ago. Paid for a week's sailing,' He pointed to the sea. 'Went in that direction.'

'That's her, it has to be. We took that yacht for a memorable sail,' he explained to James. Looking around, he asked, 'Can we hire a powerboat?' The sea was getting wild. His only hope was that she could handle the *Adonia*. Deep inside his heart he knew she was a good sailor. She'd sailed with her father and Petros many times.

The *Adonia* was teetering about in the slight roll of the waves whilst tied to the private jetty just out of the harbour at Alonnissos. It was a refuge that would give Carrie the solitude she craved, and still remind her of the few precious days she had shared with Alexis.

The wind had gathered in momentum and was blowing gently around the island, its effect cooling the heat of the afternoon sun. She had had a bracing sail this morning, though it had not been as bad as the day she left harbour in search of the dolphins. She sighed; she didn't want to face the truth that she was running away from Alexis. But this was where she needed to be, the place where Alexis had really been himself. The paradise where he had truly shown that he cared.

Precariously she stepped onto the gently swaying deck, the motion knocking her off balance momentarily. The last time that had happened Alexis had caught her in his arms, and had almost kissed the life from her body, while he ignited the fire in her soul. Looking out across the harbour she smiled, her thoughts happy until she went below to put her meagre shopping away.

Placing the fresh cherries she'd bought in a bowl on the draining board she pulled a bunch off. Fruit had been the only thing she could eat, and that was for the child growing inside her. Carefully she sat on the dining seat, the small bump in front of her already hampering her movement in confined spaces. She touched the yacht's wall with loving fingers. This was where she'd conceived, not that it mattered. It would seem that only she cared about this child. She rubbed her hands over the small bump affectionately. Boy or girl, it wouldn't matter to her.

Funny she thought, once she had realized she was pregnant, she'd suddenly developed all the symptoms. Sickness had come from almost day one, together with tiredness, lethargy, a weakness that suddenly washed over her. That feeling came again now; she needed to lie down if only for a minute or two.

It was dark when she opened her eyes. She struggled to sit up on the bunk, though she felt a little better now. Tiredness had crept up on her so quickly she knew she had had to rest or she would have fainted like she had in Alexis's office weeks ago.

Her brain acknowledged that she wanted a drink. She could hear the Greek music coming from the tavernas nearby, but she couldn't face people yet. It was then she heard someone walk along the gang plank. Whoever it was had a determined step and one that was very familiar. She looked up knowing exactly who she would find standing there.

'What the hell do you think you've been doing?' came the scathing question from the doorway. The low angry voice forbade any form of protest from her dry, thirsty lips. Alexis was in a blind fury; he'd obviously just arrived from Athens!

He stepped forward, towering over her, his angry stance full of silent rage. Each sinewy muscle was taut under the olive shirt and trousers. He stood with his legs slightly apart, looking every bit the angry male predator, but suddenly she didn't care. She was still too numb, and it was all his fault.

She sat silently on the bunk bed, full of pain. Just at the sight of him her heart was breaking. Even in anger he was a sight her hungry eyes longed for.

'I asked a question!'

Of course! It came to her now. She should be obeying, succumbing to him, being subservient. Running a hand through her damp, lifeless hair she looked at Alexis and shrugged her shoulders.

'I'm sorry. I . . .' She stumbled over her words.

'Sorry is no good! Get yourself up, we are going back to Athens.'

Carrie looked up into his tight, strained face. 'Oh please Alexis, I can't. I can't do this any more,' she pleaded, searching his face for some hint of compassion, but it was empty, devoid of emotion.

'You can and you will!' He pulled her swiftly to her feet. 'How could you be so thoughtless, Carrie? Petros and my mother are old, too old to be worrying their heads about you! What on earth were you thinking about?'

Tears stung her eyes. There was nothing said about *his* concern: obviously there had been none. 'I'm sorry, I lost track of time. I needed to think.' She sank down onto the bunk again. 'I'm so confused.'

'Crying will do no good. We've had the whole police force looking for you, do you realize? The whole of *Athens* has been out searching for you! Now let's get back, everyone is worried about you. I' – he stabbed his finger at his chest – 'I am just really angry with you. I suggest we get a move on, because if I stay here much longer I will do *something* we both might regret!'

Carrie moved. She was about to gather her shopping but Alexis took her arm and propelled her off the yacht, though not before she'd reached her cherries. She could feel his temper simmering in the darkness of the night.

'Leave the shopping!'

'But I . . .'

'I said leave it.' Alexis pushed her towards the harbour where the *Challenger* was docked. The same harbour where she had seen him kissing Marsha.

Realizing what was happening, Carrie stopped dead, turned and attacked. She didn't care any more and she wanted to hurt him too. 'I heard what you said. *I wouldn't have had it happen this way!*' she mimicked, suddenly wide-awake and angry herself.

A dawning light shone through his eyes and he laughed bitterly, still gripping her arm. He'd been to hell and back this last couple of days, thinking she was dead, thinking all sorts of atrocities could have happened to her, so yes, he was livid with her all right. 'So that's what all this is about? An overheard conversation?'

'Yes! You . . . bast . . .'

Alexis tightened his grip on her arm, ruthlessly halting her biting words. 'I suggest you stay quiet! I did say that, yes. I also said a lot of other things too. Now, move! Believe me, Carrie, I've really had enough!'

Carrie gave in only temporarily and moved forward one step. 'You don't love me, do you?'

'Don't I?'

'Don't answer my question with a question, damn you! Of course you don't. You said you didn't,' Carrie slammed back at him. 'I just wish you could have been ...' She threw her hands in the air. 'Oh I don't know, I just wish my heart wasn't involved.'

She stifled a sob and moved on.

'Yes, I too wish I'd been honest with you, but don't be so naïve as to think there would be no heartache. When the heart is involved there is always pain,' he declared harshly.

Well, at least he knew she was suffering! At least he knew he had caused that pain. There was solace in the fact that he also looked hurt, and yet she was being made to feel guilty because he had caused all this needless heartache.

She needed to get away from Greece. Once everything was out in the open. Tomorrow, when her heart would be in complete tatters, she would go back to England, back to her only other love: Peter.

'Get on the yacht,' he ordered, his bossy manner irritating her. She shrugged his hands away.

'Leave me alone!'

Without uttering one more syllable she stormed up the gangplank, and into the lounge area, where she sat straight and rigid on the pink sofa. Alexis reached into the fridge for a drink. He placed an orange juice in front of her, picked up the telephone and gave orders for the vessel to leave harbour. He chose a brandy for himself.

The journey began in stiff silence. All Alexis did was frown at her. Quietly she sipped the orange juice, not daring to say a word because underneath the dark angry stare, she saw something else. A look of relief. She didn't understand him.

Alexis looked at her; all he wanted to do was to take her in his arms. But he mustn't, he reasoned with himself. Everyone he'd seen these past few days had imagined her dead, lost on the high seas of the summer storm. He thanked God she wasn't; he'd prayed enough in the last few days.

He was tired too. He hadn't had any rest at all for days and was now so tired he wondered if this scruffy figure was truly her or a mirage. He remembered the radio call stating they'd seen the *Adonia* in the harbour at Alonnissos. At last he had her back again.

Carrie sat and fumed; she realized she had reached the end of the line. She became aware of Alexis's eyes, flicking over to her now and then, looking concerned. Watching silently as she battled with her raw emotions. Eventually the first tear trickled down her cheek. Then more tears followed; she just couldn't stop them. Now they were coursing freely down her face. Unbidden they flowed as if they would never cease, until she began to gulp back her sobs. Her shoulders were shaking hard, wrenching with each heart-rending tear. She couldn't help it, everything was lost. Lost forever!

Her crying was so out of control she failed to notice that he had swiftly moved to sit with her, that he was dragging her to him, kissing her wet, salty cheeks, murmuring for her to stop, holding her so tightly that she finally felt safe within his strong arms. She felt safe and warm, but reminded herself it was a false haven here in his arms. Especially now, when he'd admitted to not loving her. Or had he? She couldn't even remember.

'Come on, sweetheart, no more crying. I can't bear to watch you pull yourself apart like this.' His voice was gentle, no longer angry. Tears like this crippled him.

He began brushing back the hair from her face so delicately she shivered with desire. He dropped endless kisses over her eyes. Reaching inside his pocket he wiped her face with his handkerchief, so tender and gentle, so lovingly expressive. He held her until the tears had stopped, and this only made her more confused than ever.

Settling her back in the seat, he whispered, 'We must talk now. Let's go somewhere more private.'

Carrie looked across at him, confused. Sniffing back her tears she breathed, 'Where?'

CHAPTER 18

Alexis sat her down on the striped *chaise longue* and took hold of both her shaking hands. He shrugged his broad, strong shoulders. And she noticed now just how tired and drained he did look, and her heart went unselfishly out to him.

'Where do I start?' he asked, his hands tightly clinging to hers. He was shaking too, as nervous as she was.

Swallowing convulsively, Carrie suggested quietly, 'From the clinic, with Helena.'

Alexis smiled. 'Helena has been very, very naughty. I'm afraid she felt the lash of my temper the other morning. You only heard half the conversation, before you ran out.'

Half the conversation, she thought tiredly. She looked into his eyes; as in most of their exchanges there was nothing to read in them. He was well and truly locked in his shell. Confirming what she'd heard Helena say was easy. 'I know she manipulated us. She *bought* me for you.'

'You could say that, yes. But she had her reasons.

My mother has lied about it all these years.' Alexis halted her outburst. 'No, listen to me. I knew nothing of my mother wanting us to have a child. She pleaded with me before to court you, to take you out, but I wouldn't be manipulated by her. I'm responsible for my own actions. You know that. And besides, I was fighting the very attraction she wanted me to cultivate.'

Carrie opened her mouth to utter something, but her words were stuck in her throat. Surely this wasn't true? Helena wouldn't do that, and was he saying he went along with this for himself?

'I'd thought all along it was Petros. He'd been so instrumental in our relationship.' He shrugged. 'Besides, I found the situation very tempting, as you know, and since it gave me a prime opportunity to get you to myself, I took it. I forced your hand and brought you here.' He was frowning now.

'But why?' She croaked, not believing the words she had heard. 'Why did Helena do it? Why did you go along with it?'

'Helena – ' he smiled again – 'was matchmaking, for a reason. A selfish reason.'

'Oh?'

'She had an old-fashioned idea we would fall in love, though that doesn't mean she's vindicated.'

Carrie coloured under his watchful eyes. 'I did fall in love.' She struggled to release her hands but he wouldn't let go.

His voice deepened, lowered dangerously until she looked up and stopped her struggles. 'Don't fight!

It's time for the truth. We owe ourselves at least that.'

This was it. Rejection time. Carrie let out the breath she'd been holding and smiled unsteadily. 'And your reason for bringing me on the yacht? Tonight?' She pursed her lips together. Where was this conversation going?

'My reasons are my own for the moment. You're my wife.' He saw the quizzical arch of her brow but carried on regardless. 'I want you back in my bed, and in my life. But let me explain about Petros and Helena.' Alexis looked down at their hands, his face growing dark red under his tan as he continued. It was as hard for him to explain to her as it was for her to comprehend.

'My mother arranged for Petros to use his illness and tell me this ridiculous tale so that I would help him.' He looked slightly embarrassed as he confessed, 'She knew I wanted you; apparently it shows in my face.'

She couldn't help the bitter little laugh. 'But how did she make Petros do it?'

'Because he would do anything for her. Plus the fact he felt he owed her for the Theo affair five years ago. He was a fool to ever promise your hand to a man of Theo's reputation. My mother's wasn't the greatest crime however. She merely wanted me to make you pregnant.' He looked her straight in the eye. '*Mine* was the crime, Carrie. Blow Petros and my mother. *I* wanted our child, Carrie. I wanted a chain around your neck that you couldn't break. And what's more, the thought of marriage became more and more enticing.'

'This is too much. Don't I have a say in the matter?' she cried.

He had the decency to look embarrassed. 'When my mother planned all this, marriage was her ultimate aim. She wanted half a dozen children for us both.'

Carrie stared in disbelief. Anger raged in her heart. 'I've been well and truly had, haven't I?' She struck out at him, punching ineffectual blows against his chest, 'My godfather, your mother. You! You must all be laughing behind my back! What's it like, Alexis? You've got your revenge. I insulted you in London and you've made me squirm, treated me like a brood mare.'

'No! Carrie, it isn't like that, believe me,' he moaned softly, almost like a wounded animal.

Carrie moved to the window to look out over the darkened sea. How could he? She turned back, her eyes blazing her anger and hurt right through him.

'And have you got your revenge? Do you now have your pound of flesh?' Taking a deep, steadying breath to calm the storm within she whispered faintly, 'I want to get the next plane home to London! No one loves me here.'

'No! Your home is with me.'

'Try and stop me, Alexis, and I'll have you arrested,' she seethed. Her breast was heaving, her heart slamming against her ribs, but he was smiling!

She flew at him again. 'Don't laugh at me!'

'Stop it, Carrie. I'm not laughing at you, just your foolish comment. Of course people love you here. Stop and think what hell we've all been going through while you've been missing. And you haven't even asked about Petros. For all you know he could be dead!' It was cruel, he knew, but at least it got her out of this hypnotic trance she seemed to be in.

Dragging air into her lungs, she cried, 'Oh God, is he OK?'

'He'll be better now he knows you're safe.'

Putting a hand to her lips, Carrie sighed. 'You must think I'm awful. So selfish.'

'I think you're tired, and anything but selfish. I'm the wicked one. I accused everyone of trying to manipulate us, and I unforgivably manipulated you – my darling wife.' He grabbed her hand and kissed it, his lips lingering. 'If you insist on leaving, I won't stop you, but I insist you hear me out first. Unfortunately, that will have to wait until we are alone, in bed. We have visitors aboard and dinner is in about half an hour.' He offered this news gently to her, his eyes never leaving her tortured face.

'Visitors?' She shook her head. 'I can't cope with visitors. Not even the dolphins.'

He smiled, how could he be angry with her?

'Come, I am sure you can make an effort for these visitors.' He lifted a strand of her limp hair. 'But first I think you need a shower. My guests would be offended to see you in such a state, I fear they would blame me.'

Her eyes flew to his. If she left in the morning, she would never see him again. Never be able to touch him, to kiss him softly on the brow when he slept. Or creep up behind as he shaved and touch him intimately, only to receive a look of mock severity through the mirror; he took his shaving seriously.

Pain rocked her and she closed her eyes. Since their visit to the clinic she'd felt devoid of hope. Each time she opened her eyes after sleep, she would feel happy for a moment, and then she would remember, and a feeling of great loss would enshroud her. She needed him just one more time. Needed to feel him hold her safely, just one more time.

'I feel too weak to shower. You'll have to help me,' she whispered breathlessly. He nodded, his frown barely visible.

Turning the shower on in the bathroom, he sat her down on the bed. Without words he helped her undress to her underwear. He'd never seen her like this, so passive, so empty of fight.

'Can you manage the rest?'

She shook her head. 'Please, Alexis, help me.'

He did, gently unhooking her bra, easing the straps down her shoulders until it fell on the floor. Willing himself not to touch her intimately yet, he pushed her softly back on the bed. It would be so easy to take her like this, but he wouldn't do it. Not until they'd talked properly. She lay still while he took her panties off, her eyes almost imploring him to touch her.

Dragging himself away, he told her to sit up, his tone harder than he intended.

Placing a towel around her he helped her towards the shower.

'You're not attracted to me any more, are you?'

His eyes widened as he looked down into the pained expression on her face. He put his head slightly to one side, baffled by the question. What more should he do to express his love? He'd come after her, been searching for her for days and nights and besides he couldn't make love to her until everything was completely out in the open. Surely his anger when he'd found her was proof of his feelings?

Clamping his lips together, he said a little harshly, 'That's rubbish, Carrie, and you know it! I won't give you the satisfaction of using me again and then disappearing tomorrow. If you want me to make love to you, you promise me you won't run out on me again. Don't forget we'll soon have a child to bring up.'

'You said you wouldn't stop me from leaving. You promised,' she accused, her weariness submerged in waves of anger. 'As always you go back on your word.'

'When have I gone back on my word?'

They were facing each other like two avenging angels, flames flashing from their eyes, the atmosphere far from erotic. And yet still . . . The very air around them seemed to throb with sexual tension.

The look in her eyes said it all. She wanted him. He shook his head, trying to blot out this image.

'This is ridiculous,' he said but even as he was saying it his hand reached for the towel and pulled it free.

'Alexis,' she pleaded, only because she saw something in his eyes, something she thought she recognized.

Closing his eyes, he touched her. He wanted to savour this chance to touch her, but he couldn't. Dragging her to him, he lifted her into his arms.

Hot hungry lips met his, kissing him in a way she'd never kissed before. She was so hungry, and he was there to satisfy that hunger. Leaving her lips briefly, he carried her into the shower, resting her against the cubicle side.

She laughed against the velvet softness of his cheek. 'You still have your clothes on.'

'I'm too weak, you'll have to help me out of them,' he mimicked, his eyes shining with this new feeling. Whatever it was, it excited her.

Together they exploited the shower cubicle to its limits, and when they were both sated he washed her hair, her body, her enchanting face, anywhere his hands could reach.

'Where are we going?' she whispered, still following him up the steps. Pulling her short skirt down she wished he had brought her some of her clothes instead of Maria's. This bright pink dress did nothing for her but show off her bump.

'The bridge.' His dark eyes shone with devilment.

'What or who is on the bridge? And don't tell me Captain Savidis is there. Is he?'

'Hush.' He put a finger to her lips, 'I'll tell you about all that later.'

Carrie saw the little figure perched high on a young man's knee. Peter was at the helm! She gasped, and as she did, he turned, his face lighting up as he saw her. She threw a look to Alexis that relayed her thanks wordlessly and ran to him.

'Oh Peter!' She held her arms out to him for a cuddle.

'Hi, Carrie,' Peter sat there on the bridge with the captain's hat on. He was sitting on Yanni's knee, steering the *Challenger* and looking decidedly pleased with himself.

Carrie looked at Alexis questioningly. He shrugged. 'I promised him. I don't break a promise.'

Peter tucked his arms around her waist and rocked gently against her. 'I love you, Carrie,' he said softly.

Carrie hugged him and then stopped. 'You said it right, you said my name properly. Oh Peter, sweetheart.'

He grinned up at her, saying smugly, 'I love you, Carrie.'

She laughed, her eyes catching Alexis's as she mouthed, 'Thank you.'

He smiled, and nodded. 'Audrey and Graham are in the dining room. Peter has had his tea and Yanni is in charge up here. I'll be down in the dining room. Come down when you've had a talk.'

She shook her head. 'Wait for me. Peter is more interested in manning the helm. I can see him before bedtime.' She kissed the top of Peter's head. 'See you later.'

He grinned, 'Bye bye. Love you.'

Carrie took Alexis's hand, daring herself to act as if nothing had ever happened.

He squeezed it. 'When we've had dinner we must talk. There are things I want you to know.'

'Yes. I won't get angry this time. We should talk, it will be better to get things sorted.'

'There is one thing you should know now though. I won't give you up without a fight. I l . . .' He didn't finish.

'Carrie! Oh how lovely to see you. We have so much to tell you. The first is that Alexis has offered Graham a job, here in Greece,' interrupted Audrey. Grabbing Carrie by the arm Audrey sat her down next to her at the dining table.

Carrie looked at Alexis. She was sure she knew what he'd been about to say. She giggled, her heart lifting cautiously.

'He's offered Graham a job? He never told me.' She turned to her husband. 'Alexis, you never told me. It would seem there are several things you should be telling me.'

'Yes, my love, there are. Including the new villa I'm having built. You thought it was for a complete stranger but I did it for Audrey and Graham, and little Peter.'

'Thank you.' He'd never said anything about this to her, it was obviously meant to be a surprise. Compressing her lips to supress a cheeky smile she decided she would take him to task later. This man was someone entirely different to the one she'd known when she was a teenager.

'Champagne, anyone?' Graham said as he popped the cork, 'By the way, congratulations, love. I'm pleased all's going well with the baby.'

'Thank you.' She knew he was a man of few words so his good wishes meant a great deal to her. He lifted the bottle of champagne at her. Carrie shook her head, 'I'll have fruit juice.'

'Peter has been so looking forward to this. He's going to love living next door to you. We're just so grateful.' He looked at Alexis. 'You really don't know what you've done for us. We love Peter, we'd do anything for him.'

'Oh, don't you worry, you'll work hard at the sanctuary.' Alexis drank from his champagne flute. 'I couldn't believe it when Carrie told me you were with the police, working within the dog-handling section. Your experience is bound to come in handy.'

'I'm pleased you think so, Alexis.'

The young crewman came in to serve dinner, but Carrie looked away, not sure she could eat anything at the moment, even though everything looked so deliciously appetizing.

She managed to nibble on the fresh bread, the cool Tzatziki. She drank fresh orange juice until she was nearly bursting.

'Helena was telling us your godfather has had a heart operation. He's doing really well, isn't he? And he and Alexis's mother are getting married,' said

Audrey as she finished her main course of lobster with fresh vegetables. 'Now isn't that a nice surprise?'

Carrie looked at Alexis questioningly. From the look on Alexis's face, it seemed Audrey had jumped the gun a little.

Alexis explained: 'Carrie, they phoned while we were on our way here to tell us the news. My mother wants to be married soon.'

'I didn't know. I never even suspected.'

'No one did!' He laughed. 'Well, actually that's not true. I went to his bedroom to talk to him, the morning after our engagement party and I thought I could smell that expensive perfume my mother uses. Apparently they've been seeing each other for quite a few years.'

'It's sad about your mother though. I can understand why she wants you to have babies so soon in your marriage.' Audrey ploughed in again, spooning hot chocolate souffle into her mouth.

Carrie look dumbfounded again, but Alexis filled in.

'She thought her eyesight was going to be lost again soon. Now the consultant thinks it will take a few years longer for her eyes to deteriorate. She's not exactly blind yet, you understand, she just has a wish to see her grandchildren before she is.' He threw Carrie a look that should have relayed his thoughts but she still looked shocked. 'She's hoping we get those blue eyes in the Stephanides family.'

So that was why Helena had set this whole thing up! She'd gone behind both their backs and Carrie could see why now.

'And then she was telling me . . .' Audrey took another mouthful of souffle and paused.

Alexis looked helplessly at Carrie. Carrie wanted to laugh. If he wasn't careful Audrey would be stealing his thunder. There would be nothing for them to talk about.

'Where was I? She was telling me all about this drug thing. I have to say she's very proud of you, Alexis, helping like you did.' She nudged Carrie. 'He's a hero, isn't he? Someone tried to kill him too, you know. I bet you were petrified, weren't you, dear?' She sighed, obviously the champagne had taken its toll. 'Life seems to be much more fun over here, doesn't it, love?'

Graham smiled, pouring more champagne. 'Much more.'

'Have you missed anything out, Audrey?' asked Carrie.

Audrey looked at her friend. 'I don't think so, dear. Let me see? Petros sends his love; of course he's not out of the woods yet but he's certainly responding well.' Her eyes sparkled. 'Ah, there is one thing. Before we left England we saw Maria at Heathrow, in Arrivals. She told me she was expecting a man from Greece. We got chatting, as you do –' she pursed her lips together – 'and she told me he was an old flame. Didn't look an old flame to me, not with the way they were carrying on! Mind you, I wouldn't blame anyone for going two rounds with him.'

Carrie burst out laughing. 'Audrey!'

'A man?' Alexis responded quickly: 'Which man? Did you see him, Audrey?'

'I did. He's was big with blond hair, good-looking brute, too, like I said. American I believe.' She leant over towards Alexis. 'They were all over each other, like butter on bread. Sliding up and down each other as they kissed.'

'Butter on bread?' questioned Alexis with a frown. He'd heard some strange English expressions when he'd been at university but this one was new to him. He got the gist of it before Audrey went into a full-blown explanation.

So Maria and Garry were seeing each other again. He smiled. Garry had been so casual about the relationship. Maybe Maria's hold was tighter than he'd realized.

Carrie was pleased when Peter came in to say goodnight. Audrey, who'd been on top form this evening, was now flagging. Peter sat on her knee for a while, eating ice-cream and pineapple, but eventually he was yawning, asking if he could go to bed. At the same time Audrey and Graham said they would retire.

'Alexis, tuck me in?' asked Peter with that cheeky grin.

Alexis smiled. 'Do you mind?' he asked his wife.

She smiled and shaking her head, she kissed Peter goodnight.

Looking around the empty room, she began eating the ruby red cherries. She had a craving for them. Each one tasted fruity and sweet, the juice and flesh so special she took her time with them.

What had he been about to say earlier? Before Audrey had opened the door and interrupted them. Poor Audrey, she loved to tell all the gossip.

If he loved her, the question was, could she forgive him for all this deceit? But it wasn't all his, she supposed. He'd come clean about Petros early on in their relationship, and he'd said *he* wanted their child. Obviously he'd been going through his own personal torment. No, most of the blame should be placed on Helena's shoulders, but how could she blame her either?

Soon there was a plate full of stones. She looked around, wondering whether to stay or go to back to the state rooms. Peter must be keeping Alexis busy with a bedtime story.

Musing, she began lining the stones up. What had she seen in his eyes? Did he love her? One by one she recited the old saying. 'He loves me, he loves me not. He loves me, he loves me not.' On the twenty-fourth stone she stopped.

'He loves me not!'

CHAPTER 19

'Hey.' She looked up as Alexis threw her a cherry. He'd been standing there watching her. 'Catch.' He smiled that devastating smile at her. 'He loves you, *very much.*' His words were said slowly, and simply because he meant them.

The shaky smile that appeared on her lips revealed the extent of her joy. Looking at him, she realized that a love like this was far too precious a thing to lose over a few misunderstandings.

What was it she'd preached to Stephan? *Get your head out of the sand.* Well maybe, just maybe, she and Alexis had been guilty of that same blindness.

Alexis came and sat with her, reaching for her hand. 'He's been a fool, a blind and stupid fool, and he asks your forgiveness. He knows there is a lot to forgive, but he promises to spend the rest of his life making you happy.'

Carrie watched him as he took her hand to his lips. He bit her palm softly, then pressed his other hand to her belly. 'This is a big baby, Mrs Stephanides, for only four and half months. Are we sure we're not having twins?'

She shook her head. 'No, just the one, Mr Stephanides, just the one.' She yawned. 'I'm tired, can we go to bed?'

He shook his head. Moving over the room he switched some dreamy music on quite low, and turned. 'I want to dance with you, while I can still get my arms around you.'

She grinned. 'Really, it's *your* fault I'm getting bigger.' Her look softened. 'If you insist.' She walked into the circle of his arms.

Tipping her chin up, he looked down into her face, 'Am I forgiven?'

Carrie mused over this evening's events. She shook her head. 'I'm still confused. I don't know why you were angry this evening. I ran away, yes I know, and maybe I shouldn't have.'

Alexis brushed his thumb over her lips. 'Hush. I'll tell you why I was angry and maybe then you'll understand my anger was connected to how much I love you.'

'Intriguing!' She bit his thumb, holding it firmly in her teeth, licking the edges with naughty intent.

'And no cheating. I need concentration for this, not silent erotic suggestions,' he scolded softly.

Carrie listened, watching his expressions as he went through the events of the past few days. She began to feel very guilty. She'd been selfish, staying out of contact.

'When we saw you running away from the clinic, at first we thought Petros had had another attack, but we dashed in to find him crying. He was so upset, quite devastated, in fact. He told me what you'd heard.' Shaking his head, he said, 'Eavesdroppers don't hear good of themselves, do they?'

'I don't suppose they do, no.' Carrie smiled, pressing her tummy against him as they danced. She was playing with him, but still listening.

'Well, you certainly got the wrong end of the stick.'

'Did I?' She laughed. 'Guess I should have hung around.'

'I love you,' he scolded as if she should have known, 'and I thought my actions over the past few weeks would have told you that. Apparently my mother has known for years. To be honest, *I* just used to think I had a thing about you. You know, a sexual thing.' His eyes shone darkly wicked.

'I hope you still *do* have a sexual thing about me, Mr Stephanides,' Carrie laughed, seeing her answer in the way he looked at her. 'So go on, that doesn't explain your anger toward me this evening.'

'Well, I chased you, from the clinic.'

'You did?'

'Yes. I lost you somewhere near the *plaka*. I searched all afternoon but it was hopeless. There were so many people about. Eventually I went back to the bakery. I just sat there, until James came back. I was lost, Carrie, absolutely lost without you.'

Carrie's face went serious and she tightened her hold on him, but let him continue.

'James was great, he got a search party organized for you. We tracked you down, traced you as far the harbour. Then the most awful thing happened.' He closed his eyes, pain visible on his face. 'I feel terrible about this. Garry came and told us a woman's body had been picked up out of the water. I was asked to identify the body, *your* body, so everyone believed.'

'Oh God, Alexis. I didn't realize. How could I?'

'Not your fault. You were hurting.' He paused, as if this was hard for him too. 'When we arrived at the harbour where the coastguard had brought the body in, I couldn't do it. I felt sick. If you had been under that blanket I don't know what I would have done.'

They clung to each other. She was beginning to understand his anger, his worry. Now that understanding went so much deeper.

'James identified the body.'

Carrie frowned. 'How could he? He's only just flown in from the States. He doesn't know . . .'

Alexis sighed. 'It was Marsha, and it turned out that she hadn't drowned. She was murdered.'

'Oh no! Oh God, Alexis. I'm so sorry,' she whispered. How must he be feeling? He'd cared for her once.

Alexis saw the look on her face and jumped in quickly. 'Look, Carrie, I know it's a shock and I wouldn't want this to happen to anyone, but she didn't mean a thing to me. Not a thing! She got herself in too deeply with the wrong people. I can't even say I liked her, not without lying.'

'But you had an affair, didn't you? You must have . . .'

'Come on, let's go back to our room. I need you to sit down, and make you understand all this.'

Gently he took her somewhere more comfortable, clearly in a hurry. He was in a rush for her to know, and understand. He didn't want any more misunderstandings left, none at all. The whole sordid story had to come out about Marsha.

'Sit down, my darling one.'

She did, and he sat down with her, next to her on the *chaise*.

He took a deep breath, in the knowledge that this was going to be hard to explain. Softly he began. 'Marsha has been involved in this drugs thing for quite some time.'

'I'm sorry. I didn't realize. Did she take it herself? You know?'

'Apparently so. In her feet, she used to inject into her feet. The thought frightens the hell out of me! Of course that would account for her erratic behaviour.'

'I know. Funny, I always thought she was drunk when she phoned me,' she remarked.

'Phoned you? When?'

'You didn't know, did you?' she said when she saw the surprise on his face.

He shook his head. 'Not that it matters now.'

'No, I suppose not. How did you meet her?'

'I met her through her husband really, at a dance. You know the kind, the ones you never want to attend, but good manners dictate otherwise.'

Touching her cheek as if he couldn't resist, he smiled. 'I'm not a fool. I knew she was interested in me. I've seen that predatory look before in women, and I've usually steered clear. Before you, I bedded women who knew the score; some of them were married, but not that many, believe it or believe it not!'

'How many?' Then she backtracked immediately. 'No, don't answer that. It's none of my business.'

Alexis touched her cheek. 'I think it is and I want to answer it.' He paused, saying at length, 'Over the years, three, maybe four. We mutually used each other. Marianne being one of them,' he added quickly. He bit his lip; he'd promised himself he was going to tell her everything. 'I wanted to drive you out of my mind. You've been haunting me for years.'

It was obviously a time for truth, Carrie realized. 'So have you, been haunting me, I mean. Why do you think I left so eagerly for London at Petros's insistence. I knew nothing of this threat from Theo. It was you. You were visiting more and more and I was afraid of what I would do. You made me feel like no other man has ever made me feel. I was young, confused. I wanted to hate you, I really did, and yet I was so attracted to you. I found hating you easier to contend with.'

He smiled, his voice a soft rebuke: 'Tut, tut, why didn't you tell me? I could have saved us both the heartache and swept you into my arms. We've wasted a lot of time.'

Looking down at the short dress she was wearing which had ridden up enticingly as she tucked her legs underneath her on the *chaise*, he almost cried with need. The way it clung to her slightly larger breasts, the seductive way it fitted, it was almost too much. But no, she'd fooled him once already today, had whistled her little tune in the shower and he'd succumbed, but not again. He wanted everything resolved now.

She'd seen the approving look he swept over her. They could talk later. 'Shall we go to bed?' she asked, her blue eyes filled with fun.

'No! I want everything out in the open, *everything*,' he said, then cleared his throat. 'As I was saying, Marsha was at a particular function in America. I made the mistake of telling James I knew her.' He flexed his large athletic shoulders as if they ached with tiredness. 'She was under suspicion already, so he asked me to get to know her a little more intimately.' He looked at Carrie. 'I danced with her, and chatted, and I believed I'd done my job well. During that night, however, whilst I was staying at the hotel, she crept into my bed. There was an ugly scene when I threw her out.'

He shrugged. 'For all I knew it could have been her who tried to kill me only a few months ago on board ship. She certainly had no compunction about throwing Saffy into the sea and letting you follow when she knew damn well there was a shark basking.'

'But why did the captain sound the horn? He was in on it, wasn't he?'

'Yes, but I didn't know that at the time. 'Maybe he had a soft spot for you or Maria. He was involved with the arson, we do know that. We found a message had gone to the ship from the *Challenger*, weeks previously, telling someone when I was to be on board. We didn't know who it was, so I checked the yacht for something being planted.'

'What? Drugs, you mean?' He nodded.

Grinning, he looked at her. 'You remember that night I attacked you from behind with my wetsuit on?'

Carrie laughed, the sound soft and husky. 'Wasn't the kind of attack I was looking for,' she grinned.

'Will you concentrate, woman! The reason I was below the yacht was that I felt I had to check for drugs. You have to remember that I had Marsha on board, who was the number one suspect then.'

'And when you were in America. You say you were hit from behind, right?'

He nodded. 'Yes.'

'What with? Do you know?'

'An iron bar, I think.' He rubbed the spot where he'd been hit on his head. 'They believe the murderer swam to the ship, belted me and the other poor fellow and swam back across the docks.'

'Then it wasn't Marsha. She was petrified in the pool on deck; she would only ever dip herself in and then get out. She really was petrified. Poor Marsha, she wasn't a murderer.' The compassion in her voice relayed the empathy she felt for Marsha. 'The thing is, will we ever know who tried to kill you?'

Alexis frowned. 'Maybe not, but it's all over now. Theo, Captain Savidis, the senator and several others have all been caught and jailed. They've had extradition orders issued for the trial to be held in America.'

'And Petros and Helena? Have they been exonerated of any involvement?'

'Completely. They have been very helpful to James.'

Looking across at her, he couldn't wait any longer; he had to touch her. Dropping his head, he carefully covered her lips with his, gently easing them open, and kissing her before saying, 'I need refreshment for my soul.' He took her into his arms again, thirstily feasting upon her.

He lifted his head. The phone was buzzing its interruption. 'Am I forgiven? I was out of my mind with worry about you.'

She nodded. He sighed with relief then grabbed the phone. 'Alexis here. Hi, James. Yes you'll be pleased to know that she is safe and sound.' He pulled a face at her whilst he was listening to James and she giggled. 'Really, so that ties it all up. Yep, thanks, buddy. We'll see you back at the villa tomorrow. Thanks a million.'

'Well, Carrie, my love, we have our murderer.'

'We do?'

'Theo has confessed to it all. Apparently he killed the man on the ship and Marsha. He reckoned if I were off the scene altogether he could make his move on you. The man must be besotted with you.'

'But why?'

'Marsha had orders from Theo to get me any way she could, and when that didn't work, he tried to kill me himself.'

'How did he know?'

'You heard Captain Savidis talking to Marsha, the morning before I left? I'd already told Marsha to leave, and she'd told Theo. I told her I wanted nothing more to do with her.' He grinned. 'Theo must have been desperate to have you.'

Carrie cringed. 'Don't you dare say it! He once nearly assaulted me when I was young. I'm glad he's going behind bars. He deserves all he gets.'

She shook her head. 'We were at one of Petros's parties. I'd gone to bed and he came into my room. He'd just taken my covers off when I woke up. Luckily my mum came in. He told her I'd been crying in my sleep, but she didn't trust him. She didn't leave me that night; she hated Theo too.' She smiled. 'Let's change the subject.'

Looking at her breasts in the clingy dress, Alexis whispered suggestively, 'It can't hurt. Looks like everything is out in the open now. How about we go bed?'

Carrie shook her head, her eyes serious for one long awful moment. 'There is something else to come out.' Then her face cracked up as she reached for his zipper and she burst out laughing. '*This*!'

EPILOGUE

Four months, ten days later Carrie gave birth to a blue eyed little girl named Dionne Alicia Stephanides. She weighed seven pounds, five ounces. Dionne meant '*The daughter of heaven and earth.*' Aphrodite's mother. At least that was what Petros had told her. Petros and Helena had just left the clinic but had insisted he see his 'grandaughter', even though he was only allowed light exercise.

Alexis looked down proudly into his daughter's blue eyes. 'All babies have blue eyes, don't they?' he asked his wife. He stroked the short cap of blonde-hair, and smiled. Bending his head, he kissed the baby's tiny little lips.

Reaching for Carrie's hand, he said softly, 'I'm glad you understood that I couldn't be at the birth.' He rocked his daughter.

Carrie laughed, exhausted but not at all angry with him. 'I'm pleased you were honest with me. I would have hated for you to pass out. Loving each other means we should try and understand each other's feelings too.'

'Which reminds me,' said Alexis, reaching into the envelope he'd brought with the flowers, 'this is for you.'

Carrie frowned. 'What is it?'

'Open it and see.' He smiled whilst rocking his daughter and hummed a nursery rhyme, all the while watching for Carrie's expression.

Carrie opened the envelope. 'These are deeds?' She looked up.

'Yes, they're for you.' He smiled again, wishing she'd just read it.

'But why?' She looked confused.

'Look at it, woman!'

Carrie stared at the words. Oh Lord, she was going to cry! She bit heavily on her lip. The deeds were for Killcarrie farm, on the south east coast of Ireland. The house where she'd been born.

'Surprised?'

She nodded.

'Happy?'

She nodded again. Words seemed so unimportant for a moment, then curiosity got the better of her.

'Why?'

'Because I love you.' There was a softness playing around his mouth. 'Because I wanted to give you something that you felt you belonged to. Your heritage, your past. Something solid in your life.' He shrugged, 'I want our children to see where their mother was born too. To be proud of their roots, both here and in Ireland.'

She breathed deeply. 'OK, so when did you buy it?'

He laughed. 'Now that was more difficult. I've been trying for four years now.'

'Four years?'

He nodded. 'I finalized the deal the day you insulted me in London. I flew to Ireland that morning and would have taken you with me, had you not . . .' He didn't finish.

'Been so awful to you?'

'You weren't awful, you'd just not grown up properly. Thankfully I had an input in that.' He rocked his daughter.

They both laughed as she said, 'Quite an input if I remember rightly.'

Minutes later Alexis said, 'Carrie, just look at how small her hands are, her feet too. She's perfect.'

'Say that when she's fifteen and being rude to you. When she marks your best dining table with a knife. Then tell me she's perfect.'

They looked at each other for a neverending moment.

'She's perfect, just like her mama.' His eyes shone. 'I must be the proudest man on earth.'

Reaching over, he kissed her. It was a kiss that held the promise of more children to come. For Carrie, one was definitely not enough. After all, she'd promised him a boy!

THE EXCITING NEW NAME IN WOMEN'S FICTION!

PLEASE HELP ME TO HELP YOU!

Dear ***Scarlet*** Reader,

As Editor of ***Scarlet*** Books I want to make sure that the books I offer you every month are up to the high standards ***Scarlet*** readers expect. And to do that I need to know a little more about you and your reading likes and dislikes. So please spare a few minutes to fill in the short questionnaire on the following pages and send it to me.

Looking forward to hearing from you,

Sally Cooper

Editor-in-Chief, ***Scarlet***

P.S. Make sure you look at these end pages in your ***Scarlet*** books each month! We hope to have some exciting news for you very soon.

Note: further offers which might be of interest may be sent to you by other, carefully selected, companies. If you do not want to receive them, please write to Robinson Publishing Ltd, 7 Kensington Church Court, London W8 4SP, UK.

QUESTIONNAIRE

Please tick the appropriate boxes to indicate your answers

1 Where did you get this Scarlet title?
Bought in supermarket ☐
Bought at my local bookstore ☐ Bought at chain bookstore ☐
Bought at book exchange or used bookstore ☐
Borrowed from a friend ☐
Other (please indicate) ______________________

2 Did you enjoy reading it?
A lot ☐ A little ☐ Not at all ☐

3 What did you particularly like about this book?
Believable characters ☐ Easy to read ☐
Good value for money ☐ Enjoyable locations ☐
Interesting story ☐ Modern setting ☐
Other ______________________

4 What did you particularly dislike about this book?
____

5 Would you buy another Scarlet book?
Yes ☐ No ☐

6 What other kinds of book do you enjoy reading?
Horror ☐ Puzzle books ☐ Historical fiction ☐
General fiction ☐ Crime/Detective ☐ Cookery ☐
Other (please indicate) ______________________

7 Which magazines do you enjoy reading?
1. ______________________
2. ______________________
3. ______________________

And now a little about you –

8 How old are you?
Under 25 ☐ 25–34 ☐ 35–44 ☐
45–54 ☐ 55–64 ☐ over 65 ☐

cont.

9 What is your marital status?

Single ☐ Married/living with partner ☐

Widowed ☐ Separated/divorced ☐

10 What is your current occupation?

Employed full-time ☐ Employed part-time ☐

Student ☐ Housewife full-time ☐

Unemployed ☐ Retired ☐

11 Do you have children? If so, how many and how old are they?

____

____

12 What is your annual household income?

under $15,000	☐	or	£10,000	☐
$15–25,000	☐	or	£10–20,000	☐
$25–35,000	☐	or	£20–30,000	☐
$35–50,000	☐	or	£30–40,000	☐
over $50,000	☐	or	£40,000	☐

Miss/Mrs/Ms ________________________________

Address ____________________________________

____

____

Thank you for completing this questionnaire. Now tear it out – put it in an envelope and send it before 31 August, 1997, to:

Sally Cooper, Editor-in-Chief

USA/Can. address
SCARLET c/o London Bridge
85 River Rock Drive
Suite 202
Buffalo
NY 14207
USA

UK address/No stamp required
SCARLET
FREEPOST LON 3335
LONDON W8 4BR
Please use block capitals for address

ANIMP/2/97

Scarlet titles coming next month:

TIME TO TRUST Jill Sheldon

Cord isn't impressed by the female of the species! And he certainly doesn't have 'time to trust' one of them! It's just as well, then, that Emily is equally reluctant to let a man into *her* life – even one as irresistible as Cord. But maybe the decision isn't theirs to make – for someone else has a deadly interest in their relationship!

THE PATH TO LOVE Chrissie Loveday

Kerrien has decided that a new life in Australia is just what she needs. So she takes a job with Dr Ashton Philips and is soon hoping there can be more between them than a working relationship. Then Ashton's sister, Kate, and his glamorous colleague, Martine, decide to announce his forthcoming marriage!

LOVERS AND LIARS Sally Steward

Eliot Kane is Leanne Warner's dream man, and she finds herself falling deeper and deeper in love with him. When Eliot confesses to having memory lapses and, even worse, dreams which feature . . . murder, Leanne begins to wonder if she's involved with a man who could be a very, very dangerous lover indeed!

LOVE BEYOND DESIRE Jessica Marchant

Amy is a thoroughly modern woman. She doesn't want marriage and isn't interested in commitment. Robert seems as happy as she is to keep their relationship casual. And what about Paul – does he want more from Amy than just friendship? Then Amy's safe and secure world is suddenly shrouded in darkness and she has to decide which of these two men she can trust with her heart . . . and her future happiness.